THE SECOND ONE WAS DEAD

The first youth still breathed, but there was a funny sound coming from him. After a moment she realized that the human inhaled at three places—mouth, nose and the hole in his chest. Not good; this one would die soon.

Dove will not. Determination hardened in Windwhisper; she would not think about how serious a shoulder wound was, about the bleeding inside. . . . "We must go, before more humans come. Do you need help?" *Can you walk?* was what Windwhisper wanted to ask, but she was afraid to hear the answer. Slowly she turned back toward Dove, but the deed was done, Whiskers lay peacefully on his side. *We cannot mourn you, not until we are sure the others are safe.* With so many cubs in camp, and so few adult Wolfriders, they might not risk coming to help.

They had to protect the cubs. . . .

**Other Elfquest titles
published by Tor Books**

ELFQUEST Dark Hours

The Blood of Ten Chiefs

Vol. 5

Edited by
Richard Pini

TOR
fantasy

A TOM DOHERTY ASSOCIATES BOOK
NEW YORK

*To the healers, the dreamers,
and Dmitri.*

DARK HOURS

Cover art by Wendy Pini

A Tor Book
Published by Tom Doherty Associates, Inc.
175 Fifth Avenue
New York, N.Y. 10010

Tor® is a registered trademark of Tom Doherty Associates, Inc.

ISBN: 0-812-52341-5

First edition: June 1993

Printed in the United States of America

0 9 8 7 6 5 4 3 2 1

Contents

Timmain —— true wolf

TIMMORN —— Valloa / Murrel

RAHNEE —— Zarhan Fastfire

Prunepit / PREY-PACER

Wreath —— PREY-PACER —— Softfoot

SKYFIRE

Swift-Spear / TWO-SPEAR

SKYFIRE —— Dreamsinger

FREEFOOT —— Starflower

TANNER —— Stormlight

GOODTREE —— Lionleaper

MANTRICKER

MANTRICKER —— Thornflower

BEARCLAW —— Joyleaf

CUTTER, Blood of Ten Chiefs

Prologue

Blood of Ten Chiefs
#5

The tribe's nascent storyteller was in a worrisome frame of mind.

Pike, usually the most happy-go-lucky of the Wolfriders, was not really aware that Longreach's mantle was being fitted for his shoulders by the elder storyteller. Pike only knew that he enjoyed listening to the tales that the others spun during the tribal howls. It seemed he could call any story to mind with ease whenever he wanted to experience it, and this gave Pike a great deal of pleasure. He knew that Longreach would spend a lot of time with him, telling him of the exploits of past Wolfriders, and that was enjoyable too—but he always figured that the elder did the same with the other elves as well. Pike never knew—and Longreach had not told him—that he had a special talent, the natural ability of the storyteller.

Reaching into the dim past for tales of long-gone chiefs and kin might have seemed an odd thing for a Wolfrider to do, for the forest-dwelling elves spent most of their lives as their brothers the wolves did—in an eternal present, the "now of wolf thought." Sometimes, when both moons were full and bright in the sky, the entire tribe howled to the heavens along with their four-legged friends, and reminisced about this or that event and the lessons it might have for the elves. But the tribe had no real history, and certainly not a written one, for the Wolfriders had been a part of the World of Two Moons for more than ten thousand years, though none of the elves could even conceive of a number that large.

And yet, without even knowing it, the Wolfrider tribe carried with it through the endless turns-of-seasons a kind of history. Even before the time of Timmain and her wolf-son Timmorn, the very first Wolfrider chief, there were the storytellers, though they did not call themselves that. They were the ones who, through some subtle and long-forgotten magic, could dip into the neglected pools of deep, dark tribal memory and pull forth tales of long-ago times. Not all elves could use the ancient magic, though all could feel it and be affected by it . . . for who among the Wolfriders did not delight in the pleasant, drunken sensations brought about by dreamberries?

Dreamberries. Not one of the elves could have said where the plump, purplescent berries came from, or why they were never found except where the tribe settled, or why they had such a different effect on the tummy and brain from all the other berries to be found in the woods. But dreamberries had followed the Wolfriders from the beginning of the tribe. And for those few elves who responded in a special way to the intoxication, dream-berries opened the floodgates of memory and allowed a glimpse of lives and events long dead and gone. The dreamberries both planted and nurtured the seeds that became, in the minds of the storytellers, stories to tell.

Pike knew little of this, however. The fuzz-cheeked Wolfrider knew nothing of magic or tales, though Longreach was taking time with the young elf, guiding him, preparing him. Pike really didn't care about any of that at the moment. What he cared about right now was dreamberries, and there was something wrong with the dreamberries.

Or rather, there was something wrong with the dream-berry bushes. Perhaps no one except Bearclaw, the tribe's chief, might have noticed it, but Pike fancied himself the keeper of the harvest, and he knew to a berry how many of the succulent fruits hung from each branch of each bush in the woods, and there were berries missing! More —many more—than could be accounted for by the occasional bird or treewee. This was worrisome indeed.

Pike's brow furrowed. Should he try by himself to figure out what was happening? Should he say something to Bearclaw? Maybe he should bring his concerns to Longreach; after all, the elder always seemed to be able to dip into his pouch of dreamberries and call forth some wisdom. Pike decided: Bearclaw might go into a rage or funk; Pike would confide in Longreach. He hoped the storyteller would have some comforting answers. What will happen to me, Pike wondered, if I can't get any more dreamberries?

And what would happen to the stories?

In Memory Green

by Alice Cascorbi and Richard Pini

"Will we stay in this world long?" asked Almeck anxiously, gazing down at the brilliant blue sphere that hung suspended in the velvet void of space. Two satellites circled the planet, though the spherical craft of the star-travelers, self-contained and self-sustaining, would now show in its skies as a third, unnaturally brilliant small moon. Through the swirling clouds that veiled the planet's surface, oceans and continents slowly revealed themselves and then retreated again from view. Almeck's wispy form, frail even for one of the wanderers, showed his tension as he leaned over the railing of an observation place. His large green eyes were troubled, and his friend Seeree could feel his apprehension. Telepathically sensitive, their people were attuned to the life-energies of others—not only members of their own kind, but even the minds of alien beings. And to both travelers, suspended though they were, miles above the storm-studded atmosphere of the two-mooned planet, came the unmistakable presence of intelligent beings on the planet below. Intelligent, but primitive.

Seeree raised a slender, four-fingered hand to straighten her simple garment. She was not unduly bothered by the rough touch of the alien minds; unlike Almeck, she loved the play of the senses and was often to be found in sturdy animal shapes, scampering up the walls of the castle-ship with tree-frog toes or racing on four legs down the long, sweeping halls of their star-traveling home.

Almeck, on the other hand, loved tranquility and contemplation; among all physical creatures his favorite forms were the sun-loving plants. Their quiet, steady joy in living was untroubled by the clashing, all-at-once, blood-pumping needs and drives of the animals. Almeck spent many hours meditating, hovering lovingly in spirit over the ship's vast collection of plants from many worlds. Free of his physical body, he could travel at will, insinuating his consciousness between the living cells, feeling the life-spirit reverberate from the embryonic tips of the new green buds to the dark, calm, hollow centers of the woody inner core. The lives of plants were lives of balance and harmony—they might crowd each other for light, even fight each other for soil, but their malleable bodies and simple needs freed them from the fear and scrabbling that was the way of the animals, the "eat or be eatens." Seeree would have said it also robbed them of the joys of passion and movement, but to Almeck that was immaterial.

It was those same passions of rage and movement, emanating from the minds of the humans below, that frightened Almeck and made him wish they had not come this way on their travels. The intelligent beings native to the two-mooned world were still perilously close to the savagery of their animal origins; in Almeck's estimation they were probably more dangerous than any true beast, whose cruelties would be unintentional and limited to the necessities of survival. Human consciousness still reeked of violence and deception, lacking the refinement and reflection of older, more mature intelligent races. Yet studded throughout the collective memory of this infant intelligence were references to higher beings, angels, sky-spirits, who had come from realms unknown and performed wonders on the two-mooned planet: feats of magic, miraculous healings, beautiful transformations. The legends and crafts of the human creatures gave these spirits faces and form. In their eons-long search for any trace of their fellow wanderers, the inhabitants of the life-sphere had chanced upon this clue that hinted that at some time, perhaps, others like them had visited the two-mooned world.

Almeck turned away from the observation window and paced the length of the balcony, hands knotted behind his back. Seeree watched him with a quizzical expression. He was no coward, but his quiet, contemplative nature was the opposite of her reckless, experiential temperament. He was her dear friend, she loved him, and she didn't like to see him troubled. Coming up gently to touch his shoulders, she sent a warm wave of reassurance into his mind. "It will only be a little visit. See, we grow closer now." He allowed her to pull him back toward the window, still skeptical, but somewhat comforted by her touch. "We will only stay as long as it takes to find out whether our kindred *did* pass by here. See, let me show you the form I shall assume." And her smiling, delicate alien-face shimmered and re-formed into a sturdy humanoid one, with wide blue eyes and pointed ears under a thick shock of red-gold hair. "The creatures seem to revere these images, so we will be welcomed, will we not?" Seeree dimpled, then her new face relaxed into a warm smile. "What makes this planet so different from all the others we have visited? Tell me, how could it possibly harm us?" Seeree paused to let a pair of butterfly-winged Preservers settle on her outstretched fingers. "Almeck, you mustn't fear. You know our magic will protect us!" Buoyed by the thought, she rose to her toes, testing her new body with a little dance step. Her charm was, as usual, irresistible, and Almeck found himself giving her a soft half-smile despite his consternation. Her smile widened and she hugged him, then turned and tripped away in a breeze of joy. The two Preservers flew up, scattering in her wake, echoing her happy mood with their tiny giggles. Almeck looked after them and wished he could be as confident.

The elf shook his black hair out of his face and rubbed his wide green eyes open again. Seeree—he had been dreaming of her again. Seeree, who had been his friend so long ago. She had not died at the sky-mountain when their craft, betrayed, crashed headlong in the wrong place and time, when so many fell to the brutal human horde. Both of them had been among the few who fled, bleeding, into the alien forest. The terrible accident on the two-mooned world had robbed Seeree—robbed all of them! —of most of her magic, and had changed her joy in living into a fierce determination that she and her kind should not die. Desperately, she and others began the struggle for survival in this animal world, painfully calling long-forgotten skills and drives back into existence. For the sake of bare survival, the life-loving sky-travelers had learned to kill for food, those such as Menolan with his fire-talent and Seeree with her floating skills and Timmain with her ability to sense the forest's secrets providing sustenance for others who could not even begin to accept the dirty work of living. Almeck could do a little bit, too, for though he could never bring himself to hunt he could sometimes shape a shelter from a tree trunk or bring reluctant fruit from a berry bush out of season.

Almeck felt the cold breeze on his damp skin. He rose from the leafy ground at the base of an old ash tree, where a welcome patch of autumn sunshine had tempted him to nap, and looked around at the camp his people shared. A collection of tree-bowers, crude stick lean-tos, and stiff leather tents was scattered around a clearing in the ancient virgin forest. Here, as every day, some three-eighths of beings cooked, scraped fresh hides, and other-wise attended to the daily business of survival. There was Rellah, long-leggety maiden, helping her father drag bunches of reeds for baskets into the camp. Drained of the power to change their shape, the sky-travelers lingered in the not-quite-human forms they had adopted just before their starship fell. The deaths of so many, at the sky-mountain and in the harsh years since, had left places that a new generation, young born on this alien soil, were just beginning to fill.

It had not surprised Almeck when Seeree and Menolan had been among the first to experience the urge of Recognition in this new and alien form; they were alike in their determination to survive but they needed each other's gifts to do so. Seeree had died giving birth to their son, Enlet, when even Segray's flesh-mending powers could not save her, could not stop the red rush of her life-blood into the ground. But Segray had taken the child, nursed him at her own breast—a perilous beginning for any child, even when magic did provide the milk the baby needed. But Enlet had been gifted with the strong will of his mother, along with her flaming crown of auburn hair. He had lived, and when Segray Recognized the following year he had grown up as a brother to the healer's own little son, Samael. Now, in early maturity, he was beginning to show signs of his father's fire-talent.

There he was, mending a spear by Segray's lean-to. Almeck felt a surge of affection, a kind of wistful avuncular pride: what a fine young lad Seeree's son had grown into! He could not help but wonder where the little child, so lately born, had gone. Even before Enlet could speak, the red-haired child had sought out the quiet treeshaper with a stone or pretty feather in his hands, smiling up at the green-eyed elf in pure delight and innocence. With Samael, his brown-haired foster brother, firmly in tow, Enlet had joined Almeck on great excursions into the vast provider forest, to gather mushrooms in the dappled clearings or to pluck fresh greens in the sunny river meadows. Though the elves had rather fluid concepts of parenthood, if there was one the young Enlet loved most as his father, that one would surely have been Almeck.

But Enlet learned, as he grew older, that he had another father, Menolan, whose devastating fire-talent ensured success for the elfin hunters. Menolan, who sometimes smiled at him, yet remained always distant, who would never sit at Segray's fire when his red-haired son was also there. Sometimes Enlet would turn his head and catch Menolan staring at him. The older elf always looked away quickly, but not before Enlet caught the stricken look of mingled blame and pity on his face. And so, though Enlet grew to admire his true father and sought always, in a haunted way, to please him, the older elf was ever and always out of his son's reach. In truth, Menolan retreated not only from the child whose birth had taken Seeree's life and whose face reminded him daily of his grief, but from all his people. He wandered gradually from the company of his fellows, his magic unaffected, his vigor unchanged, but his eyes held a queer light and he spoke less and less to the others, wrapping himself in silence.

Today, Menolan had come into camp from the forest, twirling a long frond of leather-fern between his fingers. He sat alone for a long time by his bower and was lost in thought when a shadow fell across him. He looked up, startled, to find a lanky red-haired youth staring down at him.

"Well, what do you want?" growled the older elf, looking away from his son. The young elf's shoulders slumped. "I— I just came to see if you needed anything," the youth began lamely. "Maybe some willow tea? Segray's steeping a bowl of it right now . . ."

"If I needed a medicine, I'd go to the healer myself!" snapped Menolan. Enlet fell back, tight-lipped. "I can do without it—and without your useless concern today!" Menolan got to his feet and began to pace around the clearing, punctuating his words with stabs of the fern frond. Almeck was not sure if his words were directed at his son or to the tribe in general, but it was clear the firemaker was working himself into one of his rages—on little provocation as usual. "Why can't you leave me alone when I want a little solitude? It's always 'Menolan, start this cook-fire for me' or 'Menolan, we're cold, come spark the hearth fire in our lean-to' or 'Menolan, we're hungry, come toast a patch of forest and scare us up some game!' And then, when you're warmed and fed, when you've got a bellyful of game and a good fire blazing in your pit, you whisper behind your hands and come creeping around trying to tell me something's wrong with me. Take it to the five-fingers, all of you! You—" Menolan's eyes flew to the fern frond, which had burst into flames in his hands. He had not consciously willed it to ignite. He dropped the burning thing with a gasp and stared at it. "Father," Enlet began, taking a step toward him. "Menolan . . ."

"Don't touch me!" the older elf said furiously, backing away. "Stay away!" In his divided brain, Menolan felt a stab of shame as he saw Enlet's face fall, the hurt plain in his eyes. But he too was in pain; he had to push pain away, he had to provide meat for the tribe, he had to . . . Menolan's mind began to trace its path back into despair. Suddenly, warm hands closed upon his shoulders from behind. A bolt of sweet energy surged into him, at once warming as summer honey and bracing as spray from a snow-fed spring. It was as if a blast of cold, pure air rushed into the chambers of his mind, driving out the spirals of paranoia, whirling away the fog of his unreason. In a moment, his clarity returned. Tension left his body; he slumped for an instant in the arms of the elf behind him. To Enlet the change was visible; a dark shadow, like a cave's mouth, seemed lifted from his father's face. Menolan sighed, shook his head. "Timmain . . ." he said, turning grateful eyes on the tall elf-woman behind him. She gave him a gentle smile. Almeck let his breath out. Once again, Timmain had averted a crisis.

Timmain—the beautiful one with the white-gold hair, the only one who felt at home with this world and all its rhythms. She alone of the refugees retained nearly the full measure of her mental powers, and she alone could help the others rediscover the keys to their own powers when, confused by hunger and the new rules of this world, they lost their magic. She was like a mother to them all nowadays, comforting, providing, advising.

Because of this, the others had begun to look to Timmain for leadership—an antique concept to a people whose society had been based for eons on equality, unspoken consensus, and mutual understanding. But, Almeck mused, it had been the free and effortless clarity of minds touching between the stars that had made this possible and here, on the world of two moons, mind-touching was like trying to see one's feet while wading through a muddy river. Only glimpses of the truth filtered through. So the refugees made do with outlines of thought and heavy, spoken words, and mourned not only the loss of physical security but the loss of their community as well. Their understanding of each other, their not-aloneness, was, like their magic, a casualty of their fall.

Almeck felt this keenly as he and Timmain bent together one day to gather clams in the freshets of the stream. There was no conversation between them; the stillness of the forest was broken only by the babbling of the cold, clear water. The silence pressed on Almeck like a stone.

I'm worried about Menolan, he sent to her at last. **Do you understand what's wrong with him now? The other day I tried to ask him something and his eyes looked like he was an eight-day's walk away in spirit! Ever since Seeree died . . .**

Timmain straightened abruptly to look at Almeck. **I know.** She sighed, then looked over his shoulder at the forested hills beyond. **He feels the sickness of the spirit. This world will drain the life out of us if something cannot be done.** She shared with him foreboding at the strange, twisted paths the world was beginning to lead their people down, one by one, always one by one. Almeck became very still. So it was not just his own apprehension. If Timmain, of all people, feared for the future sanity of their tribe . . . As they bent back to the clams, he felt a cold wind blowing down his soul.

Some days later, curled in the safety of his oak-tree hollow, the bite of apprehension had faded to an occasional uncomfortable pang at the back of his mind; a good day's worth of gathering and a good evening meal round a roaring fire had put him in a comfortable mood. Dusk was falling and the warm summer air was full of fireflies, dancing like a second tier of stars against the darkness of the forest. Back and forth they wove their web of light, a soothing bit of beauty that sparked an echo of joy in the star-traveler's heart. He was just beginning to relax when he saw Oraynah stalk by, head forward, her lank blond hair hanging in her face. Oraynah was one of the elves who hunted. She carried her crude spear in one hand and the body of a ravvit hung by one leg from the other.

At first glance he saw nothing unusual. But, reaching out reflexively to sense the situation, a sudden knot of horror formed involuntarily in Almeck's stomach. His mind had touched a cold ribbon of death-fear and lingering agony snaking out of the animal's mind: though wounded and paralyzed, the ravvit Oraynah held was not yet dead. Shocked, he drew back into concealing shadows. His eyes widened as he sensed the huntress's extreme anger. She strode to the grove's center, threw back her head, raised up both arms with an ominous slowness. She was at the breaking point, like a black cloud full of skyfire; in the next heartbeat her storm exploded, her bloody rage-thoughts finally forming words in sending strong enough to hurt his mind as, oblivious to Almeck's presence, she sent and shouted through the glade: **Where are they? Your kin! Miserable wretched *animal*—** and she twisted the ravvit's mind with her raging magic as she twisted its broken hind leg, and it screamed a scream of tortured agony that Oraynah caught up, broadcast, magnified until the whole glade pulsed with agony and terror and three more ravvits leaped up from hiding, screaming too, and quicker than skyfire Oraynah found them with her mind and paralyzed them, blasting them till blood vessels exploded in their brains and they fell dead, glassy-eyed. Almeck was struck dumb with horror, unable to move or even wet his dry lips as Oraynah moved forward matter-of-factly to collect the bodies. Darkness swirled before his eyes. His first returning sensation was nausea and he retched involuntarily, betraying his hiding place to the huntress. She turned to look up at his tree-bower, four dead ravvits hanging from her spear. **Why, Almeck! What are you doing here?** She took a step toward his hiding place, pushing the lank hair out of her eyes again. **Come, I have meat here that we can share!** She loosed her prey from the spear and came toward his tree with a vacant smile, a bloody carcass dangling from her outstretched hand.

After that, Almeck could not eat. He mourned for two days in the shadow of Segray's lean-to, unseeing, as the healer and her young son Samael gathered roots and berries and tended to the business of survival. He did not notice when Segray set food and water near his hands, or when Samael collected a big pile of brushwood in front of him and Enlet set it alight, warming his body and casting strange shadows on the worried faces of his friends. The healer's heart ached, for her powers could mend only wounds of the flesh and Almeck's sorrow lay far deeper than that. Perhaps Timmain could have helped him, but she was gone on one of her private wanderings and no one could say when she might return. (At such times, Timmain could not even be found by sending; her folk could only watch and wait for her to come back to them.) And so wait and watch was all Almeck's friends could do.

Retreating from the world and its all-too-ugly battle for

survival, Almeck sent his spirit "out" until it all but abandoned its weary shell. Recoiling from the madness of the world, he found himself lost instead in its life-web, a mote of soul wandering aimlessly in a vast forest of shadows and presences. The endless green of the plant-consciousness called to him, soothing like cool water as he slipped into its embrace. He fled the ugliness of the animals and forgot his life as an elf, drifting into the green, his soul at peace at last.

Unexpectedly, in that world of alien consciousness, amidst the music of its unfolding secrets, he caught the sound of a familiar voice. Who? He drifted closer, brushing past thickets of the mind until at last in a formless bright shadow-grove he caught sight of Timmain. Her feet were rooted in the soil, her mind open and singing, reaching up to learn the song that the forest reached down to teach her. Shapeshifter that she was, her power could make her one with the world-mind's song even as her body remade itself into one of the world's tree-children. Hearing, seeing, Almeck was filled with an admiration tinged with equal parts of love and longing. If only *he* could escape forever into the green! But Timmain, who had the power to become one with the world, did so only to benefit the rest of their people. Life outside was not her enemy; she sought within so she could teach her kind the ways of the seasons, or the patterns of prey migrations, or which plants would have healing or nourishing effects on their bodies. Almeck moved to withdraw quietly into the stiller depths of the world-mind, but Timmain had already sensed him near. She looked up from the song she was singing. "Stay, friend!" she called to him, extending her spirit hands.

Reconsidering, Almeck smiled and took them in his own. Images flowed between them nearly as freely as before, on the sky-mountain. Images of Timmain's present search, for a clue to the cause of the increasing cold, and of Almeck's fear at what had befallen Oraynah. The wholeness of his wonder at her communion with the world. Holding her hand, one with her spirit, Almeck felt a subtle texture to the planet he had been unable to perceive before. Noting his surprise and delight, Timmain spirit-smiled. "Would you like to see more?"

Withdrawing from the sun-bright glade of towering ancient trees, she led him by the hand along a path through the world-green. The green-eyed elf was enthralled, his wonder at her skill exceeded only by his delight at what he saw and felt around him. The two-mooned world was *not* ugly, just exacting; its rules were its own and its children were expected to dance to its tune. Timmain parted the veils for him, and Almeck saw into the life-codes of the planet, how the rocks ground in its belly and the oceans rippled over its surface like a living skin. He felt the give-and-take between plant and animal life, how each twined about the other in mutual dependence and mutual support. Allies and enemies faced each other in the long dance of changes down the centuries. Beetles chewed on leaves and built up poisons in their gut. Flowers offered nectar to lure the eager bees to waiting pollen. Almeck saw how plants produced strange substances to attract or repel animal creatures, how some made poisons and others intoxicating sweets. For the first time, he *understood* the interplay of the green-and-red life of the two-mooned world and his heart, often wounded in the melee of the world's rough pageant, began to sing with a heady joy.

Timmain was smiling at him, a smile that warmed his heart, a smile that spoke of her joy and his. "But I must return." She withdrew her spirit from his until he could again see plainly her beautiful brown eyes. Behind her her rooted body waited. He understood then that she must continue her quest, for the life of their people, and as she stepped away and lifted her head once more into the smooth current of the world-song, he understood something else about his old friend: her monumental sadness. As she lost herself in union with the forest her grief dissolved and she was whole again. For the first time since before the Palace fell, Almeck saw an elfin soul enrobed in joy.

His own soul circled round and found its center, like a weary swan to still waters in the evening. But as calm seeped in, so too the remembrance that he was more than just a soul. However he might wish it were not so, Almeck was still bound to his body. After three days of spirit-wandering, his flesh cried out for food and water, and the stubborn spark of survival instinct that had kept him alive so far wouldn't let him simply cut his bonds and drift free of it forever. If his journey out had been a headlong flight into the groves, coming back to consciousness was an uphill struggle through thorn thickets, a long and achy process of subtracting himself from the great green harmony. Part of him wept to leave the realm whose true beauty he had so lately come to see. When he finally opened his eyes to see Samael and Enlet's anxious faces bent over his own, it was with a surge of sorrow. He remembered the fall, his grief, the spirit-sickness of the tribe. It was like waking from a beautiful dream, and his whole body ached.

Almeck was thinner than ever. Some days after his painful return to consciousness, Timmain had quietly returned to camp. She and the treeshaper exchanged a secret smile but Almeck did not seek her out for conversation. Rather, he kept to himself, exploring every detail of the little grove by his hollow tree with his newly sharpened senses. Fascinated with the beauty of even the simplest creatures, he could spend a day experiencing the swelling upgrowth of a mushroom or tasting the movement of light over the bronze leaves of a great beech tree. Arising one morning to find the first autumn starflower nodding by the roots of his oak tree, he spent the whole day seated next to the delicate plant, spirit extended to feel the purple petals swell and slowly curl back from the golden center, one by one.

He found himself with little desire for the maintenance of his body. It had called him back from the green, but he was no longer so protective of its fragility. He dwelt alone in his tree-bower, slept but little, and ate even less. He accepted no more meat and sought out for himself only those few vegetables that could be gathered without taking the life of the whole plant. Even the mealy cattail roots, which all his folk loved to eat wrapped in leaves and roasted in the coals, he turned away uneaten. He was tired of suffering and causing other things to suffer. But the autumn nights were growing cold, and stormy skies began to threaten. In the way of things, Almeck himself began to suffer for his new resolution. It was a meager diet the forest yielded when one cut out roots and meat and mushrooms. He fell sick with chills and fever.

"Such foolishness," Segray scolded. She was spooning a bitter brew down Almeck's throat as he sat, huddled in the healer's big bearskin robe, by her fire. He was thoroughly bedraggled; heavy rains and gusty wind had soaked him to the skin the night before and finally sent him staggering out of solitude back to the healer's camp-fire. His black hair fell in tangles down his back, and he huddled miserably in the thick robe, eyes downcast like a sulky child as he swallowed the hot herbal tea. "Bad enough that you should trance off for three days and give the rest of us no sign but that you'd gone forever, and now to try to live on nothing but leaves and berries . . . By the wandering stars, Almeck! You're not a ravvit!"

Almeck could not suppress a smile at the healer's fussing. "If I were, I wouldn't have to listen to this kind of scolding . . ." He caught her hand, making a sour face. "Enough of that foul brew for now! It's as bitter as redroot leaves in summer!" But under his words he sent a warm wave of gratitude, gentle acceptance of the wisdom of Segray's words. His deep green eyes caught her anxious blue ones, and she squeezed his hand and smiled back. "It's *made* from summer redroot, silly. But by guiding powers, Almeck, eat something! We've lost enough to hunger without elves deliberately starving themselves to death. Your body won't forgive you if you don't get some solid food into it soon!" Almeck had just opened his mouth to promise he would when an open sending blazed through the camp.

The hunters have prevailed! Deer hunt successful!

Segray started up, delighted, and all the camp was instantly abustle as children and elders emerged from dens and bowers gathering up knives, and hides to sit upon, hurrying excitedly into the forest. For this was not a feast the hunters could bring back into camp.

Samael came running to the healer's lean-to. "Mother, did you hear? The hunters have downed a herd of blackneck! We feast in the gully by the Hidden Gorge!" Enlet ran up puffing, a few breaths behind his foster brother. "Father just sent to me, too. We won't be waiting long. They butchered a deer and started the cook-fires before they gave us the open summons!" Segray hugged the boy, crowing with delight. Such a feast was overdue around their camp, and the deer of early autumn would be at their peak for fat and flavor.

Samael turned to the treeshaper, as if noting for the first time Almeck's haggard condition. "Almeck, how are you feeling? Could I offer you an arm to lean on as we walk?" The boy was courteous, as ever. Almeck knew the green-eyed youngster looked up to him, found in him a mentor's figure, though how his frail and unworldly nature could inspire a youngster's admiration was unclear to the treeshaper. Smiling, he took Samael's proffered arm. "Weak as a waterweed, useless as a treewee, that's me, Samael—but your mother has done her best to talk some sense into me today." The elves smiled at each other and set out slowly for the feasting circle.

It was not a long walk, perhaps a bit of a scramble through the briarberries near the river, then over a rise, down a valley and across a second rise, where beech and oak grew tall and the stone bones of the land cropped up like yellowed molars. The limestone cliff was sheer on one side of the gully, but on this side the slope was manageable and most of the elves had already clambered down to gather in the valley below. This was an excellent feast-site, for not only was there wood for many fires, but also a spring of good clear water, bubbling down in a little freshet toward the nearby river. The four had traveled slowly in deference to Almeck and late afternoon was giving way to evening when at last they stood together on the rise above the cook-fire site. They could see flames winking orange through the trees and caught excited elfin voices rising up the slope from below.

Almeck halted, placing a hand to his head. He must have looked as dizzy as he suddenly felt, for Samael caught him around the shoulders and held him up anxiously. "Almeck, are you all right? Do you want to sit down here and I'll bring a leg joint up to you?"

His stomach rumbled at the thought of plentiful roast meat, but the memory of Oraynah came into his mind and he recoiled, grimacing. "Thank you, youngling, but I . . . I think I couldn't stomach deer tonight. Perhaps I should go back to camp . . ." Segray stepped toward him, hands on hips. "Idiot. Treewee. What did I tell you just this afternoon? You will not starve yourself while I'm around to do something about it!" Almeck sank to the ground, unable at last to keep his footing. "Segray, I can't eat deer tonight, I'm sorry. I'd throw up. That's worse than not eating anything at all, now, isn't it?"

"How about some berries?" Samael stood forth, solemn compassion knitting his brows together. "There's a good crop of them by the stream—I gathered them there yesterday. It's not far from here, or from the feast-fire either . . ."

And so the four turned round and wove carefully down the slope behind them, circling around the foot of the rise to reach the thick vegetation on the banks of the spring-fed rivulet. The brown-haired stripling helped his fragile mentor to a comfortable spot within easy reach of several berry-laden bushes. The summer night was fine and the moons were just rising full over the horizon. Samael helped Almeck arrange his long limbs into a comfortable position and, as the older elf reached for his first plump berry, took his leave and crossed the little ridge to rejoin the feast.

It was a fine crop of berries at that. Along the riverbank, under the scattered pines and among the gray-green clumps of lichen, the round blue ones were deepening from red to purple as their sour taste mellowed into piquant sweetness. Briar patches too were heavy with their black, tangy berries, and during the daylight hours of toil, slender, pale forms would reach long fingers between the thorns to gather the ripe ones.

Now Almeck extended his weakened hands carefully, slowly relieving first one bush, then another, of its sweet burden. Even the mild tartness of the blueberries seemed a bit too biting, an assault upon the senses of a body too recently ravaged. He sighed. Settling back to rest—perhaps a double handful of berries later—he scarcely noticed when his eyes closed and his spirit slipped free of its weary shell. But suddenly he found himself with the revelers on the other side of the hill, surrounded by the smiles and doings of his kin. There was Talen, his face smeared with deer grease, lying contentedly in Selnac's arms. Marreck cracked a marrowbone to share with Jennah, while Menolan amused others by setting fire to a boulder that inconveniently blocked the shortest way from the cook-fire to the spring. Enlet, returning to the feast-circle with a drinking gourd full of water, halted to watch his father with admiring eyes. His own fire-magic was still weak and unpredictable, and such flourishes were generally beyond him. Almeck even saw Oraynah hunkered down happily next to the cooking fire, one hand brandishing a roasted rib, the other making stabbing motions to punctuate whatever hunting tale she was telling. Beyond the circle of firelight and feasting, the moons rose over the forest. Behind the gathering of his kin, Almeck could see many dark hummocks scattered at the base of the cliff. Some reached for the sky in odd, upward-pointed shapes, like the branches of fallen trees. These were the corpses of the blackneck herd, littering the glade at the base of the rock wall. The moons rose silently over the carnage scene.

The herd had numbered perhaps forty, including fawns and a smattering of gray-chins. Now all lay broken together where they had been driven to their deaths by the elfin hunters. Two or three had been butchered to provide the night's feast and, of the others, perhaps a dozen could be stripped and the meat preserved before rot and wild scavengers rendered the kill unusable. Some of the hides would be removed and tanned by magic, but many deer would lie unclaimed and unused, except by the foxes and the vultures and the carrion crows.

In the glade where Almeck's body lay motionless, a shadow detached itself from the forest and glided cautiously into the clearing. A young bobcat, a male, sniffed suspiciously at the unfamiliar scent of elf. Unknown to Almeck, he had chosen a resting place near the edge of the small predator's territory; the berry-rich glade was also home to dozens of ravvits, the small cat's most favorite food. The scent of an unknown larger creature might be enough to keep the shy feline from following his course toward the river. But elves were not habitual hunters of bobcats, and tonight the young male had other things to concern him. He circled the grove on huge, noiseless pads, giving Almeck's body as wide a berth as possible, then disappeared down the slope toward the river. A sweet scent, borne on the breeze wafting from the riverbank, touched and tantalized the deepest part of his wild brain. It would take more than the presence of an unconscious elf to keep the cat from answering that sweet lure tonight.

In spirit-form, Almeck was attuned to a depth of things not usually visible to him. About each body of a feaster glowed the bright aura of his or her living spirit. The life-forms of the ground and forest glowed with a different light. Recognizing the comforting presence of his plant acquaintances, Almeck drifted closer, close enough to catch an occasional flicker of sending as thoughts made their way from one elfin mind to another. Suddenly several minds paused, and all focused their attention upon one child, Khyra. That youngling had not yet seen eleven summers, and now her wide blue eyes were fixed expectantly upon the face of her mother. Her aura was bright with a question and a longing. The faces of her elders reflected pain, and also guilt; several of them slid their eyes away. Almeck puzzled. What could the child have asked? Then, slowly, faintly, one mind began to answer. An image of their sky-ship was held up in their midst. It was Samael, and he was not projecting his own memories (for he was one of the earth-born) but relating his version of a story once given him by an elder.

Khyra had a remarkable gift of projection. The images she received she held up in her aura to study with her intense need to know, so clear that even Almeck could perceive them. A flying ship was beyond her, so she imagined a great rock like a mountain hanging suspended above the clouds. Time travel? Shapeshifting? To this child of the mud and cold of the two-mooned world, these concepts had no reference or meaning. Samael's sending faltered and came to an end. The firstcomers turned their heads away, their minds closed up in pain and in shame that they could not answer. They could barely face the memories of all they had lost, let alone communicate them to this bright, asking child. Khyra was unsatisfied; he could feel her curiosity gathering again in another brilliant burst. Then Almeck saw Nefahrin steel herself mentally, slide her eyes back to meet Khyra's, and begin to speak. She began to describe their ship, their quest, their accident, using words without sending images behind them. Her mind was strong and disciplined, and she held it completely closed. Before the Fall she had been one of the Sighters, those who reached out through time and space to find worlds the life-sphere might like to visit, providing direction to the motive power of the Guiders. Now her power served her for nothing. She was a decent basket weaver, here on the world of two moons, and she used only the words of her lips to give some sense of their origins to Khyra. Honorable, unswervingly responsible, she could not leave the child completely in the dark. In spirit-form, Almeck could not hear the exact words Nefahrin spoke. But he could watch their effect upon the mind of Khyra, whose life-glow momentarily darkened and brightened, with confusion or understanding. And now the child formed no images at all. She could only imagine, not see, the story Nefahrin told her.

For one time in his tranquil life, Almeck was filled with a tearing, helpless rage. His spirit blazed like skyfire as he sent it swirling into the treetops in frustration, sent it pulsing along the life-lines of the forest around the cook-fire. His kin were sick, they were losing the life of the mind in the mud of this alien planet! Cut off from its healing teachings by their crippled powers, most of the elves never felt connected to anything anymore. The creatures of fire who had survived the Fall were dying inside, and their children, born on the two-mooned world, were growing up in puzzlement and ignorance. Only Timmain could tap into the new world's life-currents, and the measure of healing she brought to her kinfolk was short-lived. Almeck's spirit pooled in a wide circle of green light round his still and darkened body. Healing—his people needed healing in spirit and in mind! They needed a way around their pain, as he had his way through the plants—some way to make the pain disappear, to let minds fly free again without fear. But how? Neither he nor Timmain could transfer their powers to any other elf, just as one could not drink water for a thirsty friend or eat for one who was starving. He knew of no way he could help them. No possible way. He turned away in frustration, feeling there was nothing else to see among the feasters. He gathered his spirit and prepared to reinhabit his still-quiet body.

Something caught one edge of his spirit-circle as he was drawing inward, as though a thorn had hooked the hem of a leather cloak. It was a little bump or ripple in the otherwise serene web of plant life-spirits he could feel. In and out of the pale green glow of the plant-consciousness wove a cheerful purple thread of—something else. Not the normal, red-orange glow of animal life, but an aura altered, *merged* with the plants'—an animal note, but sounding in harmony with the green. What was going on? His return to form momentarily forgotten, Almeck drew himself over to concentrate on the little patch of mossy ground.

The bobcat crouched in a pile of crushed herbage, eyes narrowed to slits of pure bliss. A raspy purr rumbled in his throat. The potent scent of wild catnip hung heavy in the moist night air. Growing in profusion among the nettles on the riverbank, its scent was irresistible to most wild creatures of the cat family. Its essential oils, inhaled, touched the most ancient parts of a feline's brain, setting off a cascade of emotions and responses. Earlier the woods along the river had been witness to a most extraordinary scene: the normally reserved and graceful young bobcat pouncing like a kitten into the patch of catnip, biting eagerly at the minty leaves, releasing more of the intoxicating scent with every stem he crushed. He rolled and wriggled on the ground, strangely reminiscent of a female bobcat in heat, and indeed the sensations coursing through his brain might well have resembled those of a female in the grip of sweet spring mating madness. His initial euphoric energy spent, the cat was content now to remain blissfully still, enjoying the strange state of catnip catatonia.

A beautiful incongruity—a feline spirit wandering freely in the world-green! Almeck had not seen anything like it before on this planet—but then, how often had he truly seen the green before Timmain showed him the key to its secrets? Hovering by the bobcat's entranced body, he sensed its life-force near, its spirit padding lazily through the forest's essence as its body would in life. He had an impression of great eyes turning to regard him. The cat was aware of him, but unconcerned. The cat drew Almeck's attention back toward the life-glow of the forest. The music of the world was open to him; he could catch it in his claws like little rodents, romp through it like a pile of autumn leaves. Almeck felt the tug of that song on his own heart. He smiled sadly at the irony. Now here was a mortal creature born to live a few seasons at best on this primitive world; for all the subtleties of the elfin people, for all their ages of sentience and eons of complexity, his folk could not equal the simple wisdom of the cat. Once his people had had community—as "one heart and one mind" had been their separate hearts and minds, and no heart needed to shut itself up in grief when, ever and always, comfort was as close as the touch of a neighboring mind. Now comfort was elusive, misunderstanding flared and smoldered, and madness stalked their grief-enshrouded souls. Unlike the earth-born cat, the elves no longer knew their road to unity.

The bobcat's spirit was returning; the simple power of the catnip was clearing from its brain. It stirred in its trance. Now himself, now one with the world, the cat blinked. A good night's wander was coming to an end as the drug wore off. Almeck sensed that perhaps he, too, should take up his flesh again. The eyes of the cat's settling spirit met his once more as he backed from the bobcat's grove. How could he help but envy this animal, who was at peace with himself in a way the elves could not match anymore? One heart and one mind, thought Almeck as he lay back down into his body. One heart and one mind—not anymore! Almeck felt the tingling of his spirit's return to flesh.

Suddenly, revelation struck! Heedless of the spots that swam before his eyes, Almeck started up so suddenly that he lost his balance. He stumbled into the bushes with a resounding crash. Ten feet away a bobcat jumped up, eyes round as the two full moons, and fled away like skyfire into the darkened forest. The answer was before him! Bodies: it was their bodies that were the problem. And plant essences could influence their bodies! He felt like running over the hill, shouting the news to his ailing kinfolk. The answer! The cure! The end to all our sickness! But telling them without showing them would not bring them the certainty that he suddenly felt—he had seen things most of the others had no inkling of, and in their weakened state he might seem merely another madman in their midst. He would do his work and set it before them finished, smiling. He looked around the grove. Was there something he could use? Yes, here was something right at hand that would suffice! A tremendous joy ran through him. At last, perhaps, he could use his powers for lasting good for his friends and kinfolk. He knelt on the soft green moss and took one berry bush's slender twigs between his fingers. He took a moment to discipline his mind, then slipped into a shaper's trance and felt his life-force flowing out into the green, mingling with the pulsing life around him. His mind and body reverberated with the opening music of the world-song, and now he joined his spirit-voice to that song. He was being swept away in a river of green, and he reveled in that river. He bent his will to teach the little plant to sing in harmony with the alien voices from the stars. The living wood responded; he could feel the change imprinting on the life-codes of the green being he held in his hands. Mutation moved like sunrise, first lighting one bush, then the next in the small grove around him. He did not notice when his spirit danced free of his body, set free by his shaper's magic. The green glow faded from his hands and from around the berry bushes. They held their fat and juicy cargo with new dignity, as though keeping a pregnant secret within. Almeck's soul shouted and ran through the world-green, reunited, at one with the world and with joy. There was nothing he could not do, all places in the world were one. He gave a thought to the land of frozen mountains, and to his surprise he seemed to see the Palace, as if from a great height—was it full of ice? No, that was a mistake—his vision cleared and it glowed with its warm and welcoming light—and in the doorway, arms wide—was that Seeree? In the green?! He laughed, and flowers climbed the walls; behind Seeree, a throng of old friends and companions, waving up at him, laughing and shouting. Dimly he felt a tug from another place, a pale elf-body slumped on a carpet of moss in a twilight forest far away. But why the hurry? All time and space had opened wide for him, and here and now were his old friends, welcoming him back, alive, rejoicing, and the Palace, long-lost home, warm and golden as the summer sun! There was no one left in the grove to notice the subtle change in the glossy leaves, in the way the heavy purple berries gleamed ripe in the moonlight. Almeck had so much to tell his old friends!

It was only later that Samael, coming over the hill with a bowl of steaming broth, found Almeck's still form slumped beside the berry bushes. At his cry, Enlet and Timmain were the first two over the hill, and Segray came running with her bag of herbs. Samael watched with tears starting as the healer knelt beside the body, only to confirm, as she touched Almeck, what the three knew already: these Fallen had seen death much too often not to recognize when it claimed one of their own. Almeck's body lay still in the quiet moonlight as the tribe straggled over the hill to gather silently about him.

The faces of the firstcomers were frozen, numb, perhaps, to new grief in a world that seemed to hand them nothing but endless cause for sorrow. From the younger, questions and confusion filled the air: **He wasn't that ill! How could he die from sickness?** **Who saw him last? Was anything wrong with him this afternoon?** **He'd been a bit touched for a while, you know.** **Yes, and now the white-cold's coming! What will we *do* when summer tree-bowers need their winter mending?**

Samael bent to the vegetation. "But—look—Timmain —these bushes!" Samael had noticed the subtle change in the ones closest to the body. The berries gleamed fat and purplescent, larger than before, and a faint magic vibration still clung to the leaves. As Timmain broke a twig off the nearest bush, twirling it thoughtfully between her fingers, Enlet pushed forward. "To use his last strength to shape a *berry bush?* Instead of calling for help? Why, Timmain? What could he have been thinking?!" The red-haired youth was close to tears. Handing him a purplescent berry, she stared thoughtfully at the juice now staining her fingers. Samael looked on, confusion knitting his brow. "Timmain, why do you think he *made* these? So— So we would remember him?"

Timmain looked around the grove, noting the many bushes that now gleamed with that new, changed light. Fat, juicydark berries nestled under every leaf. Her eyes acquired a far-off expression, as though recalling a green place where fear and sorrow were forgotten. "Yes," she said. "We will remember."

Starting Over

by Lynn Abbey

Spikes of hoarfrost clung to the underside of the withered leaves that had not yet fallen. The stream beneath the leaves and branches was every bit as cold as the ice crystals promised. Zarhan Fastfire scampered out of the water and up the rocky bank. Shivering from top to toe, his clashing teeth the loudest sound in the nearby forest, he spun the water from his hair and stumbled toward the daylit stone where he'd left his clothing. Though the slender elf had lived his entire life in an ice-bound world where the green warmth of summer meant only that winter was preparing for its next onslaught, Zarhan had never developed a tolerance for cold. He fought it tooth and nail; with every fiber, every nerve; with every mote of magic in his soul.

In a few moments Fastfire's shivering ceased. Water no longer trickled around his delicate ears, down the twin channels along his spine, or pooled beneath his four-toed feet. Thin tendrils of steam rose from his shoulders and scalp. His dark, wet hair grew as red as the leaves on the bushes beside him. A sigh pushed through his lips. He sat down heavily on the stone.

Now—exactly now and not a heartbeat earlier—Zarhan Fastfire felt good: alive, cleansed in spirit as well as body, as if he had been reborn.

Conscious of nothing but himself and the light, Zarhan opened his arms to the daystar. He arched his back until his long hair touched the stone and made a cushion for his head. Like all his kind, he was small-boned and lean, deceptively frail. Zarhan Fastfire hated the cold, the ice, and the snow, but he'd survived more winters than the stoutest tree in the forest. And yet, by the reckoning of the ancestors who dwelt in his memory, Zarhan remained immature and foolish.

An eternity of elders chastised Zarhan Fastfire. They did not approve of the uses to which he put the magic they bequeathed to him: *Only a fluff-eared fool would lie naked beneath the daystar when his outstretched toes and fingers touched unmelted frost. Only a fluff-eared fool would squander the strength of his body and soul to create a moment's pleasure. Hadn't he learned anything? When was he going to grow up? He'd regret this foolishness. He'd be bone-hungry, bone-weary, and bone-cold by nightfall—*

With a second sigh, the elf released his magic and sank flat on the stone. His unnaturally warm cocoon dissipated. In that small corner of his memory Zarhan reserved for his own life, he had always and stubbornly wished to live among his own kind, among pure-blooded elves, rather than in the shadow of Timmain's hardier, wolf-and-elf children: the Wolfriders. He'd gotten his wish a few turns back, with consequences that were less than satisfying.

I want to do what I want to do, he told the stern-voiced elders judging him from the depths of his memory. *When and if I want to do what I should do, then I'll do it. The Wolfriders survive without all this worrying, and I survived without it, too, while I was with them.*

The clamor ebbed, but Zarhan was cold. Angrily, he snatched his tunic and breeches and pulled them on. The blissful oblivion of wolfsong, about which he'd complained for his entire life, seemed wiser now that his own awakened consciousness had discovered both guilt and shame.

He yanked tufts of dry grass from the ground and used them to dry carefully between his toes before lacing his feet into waterproof moccasins: there were some things that a wilderness-dwelling elf knew that his ancestors had not. There were some things that he did without the prick of conscience, if he valued his ability to forage for his next meal.

Zarhan had the second moccasin snugged around his ankle when he heard rustling on the far side of the stream. Instinct and experience both proclaimed that he was about to have a visitor roughly his own size. Swiftly and without thought, he grabbed his flint-studded club. He was poised to flee or fight when he saw a flash of bright, fluttering feathers and a cascade of sable hair. His visitor was his own size, all right—his visitor was another elf who'd come, as he had, to bathe in the stream one last time before winter locked it beneath a sheath of ice.

He dropped the club and cinched his breeches cruelly tight. Instinct said something that was neither fight nor flee and, in this one matter, his burgeoning conscience agreed, but Zarhan resisted all temptations. He found himself standing stock-still with his mouth open when Cheseri burst through the underbrush. Their eyes met. Zarhan's heart pumped like a pair of bellows. His magic kindled; his gut and groin were searing. He swallowed—a useless, painful gesture—but couldn't quite break away from Cheseri's silent stare.

The elf-woman hooked a finger in the lacing of her tunic and with a single, smooth movement pulled it free. The soft doeskin split across her shoulders, slid down her arms, and gathered around her already naked feet. Zarhan did not doubt for a moment that she'd spent days practicing the elegantly defiant gesture. Cheseri's expression remained focused and cold as she stepped out of the doeskin circle and dove into the frigid water. Her arms pointed like arrows toward the place where he stood gaping.

She was one lodestone, he another, and the attraction between them sent bolts of agony down Fastfire's spine. With a raging shout, he turned away. He escaped into the woods, leaving his club behind. Branches snagged his hair, his clothes; he slashed them aside with his hands as he ran blindly from the stream. Leaves swirled and smoked in his wake. His hands were bloody when he finally came to a breathless stop. His lips worked, but several moments passed before they shaped a coherent sound:

"Rahnee . . . Rahnee . . ."

Fastfire called his lifemate's face to the center of his memory and made it grow until everything else was crowded into the shadows. He sank to his knees. His pulse slowed, his muscles relaxed; the Recognition crisis passed. He remembered the club lying on the daylit stone. There was no point going back after it. Cheseri would have already found it, would be planning how best to return it. After taking his bearing from the daystar, Zarhan began the long walk home. He no longer felt cleansed.

"You're late. You said you'd be back before the daystar touched the treetops."

Firelight shining through the open door exaggerated Zarhan's scowl. His lips and nostrils were flared. His lower jaw thrust forward, to bare both upper and lower teeth. After so many seasons among wolves and Wolfriders, Zarhan was utterly unaware of how many of their rituals he'd made his own.

The other elf scuttled sideways, giving Zarhan all the room he wanted in the cramped tent.

"It's over," Delonin said, half defensive, half apologetic. The healer's eyes were swollen and leaking. He sniffed and winced as he wiped his sleeve against his tender nose. "Finished."

Zarhan emptied his lungs through tightly clenched teeth. When the air was gone, so was his anger. Crouched beside the dejected healer-elf, he reached tentatively toward his lifemate's face. Her flesh was warm and lively beneath his fingertips, but she gave no sign that she felt his presence. Zarhan shaped her soulname.

Rahnee?

His sending was a whisper filled with love, borne on hopelessness. There was no answer, only a steady, swirling rhythm Zarhan likened to water flowing through gravel. It was a rhythm he knew all too well, and one that he'd learned to dread.

"I don't understand," he complained to no one, no thing. "We did everything we could do. We made no mistakes. We never tried to move her, not even when we raised the tent. She's been safe, still, and secure right here since the shaping started."

Delonin sniffed again in avid agreement. The trees above them had been naked and dormant when he and Zarhan erected the shelter over Rahnee the She-Wolf. The little healer had not noticed they were oak trees until it was too late. He wrapped his hand over Fastfire's and brought it away from Rahnee's face. "It was nothing we did or didn't do. It was only a mistake—a mistake . . . inside, in the shaping. Your lifemate, you know, she is . . . *different.*"

Fastfire freed his hand. Timmorn had been chief of the not-yet-Wolfriders when he was born. He'd grown up amid wolfish elves and elfish wolves. At the very back of his own mind, he was convinced that he was the one who was uselessly different, with only one set of instincts and abilities to draw upon, rather than two like Rahnee and her kindred. Here, among Cheseri, Delonin, and the others, their positions were reversed. He was one of the like-blooded, and Rahnee was the one who seemed unnecessarily unique.

"If the She-Wolf were not Timmain's granddaughter, she would have died when the thunder-feet trampled her," Fastfire insisted, as much to himself as the healer. "Timmain bequeathed her shapeshifting magic to all her children so they could keep the elf and the wolf balanced within themselves. The She-Wolf uses it to reshape herself."

Delonin stroked his lower lip. *"Rahnee,"* he corrected, "does not use anything. Her magic acts upon itself. It, and it alone, sought a shape—sought it longer than it has ever done before because we stayed here, in one place, longer than we've stayed anywhere since . . . since that day we found her. But it was not a good shape, not the right shape for legs, or hips, or spine, and so the shaping magic abandoned it."

Anger crystallized Fastfire's vision. His skin flushed and grew warm to the healer's touch. Any other elf, even the She-Wolf, would have left him alone, but not Delonin.

"I felt within her, Zarhan. Yes, the bone grew, but it grew wrong, and now it's gone. Magic's taken it back— just like it's taken the bone before. It was wrong, Zarhan. Trust me. If the shaping had continued, if the bone had hardened, she could not have stood or walked." The healer's grip was firm and cool.

Zarhan fought Delonin, but the healer was armed with the truth as well as magic. Swallowing a child's cry of anguish, the red-haired elf withdrew his fire, as he'd withdrawn it by the stream. He collapsed against Delonin's shoulder.

"I can't wait much longer."

Delonin shook his head gently. **Why wait at all?** His sending was soft as thistledown.

Zarhan shuddered but said nothing.

With a deliberate sigh the healer found his voice again: "She left here looking for you and came back with your stick against her shoulder and midnight in her eyes. Zarhan, friend, I need all my fingers and half the toes on my right foot to count the winters since you came seeking your lifemate and found her with us. Throughout all that time Rahnee has been helpless and Recognition has been an open wound between you and Cheseri. None of you is healing. Why do you fight something so clear, so simple?"

"I made a vow," Fastfire explained, straightening up and bumping his head in the peak of the tent. "I had never felt Recognition before I Recognized the She-Wolf. Together, we found her name, and she found the strength to take Timmorn Yellow-Eyes' place. We were rarely more than a day's walk from each other's side, but always I shared her with something I was never a part of: the tribe, the wolves, and especially the wolfsong—winters, summers, one after another when they live without memory. You can't imagine it, Delonin. With their wolf blood, Timmain's children can be with you talking, eating, lying beside you in the moonlight, and you remember all of it, but they don't.

"One day Journey stood in front of me with that midnight look in her eyes. Recognition—hotter, fiercer, and more brutal than I had imagined it could be. I called out to Rahnee but she only heard her wolfsong. She couldn't remember my name. She didn't recognize me.

"That was the first time. It was far from the only time. But now I've made a vow. We will Recognize each other when she is healed—we have always Recognized each other when she awakens from the wolfsong—and this time it will be forever. We're not among wolves or Wolfriders. Merolen is chief and a full-blooded elf; she won't challenge him. We'll finally have what the high ones intended for themselves when they came here; what my elders had—and yours. Just as soon as she heals herself and wakes up. I won't spoil it, Delonin. I won't Recognize another elf. Cheseri doesn't hear the wolfsong and our passion might not fade."

The healer was incapable of deceit or deception. Disbelief tempered by amusement pulled the corners of his mouth into a grin. He bit his lips together to keep the words inside. Zarhan was his friend: the only elf he knew with manifest magic and the only one who shared his bone-deep aversion to killing. Moreover, he looked to Fastfire for wisdom. If the four surviving elves of Trickster's clan put their ages together, they were still a child compared to the fire-haired elf. No, the healer didn't want to endanger friendship or future wisdom with a blunt opinion, but minds weren't mouths and in shoulder-rubbing closeness, thoughts had a way of leaking out:

Recognition doesn't work that way. You've already Recognized Cheseri; denying it doesn't mean it hasn't happened. She's miserable—she can't think about anyone but you. She never has time for Kelagry anymore, or me. And the daystar could become a stone-cold cinder before your lifemate heals—

Zarhan was shamed. **I'm sorry,** he sent, but that sentiment, sincere as it was, couldn't conceal the doubt, anger, and ambivalence in his mind. He reverted to spoken words because they were so much simpler and more opaque: "I could understand how Recognition moved through the Wolfriders. Timmain *became* a wolf; that was too much. Timmorn Yellow-Eyes was wolf and elf equally. Rahnee and the other Firstborn are more elf than wolf, but the children of the Firstborn are the true Wolfriders. They needed us elves for our elfness—for balance and serenity, for the memories of the elders they lost when Timmain became a wolf. As time went on, I was the only one they could Recognize.

"But I do not understand Recognizing Cheseri. I've sought out every name in my soul's memory. I've found the names of elders my parents had forgotten, but nowhere have I found your names. We are elves, but we are not kin. Delonin, I ask you: What purpose could possibly be served by Recognizing an elf whose memories must be utterly different from my own?"

The healer's eyes widened. A reply had formed at the front of his mind and his own seldom-heard elders had snatched it safely away. If Zarhan Fastfire did not know the answer to that question, no blundering child of Trickster's clan would reveal it by accident.

Zarhan watched and misunderstood. "There's so much

left unanswered. I've asked my memory so many questions since that moment when Cheseri aimed an arrow at my heart. Most of them remain unanswered. My elders can't tell me who you are. There are the stars, the star-mountain, the nightmare, and the darkness—but no other elves, anywhere. The high ones don't seem as perfect or powerful as they used to; Timmain thought we were alone when she submerged herself in her magic to give us Timmorn. Not like you. You had the Trickster; your clan found a way without sacrifices or compromises—"

"Your lifemate's weak." Delonin put an abrupt end to Zarhan's musings. "Kelagry brought the bowl just after day's end." He tipped his head toward the other side of Rahnee's pallet where a clay bowl held a lumpy mass that glistened in the firelight. "I'll go now, while you . . . eat. I'll be in the house with the others, if you need me. I'll tell Cheseri to leave you alone." He worked his way past Zarhan and untied the leather door after he left.

Fastfire blinked once, twice. He couldn't see as well in darkness as Rahnee or the wolves. Of course, the wolves couldn't see as well as tuft-cats or owls. But he didn't actually need his eyes to find the bowl; the scent was enough to guide his hand. His fingers slid across the slick, cool surface; his gut clamped tight and took a dive toward his knees.

When the healing, shifting magic had her body in its grip, Rahnee was as helpless as a newborn. More helpless. A newborn elf or wolf would mewl until its hunger was sated; it would writhe and wiggle to the sweet-smelling teat and cling there tenaciously. While her body shaped or unshaped bone, Rahnee could not move or make a sound.

She was that way when Delonin and his three companions found her in the grass with a scrawny wolf standing guard over her scarcely living body. The wolf ran as soon as it saw them and they, having lost all their kin to the same creatures that had crushed her bones, took up the vigil. The enormity of Rahnee's injuries confounded the young healer's skills, but he heard her hunger and answered it as best he could.

When Zarhan finally found his lifemate she'd been in the care of Trickster's clan for three winters. They fed her milk from a cow-ox and a pungent, gooey concoction they called *cheese*. The She-Wolf was conscious, but from her navel to her thighs there wasn't a bone in her body. Zarhan told Delonin and the others the truth:

She needs meat: raw meat, black meat with the thick blood still in it.

The four strange elves, whom Zarhan had known less than a moons-dance at that point, exchanged dark glances until Delonin found the courage to speak: Didn't he know the danger raw meat posed? Rot worms, gut worms, and a horde of invisible, gnawing things that would transfer themselves from dead meat to living elf unless light, wind, or boiling fire rendered them harmless.

Zarhan replied that the She-Wolf and her tribe knew the dangers, which was a lie, but that parasites didn't bother them, which was almost the truth. Every eight or so winters, Rahnee and her first born kin developed cravings for certain barks and bitter roots. She'd gorge herself on the foul-tasting, indigestible stuff and be sick for a moons-dance, then she'd be ready to eat raw, bloody meat for another eight winters. The purging was more frequent, less profound for the young ones, the Wolfriders, but none of Timmain's children believed there was a connection between the meat they loved and the days when their bellies were sore and swollen.

The wolf keeps the elf alive, Fastfire had explained to his dismayed, disgusted companions. *And the elf returns the favor. Rahnee needs raw, black meat.*

How will she eat it? Kelagry had demanded. He was the wildest of the youngsters, the boldest hunter, the most forthright speaker. He was the one the She-Wolf would feel kinship with when her healing finally ended. *Gut meat doesn't tear easy like red meat—especially when it's raw.*

I'll share it with her, the way the wolves do.

Zarhan would never forget their responses when he told them what the wolves did. Cheseri had actually covered her mouth and bolted into the bushes. Merolen clung to his bow and his dignity, but he'd been as pale as a dead fish's belly. Delonin was appalled; the She-Wolf was different, but Zarhan was an elf. Kelagry was insatiably curious. None of them guessed the sinking hopelessness Zarhan himself felt, as strongly now as he'd felt it that first time, when he forced his fingers around the slippery offal and lifted it out of the bowl.

Breathe through your mouth—he told himself, as he did each time he performed this little ritual. *Steady in, steady out. Don't think what it is, what it was. Don't think at all, just chew and swallow.*

It was a rare storm that blew no good to anyone, anywhere. The vile taste and texture removed the last sting from Fastfire's thwarted Recognition passions. As night deepened and the other elves slumbered together in their felt-walled house, Zarhan was numb to the heart and at peace, crouched beside his lifemate, living like a wolf. Rain pattered gently on the roof of the tent, obscuring all other sounds. It didn't disturb Rahnee or Zarhan, who unconsciously licked the blood from his fingers before placing his lips against hers for the last time.

Trickster's clan kept a herd of shaggy oxen. They wove soft cloth from the undercoat wool and felted the upper layers with animal grease to make fine, waterproof tents. With the casual ease that arises only from seasons of practice, Fastfire wrapped himself in furs and blankets and stretched out beside Rahnee without jostling or touching her.

The rain stopped. The sun rose and so did the four

young elves of Trickster's clan. Fastfire would have awakened if he had not heard them moving through the camp, but their conversations assured his guardian-self that he could sleep a while longer.

Zarhan! An acorn bounced off the sleeping elf's forehead; it came to rest in his ear. "Psst! Wake up! Merolen's waiting for you!"

Zarhan was cross-grained in the morning. He recognized the silhouette and the voice well enough not to panic, but not well enough to know who it was. Until he'd been upright a few moments, he wasn't always certain who *he* was. And some mornings—like this morning—he felt very, very old.

"Come on. Get up. Merolen's waiting. He wants to speak to you. I think it's important. He and Delonin were up before dawn and talking ever since."

"Go away, Kel. I'll see him later."

"He won't wait until later, Zarhan. You better come unless you want him barging in here."

Disentangling himself carefully, Fastfire wriggled down the tent to the opening. He swore when the bright daylight lanced his eyes. "Puckernuts!" was the curse he uttered, but the thought beneath it was considerably more potent. He staggered to the far side of one of the huge oaks, relieved himself, and, circling back toward the camp, paused by a leather bucket. He splashed handfuls of ice-cold water on his face, shuddered, and swirled a few mouthfuls around his tongue.

"This had better be important," he groused, finger-combing his hair. One foot remained resolutely asleep; he limped alongside Kelagry.

The hunter led him past the fire pit where they cooked their food and toward another spindly column of smoke on the far side of the big tent-house. "I'll let you borrow my cloak, if you want. The one with the speckled shells and the sky beads—"

Zarhan flared his nostrils, filling his breast with the

morning air. Trickster's clan was burning ox dung again, the way they did when they wanted to commemorate something important. Fastfire supposed it was no different from the Wolfriders gathering to howl a birth or a death, or the times when Samael passed around the dreamberry bowl. But the howls and the berries were real. Trickster's clan, reduced by the thunder-feet to this handful of children, mimicked customs their own lives could not remember. "I don't want your cloak, Kel."

"You should," he scolded. "You shouldn't stand before the fire looking like nobody. My cloak— Those sky beads, they're forever-old. They came from the stars. My mother had them from her father and he had them—"

"I don't care if they came from your Trickster himself, Kel. If Merolen wants to talk to me before the daystar climbs above the treetops, he can talk to me exactly as I am."

The pair passed around the large tent, into clear view of the ceremonial fire. Cheseri and Delonin got to their feet but Merolen stayed as he was, seated on a woven mat, hands palms-up and resting on his knees, eyes transfixed by the curling smoke. He was, as Kelagry promised, robed in the clan's finest panoply. A cloak of iridescent feathers spread out from his shoulders. White-weasel tails dressed his thick, sable-colored hair. Painted blue patterns swirled across his face and neck; the markings became bolder and mixed with other colors as they descended onto his naked chest. None of this disguised the fact that he hadn't yet outgrown his adolescent awkwardness, no more than the She-Wolf had when she took Timmorn's place as chief.

That morning burst into Zarhan's consciousness as bright and sharp as if it were only yesterday and not an ancient day long before any of the nearby oak trees had sprouted. He'd used his magic to ignite Timmorn's spear while Rahnee held it, making the tribe believe she was a chief, making her believe it, too. He'd forgotten how

young she was. He regretted that his own appearance
showed no respect for Merolen's authority or wisdom.

"I came directly," Zarhan said. He met Merolen's stare
without flinching but let his arms hang limply at his
sides. "I should have taken a moment to prepare myself.
But I'm here *now*." *Now* was more important to the
Wolfriders than either the past or the future. Zarhan
couldn't help assuming it was important to Merolen,
chief of Trickster's clan.

"The time has come to speak of the matter of your
lifemate and her fate—"

The youth's calm, coldly spoken words rocked Fastfire
onto his heels. He was speechless; his thoughts were
severed from his body.

"It will soon be twice-eight winters since we took
Rahnee to shelter with us. Her injuries were grievous; she
should have died long before we found her. But her will
was so strong, and we had lost so much ourselves to the
thunder-feet, that we could not give her the mercy her
crushed bones deserved. She would heal, we thought, and
we would heal in the new house we built around her. We
tried, by the Trickster's cunning, you know we tried, but
she did not heal and yet she did not die either, then
fireblight withered the meadow grasses. Those oxen in
our herd that did not die outright grew weak with hunger
and illness—"

Suspended in his thoughts, Zarhan knew exactly what
Merolen was going to say next; on his command they
collapsed their tents and went looking for another home.
They were still looking. Perhaps it was just as well that
Fastfire's tongue was not in his mind's control, for if he'd
been able to speak, Zarhan would have countered that
every time Trickster's clan found a hospitable place it
roused too much pain for the youngsters. And, of course,
the places that did not evoke those memories were
ill-suited to oxen or elves. Even this grove where they had

camped since ice-thaw was a half day's walk from the nearest stream and two days from the meadow where their herd grew fat and shaggy on sweet-grass.

"Delonin told me that late yesterday afternoon Rahnee's healing spirit let go of the bone it had been weaving and that by midnight she was as hollow as she was the day we found her. He says there was nothing we could have done. Her healing spirit missed its mark. He says it will try again because her will remains strong and you . . ." Merolen hesitated and swallowed his distaste. "You sustain her."

Sweat erupted on the youth's skin. It muddied the carefully painted patterns. He seized his fleeing composure with his fists and continued in a slower, deeper voice.

"The high ones, our elders, brought magic to this world, Zarhan Fastfire. It belongs here no more than we do, and sometimes it loses its way. We have all seen the purest spirits turned to fume and mire. Most of us have no magic now except to share our thoughts and memories. Rahnee is different, and full of magic. How long has it been since she has spoken a word or sent a thought meant for any of us? Delonin says her magic will find the way back to her one right shape. He has magic. She has magic. You have magic. I am as ordinary as an elf can be and survive, and I am not so certain. I'm afraid of what Rahnee might become if her magic sours. We can't shelter Rahnee any longer. We can't wait for her to heal. Trickster's clan must search for its home."

The timeless, paralyzing moment came to an end. Zarhan was aware of his tingling fingers, his cramped toes. He saw the astonishment on the faces of Delonin and Kelagry and knew the young chief had not taken them into his confidence. Fastfire did not look at Merolen's sister, Cheseri. He squared his shoulders within his wrinkled tunic and looked down at Merolen with all the disdain he could muster.

"Rahnee would not abandon you."

The youth trembled; he nearly cracked. Sendings flew thick and shielded between the siblings. Then, once again, Merolen found his voice:

"Let her go, Zarhan. *Help* her go, if you must—"

"No! Never!" Zarhan's face went livid. He kicked a rock into the fire pit, raising a column of pungent sparks and dislocating his toe. He meant to show Merolen his back, for now and forever, but his foot wasn't listening to his will and he had to use words, instead, to express his outrage. "Go ahead, leave if you want. Chase your dreams from one horizon to the next. You're shut out of your own heart, Merolen. You and your clan will never find a home! If any elf's lost the way, it's not Timmain's granddaughter. The Wolfriders know the way. Trickster's clan . . ." The rest of Fastfire's insult never reached his lips but was replaced by an entirely different jibe: "Trickster's clan has the name—and the way—it deserves!

"Go where you will. I'm staying with my lifemate and my chief. We'll meet no more in this life."

Zarhan made his foot bear his weight and beat back its savage pain. He was light-headed before he'd taken two steps and prayed his will was strong enough to carry him into the little tent, to Rahnee's side where he belonged. Where he'd stay until she healed—or at least until these strangers were gone.

"He can't hunt," Kelagry said loudly. "He'll *starve* if he stays here along with Rahnee."

"The wolves might return after we leave and hunt for them both." That was Delonin's voice.

"I'll hunt for Zarhan Fastfire. I'll stay with him, and her, for as long as it takes."

"Cheseri—"

Zarhan heard the astonishment in Merolen's voice and the rustle of feathers as he got to his feet. He heard a light-footed hunter's tread race across the fallen leaves and heaved his throbbing foot forward. His knee buckled from the pain, but a strong pair of hands seized his arms before he collapsed and kept him upright. Before Fastfire knew whether to be grateful or to struggle for freedom, Merolen was in front of them, blocking their path.

"Seri, I can't believe you'd do this!"

"When he owes me his life, perhaps he will find it easier to give me a piece of his," she replied, adjusting her grip on Zarhan as if he were just another bundle to be tied on the back of a musk-ox.

"This is madness, Seri. Recognition madness. There's nothing between you. You can leave him behind. You can put him out of your mind."

There was an edge of desperation in Merolen's voice. It gave Zarhan the answer to a nagging but unimportant question: Merolen might be the hereditary chief of Trickster's clan, but he lived in his older sister's shadow.

"There is a child between us. A girl child with our hair and our eyes; his magic. It is not her fault that she's grown shrill and prickly waiting all these winters to be born. I will not cut *her* out of my mind and so I cannot put this worthless lump of elf-flesh behind."

Zarhan caught a flicker of movement in the distance, behind his shoulder. It startled him and pulled his head around, but there was nothing to be seen—not with his skull's eyes. With his mind's eye he'd seen her clearly, almost full grown and very angry.

"Anaya—" The syllables, her soulname, seeped into his thoughts and off his tongue.

"So, you are not completely blind after all," Cheseri jeered.

Between them, Fastfire and the She-Wolf had brought a handful of cubs into this world. Through the momentary passion of Recognition, he'd sired a double-handful who belonged completely to the Wolfriders. Names still swam in his memory, full of potential and yearning, void of personality—he hoped that he and the She-Wolf would have one last child whom he would not lose to the tribe. Anaya's name was not among them. Zarhan knew with utter certainty he'd never heard of her before, but once he had, all the other names, all the other possibilities vanished from his mind. There was only Anaya, and her yearning for life was worse than any imaginable Recognition pang.

Zarhan very nearly strained his neck staring past Cheseri into the silent forest where Anaya wanted to be but was not. A fire kindled in the pit of his stomach. The short hairs on Fastfire's arms and neck stood erect: the fire was not his!

Timmain had given her children all the magic they'd need on this world of two moons. None of Zarhan's Wolfrider cubs inherited his particular magic. They were satisfied with wolves and wolfsong and more than a few of them preferred to believe that their father was someone else. Zarhan disciplined himself to believe he didn't care. The She-Wolf was always a chief first and a mother second; she surrendered their cubs to the tribe as quickly as she could.

But Cheseri was an elf, like himself, not a Wolfrider, and Anaya would inherit his magic—if he broke his vow and allowed her to be born.

Zarhan smothered the flames reaching for his heart. He shivered uncontrollably and, once again, Cheseri's hands kept him on his feet.

"You vile, unnatural creature," the elf-woman hissed, but there was another word seething in her thoughts: **Trickster!**

The enraged sending stunned them all. Merolen recovered first. He shoved Zarhan and his sister forcefully apart. "Enough!" he both shouted and sent.

Fastfire collapsed to one knee and stayed there. He'd heard that imperative tone many times before from

Timmorn and Rahnee. He knew a chief when he heard one, and was wise to their power. Despite his youth, Merolen was the right elf to lead Trickster's clan and woe betide his sister if she thought she was dealing with a half-grown sibling instead. Cheseri got one snarled syllable in rebuttal before she realized her mistake.

"But I cannot leave," she said softly after shielded sendings had flown between them. "Unless you force me to." She lowered her head, hiding behind the fall of her hair.

For one brief moment Zarhan expected Merolen to throw back his head and howl. Rahnee did that sometimes when a simmering conflict would neither sharpen into a challenge nor fade away. That moment passed. Kelagry and Delonin crowded close, their anxious faces elegant mirrors of the struggle going on in Merolen's mind. Always a witness, never a participant even during his lifetime among the Wolfriders, Fastfire remained on one knee and pondered whether any vow could be correct while causing this much pain and misery.

Merolen acted before Zarhan reached any conclusion. "I won't use force. I won't abandon anyone. I won't separate my kin." The emerging chief drew confidence from the sound of his own words. "One chief. One clan. One roof. We'll stay here. Right exactly here—"

"But, Merolen—" the itchy-eyed healer objected.

"We'll build our winter house right here. We'll lay the stones around the She-Wolf's tent so she doesn't have to be moved at all. We'll make it large enough for all of us and we'll stay here, together, until we can leave. Until *all* of us are ready to leave."

The three elves of Trickster's clan exchanged anxious sendings without glancing at their newly implacable chief. Zarhan, in contrast, relaxed; his toe had snapped into place, for one thing, but the relief went deeper than muscle and bone. He still didn't understand who or what the Trickster had been, but for the first time he felt that he belonged: one roof, one clan, one chief.

"If we filled the walls with clay, the fiercest blizzard couldn't bother us," he said, including himself in the proceedings as he had never done before, not even with his lifemate and the Wolfriders. "There's good red clay between here and the meadow. It would make a fine stone with a little fire-heat—"

"Clay-stone walls! A winter house of mud and sticks isn't strong enough for you—you want to turn clay into stone!" Kelagry interrupted. "Stone lasts forever. Just how long do you think it's going to take the She-Wolf to heal herself strong?"

Zarhan couldn't answer, but Delonin could. The healer stared up at the frost-withered leaves clinging to the oak branches. He sniffled wearily before opening his mouth. "A lifetime," he whispered. "*Your* lifetime anyway, Kel. As long as you've been remembering your own life."

The young hunter let out a horrified sigh. His eyes lost focus as his thoughts raced backward. "One hand . . . two . . . three— We left home because the thunder-feet had trampled everything . . . everyone. I was almost grown then." Profound disbelief formed on his face as he finished counting. "Five-of-eights! Merolen—do you hear what Delonin's saying? Five-of-eights winters!"

Fastfire hadn't given a measuring thought to Rahnee's healing, but now that he did, Delonin's estimate felt about right. Elves were unaffected by the ravages of time; they died by accident or by choice, but never from age. Rahnee, of course, was Timmorn's child, and Willowgreen, the elf-healer of the Wolfriders, asserted that the wolf blood aged inevitably to death. But Rahnee was not yet old and neither, for that matter, was Timmorn Yellow-Eyes, whom Zarhan had met in the forest not long before he met Cheseri. Five-of-eights winters—to any elf, with or without wolf blood, it was longer than a sneeze but less than a yawn; unless that elf remembered only five-of-eights winters, in which case it was, as Kelagry continued to repeat:

"A lifetime. A whole lifetime—"

"Be quiet, Kel," Merolen chided, though the measurement had left its mark on his own, slightly younger face. "Our old clan-house was eights and eights and eights of eights old. Five-of-eights is nothing, no time at all. Our feet will hardly have time to feel rested. Maybe we need a rest," he concluded without confidence.

Cheseri brushed imaginary grit from her sleeves, then began to roll them up. "Unless you want to rest forever we'd better not rest at all until we've made those clay-stone walls Zarhan's talking about, and everything else, too. I saw rings around the moons last night. They might crest twice more before winter sinks her fangs into this forest, but I doubt it."

They worked with diligence while the daystar shone and the leaves continued to fall. The oxen wore trails into the ground between the trees bringing flat stones from the stream and heavy baskets of clay from a marsh near the meadow. The clay-filled walls were up and a thin layer of twig-thatch spanned the roof before the lasting snows fell. The oxen foraged for themselves in the nearby forest while Kelagry set snares for small game. Winter itself was not as hard as it could have been. The elves were cold and hungry when the snow was gone, before the first hints of green had yet to appear in the tree crowns, but spring kept its timeless promise and the season of starving passed without incident. The ox cows dropped their calves and the herd stripped the nearby forest to deadwood before Merolen and Kelagry took them to the sweet-grass meadow for the growing season.

Rahnee had lain silent and unmoving since they began to build the house around her. Zarhan watched the moons and counted the winter days as they passed. It was the longest sustained healing and shaping his lifemate had undergone since her terrible injury. He was certain he saw bone rising beneath her hips when he attended her. He allowed himself to hope; then one night when the trees and berry briars were in blossom, the She-Wolf woke them all with a bloodcurdling shriek.

Delonin pressed his fingers against the throbbing veins of her neck. He didn't need to peel back the fur blankets, but simply shook his head. "There was something wrong when the bones began to harden. They weren't in quite the right place. Once her body makes a mistake, even the smallest mistake, it starts over from the beginning."

"One mistake!" Cheseri's hair and eyes were wild with interrupted dreams. The pangs of thwarted Recognition ebbed and flowed with the seasons. Winter was a quiet time; spring saw the return of the symptoms. Cheseri strode to the earthen platform where Rahnee lay, where she seldom ventured. She opened the blanket cocoon and stared at her naked, hollow rival. "Fix it! Don't start over!" she shouted. "We'd all like to make our kill with our first arrow, but sometimes you need two or three. Even your precious wolves didn't bring down their prey with the first rush. They never gave up! If I knew how, I wouldn't let you give up so easily, either!"

She stormed out of the house before anyone had the presence of mind to restrain her. The bear-pelt door flapped in the raw midnight wind. Kelagry chose to join Cheseri outside the shelter rather than remain inside with the others; he paused to carefully secure the bearskin before he disappeared. Delonin had a similar idea. He bolted toward the opening at the narrow end of the house, but Merolen and Zarhan both lunged after the healer and surprised each other with their apparent common purpose.

"You first," the clan-chief said, looking into Zarhan's eyes as he kept a firm hold on Delonin's upper arm.

"Cheseri's right, that's all. Maybe Delonin isn't a

shapeshifter like Timmain, or Rahnee, but he's a healer, and a healer should have known that the bones weren't growing right, and should have been able to fix them."

Merolen nodded curtly before turning to Delonin and releasing him. "Well?"

The healer stared at his feet, wishing that the ground would swallow him whole. It didn't, and he began to speak in a painful whisper. "I don't know anything until it's already happened. I try, but I don't understand what the magic does within her. I think, maybe, there's a pattern to it; maybe next time I'll know what's important and what's not. There's so much I don't know, Merolen. Hestawai and I, we thought we had forever. There's so much I wasn't taught."

Delonin's answer satisfied the clan-chief, who sighed as he fumbled a corner of the blanket under Rahnee's chin. Fastfire tapped his fingertips together, counting backward from eight to one, then he exploded:

"Taught! Since when did any elf need to be *taught* his magic? Magic's inside you from the very beginning. I imagine fire, I dream fire, I know fire. It was inside me before I was born—" Zarhan's thoughts slewed toward Anaya, his unborn, unconceived daughter. Frantically he covered her accusing face with another equally ill-tempered and magical one: Willowgreen, the Wolfriders' healer, who denied her elfin heritage in her efforts to belong to the tribe and hear the wolfsong. "Willowgreen was a healer whether she wanted to be one or not. No one taught her anything; no one could. When a Wolfrider was hurt or sick, she reached into the part of herself that she hated, and healed them. Sometimes she failed because she lacked the strength, but never because she lacked the knowledge. You're a fluff-eared fool, Delonin, if you think an elf with the right magic has to be taught how to heal."

Delonin's face froze into a mask of shame. Zarhan could not have pierced him more deeply if his words had been laced with fire and bound to an arrow shaft. The would-be healer's eyes glistened, and tears had begun to stain his cheeks before he threw himself into a shadow-filled corner. It wasn't the first time Fastfire had gotten himself in trouble by taking Willowgreen as an example. He would have apologized immediately, but a word—that mysterious name, Trickster—seemed to hang in the place where Delonin had stood, and with it an aura of betrayal.

Trickster? Zarhan sent cautiously, not knowing who, or what, might respond.

You'll get no answer, Merolen replied. **He's long dead, and no kin to any of us.**

Implications came together slowly. The border between life and death was clear enough in the ordinary world. When an elf died, his body was stilled forever, and his body's voice as well. But in the almost-magic realm of thought and memory, the border could be blurred, and crossed. In an essential way, Zarhan Fastfire retained ongoing kinship with Timmain and the High Ones who had accompanied her out of the ruined sky-mountain, and with all their direct descendants. Merolen and Trickster's clan were obviously elves but, just as obviously, not kin. Zarhan accepted that, although it threw his understanding of himself and his universe into a turmoil. Now Merolen claimed—or seemed to claim—that Trickster's clan was not kin within itself.

What is Trickster's clan? What was the Trickster? What are *you*? The questions belched out of Zarhan's thoughts, leaving a foul trail of doubt behind them.

Shades of silver coalesced in the featureless place where Zarhan received another elf's sendings and, on occasion, glimpsed the faces of his conscience. The fast-emerging figure was like no other in Fastfire's experience. Gross and misshapen, with heavy brows and limbs, and teeth crowding its mouth like grinding stones, Fastfire thought that he beheld one of the five-fingered demons.

A human? Your Trickster was a human? You let yourselves— With a *human?*

Merolen would not answer with coherent thought. Another silvered cloud grew out of the darkness, beside the brutish face. It became a lumpish sphere, then a fist, then it opened: a hand as gnarled and swollen as the face, yet proportioned exactly like Fastfire's own, with four fingers, one of them opposed to the other three. Zarhan recoiled and, realizing that Merolen had hold of his wrists to facilitate the image-sending, wrested free. The silver clouds dissolved immediately, but the images were part of his own memories now and could not be so easily banished.

"What?" he sputtered, rubbing his wrists frantically and beginning to shiver.

"Trolls. Like us, they kept the name the humans gave them because, like us, they lost something vital when the sky-mountain fell."

The shivering became uncontrollable. Zarhan lowered himself awkwardly to the ground and reached beneath Rahnee's blanket to clutch her hand. Merolen's words continued to assault his memories like lightning in a thundercloud. When the tumult ceased, nothing remained as it had been. Timmain's haunting voice, and many others, had risen in a chorus, affirming Merolen's claim: when the elves had come to the world of two moons they had not come alone and, more importantly, they had not come where or when they had intended.

"They betrayed us!" Zarhan shouted the implications of his reconstructed memories. "The *trolls* betrayed us. Your Trickster betrayed us!" He warmed himself with the fire of righteous rage.

The young chief offered no defense. His body was limp, his face impassive, and his thoughts—which Zarhan barely perceived—welcomed Fastfire's anger. At length, Merolen moistened his lips and began to speak:

"Much was lost—" He shrugged his shoulders ruefully

and shook his head. A thick lock of sable hair fell across his face; he let it be. "Our clan began with children and ends there. We had no one like Timmain to hold our memories until we were grown enough to hold them. All we had, and have, is what the Trickster told the elves he rescued and sheltered in his cave.

"He said he had not been part of the rebellion"— Merolen's tongue stumbled over the un-elfin word—"He said he'd been loyal to the high ones, that he'd tried to prevent the catastrophe"—another awkward word— "He said he'd tried to befriend the firstcomers, but the few who survived the Fall ran away from him and from each other. Within the clan, my grandfather remembered the cave; my grandmother remembered Trickster rescuing her. Those are our oldest shared memories; before them is only nightmare. When Trickster had rescued three hands of elves, Trickster led them against the humans; that became our second nightmare. After that he led those who were left to a place where the grass grew tall and stretched to every horizon.

"Trickster showed the clan how to hunt the great ox and, later, how to capture their calves, and raise them. Finally, the thunder-feet came. They were mindless beasts, but mightier hunters than elves would ever be. The Trickster was still alive when the clan abandoned the grasslands and drove the herd back into the forests. He feared the humans would hunt us again, but they had abandoned the forest and we were alone. The Trickster showed us how to make houses like this one. He would leave in the summer, searching for elves, he said. One winter he didn't come back.

"My father became clan-chief and the clan became the clan I remember from my own birth. We lived well, without remembering, until something drove the thunder-feet off the plains, into the forests. The rest you already know."

Zarhan listened deeply, allowing Merolen's words into the faded memories he shared with his ancestors. He waited—expecting another tumultuous assault. The only response was an age-old sigh. Children were the single joy this world had shown the firstcomers, but children without their elders—without their communal wisdom—was unmitigated tragedy. Zarhan yearned to take Merolen in his arms, to fill the youngster's emptiness with his own memories. It was not Recognition, but it was almost as strong and, looking at the young chief, Zarhan saw that Merolen felt the yearning, too.

"Cheseri," he murmured, finally realizing what she must feel when she looked at him.

"From you to Anaya, from Anaya to my sister, and from her to all of us. We would know the truth, not just what the Trickster taught us. We would be complete."

Fastfire retreated unconsciously. He struck his head against the wall, releasing a shower of grit from the roof. Sharp bits entered his eyes, where they became both cause and excuse for tears. The same ancestors who had made themselves into his conscience abandoned the niceties of vows, oaths, and lifemate loyalty. They raised a wild howl of Recognition instead.

"You'd have me. You'd have my lifemate, Timmorn, and the Wolfriders. But you wouldn't be complete." His desperate words were meant for his own ears and elders more than they were meant for Merolen and Delonin, who'd risen to his knees and stared at Zarhan with wide, hopeful eyes. "My memory is like the sky on a storm-cloud night: I know the stars are there, but I can't see them."

"Knowing would be enough," Delonin responded from his corner.

The red-haired elf wanted to run until exhaustion quieted the clamor inside his skull. If the path to the door had been clear—if that path had been blocked by Merolen rather than Rahnee's fur-strewn pallet . . .

Rahnee! She-Wolf! Help me. Set aside your wolfsong just this once and Recognize me. Tell me who I am and that we belong together—

Fastfire followed his sending into the silent depths of his lifemate's soul. She was all around him. In ecstasy, he Recognized her, but for her part there was only the self-absorbed pulse of her body as it shifted and shaped.

Rahnee!

Their souls quaked; the She-Wolf's inner eye opened, bathing Zarhan Fastfire in gentle light.

Beloved? The sending came from the unfathomable place where her body reshaped itself. It began as a whispered question, swirling around him, probing his soul with a feather-light touch. The light strengthened. **Lifemate.** It was no longer a question. **Zarhan!** The caressing light became the irresistible radiance of Recognition.

I'm here. With you. *Forever*—

Zarhan . . .

The She-wolf Recognized her lifemate, then just as quickly, released him. Zarhan surged forward, but his striving could not confine her. She slipped away and her soul was dark again . . . dark and silent until he filled it with orphan wails. His body demanded his return; he exercised his will and refused. He would stay where he was, in the middle of absolute nowhere, until his lifemate returned. He did not want his body; its pains exceeded its pleasures. He did not care about its fate. It would and could resolve into the dust and dirt of the world of two moons while he waited . . . waited forever, if he had to.

It was not easy for an elf to abandon his physical self. Zarhan possessed will, strength, and stubbornness in sufficient measure, but he had failed to reckon with the will, strength, and stubbornness of his clanmates. When Fastfire's body fell to the ground and his pulse fluttered wildly, Delonin discovered that desperation was the only teacher he truly needed. He commanded Merolen to take

Zarhan's other arm; together they dragged the dead-weight elf into the night air.

Fastfire's limp arms and legs folded against his torso and became rigid.

"He's going to die of cold!" Merolen exclaimed when his frantic chafing brought no warmth to Zarhan's flesh.

"There's fire-magic in his soul. He *can't* freeze. The fire won't let him."

There was a cistern sitting in the dirt beside the door—one of several Zarhan had made to catch water as it flowed off the roof. Delonin wrestled it loose and moved it toward Zarhan. When the surface ice cracked and water splashed over the rim, the healer's hands numbed instantly.

Grunting with triumph, Delonin tipped the cistern; frigid water cascaded over Zarhan Fastfire. The healer had no time to savor his satisfaction. Merolen seized him by the shoulders and braced him hard against the nearest oak tree.

"You're mad! He'll never come back now. You might just as well have put your knife between his ribs!"

Delonin squirmed in his chief's grip. Words failed him and so did his newfound confidence. He was ready to beg for mercy when they heard a piteous moan in the mud. Merolen let go.

"What now?" he demanded.

The healer bounded to Zarhan's side and pressed his hands into the hollows of the elf's neck. Fastfire had been sucked into his body by the ice-water shock—that much had gone according to Delonin's plan—but his magic hadn't kindled. The red-haired elf was slipping into an unchosen death.

"Make fire!" Delonin commanded, pinching Zarhan's cheeks. "Make yourself warm."

Zarhan moaned. There was no guessing if he'd heard Delonin's commands, or if he could obey. Merolen shoved the healer aside.

"Back under the roof."

The chieftain hooked his hands under Zarhan's shoulders and dragged him halfway to the door before Delonin lifted his ankles. When they crossed the threshold, lamplight fell on Zarhan's face, revealing a death-mask grin. Merolen sent his thoughts in a wide arc through the forest.

Kelagry, come back. Sister, I need you.

There was no time to confirm if the sendings found their targets. Fastfire's eyes were open and completely white. He was breathing, but it didn't seem likely that he'd breathe much longer. There were sleeping furs and ox-hair blankets in abundance on the four stick-and-straw pallets around the glowing hearth but, whether attached to hide or felted into cloth, the fibers could only retain warmth, not create it. Once they'd ripped Zarhan's sodden clothes from him, Delonin and Merolen wrapped the nearest furs over their own shoulders and then wrapped themselves around Zarhan.

"Whatever *possessed* you?" Merolen demanded, barely able to keep his teeth from chattering.

"I did exactly what he said to do. I looked deep into myself. I imagined healing him: bringing his soul back to his flesh, and suddenly I knew what to do, or I thought I—"

Kelagry burst through the door and stopped short. His eyes and his mouth opened wide as he panted and stared.

"Grab a blanket," Merolen said. Kel obeyed his chief, who raised a winglike arm to make room for a third warm body on the circumference of their circle. "Did you find Seri?"

The hunter shook his head slowly. He was pulling the immediate past from Delonin's mind as fast as the healer could send it. Answers took shape before he could conceive the questions. He draped a blanket over his hands and studied Zarhan with awe. "We can't let him leave." He draped the cloth and yanked the laces from his tunic. He shed his clothes completely before joining the circle and gasped when Zarhan's cold, damp skin touched his. "We need Seri. She's the only one who can pull him back."

Their hearts and minds joined for one sending. It didn't seem possible that Cheseri had outrun their combined strength, but they could not find her. Delonin withdrew first.

"The way was clear," he murmured. "My healer's sense has never been so clear. I knew where he was and what he'd done, and I knew what had to be done to bring him back. The way was clear—it couldn't have been the wrong way."

The three in the outer ring remained huddled beneath the furs and blankets, holding the fourth between them. Zarhan could not slip further into oblivion, but his companions were unable to restore his consciousness and life—until the door leather moved again. The young men of Trickster's clan opened their thoughts to Cheseri.

Sister—help us.

She strode through their sendings as she strode from the doorway. Her face was grim as she shook the tangles and dampness from her dark hair. Without a word or thought, she peeled her heavy tunic over her head. There was a long tear on the sleeve and a matching crusted gash on her forearm. It opened and bled freely as she wormed between her brother and the healer. They both sent a gentle question; she shut them out with a thick, black wall.

Zarhan. Cheseri's sending rode a brilliant, searing light. **Zarhan Fastfire. Enlet's son—** She recited the names of all his elders, and, of course, Anaya's name, too. **I Recognize you! You cannot leave. You cannot pass into memory until you Recognize me. I will not allow it. I will pursue you across time and the stars. You _will_ Recognize me. Zarhan!**

Within the warm arms of the circle, Cheseri reached

for Zarhan. She laced her fingers into his hair, pulling his face to hers. A low moaning vibrated in Fastfire's throat, dying before it reached his lips. Cheseri wrapped her arms around him. Her blood smeared across his cheek and shoulder.

Come to me. Come to me *now*. Recognize me, or I swear by my last breath: You will never know peace.

Cheseri squeezed with all her strength. The breath came out of Zarhan's chest with a sigh; his conscious self followed, like any drowning creature seeking life and air. He threw his head back—after a life among wolves, Zarhan Fastfire had learned how to howl. The raw sound shattered the outer circle, but not Cheseri's inner one.

Rahnee!

The wolf-soul of Timmorn's daughter answered her lifemate's call. It touched the elves and tasted their thoughts, then withdrew. Defeated, Zarhan opened his eyes. Everything was gray—even the hearth fire. Cheseri was a gray shadow, and Merolen beyond her. The smoke shaped itself into the solemn faces of Timmain and her star-wandering companions. They were solemn, watching the least among their children, nodding slowly with approval.

Zarhan remembered the rough-hewn word Merolen had used and he tried to rebel. "I'm not just flesh, blood, and your memories. I'm one living creature, one elf. I was born. I *will* die . . . Because Rahnee will die. I will die here with her when she dies. It is my choice, my will: to be remembered, forgotten, by the Wolfriders. Do not make me do this. Do not bind me here forever."

Cheseri smelled the smoke from the hearth. She saw pale ivory skin and the ruddy reflection of firelight in Zarhan's black eyes. She saw Kelagry and Delonin, and the She-Wolf still as death on her pallet. For Cheseri, there were neither ghosts nor memories in the shadows.

"You flatter yourself," she said coldly. "I will bind you for one night only: until Recognition is sated and Anaya is my daughter, to grow within me. I would not have you for a heartbeat longer."

"This is true." Delonin freed his hand from Merolen's and placed it gently on Zarhan's shoulder. "You have nothing to fear. Recognition is for the moment, for a child. It is mating without life or love. None of us will keep you from Rahnee; Cheseri least of all. When the She-Wolf awakens, or if she does not, you will be free to join her."

The healer told the truth, but not all of it. Nothing could bind Cheseri and Zarhan together against their mutual wills, but Recognition could, and probably would, recur. Zarhan heard what had not been said—after all, he'd felt Anaya emerge from the unanticipated future. His soul knew she was not alone. But he was weary and chose the comfort of Delonin's spoken truth.

Beloved— Fastfire stopped fighting the arms around him and the needs within him. **I'm sorry.** He was exquisitely aware of Cheseri's presence. It transcended pleasure and pain. **Forgive me.** And became life itself.

The days and nights that followed were peaceful, even serene. The tensions of thwarted Recognition vanished as abruptly as they'd begun so many winters earlier. Cheseri kept her promise: once her daughter was smiling within her, not wailing in the unformed future, she lost interest in Zarhan Fastfire. She treated him no differently than she treated Kelagry, Delonin, or her brother—which was to say she ignored them all.

Summer ascended in long, warm days. The forest berries ripened, and Cheseri, who had always been sleek and feral, underwent her own shapeshifting magic. She grew softer, rounder, as Anaya swelled within her, and rarely strayed from the oak grove except to bathe in the stream. She had not hunted since Zarhan Recognized her, but appropriated the pelt of every beast Merolen and

Kelagry brought home. Throughout the summer she scraped, dried, buried, and pounded, transforming the raw hides into suedes soft enough for an infant's skin. She sang as she worked, and sang to Anaya each night before she slept. The days were growing short again when Cheseri began to sing to Rahnee as well.

She no longer saw Rahnee as a rival. When she looked at the pallet where the She-Wolf lay, Cheseri saw a helpless elf, to be comforted and nurtured until she held her own daughter to her breast.

The daystar had set; the sky was a warm, pale lavender. Cheseri stood in the doorway, waiting for Zarhan and Delonin to return from the meadow with sweet-grass for the roof-thatch.

"Rahnee no longer needs you," she announced when they entered the grove. "You have done your best. Blood and black meat were good, but I can give her more than that. You'll only be in the way."

The sweet-grass sheaf slipped through Zarhan's arms. He looked past the healer to Kelagry and Merolen squatting hunch-shouldered at the outdoor hearth. Kel shrugged, and nearly lost his balance. Merolen didn't twitch.

Fastfire marched toward the door. He was three strides short when Cheseri blocked him with her will. Stymied—feeling foolish because he'd forgotten everything he'd learned about women as their birth-time approached—Zarhan smiled and shrugged and, finally, retreated in silence. He spread the sweet-grass out to dry in the next day's light, then joined his unhappy fellows at the fire.

Merolen spoke first. "She is not Seri any longer. She says we must build ourselves another house, a fathers and sons house apart from mothers and daughters. This has never been done. Never. Something possesses her soul. She is not my sister."

"She's broody," Zarhan replied, coaxing more light, less heat from the fire as he spoke. "It could be worse."

Most of the Wolfriders bore their cubs easily; most of the elves and the Firstborn, too. Most, but not all. A smile tugged at his face as he remembered the transformations that invariably took Rahnee by surprise. His three companions were little more than cubs themselves, unprepared for what was coming. They were without elders to show them what to do. The smile became a frown: He was their elder.

The fire nearly died. Kelagry prodded it with a charred stick.

"I thought when she was done with Recognition she'd be—well, done with it. She'd have a smile for the rest of us. When Zarhan wouldn't Recognize her, everything was his fault and everything made sense. But now she doesn't want us around at all, and nothing makes sense. I keep waiting for everything to be the way it was . . ." The hunter's voice caught in his throat. There was no way back to the time before the thunder-feet except through memory. "The way it was when there were just the four of us."

The stick began to burn. Kel watched the flames a moment before stifling them in dirt.

Zarhan remembered something his father said: "Life is like a stream. It can't flow backward; it can't stay the same. Even when life seems the same, it has changed."

"Is that your way of telling us that we should do what Seri says and build another house?" Merolen muttered without raising his head.

The elder elf was nonplussed. He'd been thinking of new children replacing old children, not houses. Merolen got to his feet, facing the house. A wordless lullaby wafted out the still-open door.

"If that's your advice, it rots my gut. I do not intend to be chief of half my clan. Seri could have been chief, if I hadn't been born after her. She would have been chief if I had died with the others. But I'm here and I'm chief. One chief, one clan, *one roof!*"

Fastfire never remembered leaping to his feet or grabbing Merolen's arm and spinning him away from the house. On the other hand, he'd never forget the look in the young elf's eyes, either. Chiefs and challenge, he realized, were what wolves and elves had in common; they were, perhaps, the reason Timmain had chosen the wolves. Unfortunately this realization occurred because Merolen looked exactly like a dominant wolf about to tear the throat out of a too persistent, too stubborn rival.

Get out of my way.

I'm no threat to you. I just don't want you to do something you'll regret. I'm no chief—not the way you and Rahnee are—

Get out of my way. NOW.

Cheseri's no threat to you, either. Let her be. Anaya will be born before the snow comes to stay—

NOW!

Merolen surged forward; Zarhan braced himself.

Only a fool would challenge a mother in her milk-lair. You'll start a fire you can't put out. Do you want to be chief of ashes? Fastfire called on his magic to sustain him. The ground smoldered beneath his feet. He had a heartbeat, maybe two, before the fire would grow too strong and Merolen would truly be the chief of ashes. But another heartbeat was enough. The pressure of mind and muscle eased.

"One chief. One clan. One roof." Merolen backed away. There were blisters swelling on his palms, but he had not felt them yet.

"One moons-dance, two at the most. Once Anaya's born, Cheseri will welcome all the help she can get. We can sleep under the stars, in tents, until then. We don't have to build anything."

"One house for all of us, no matter how many—" The young chief tried to move his fingers. Pain drove all other thoughts from his mind. He stared at his hands. They began to shake; the quivering quickly spread up his arms and down his spine.

"Delonin," Zarhan called with unnatural calmness. "Come here—now."

The healer hurried. He took Merolen's right arm and gently pressed his fingers over his chief's inner wrist; the trembling stopped. He did the same with Merolen's left arm and, after the pain was grounded elsewhere, began the healing.

"I didn't mean to injure you, but I couldn't let you go into the house—"

Merolen felt Delonin's increased confidence. His weepy, ruined palms repaired themselves as he watched. The agony was already dispersing. "You meant to keep me from greater harm. If I'd gone in there— If I'd raised my will against Seri, I'd have made injury to myself and my clan that no healer could heal." He wove his restored fingers through the air while Delonin wrought similar magic on his numb right hand.

Kelagry would not stay by himself by the fire. He appeared silently, suddenly, among them and whistled through his teeth when he saw what Zarhan's magic had done and what Delonin's was doing. "So—who won?" he asked. "Are we going to tell Seri that she's full of wind, or do we do what Zarhan says and sleep in the trees? Is he chief now? Are we still Trickster's clan or are we Zarhan's?"

The erstwhile challengers looked quickly at each other. Merolen's expression showed a hesitant question and a glimmer of doubt that Zarhan deflected with a shake of his head; that was all the reassurance the chief needed. His smile broadened as his eyes narrowed.

"You belong to my clan—to Merolen's clan—and you'll sleep wherever I tell you to!" He launched himself after the hunter who wisely—albeit noisily—retreated into the forest.

Delonin raised his voice in protest: "Wait! I'm not finished!"

"You're wasting your breath," Zarhan advised as the sounds of laughter and broken branches echoed through the night. "There's no stopping him or calling him back. He's got a chief's spirit."

The little healer led the way back to the fire. "Chief's spirit," he muttered. "I'd sooner believe a rascal's spirit —even a trickster's spirit. He and Kel were a pair— running wild like ferrets. No one knew where they were half the time—" Delonin fell silent as Zarhan tended the fire with his magic. "Listen to them out there. We're all children to you—but those two, they were born in the same summer and they've never seen another elf born. They *are* children. No wisdom. No restraint. It would be better if you were our chief—"

"No it wouldn't," Zarhan countered as he rocked back on his heels. "I'm no chief—I learned that a long time ago. Being chief has very little to do with wisdom or restraint. I learned that from Rahnee."

"Then maybe she'll teach Merolen. Maybe she'll be our chief."

Fastfire brought the two personalities together in his mind, face to face, will to will. The fire collapsed with a shower of sparks, leaving him and Delonin in darkness.

Cheseri never mentioned a separate house for fathers and sons again. So long as none of the menfolk crossed the threshold, she did not care where they slept or what they did. Merolen and Kelagry—as if confirming Delonin's worst fears—ranged farther and farther from the oak grove. They were gone for days at a time and the task of gathering sweet-grass, drying it, and tying it into thick bundles for the roof fell entirely to Zarhan and Delonin, who spent as much time chasing away the birds and squirrels as they did thatching the house.

The work was special misery for Delonin. In the short time since he'd healed Merolen's hands, his mastery over his magic had increased dramatically. He understood that he was a warrior in his own way: a vigilant guardian, ready to defend the clan from the ravages of injury and the invisible perils of bad water, bad food, bad air, and the myriad other dangers he knew but could not name. Delonin understood, as well, that his healer-self was sometimes overvigilant. Sometimes it saw danger where it did not truly exist. The oak trees were one such nondangerous danger; his healer-self treated them as if they were deadly poison. The sweet-grass was another.

Delonin's eyes were dry and scratchy, his nose raw and swollen, and the itchy roof of his mouth was enough to drive him to distraction. And all for nothing. Sweet-grass wasn't poison. He'd get himself convinced of that eventually—he'd pretty much conquered the oak tree menace—but until he did, Delonin's conscious wisdom and innate magic were in ceaseless conflict.

When a huge crow had the audacity to swoop down behind Delonin and cackle loudly in his ear before ripping a seed-ear out of the heavy bundle he was trying to pass to Zarhan on the roof, the frustration and weariness finally got the upper hand. The normally placid healer shed his self-control. Shrieking like a winter storm, he charged across the grove and flailed the bundle of dried grass against an oak tree trunk. Grain flew like wind-driven hail. The crow that had precipitated the outburst, and a handful of its companions, sought shelter in the branches.

"Go ahead—fill your bellies! Eat it all!" Delonin roared at them. He pointed at the kernels and chaff scattered on the ground. "Stuff yourselves until you're too fat to fly away. I'll smash your noisy heads in with a stone. By the stars and the moons, I promise I will!"

It was an idle threat—the healer never killed anything

more soulful than an insect—and the crows seemed to know it. They raised a ruckus; eights and eights of birds flew in from everywhere. Big birds, little birds, chirping birds, honking birds, and the original handful of insolent crows joined the pecking, squabbling throng. When Delonin had beaten all the grain out of one bundle, he grabbed another and started again.

Zarhan planted his fists on his hips and watched the spectacle from the half-thatched roof. As still more birds materialized around him he had an idea:

"No sense feeding and killing them now." He leaped down from the roof, scattering the birds enough to gather a handful of grain for himself.

Delonin glowered at the interruption.

"They're hungry—but we're not. If you can draw this many now, think how many you could get when the ground's covered with snow. We might be glad of an easy meal then."

The healer thought about it. Merolen and Kelagry had been gone for three days. When they got back they'd have meat for Fastfire to smoke and pelts for Cheseri to cure. But there was always the unspoken chance that the twosome wouldn't come back and there was no guessing when, or if, Cheseri was going to pick up her hunting gear again. Even so, Delonin was unconvinced.

"There aren't any birds around here in the winter. They've all flown away." He raised the grass to shoulder height.

"Not all of them. I think it would be worth waiting. Who knows—maybe we could eat this stuff. Maybe there's something to be learned here."

"It's *grass*, Zarhan. What is it that the Wolfriders said— 'We don't eat grass, we eat the animals that eat grass'? You might as well try eating bark or branches."

Delonin swung the bundle of grass into the tree. Kernels scattered. Zarhan caught some while protecting his face. He popped them in his mouth and began to chew and crunch. The hard bits had the taste and texture of pebbles, but Zarhan was persistent, grinding them on his back teeth until the husks opened. He mashed the husks and grain around in his mouth, then spat everything out without swallowing.

"No good, eh?" The healer flailed as he spoke. "What did I tell you?"

Zarhan shook his head and tried to get a sharp-edged scrap dislodged from between his teeth. His tongue wasn't equal to the task. He used his fingernails instead and stared at the golden husk a moment before flicking it away. "Not grass; grass-nuts. I've eaten worse. Probably want to pound them a bit, and maybe soak them in water to soften them up. They taste better than acorns any time, any way."

The healer clung to a tasseled ear sticking out of the bundle and let the rest drop to his feet. He separated a few grains from the ear and carefully split the husks. He rolled the kernels across his fingertips, sniffing them cautiously, then deeply. Acorns were the worst part of the oak-tree menace. He doubted he'd ever be able to eat one even though he knew, as did every other elf and animal in the forest, that acorns could be the difference between starvation and survival after a hard winter. Delonin lived with the thought that his healer-self might prefer starvation to the bitter, pulpy nuts—and that thought frightened him.

He waited, listening to his body. The gut-wrenching aversion he would have felt if he'd held an acorn beneath his nostrils did not occur. Feeling bold, Delonin caught a grain or two on the tip of his tongue. He could hear the blood pounding behind his ears, but his itchy palate was no worse than it had been. He chewed, and waited, and chewed again until his mouth tingled with a taste sweeter than honey, then he swallowed.

"Different," he conceded, half expecting a thunderclap to rise out of his stomach. When it didn't, he licked his hand clean.

Zarhan stretched his arms and back until the sinews snapped. He stared at the unfinished thatch roof. The damage the birds were causing was all too obvious. But at that moment the roof was deserted; all the birds were scratching the ground and stealing from each other.

"The birds are after the grass-nuts, not the grass. Whether we eat them or not, you've had one good idea today: beating the dried grass to get rid of the nuts and the birds." He started toward the pile of loose, dry grass. "Probably we should beat the nuts out of the grass before we leave the meadow. No sense carrying bird food all that way."

Delonin blinked and drifted out of his magic. "Better to gather the nuts and leave the grass," he said dreamily. A scant handful of grass-nuts left him hungry for more in a way that few other foods did. "This is good, Zarhan," he said, shooing the birds aside and scratching in the dirt himself. "Not just better than acorns—this is as good as meat or cheese."

"Acorns are better than cheese." Fastfire had never developed a taste for the curdled, congealed ox milk that Trickster's clan considered an essential part of every meal.

Still, the look on Delonin's face as he crunched his way through another handful of grass-nuts was a match for any Wolfrider's midway through a moonlit feast. Zarhan gave the grass-nuts another try after carefully removing the husk. He chewed and waited, as the healer had, until the grass-nuts were thoroughly mashed and their sweetness bloomed on his tongue. He thought of all the starving times when the Wolfriders hovered around his fire waiting for the elfin brew of roots, acorns, and other woody nuts to become digestible. He used grass for kindling, but he'd never once thought to add grass-nuts to the pot.

Zarhan swallowed. The sweet taste turned to pleasant warmth in his stomach. He'd soak some of the grass-nuts in water to soften them, then keep a sackful handy. Taking a sheaf of grass in his arms, he began flailing it against the wall of the house, where the nuts would fall on the flat stones around the threshold and be easier to collect.

The birds saw the advantage of stone over dirt almost immediately. Zarhan was soon shooing the birds twice for every time he beat the grass against the wall, but he persisted with single-minded determination. Delonin shuttled from Zarhan to the pile of unthrashed grass and back again, creating another pile of nutless grass midway between them. They were both paying more attention to the tasks at hand and the thieving birds than anything else. Neither noticed Cheseri appear in the doorway until it was too late.

The elf-woman was disheveled from an interrupted nap. Her hair stood in wild tufts and her eyes were filled with terror. "Thunder-feet! Thunder-feet are coming!" she shrieked, seizing Zarhan's grass-flailing arm and digging her fingernails into his flesh. "Gather what you can and run! Thunder-feet—don't you hear them? Don't you feel . . . ?"

Her voice trailed off. The sounds that had addled her dreams were nowhere to be heard—although she remained certain she had heard them. Then she saw the birds, the layer of golden kernels on the threshold stones, the dry grass that had fallen from Fastfire's hand and was tickling her bare feet. Dream memories fled like frightened ravvits. Cheseri felt foolish, and that turned her fear to anger.

"What's the matter with you?" She released her daughter's father with a shove. "Banging away against the walls!

You turned my dreams to nightmares! Have you lost your wits?—scaring me like that. What were you trying to do?"

Before Zarhan could answer—and undoubtedly make a bad situation worse—Delonin inserted himself between them. He scooped up a handful of thrashed grain and offered it for her inspection.

"Grass-nuts, Cheseri. Food. So long as grass grows, we won't have to fear the starving time again."

Cheseri stared at the insect-sized bits the healer poured into her hand. There was a part of her that understood the importance of a new food source, but that part was completely obscured by her lingering anger. She threw the grain at Delonin's face and sought words to wrap around her rage. The best she could manage was a barely coherent sending:

Useless. Thoughtless. You don't understand. What would we do if the thunder-feet did come? What *could* I do? If anything happened to me, or her. It's so easy to die, and Anaya needs so much. I'm everything to her, but I'm alone. There's no one to turn to. I'm all alone—

"By choice," Zarhan snarled aloud; there were some emotions that could only be evoked in bile from the back of the throat. "Don't forget you shut us out of your life. There's no room for us. I have to wait until you go to the stream before I can steal a moment with my lifemate. You've made it clear we do nothing right. We don't think. We don't understand. And now you complain that you're alone!"

Cheseri shrieked through tightly clenched teeth, and drove the birds high into the trees. **What do any of you know about having children?** She dismissed Delonin's half-sent objections with a wave of her hand and focused her scorn on Fastfire. **I couldn't turn to *you*. You denied your daughter for eight-and-two winters. I thought Rahnee—**

Zarhan's jaw dropped.

I reached out to Rahnee with one hand and Anaya with the other. I hoped they would grow strong together and Rahnee would help me when it was time for Anaya to be born.

"My lifemate? The She-Wolf?" Zarhan sputtered before he burst out laughing.

Stop that. Stop laughing! Cheseri braced herself against the doorway. She hung her head and sought to quiet her pounding heart. She had forged a link between Anaya and Rahnee—at least she thought she had. She'd created something, but in the pit of her heart she'd known from the beginning that the She-Wolf couldn't replace the midwives' smiles or their strong, reassuring hands. **She'd try. I wouldn't be alone. She's been through this; she'd know what to do.**

"The She-Wolf would go out into the forest, kill the biggest animal she could find, and feed you steaming black meat to make you strong again."

Zarhan knew he should have kept quiet before the words were out of his mouth. Even though they were the simple, honest truth, their images were more than Cheseri could endure. Her knees buckled and her face turned a dangerous shade of red. She closed her eyes and thought the worst had passed when a spasm raced down her spine; it stopped behind her swollen belly where it began to squeeze and twist. Every other part of her was numb in comparison—she didn't feel her knees strike the threshold stones, or her forehead.

"It's Anaya," Delonin whispered. "It's Anaya. I hear her—she's coming. What do we do?"

The birthsong rang in Fastfire's head, pushing all other thoughts aside. It pulled him close to Cheseri, as it had always drawn the whole Wolfrider tribe, elves and wolves alike, to the birth-pair. Timmain's children—the only mothers Zarhan had known—gave birth in exhilaration that overshadowed all discomfort. He had supposed it would be the same with Cheseri and was shocked to find her rigid with fright and pain when he wrapped his arms around her.

"What's wrong?" Delonin demanded when he saw Zarhan scowling. He grabbed Cheseri's hand, compounding her fears with his own until Fastfire pried him loose.

"Relax. My daughter's being born—there's nothing wrong. If this doesn't fill you with happiness, at least keep your fear to yourself. Or, better yet, just get rid of your fear and hold her hand gently."

The healer took a deep breath and found—to his amazement—that he could banish fear with a thought and Anaya's birthsong. With that echoing in his ears, nothing could possibly be wrong. He knelt opposite Zarhan and whispered that to Cheseri. She smiled, and gripped his hand until the knuckles snapped. He winced, then drew upon his healer's magic and shared it with her.

"Should we send our thoughts after Kel and Merolen?" he asked when feeling had returned to his fingertips.

"Wherever they are, they're already heading home," Fastfire replied softly.

Another spasm shook Cheseri, but she was no longer alone or afraid; the pain came and went quickly. She clung to her companions, trusting them completely as Anaya slipped from her into the daylit world.

"They won't get here in time," Delonin gasped when Cheseri squeezed and twisted his hand another time.

And they didn't. Anaya's gray eyes beheld their first twilight before the breathless hunters staggered into the oak grove. Kelagry was content to sag against the wall, one leg across the threshold, the other still outside it; but Merolen, clan-chief and blood kin, was drawn all the way to the fresh straw pallet beside the hearth. He reached down to embrace his sister, then froze when he beheld Anaya.

"She's . . . she's *tiny!* She's a tiny elf." The chief's hands dropped slowly, ignoring Cheseri. He dearly wanted to touch the infant and yet was obviously afraid to do so. "Kel. Kel, you've got to see this. She'd fit in my hands."

Zarhan turned away. His daughter was very small and he was worried about her, but he'd turned away so no one would see him smiling. If Merolen saw him, his chiefly pride would be bruised. If Cheseri saw, she might laugh with him. There was peace between Anaya's parents now; there had to be. They'd gotten a glimpse of their daughter's temper when she emptied her lungs after her first breath. They'd need each other, and the rest of the clan, to see Anaya through her childhood.

The straw crackled as Cheseri lifted the swaddled infant. "Do you want to hold her?" Cheseri said softly to her brother.

"No. Not really—I might drop her."

"I'm sure you won't."

There was more crackling and the unmistakable sounds of an infant cooing. Zarhan turned around again in time to see Merolen waggling his fingers above Anaya's face.

"Her eyes are open," the chief said in the adoring tone that forever separates adults from children. "She sees me. She knows who I am." His attention shifted away from Cheseri. "Don't you? You know who I am. I'm Merolen. I'm your chief—"

Zarhan buried his face in his hands.

If you laugh, Cheseri sent to him alone. **If you even chuckle—** Her threat was as friendly as it was sincere.

"Kel—get over here. You've got to see this. Her whole hand barely goes around my finger."

Kelagry hauled himself to his feet. "My chief calls and I obey," he grumbled—until he saw his first infant, after which he entertained her with his repertoire of silly expressions.

Cheseri begged him to stop and demanded that

Merolen return her child since he couldn't keep from bouncing her as he laughed at Kelagry. The chief understood that there were some requests he did not dare argue with, but he stayed on his knees and was radiantly happy when Anaya caught his finger again. Kelagry crowded close to his chief and, after a moment, Delonin was drawn into their gathering.

Fastfire lowered his hands. He felt them sending happiness to each other. He could have joined them. He'd be welcomed; he hadn't been deliberately excluded, but another pallet rose by the hearth and his happiness was there.

Rahnee?

The She-Wolf had benefited from Cheseri's nurturing. Her cheeks were not as hollow as they'd been, her eyes seemed less bruised. Most important, there was bone—solid, living bone—spanned between her legs and her spine. Delonin had examined it after Anaya was born.

The hardest part is over, the healer said to her disbelieving lifemate. *All the bones come together exactly as they should. All the shaping is over. Now it's just healing.*

How long? Zarhan asked. **How long until you're strong and walking again?** He caressed her cheek, not expecting an answer, nor any response at all.

But she leaned into his touch and a sleeper's smile curved her lips. Zarhan was weak and giddy with joy—then Rahnee opened her eyes and his hand began to tremble.

Fastfire? Fastfire—what's wrong? What's happened?

Nothing. A birth. A girl-cub has been born.

How many toes? Did you see its toes and fingers?

Four perfect little toes on each foot. Four perfect little fingers on each hand.

Good. I'll sleep now. I'm tired, Fastfire, very tired and weak. I could sleep clear through winter to spring. I'll sleep now.

Until spring, then, Zarhan agreed, tracing the curve of her jaw as he withdrew his hand.

She was in wolfsong; he knew all the subtle signals. She knew who he was, but she hadn't Recognized him. It was just as well. Any fully conscious creature would be thoroughly mad after waiting twice-eight winters for her bones to find the right shape. And she still had a lot of healing left. Zarhan judged he'd go mad if he had to lie on his back just one winter. But the She-Wolf could endure it all with the wolfsong, without madness. He supposed he could endure one more winter. She'd answered his question, at least; he took consolation from that. Often when she was in wolfsong she heard only her own questions.

You look sad, Delonin sent from Cheseri's cluster. **Why don't you join us?**

"No reason not to."

He snuggled in beside the healer, extending his hands to take Anaya from Merolen's arms. The chief paused in his crooning. His sending was empty; the sidelong glare from his eye said everything. Zarhan tucked his hands on his thighs.

The bloom will fade off that flower, Delonin sent again. He clapped Zarhan lightly on the shoulder. **Once it's time to change the wrapping.**

Fastfire managed a feeble smile. He told himself he didn't mind. Rahnee would Recognize him in the spring. Recognition never linked full siblings and, considering the resemblance between them, it was unlikely that Recognition would link Merolen to any of Cheseri's children. The young chief might never hear his own name weaving through the birthsong.

Merolen's patience faded with sound, not sight or smell. Anaya was a tempestuous infant, prone to thrashing and screaming until her face turned blue. She'd waited too long to be born and was full of yearnings her helpless body could not fulfill.

"She wants to run, but she can't even crawl," Cheseri explained as she rocked her squalling daughter and ignored the little hammer-fist pounding on her chin.

A storm had raged through the forest for two days. Snow had drifted all around them, protecting them from the worst of the cold wind. They were trapped together in the one-room house until the weather broke. Tempers were beginning to fray.

Kelagry missed his mark with the flint-knapping stones, shattering a knife he'd worked on all winter. He stood up—looking for a place to throw the pieces. There was none, so he lifted the leather door and shoved them into the snow wall. There wasn't a draft—there couldn't be with snow drifted over the roof—but Cheseri shot a dark thought in the hunter's direction and Anaya's screaming intensified.

"Can't you do something, Delonin?" Kelagry demanded. "You're a healer. Make her arms and legs grow faster so she can crawl if that's what she wants to do!"

"I can't do that."

"You'd do it for the She-Wolf. You were fussing over her last night. I saw you."

That drew interest from opposite corners of the room, where Zarhan and Merolen had been letting their thoughts wander as far afield as possible. The clan-chief marched over to Cheseri.

"Quiet!" He pointed a half-fletched arrow at Anaya and shouted louder than she squalled. Cheseri cocked her fist and aimed it at her brother's knee, but Merolen had sent his command also and Anaya's survival instincts were sharp as the arrowhead in her clan-chief uncle's hand. She became silent in midyowl. "That's better."

Cheseri stuttered with her fist, then lowered it. Everyone appreciated the quiet.

"I thought we all agreed that we'd let the She-Wolf heal at her own pace. I thought we all understood when

Zarhan said she'd be worse than a trapped wolf if she woke up before she could walk. Or do you really want to be under one roof with her and Anaya?"

"I was checking, that's all. I could help the She-Wolf now, if something wasn't going right—" Delonin saw Kelagry frowning behind Merolen. "Bones grow, they don't just heal. Anaya's got to *grow*, there's nothing a healer can do to change that. The She-Wolf's healing. I could do something, if I had to. But I don't have to. She knows what she's doing now. I'll be surprised if she sleeps until spring—but it won't be my fault if she wakes up before she's strong enough to walk."

The chief turned his attention to Rahnee. The She-Wolf lay on her side. She moved around on her pallet now and fed herself when they put a bowl in her hands. Sometimes she talked to them, but her conversations were strange. She remembered nothing from one day to the next. She asked Zarhan's name each time she saw him, and promptly forgot it. Zarhan called it *wolfsong*, and Merolen guessed he understood what made Zarhan act so strange. Being lifemated to an elf who thought like a wolf couldn't be easy. And she was a chief, too; there'd be no arguing with her. He was more than a little nervous when he wondered what would happen when she argued with him.

Zarhan said his lifemate had finished being chief, but Zarhan Fastfire wasn't always right. Merolen hoped with all his heart and soul that the She-Wolf would sleep in her wolfsong until the height of summer. If they argued then, they could turn their backs without one of them becoming the winner, or loser. Sometimes, when Merolen looked at Rahnee through the tail of his eye, he saw a wolf, not an elf. For twice-eight winters he'd seen a scrawny, age-grizzled wolf, but this winter the wolf was sleek and powerful.

"Rahnee would never challenge an elf."

Merolen started. He hadn't heard Fastfire approach. "How can you be certain?"

"She never challenged anyone. Timmorn Yellow-Eyes made her chief and the challenges come to her, not the other way around. She'd no sooner challenge you than she'd challenge Timmain. She'll leave before she'd challenge."

"And you'd leave with her?"

"Of course."

"Anaya—?"

"Has you, and her mother, and the others; my magic and my memories. She'll do fine."

"I'll miss you."

"I haven't gone anywhere and I don't think I will. I think Rahnee will be very happy here." He reached down to touch his lifemate. She slept lightly these days. His fingertips awakened her.

Fastfire? Rahnee raised herself to one elbow and swept her wild silver hair aside. **Zarhan?**

Zarhan's heart leapt in his throat; she'd used his elfin name, his Recognition name. She was getting stronger and the wolfsong was getting weaker. One day soon— One heartbeat, any heartbeat, and she'd be fully awake, fully alive. His life would be complete again. He knelt down and framed her face with his hands, staring into her violet eyes, waiting for Recognition's heartbeat.

I'm hungry. Where am I? The She-Wolf pushed Fastfire's hands away and flopped onto her back. "Where is this place? Who are *you?*"

Merolen stammered. He looked left and right and at his feet, which had sunk roots into the hard-packed dirt.

The She-Wolf wrinkled her brow and flared her nostrils. "I know you," she said with growing certainty. "I've seen you before." She threw aside her furs and, with miraculous agility, pulled herself into a sitting position. "Let me look at you closely." She struck fast, seizing the hem of Merolen's tunic, hauling it toward her, then grabbing a handful of his hair.

"What's going on?" Kelagry asked from the far side of the room—although it should have been obvious.

Zarhan shouted, "He's *Recognizing* my lifemate!" and planted his foot in Merolen's bent-over side for good measure.

The young chief was scrabbling for his balance before he hit the ground. He was ready and able to launch himself at Zarhan, but Rahnee had been faster. She had Fastfire by the ears. Her eyes flashed and her sendings cut like knives. When she let go, Zarhan hit the ground like one of his sacks of grass-nuts. Merolen put one foot behind the other and tried to retreat.

"I remember you. *Merolen.*"

"No."

If Zarhan had been able to talk—or if he'd cared to—he could have told the youngster he didn't have a chance.

"I recognize you. I *Recognize* you!"

Zarhan had been waiting a very long time to see that look of Recognition in her eyes. He saw it now, obliquely, as she rose to hands and knees and began to stalk her prey. Maybe Merolen would continue his retreat; maybe he'd try to deny the obvious; maybe she'd tear his wretched little head off. Fastfire could live with that, if it brought Rahnee back to him.

But Merolen didn't put up a fight. He was flushed and breathing hard, but not because he was frightened. When Rahnee tried, and failed, to stand, the young chief came to her and within three heartbeats they were both absolutely oblivious to the world beyond their own bodies and souls.

"I cannot witness this!" Zarhan grabbed a spear from the rack and swept up an armful of grain sacks. "I will not witness this!" He circled the room along the wall, being pointedly careful not to look toward the hearth. "I won't!"

He tore the door leather from its lashings and walked into the snow, which hissed and melted around him. Kelagry, Delonin, and even Cheseri called after him, but their sendings came back singed.

"What should we do?" the hunter and the healer asked together.

Cheseri pulled a blanket over Anaya. "Tie the door up again. The wind's fit for freezing!"

Zarhan Fastfire squandered his magic trudging through the snow. The faces of his conscience didn't dare show themselves. Even with his magic, walking was slow and treacherous. Ice formed beneath his feet and fire couldn't protect him from bruises when he fell. It wasn't long before he decided he was far enough away from the house—at least until the storm ended. He backed into a snowdrift, made himself a cave, and stewed in his juices.

He got hungry—ravenous, actually—and ripped the thongs out of the nut sacks with his teeth. He'd soaked the grass-nuts in water, then dried them before putting them in the sacks. Now they were wet from melted snow. He shoved a handful into his mouth anyway and retched it out. The taste was indescribable. It was like eating fire, except it wasn't hot. It was like eating ice, except it wasn't frozen. His eyes and nose watered. The tips of his ears tingled.

And he was still hungry.

Maybe if he baked the water out by holding the grain between his hands? Fastfire gave that a try, scorching his palms and dumping a hard lump on his feet in the process. After cooling his hands in the snow he looked for the clot of dried grass-nuts. He thought he'd made clay-stone, but clay-stone had never made his mouth water. He tore it in half and stuffed a steaming piece into his mouth. It was still indescribable, but now it was good: sweet and bitter at the same time, hot from his magic and warm from something else, a bit musty, and yet a bit sharp. He swallowed and filled his mouth with the other half. His ears tingled, but his eyes no longer watered from the taste.

Always curious and ever the experimenter, Zarhan scooped out another handful and set about drying it carefully. By the time he scraped the bottom of the first sack, he had his method perfected: breathing between his fingers to add more moisture even as his fire-magic dried the grass-nuts and clotted them together. By then the tingling extended the length of his ears and out to the tip of his nose. His fury at Merolen and Rahnee was muted by all the toasty, warm grass-nuts sloshing around in his gut—but he was still hungry. Making a grass-nut stone squandered as much strength and magic as eating one replaced.

He fumbled with the knot on the second sack. His fingers had minds of their own, so he ripped the thong out with his teeth again.

Zarhan was working on his fourth sack of grass-nuts when the snow cave collapsed around him. Daylight—even muted by the cloud-dregs of a furious storm—hurt his eyes. He winced and hid behind his hands.

"Zarhan. Zarhan Fastfire. I'm sorry."

The voice was hardly familiar through the roaring in his ears. Shielding his eyes with the half-empty sack of grass-nuts, Zarhan tried to see the face.

"Merolen?"

"No! It's me—Rahnee! The She-Wolf!"

"She's inside . . . with Merolen . . . may worms swim in his guts . . ."

Zarhan, I'm here. Right here, with you. Be angry with me, if you want. They told me how you waited. But don't pretend you don't know me.

Rahnee? The light was painfully bright. Fastfire
caught her hair and pulled her close until their noses
touched. "Rahnee—it is you—"

The She-Wolf wrinkled her nose and jerked away.
"What have you been eating?"

"Grass-nuts. They got wet, but I dried them out. Are
you hungry?" Zarhan fumbled through his lap, looking
for crumbs, which he offered to her.

"Ugh—keep them. They smell like the scrump at the
bottom of Samael's dreamberry bowl when he's left it out
in the daylight too long."

Zarhan's mind-fog lifted. "Dreamberries—that's what
they taste like. I've made dreamberries out of grass-nuts."

He tried to stand up, but lost his balance and grabbed
Rahnee instead. She wasn't strong enough to hold them
both upright and they wound up in the snow.

"You got drunk, that's what you did." She dropped a
handful of snow on his face. "Oh, Zarhan . . ."

"I did. I got drunk on grass-nuts. I am drunk on
grass-nuts." He swallowed the snow. "I'm going to get
sick." Fastfire curled up on his side and groaned. "I'm
going to die."

"It was Recognition, Zarhan—it happened. You know
how it happens. It doesn't mean anything—except, except there will be a cub, of course. Another girl, I think."

Fastfire rose to his knees, retched, and collapsed again.
"Good, Anaya will have a friend."

**Zarhan! You aren't listening to me. I was lost in
wolfsong forever—I barely remember what happened to
me. It's all a shapeless dream, and then, as soon as I woke
up, I saw you, but I Recognized a *boy!* If Merolen were a
Wolfrider, I wouldn't let him carry a spear in the hunt,
but I Recognized him!**

Find some grass-nuts, beloved—you'll feel better.
I won't.
**All right, you won't—but you won't care, either. Not

about the Wolfriders or wolfsong, Merolen or Recognizing Merolen. Not about yourself, not about me.**

But I want to care about you. You're my lifemate. You're the only reason I didn't die.

Then don't eat all the grass-nuts, only eat a few of them.

To Be Continued . . .

Personal Challenge

by Katharine Eliska Kimbriel

It only took a moment to change the future.

Dying time was Windwhisper's favorite season of the year. Warm days, cool nights, plentiful game; the forest painted in gold and crimson leaves, startling against brown trunks and weathered gray rock. There was time for leisure, time for thought, time for all the things, large and small, that were swept aside during the demands of long sun.

Most of all, there was time for the tribe.

Suntail! The thought erupted as a shriek of excitement in Windwhisper's mind.

Here, came a fragile mote in response.

I meant the bird! Breeze's thought sang like the gust of wind pushing past them.

Gently, Windwhisper cautioned her. The girl was a sturdy twelve turns, just coming into the strength of her sending. It was not too soon to learn that emotion could leak beyond thought, coloring the very air around them.

Silence. Dove's word dropped on their heads like a stone. Obedient to the command of one of their finest hunters, the children stilled, minds and bodies concentrating on the hunt their elders had promised them. This was a lesson that would fill both their bellies and their thoughts.

How I love this. It was a private reflection, but young Moonwalker leaned into her in response, and Windwhisper knew her wolf had understood the sentiment. Teaching the cubs was something they had fallen into, she and Dove and Willowgreen; teaching them basic hunting etiquette, tracking, and foraging. Back at the rock outcrop they called home, the graceful healer was already cooking the results of their morning quest, the youngest of the mobile cublings assisting her. It was up to Dove, Windwhisper, and the balance of the cubs to bring back the rest of dinner, for the hunters had left with the dawn, following the clickdeer south onto the plains.

A curl of wind slid past her, rich with scent. More than one suntail, plus the remains of old nests. These were young birds, born late in the season, scarcely worth catching. But one smelled *different,* and Windwhisper knew that scent promised a healthy adult suntail. It told her more, that breeze. Beyond her the suntails rustled irritably, reacting to the odor.

Suntail. Sunnyvale is moving upwind. Can you stop her? Like his mother and grandfather, Suntail was weak at sending, but already he "heard" like an adult. There was neither response nor sound, but moments later the familiar tang that was little Sunnyvale disappeared from the pulsing wind.

It would take time for the birds to settle. Silently they waited, silvery Dove above them in a tree, tiny Windy and Opal frozen below like lizards on a log. Pinecone was to Windwhisper's left, and her own son, Stars Dancing, somewhere to the right. Only Whistle was unaccounted for, but his scent lingered, so Windwhisper knew he had remained with the hunt.

They've started eating. Breeze again, this time in control of herself. Allowing herself a moment of pride in her granddaughter, Windwhisper waited for Dove's lead. To Windwhisper the stalk, to Dove the hunt . . .

Are you ready? Dove's heavy thought descended upon the group.

I can have it—him, came Breeze's strong sending. **If I miss, Suntail will have him.**

Do not miss. There was the barest touch of humor

behind Dove's tone, but the children were not old enough
to understand it.

If you do, Suntail will not. Some children were intimi-
dated by hunting with their parents; not Suntail and Stars
Dancing. They lived for the lazy days, when bellies were
full and their mothers would take them into the woods.
Then there was Whistle; his father's presence only made
him clumsy, much to Sundown's despair.

Moonwalker stiffened, and Windwhisper's thoughts
flowed away, lost in the thundering current of air that
roared about them. Instinct took over as she tried to
discern what had disturbed the she-wolf. The slanted
sunlight glinted from leaves of burning gold and deep
green, bursting like stars before her eyes. Shadows were
darker, if possible, and the soil of the deer path was
bleached from the last rays of the daystar.

A strong southern wind, whipping around them, con-
fusing sound and scent—

Then there was movement, the death shriek of a bird,
and Breeze's gasp of triumph.

"Good!" came Dove's voice from the golden canopy.
"Break its neck, quickly."

Leaping forward, the children rushed to offer their
assistance. Waving them back, Breeze set her young face
into a mask, reached with precision, and seized the
suntail by the throat. In a moment its struggles had
ceased.

FEAR

Emotion rocked Windwhisper back on her heels. It was
an echo, filtered through her wolf, coming from still
another of the pack. Was it Whiskers, Dove's tough old
male, who was alarmed? He had one of the best noses—

Suddenly the bush at the end of the clearing erupted
into another form, a tall, animated figure, part of it
shooting forth like a thrown spear.

HUMAN The warning came as a wail in her mind,
even as Whiskers charged through the underbrush, snarl-

ing his challenge. A deep-throated growl responded. Not part of the leafy apparition, but separate; one of the mud-colored beasts the elves called *dog,* a wolf perverted into a twilight existence, unable to recognize kin.

Tiny elves scattered like thistledown, scrambling to get out of the path. Ghostly Moonwalker leapt into the clearing, circling the grappling males, seeking an opening. Without thought Windwhisper reached, grabbing Pinecone's tunic and pulling him into the weeds.

The camp. *Carefully*. As if you were leading Death home. His face corpse white in answer, the youngster glided into the thicket beyond, balancing the need for speed against the possibility of pursuit.

Why didn't Whiskers smell him? There was no time, no time at all. Windwhisper tried to rise as the smiling human passed the howling, bleeding tornado of canines, leaned back to throw his spear at one of the children—

And then Dove was there. Leaping from the bough like a bird of prey, the Wolfrider ran her flawless flint spearhead into the human's chest, the force of her landing knocking them both to the ground.

Suntail! Even as Windwhisper's thought pierced him, the boy rushed across the edge of the clearing, scooping up little Opal and disappearing into the thicket with her. Another human coming through the bushes, fear and anger etched on his features, *May the High Ones give us strength*—

Then a spear blossomed in the stomach of the newcomer, and Windwhisper realized her hands were empty. Reaching to her belt, she pulled her bone blade from its sheath and ran to meet Death.

Not her Death. As Windwhisper seized her spear butt and yanked furiously at it, the skin of the youth rolled apart like soil before a ground squirrel, bloody flaps of muscle failing to hold back the offal. Confused, the human tried to hold his abdomen together with one hand while scrabbling for his knife with the other. Dancing around behind him, Windwhisper slashed her blade across the side of his throat.

The scream almost made her drop her knife. Not the work of a voice, but the sound of a soul—no! Humans had no souls! How could they have souls and kill their own, much less her people? But the scream came from the heart, and echoed as it faded, its pain as searing as a tongue of flame.

Windwhisper's knife was sharpened bone, not able to sever muscle without the work of muscle, but more than enough for skin and blood. A fountain of life sprayed over the struggling wolf and dog, squirting at Dove and the first human, who was smiling no longer, who was stabbing the elf-woman with his shiny black blade—

An anguished yelp told Windwhisper that Moonwalker's teeth had found the hamstring, crippling the dog. Then there was only the whine of a wolf, drifting with the breeze. Groping through the mental haze of pain, Windwhisper's spear was poised for a thrust, a slice, but she was not needed. Dove had finally bashed the youth's head against a rock.

Windwhisper . . . see to Whiskers . . . Faint, too soft for Dove's gentle strength, but Windwhisper obeyed her as she always had. Stepping backward several paces, she knelt by the brindle-haired wolf, letting her gaze flick from distant bush to animals, and then back. The dog was dead, its throat ripped out. Moonwalker's snowy coat was spattered with blood, but little of it was her own. And Whiskers—

His foreleg is crushed. The beast had strong jaws. Windwhisper could not bear to say the words aloud. They all had known that Whiskers' days were coming to a close, but not so soon, too soon—

"He always goes first, to scout the trail for me," Dove murmured, and now Windwhisper turned toward her friend.

Watch, the elf-woman told Moonwalker, who nudged her elbow and slowly moved out of the clearing, back down the path the humans had used. A brief call to the outcrop, to be sure they had been warned, and then Windwhisper knelt down by the mangled bodies.

Blood was weeping steadily from the wound in Dove's shoulder. What little she knew of their frail bodies told Windwhisper that it was a dangerous spot—only the High Ones' help had spared Dove's life so far. That intervention might not be enough. They needed leaves, special leaves; what had Willowgreen called them—?

Names did not matter, as long as you recognized what you sought. Stripping the leaves off several healthy plants, Windwhisper crushed them in her hands and pressed them against the wound. Then she reached for the weapon that had made the injury, squeezing the glossy stone point until it collapsed, oozing from the shrunken sinew binding. Working the blade like clay, the rockshaper began to stretch the stone, pushing it against the dirt, smoother, thinner, curving up one end and abandoning it—

"Let me," she told Dove, who was struggling to hold the leaves against her body. Gently, for fear of the heat she had released, Windwhisper pressed the stone against Dove's shoulder, molding it into depressions and over muscle like pulped squash.

"We must leave here. But Whiskers—" A soft whine answered Dove's words, as the big wolf crawled over to her and placed his head in her lap. **Dearest friend, there is only one thing we can do for you.** For a long moment the gaze of Dove and Whiskers locked, gray to gray, and then Dove pulled her flint knife from its leg sheath.

It was too private for viewing. Catching up her spear, Windwhisper moved over to the humans, inspecting them. The second one was dead, his life pumped out upon the ground. *At least you will nourish the land.* Surely she had imagined the freeing of a soul. Then again, if this was why the old ones had dreaded killing . . . The first youth still breathed, but there was a funny sound coming from him. After a moment she realized that the human inhaled at three places—mouth, nose, and the hole in his chest. Not good; this one would die soon.

Dove will not. Determination hardened in Windwhisper; she would not think about how serious a shoulder wound was, about the bleeding inside. Dove was having trouble breathing, too. Perhaps she also breathed from the wrong places. Memorizing the humans' clothing, in case Prey-Pacer asked about them, Windwhisper bent to retrieve Dove's spear. As she folded over, she noticed something odd about the youth's skin. Glossy, like grease . . . Gingerly she ran her finger down his skin, finding a pocket of the ointment at the elbow. Faint, odd odor . . . A fresh-fallen leaf made an adequate place to smear her sample. Could this be why no one had smelled them coming?

"We must go, before more humans come. Do you need help?" *Can you walk?* was what Windwhisper wanted to ask, but she was afraid to hear the answer. Slowly she turned back toward Dove, but the deed was done; Whiskers lay peacefully on his side. *We cannot mourn you, not until we are sure the others are safe.*

With so many cubs in camp, and so few adult Wolfriders, they might not risk coming to help. They had to protect the cubs. . . .

"The plantain seals the blood," Dove said through clenched teeth. "I will not leave a trail. Give me your hand." Pulling against the braced elf-woman, the chief's daughter made it to her feet. "I may need to lean on you. Quickly; the sun goes down."

I thought it was my eyes. But the daystar was already caressing the mountains above them, the hollows shadowed and silent. Too silent. Even the forest knew something was wrong.

Long before they reached the outcrop, the sound of drums murmured through the trees.

Windwhisper's fear was scarcely under control when they reached the foot of the escarpment. Darkness had settled upon their heads like a scraped skin, veiling the stunted trees and scattered boulders. Deep, throbbing drums had pounded a steady counterpoint to their journey. Although she had sent word of their progress, and of Dove's injuries, none of the tribe had come to meet them. That her daughter Dark Wind and the other young hunters had remained to guard the camp was not surprising. But why were Willowgreen and Rellah not waiting at the rocks? Where was Long Walk?—it was his lifemate that was bleeding to death!

Only the wolves had moved to greet them—the few who had stayed behind with their two-legged kin to guard the camp, and the ones who had no bonds with others than the pack. Like a warm mist they oozed past the pair of hunters, brushing their lengthening coats against battered flesh, providing a barrier between wounded elves and forest predators. Owleyes, Long Walk's great wolf, had offered his back to his friend's lifemate. In the end Windwhisper had crawled behind Dove and held her upright.

Finally Long Walk himself appeared before them, so suddenly that Windwhisper's anguish exploded in his face.

Gently! She is bleeding again from the shoulder! Long Walk swayed backward, shaking his head, and Windwhisper realized it had been her sending that had addled him.

Recovering his stance, the elf reached for his long-legged lover, lifting her as if he held the future of the tribe in his hands. *Perhaps you do.* For the first time she thought of Dove dying, and looked beyond, to what it would mean to their future. Not only the loss of a fine hunter and fertile female, but the loss of Prey-Pacer's eldest surviving child.

So far the chiefship had passed directly, from parent to child. Suntail would never possess the chief's lock if his mother died before her father. Only Swift-Spear and Skyfire would be left . . . and that thought terrified Windwhisper.

Sliding into the comfort of wolfsong, she scurried ahead of Long Walk, unconsciously deepening the toeholds she had shaped in the outcrop where the tribe lived. At the top of the curving path, Rellah and Dark Wind waited anxiously, the latter supporting Softfoot, Prey-Pacer's lifemate and Dove's mother.

Come, child, Rellah told Windwhisper, taking hold of her arm. **We are in the large cave.** Before the rockshaper had time to be surprised, Rellah added softly: "Be careful."

What has happened? Windwhisper had meant the thought to be private, but Dark Wind was always attuned to her; her daughter's long, dark braid, mirroring her own, brushed against her arm.

Swift-Spear and Skyfire are fighting, was Dark Wind's narrow sending. Then Softfoot reached over to gently touch Windwhisper's face, her gratitude palpable, and the time for questions passed.

Glowing coals sheltered by a bark screen proved to be the only fire burning within. One of the tiny stone oil lamps Windwhisper had shaped had been lit, casting flickering shadows over the gathering. They were packed like ravvits in a burrow, every elder and cub among them, including those such as Softfoot who were fighting autumn fever. Willowgreen was already in a trance, Long Walk and others hovering over the healing pit, while off to one side a furious, whispered conversation was taking place.

"We cannot leave the caves! If the humans wish vengeance, then they will brave the forest at night—and

we must be ready for them. There are not enough of us to
cover the tracks of both the elders and the cubs!"
Swift-Spear was scarcely a handspan away from his young
sister, towering over her, his face twisted with anger.

"And if we remain here we can be trapped! There is
only one exit from each of these caves. They could smoke
us out, or starve us, or simply overwhelm us, depending
on how many hunters this group has!" Skyfire was livid,
her unruly mane of flaming hair almost standing out from
her head in her fury.

"Then I will send someone to scout who they are and
how many hunters they have—"

"There is no time! Even now the drums change their
beat!" The words were full of compressed anger, but
Skyfire was clearly pleading.

Swift-Spear whirled, and suddenly Windwhisper was
pinned under his glinting eyes. "Again—what color were
their feathers?"

So they had received her sendings . . . "Yellow," she
repeated dully, trying not to give in to her exhaustion.
"Yellow with polished deer-horn necklaces and even bits
of amber. They both wore arm bands of deerskin, deer
horn, and amber."

"Arm bands?" Talen said. "Then they were on some
sort of spirit quest."

"They certainly found spirits," Swift-Spear said harshly, pushing through them to Dove's side. Kneeling by his
sister, he took in her condition, and then snapped his
head toward Willowgreen. "Can you heal her?"

Startled from her trance, the healer reached for a gourd
of bark decoction. Looking up at the towering young elf,
her eyes glistening with tears she would not let fall,
Willowgreen said: "No. She has lost too much blood. I
closed the skin and muscle, and sealed the major bleeding, but too many places seep within."

Useless! The strength of his sending blanched the
faces of everyone present and sent Willowgreen huddling

into herself. As Swift-Spear turned back to Dove, Windwhisper found it in her heart to hate the handsome young hunter. Before Swift-Spear had grown from child to adult, before Willowgreen and he had grown aware of each other . . . Windwhisper remembered days of privacy and growth, when she and Dove and Willowgreen had slowly built a friendship, and the healer's confidence in her own ability had blossomed.

Gone, all gone, now. Only time spent teaching the children remained; only praise from Swift-Spear seemed to bring joy to Willowgreen's face. *He destroys her with every thought,* Windwhisper realized, knowing there was nothing anyone else could do to stop the downward spiral. Only Willowgreen could do that. And if she did? How would the arrogant, favored, golden one respond?

"Will you stop berating the only healer we have?" Skyfire growled, her voice hoarse with prolonged argument.

This is new. Muttering to herself and her young friends, yes—but Skyfire had never argued with her older brother. Not until now. To see the still-childish figure standing up to her mature half-sibling was an unexpected turn. *Do not push too soon, young flame. The wolf that challenges too soon is broken. If we had not lost your mother last winter, even she would have counseled you to wait.* Would Skyfire listen, if haughty Wreath could reach out from beyond Death to warn her?

Oblivious to the youngster, Swift-Spear had hold of Dove's left hand, enfolding it within his strong fingers. To her right, Suntail sat in misery, clutching his mother's other hand, his gaze locked upon her pale face. Long Walk was the calmest of the three, holding Dove upright against his broad chest, methodically stroking her silver hair. Behind him, Dark Wind still supported the chief's lifemate. Windwhisper was appalled to see how fragile Softfoot looked.

"You did well today," Dove whispered to her son.

"Saving Opal like that." The huntress's eyes closed, and her thought brushed against Windwhisper's own. **I never worried about your guarding my back. But how can we protect ourselves when they depend on us?**

There was no blame there, only the anticipation of approaching loss, of all that would never be. **I will do what I can, *Eval*,** Windwhisper promised her, the tightness in her chest pushing the elf-woman's soulname from her.

Do not go beyond the limits of your own heart. In the end, *Chat,* you must choose—you must all choose. They will tear the tribe apart. Strange, how easily Dove's thoughts came now. It was as if the fading of physical strength brought other talents to the fore.

They. Windwhisper felt a chill trace her spine. A thin arm crept around her waist, and the rockshaper felt the comfort of her youngest's touch. If only the hunters were here—

Suddenly Dove's grip on Swift-Spear's hand tightened, her knuckles showing white. Her pale eyes opened, their gaze boring into her brother's face. "Take care of them," she whispered. "Take care of all of them."

There was a flutter behind Windwhisper's eyes, the passing of a lock-send. Imagination? Then why did Skyfire suddenly look so startled, so unsure of herself?

"The boy wore the claws of a golden," Dove muttered, her voice faint with the effort of speaking.

"A golden?" Swift-Spear repeated blankly, his head turning toward Windwhisper.

Nodding slowly, the rockshaper said: "Both feet, a full set of bones and talons." She had forgotten that . . . had forgotten something else. Reaching to her belt, she pulled out the folded leaf, slightly mashed but still soft. "They were smeared with this grease. We never caught their scent; could this have something to do with it?" Hesitantly she offered it to Willowgreen.

"A golden," someone muttered, and the tone was

listless, lifeless. One of them, at least, remembered what goldens meant to humans . . .

Something in Willowgreen's manner held the strength of a healer, and the others gave way before slender hands that momentarily touched. Sniffing, feeling, carefully touching her tongue to the salve . . . several moments passed.

"I know this," she said finally. "We use the leaves to purge the body after sweating fever. This is very strong— from the root, I think. The other ingredients will take some thought, but the main one is sweatbee root. Yes; this could alter scent."

"They can alter their scent," Skyfire said tightly. "*We cannot smell them.* And the dead one bore the signs of a golden—"

"Not dead," Windwhisper said quickly. "But dying, yes."

"Only the direct descendants of their totems wear symbols of their heritage," Rellah said flatly. "We are doomed. We have killed one of their walking godlings— they will not give up until they have our blood on their spears."

"They already have our blood," Skyfire snarled in turn. "On their weapons. If we are fortunate, that will be enough—"

"No," Windwhisper said softly. The word startled the murmuring group into silence. Only the drums continued their varied tempo. "I took the head of the leader's shaft to seal Dove's shoulder. I needed . . . something smooth." Touching the slash on her arm, she added: "There is blood on the other point."

"How will they respond to the missing weapon?" Swift-Spear turned to Talen, demanding knowledge from the eldest among them.

"I am not certain," the elf admitted. "But many of the humans use weapons in burial rites. If the human dies without his weapons, they believe he will lose his way as he hurries to the next life."

Swift-Spear's face was momentarily still . . . and then he smiled grimly. "If we give them something to worry about, they will have no time for rites."

NO! Skyfire's sending slashed through them like the bolt that had named her, sending them reeling. The shouts and threats that erupted surely could be heard to the edge of the forest. Hotheads among them demanded that the humans be "taught a lesson" even as Skyfire insisted they go farther up the mountainside.

Windwhisper longed to cover her ears and creep into the silence of the night. Truly, Prey-Pacer should not have left the youngest to guard the camp. Instead of fleeing she reached for the curved disk of black stone, beginning to knead it like raw clay. If she could restore it to its original shape . . . no; fresh material was needed. Too many pockets of air filled the stone, making it brittle. But if she made the point smaller . . .

Now Rellah entered the fray, trying to protect Dove from the argument swirling above them. Blocking it out in a surge of liquid rock, Windwhisper tuned herself to the shaping of stone, tiny spear points, like dolls' toys, flickering from her fingertips. Behind her she felt her son huddle against her back, hiding from the battle of words and will. Farther back she heard Graywolf's growl—her shaping had distracted him, and he had lost the train of the fight. Magic terrified him, and he shrank back against the wall of the shallow cave even as his twin Owl leaned forward to study her creation.

We must stop this, Windwhisper heard another part of herself say. *It grows worse every moment. Soon one of them will challenge the other, and that is not allowed. The chief would break the survivor.* They could lose all three heirs in the space of a day. How to appeal to this need to strike back, yet save life all around . . . Windwhisper gathered the kernel of strength within that was born of Timmain's sacrifice.

There are other punishments than death. As she had hoped, the strength of her sending, and the calm in it, slightly dampened the vigor of the fight. Idly she flipped the bits of shiny rock back and forth between her hands, letting them catch the glow of the lamp. **They are unworthy prey, these would-be cub killers. Our speed, our stealth, our knowledge mocks their existence. So let us frighten them back to the safety of their plains.** "After all," she said aloud, carefully not looking up, "we are 'elfphs,' so they say—wood spirits. We glide through the forest on invisible feet, and turn into birds and wolves at will. Fire blossoms in our hands and trees bow as we pass by." Twisting her supple body, she offered the handful of tiny black points to Swift-Spear. "Diminish them, chief's son, as only you can, and remind them how little they know of us."

Silence. Swift-Spear studied the pile of chips in her hand. Beside him, Skyfire drew a ragged breath, and slowly let it out.

Sending was one of Windwhisper's strengths. A narrow beam of thought shot to the flame-haired maiden. **Wait. He must choose for himself.** Skyfire's huge eyes promised many questions, but she held herself closely in check. Perhaps she had begun to realize that Swift-Spear would side against her no matter what she said.

A thin, tight smile crept across the young hunter's face. Ignoring Windwhisper's offering, he turned to his personal followers. "Come, then; let us lead the five-fingers a chase that they will speak of for generations. Not you," he added to Skyfire without looking at her. "You guard the camp." Nodding once, sharply, to Graywolf, Swift-Spear took his weapon from where it leaned against the wall. Most of the remaining hunters, except the ill, or the nursing mothers, followed suit. Bending one last time to touch Dove's sunken cheek, Swift-Spear made her a promise: **I will always protect the tribe. Sleep well, sister.**

Be careful. No emotion; Dove was beyond strength.

Always. A shrug of a shoulder, and the hunters followed as Swift-Spear crept from the cave into the outer darkness.

Windwhisper trailed them through the narrow entrance, pausing on the outcrop. Above them a slender Mother Moon hung in the sky . . . tonight she was a slit eye, baneful, watching . . .

Who remains? The surprise in Skyfire's sending called Windwhisper back inside.

The reason for the young huntress's dismay was evident. Of the hunters, only Long Walk, Amber, and Dark Wind remained, and Amber was currently feeding her baby. Before Skyfire's anger and dismay could form words, Dark Wind settled her bundled infant son in a nest of furs and addressed Skyfire: "Shall I go to the gnarled oak at clearing's edge? If they grow closer, I can send word."

A moment's hesitation, as Skyfire's eyes roamed over the group, and then: "Yes." Glancing at Windwhisper, she added privately: **Will you go to the creek and watch?**

Grateful Skyfire had chosen a lock-sending, she replied: **I will, but you might need me here.**

What can you do here that I cannot? This had the slightest edge to it.

Close the cave entrance.

Skyfire stared at her for a long moment, and then twisted to look over her shoulder at the crooked slit. Nodding slightly, she whispered aloud: "Amber? Is he nearly through?"

"Yes, Skyfire, a few moments only," the slender, golden elf-woman replied.

"Then give him to Breeze and go hide by the creek, in

case they slip around and come from the far side. We do not know if we will recognize that sweatbee scent." Nodding slightly again, this time as if in satisfaction, she added in tight projection: **You have studied my brother well.**

He affects my friends with his moods. It seemed prudent, Windwhisper responded carefully. She was impressed that Skyfire had chosen a momentary wait over sending Long Walk away from Dove's side. Patience was not known as one of Skyfire's attributes.

Willowgreen. She is weak. It was dismissal.

Not weak, young huntress. Different strengths.

There was no reply at all. Others called her "young huntress" at their peril, but Windwhisper had never had any trouble with Skyfire—probably because the young woman sensed Windwhisper's admiration for her growing hunting prowess.

"Shield the lamp," Skyfire finally whispered, moving to station herself by the opening. Dipping to the floor for her spear, Dark Wind sheltered the flame in passing as she slipped out the crevice. There was time to adjust to the new light level before Amber handed her baby to Dark Wind's daughter Breeze and went to the creek.

The drums rolled on, tolling now, a slight hesitation behind every beat. How would Swift-Spear and his small band attract their attention, much less lead the humans away from the hills? Sound moved slowly into the forest. After an interminable wait, Dark Wind sent word: **The drummers lead them into the forest, three lines of humans.**

How many? Skyfire asked.

I do not know; I can only tell the drums are no longer together.

Even as Dark Wind replied, the drone of the skin drums lessened, shouts and screams floating upon the steady south breeze.

It begins, Windwhisper thought, taking a moment to

rebraid her long black hair. *Where will it end?* How good the children were being, huddled together around the plucked suntail, scarcely a sound from any of them. Better than their grandsires—although the true elves were almost as noiseless as their descendants, they could not see in the dark, and found it difficult to move through the cave system without grinding gravel underfoot.

By the time Mother Moon had set, the Wolfriders knew which way the night was heading. Despite the best efforts of Swift-Spear and his small band of hunters, the scattered humans were moving inexorably into the forest, heading toward the foothills. Torches danced through leafy glades, illuminating the deer paths that all used. From the boulder before the largest lair, Skyfire and Windwhisper watched their advance.

We should have left, came Skyfire's quiet thought. **We could be hours away by now.**

North or south? Windwhisper asked casually. The chief's daughter did not reply. It was the dying time—to head north without heavy preparations was madness. And these humans came from the south; to the south they would undoubtedly return.

Is everyone comfortable? Skyfire's question was a bit sharp, but no one seemed offended. Clothing, furs, and dried food had been moved into the large, narrow cave; even the wolf-friends had helped without protest.

Come eat something, Rellah suggested. When the two women did not respond, the tall elf carefully made her way out to the boulder.

If the wind dies, they will be close enough to hear us. Although Skyfire's tone was even, the rebuke was there for those who would hear.

You must be ready if there is trouble. Food means strength. Rellah pushed pieces of dried deer meat at them both.

The Wolfriders managed brief smiles at the thought of dried meat providing anything except existence, but they accepted the offering. From the wry grin Skyfire threw her way, Windwhisper suspected that the two young women were thinking the same thing—that it was easier to give in than to argue with Rellah.

I see light. They have found the river path. Amber's sending was very loud, and anxiety threaded it.

Start back to camp, Skyfire ordered. **Dark Wind —you, too.**

Interesting how we take her direction despite her youth. It was the secret of Timmorn Yellow-Eyes and his children—an unconscious majesty that drew the eye without effort. Skyfire possessed it.

What next? Windwhisper decided to ask.

We become like the eyes of the forest, Skyfire replied laconically. **We see all, but nothing sees us. Come—you must close the entrance.**

Stifling closeness, and the burden of silence . . . the fresh air from the smoke hole was a gift of the High Ones. Perhaps Skyfire had been wrong not to warn the others of what Windwhisper was going to do; ah, the young could not anticipate everything. The cubs among them could not help but whimper, and the old ones were actually affectionate in response. Usually the true elves ignored the children, until they showed signs of learning to send.

Skyfire alone was pressed against the thin stone shield Windwhisper had created . . . she alone was truly alert. Gnawing vigorously on a scrap of deer meat, Windwhisper mentally retracted every harsh thought she had ever directed toward Rellah's fussiness. After shaping that wall, food was essential. Her fingertips rested lightly upon the granite of the mountain; that door might have to open in a hurry.

A delicate barrier . . . Windwhisper hoped it would not be necessary to tell the others how fragile. As the last grains had flowed into place, she had warned Skyfire: **If they come to the ledge, they will be able to hear us if we speak aloud.**

Then we shall not speak, had been the young woman's response.

Even the wolves, in the crevices above them, kept silent. Rellah's cooking pot and fire had been dismantled long before dusk; there was nothing to indicate that anyone had ever lived on the shelf.

Still, the humans came. One group after another, their voices low and rumbling, the light of their torches visible through thin whorls of stone. It was an eerie sensation, trapped between throbbing drums that echoed through the cavern and the faint glow that promised the dreaded men. Windwhisper divided her time with fierce concentration, one moment praying that no one would crack under the strain, the next terrified that Swift-Spear and the others would return to the ledge.

This night could mean the end of the Wolfriders. Only those who had left the tribe might still survive, somewhere . . . her children might be among them. Dark Wind's twin sister Moonfire; Godstalker, the first son she had shared with Starfall; Thyme, the fey, red-haired daughter of Sundown; Jewelshaper, the son who had followed Prey-Pacer's granddaughter Greenglow when she had led a portion of the hunt to new grounds—

Gruff human voices lingered in the air, and Windwhisper shrank deeper into herself. Why didn't they move on? Did they want this vantage point? High Ones, could she open that bolt hole in back enough for the elders to squeeze through?

Beside her, Skyfire stiffened, and Windwhisper felt a brush against her mind. Someone was sending privately to the huntress. Slowly the young elf tightened, as though restrained by wet deerskin—she was an explosion waiting to occur.

NOT YET! Not while they are on the ledge! Her response was broadcast to all, and the meaning silenced the weeping of every cub in the cave.

Will he force us to listen to their slaughter? Windwhisper had realized what the group of humans had to be: a group of male elders, initiating the young men into some level of their tribe. No women would be present, and the old ones had probably remained in the camp. *Do not harm the old ones, Swift-Spear; they would set up their next camp where one of their holy men died.*

By now the humans had found the bodies—the roll of the drums had the measured beat used during the long night before burial. What were they looking for? The signs of struggle would be clear, the mangled corpse of the dog silent testimony to a strong predator. But Moonwalker had not fed on dog or humans . . . the men would know that an animal had not killed the questers.

Either other humans . . . or wood spirits.

To her left, Skyfire sat chewing on the tip of her long braid, worrying the leather thong that held it fast. To her right, Talen had crept to the outer wall. His sending was almost a whisper, available to any who were interested.

They speak of returning to their encampment, and bringing the eldest . . . here to the ledge. They are waiting for a . . . sign . . . and think the highest spot in the region will be the safest place for their . . . shaman. This was halting; it had been a long time since the elves had had need of the language the human tribes used to trade with each other.

I'll give them a sign! The intensity of Swift-Spear's thought was frightening; just as quickly his sending disappeared.

WAIT! It was no good; Swift-Spear ignored Skyfire as he always did.

Voices faltered, volume increased—a man cried out. There was the sound of rolling gravel and scraping.

Something about a 'ring of fire,' Talen continued.

I hope he's not burning the forest down, was Rellah's acid comment.

They wait for a sign, came Skyfire's soft thought, and then she fired off a question to her wolf. The filtered response was affirmative; all the humans had left the ledge. Twisting back toward the center of the huddled group, she demanded huskily: "The lamp! Quickly!" As the adults carefully passed the lit taper down the row to Skyfire, the young woman asked Windwhisper: "Where are those tiny spear points you made?"

Wondering, Windwhisper felt around on the lip of the wall for a different type of rock. Scooping up the cluster, she poured them into Skyfire's left hand.

Taking up the lamp, Skyfire said: "Can you open this enough for me to creep out—and then close it after I jump back in?"

Flexing her fingers, gauging the composition of the material beneath her hand, Windwhisper sent a mote of assent. It would drain her, but it could be done.

"Do it."

A tingling glow that translated into sparkling light— into solid stone trickling like water— A wave of rock oozed toward Windwhisper. Slowly the heavy drops split away from the unshaped portion of the wall, even as Skyfire squirmed to the balls of her feet, crouching to spring.

Avoid the edges of the walls, Windwhisper sent grimly as she struggled to control the outpouring of energy. Better to save speed for the closing, when it could mean life or death.

Skyfire chose her own time. It was a smaller hole than Windwhisper cared for, but Skyfire popped through it without difficulty. Through the biomorphic opening Windwhisper and Talen could see Skyfire move to the smallest of the boulders piled by their lookout point. It was the flat one, which Rellah liked to use as a surface for food preparation. Swiftly the huntress set the lamp in a niche, protecting it from the south wind. Before it she scattered the shiny black points in an arc. Then her head snapped up, nostrils flaring, and she was diving headlong through the cooling, popping opening.

Hurry! A human comes!

Power answered, as Windwhisper unleashed some of what she had built throughout the long, stressful night. Strengthening her hands to challenge the mountain, she reached, pushing yielding rock up toward the opening like a wall of floodwater. Swirling, flaring stone coalesced into a smooth shield, a spatter pattern radiating from the center, and then the rock settled.

This time the wall had strength; the Wolfriders found themselves in near darkness, only their dying coals providing light. Moments later they heard a shout from a human throat, and answering voices from farther away.

Leaning against the new stone, Windwhisper pulled energy back from her actions, trying to replace some of what she had lost. A groping hand turned out to be her son's, handing her the leg of the suntail Breeze had captured hours before. Seizing the meat in her teeth, Windwhisper folded against the wall and slipped an arm around Stars Dancing.

Now, we wait, she told him. The boy wearily nodded assent, his silver hair a veil across her shoulder.

Long hours of waiting: through Dove's silent passing, through some sort of human ceremony involving endless chanting and drumming, through dawn twilight, when sounds of movement indicated the strangers were leaving the ledge. It was not until the wolves reclaimed the outcrop that Skyfire asked Windwhisper to open the crevice.

They are returning to their camp, came Swift-Spear's announcement as the rockshaper manipulated the stone. **They build a cairn for their dead.**

"A cairn?" Talen said aloud in surprise. "Then these humans you killed had high rank, indeed!"

Like water swirling down a hole in rock, the crevice expanded before the tribe. Weak in their relief, the group staggered out into the early-morning sunshine.

"Here," Willowgreen whispered, thrusting a smooth red-skinned fruit at Windwhisper. "This will give you quick energy." Biting through thin skin to firm pulp beneath, Windwhisper could only nod her thanks as she reached to hug the healer. In the slanting rays of dawn, it was apparent that Willowgreen had already offered tears to the newly dead.

A surprise awaited them on the ledge. Both the lamp and the tiny spear points had been left on Rellah's grinding surface. Embedded between the stone and the boulders surrounding it, swaying gently in the early breeze, were polished sticks with vividly colored bird feathers attached at their tips.

"So what is this?" It was Swift-Spear, gracefully pulling himself up to the ledge, the other hunters at his heels.

"They wanted the weapon," Skyfire said simply. "So I placed what was left of it where they could find it—with a bit of light to help them along."

"It seems to have succeeded better than you could have hoped," Talen said wryly. "I think they are treating it as a shrine."

"A what?" Swift-Spear's tone was suspicious; new words usually meant trouble.

"A holy place, a place to leave signs of respect. Look, they have left grain and fruit." Rellah gestured with one hand over the stone but did not touch the offerings. "Only the High Ones know what they made of these things suddenly appearing out of thin air. I think I've lost my grinding stone."

"You mean they'll be *back?*" The lift in Swift-Spear's voice was a promise of battle and, predictably, Skyfire rose to the bait.

"They were settling in on the ledge to stay! You left us no choice but to wall ourselves in—" Skyfire started.

"Now we're going to have to move the camp! How do you think the hunters will find us—"

Can't you two do anything without fighting about it? Windwhisper was too tired to speak aloud, and did not join those who would add their voices to the argument. It did not really matter; although the tribe would listen to these youngsters during an emergency, only Prey-Pacer would lead them from this place—or decide they would remain. Which meant many long nights of watching the trails for humans until—

Is everyone well?

It was an open sending, and was so unexpected it dampened the vigorous discussion. Windwhisper was on her feet in a flash, moving instinctively toward the edge of the bluff. The hunters, back? Starfall calling for their chief, as he often did?

Most of us, she replied quickly. **Why are you home so soon?**

Two reasons. We caught some stragglers, and have much meat with little effort; and we crossed the humans' trail and saw it led north. We are at the beginning of the western woods, and will be there before the sun shines in the caves.

Good. We have a pair to mourn.

Windwhisper turned back to the others and found a mingling of relief and dismay on their faces. Only Softfoot looked genuinely relieved at the return of her chief-mate. Skyfire and Swift-Spear looked . . . uncertain. *So—you do not know if you have made the right decisions. In your uncertainty, there may be hope.*

"We were careful setting the fire—only a ring surrounding their encampment. We soaked the area beyond, and dug on the forest side, to be sure no fire would jump to the trees," Swift-Spear said, gesturing as he described the scene. "It finally drew the five-fingers back to the edge of the forest."

"That was when Windwhisper opened the stone, and I set the tiny points outside," Skyfire threw in.

Leaning against one of the boulders, an arm around his lifemate and his wolf, Prey-Pacer nodded slowly at the recitation.

"They are building a cairn at the edge of the forest," the chief said aloud.

"Golden worshippers," Talen offered. "The young men who died were of high rank."

"Better them than our cubs," Skyfire said unexpectedly.

"Dove had no choice, Father." Swift-Spear's words were firm. Windwhisper was certain the siblings had not realized they were agreeing on the night's work. "Although this 'shrine' may be a problem." Skyfire stiffened, but did not speak.

"Not this season," was the tranquil response. "They will cover their dead with stone and then hurry back south. Come new leaves we will need to move, unless we wish to play hiding games with their shamans. But now?" Prey-Pacer shrugged. "We should have the snows and beyond to find a better place for our camp. Perhaps to the southwest . . . the mountains curve in that direction. With luck we can have both stone and the benefits of the plains."

Sighing, the elf hazarded a sharp glance at Windwhisper, who was nestled in her lifemate's arms. "You did well, all of you. What happened could not have been avoided, not with this ceremonial salve these humans now use. It is our grief that we lost Dove and Whiskers—it is tribute to them that we send no one else after them. Remember this moment whenever discord threatens to keep the tribe from working together." He spoke generally, but at the last Prey-Pacer's eyes were on his surviving children.

A small hand reached out to touch the chief's wrist. "Will we howl for my mother?" Suntail asked timidly.

"We will howl for her, cub. We will send her to the High Ones' arms with our music, and sing her killers home." With that Prey-Pacer stood, pulling his frail lifemate into his arms and walking toward the outcrop the pack had chosen as their meeting place. Behind him came his children, Swift-Spear alert and looking pleased, Skyfire's face thoughtful.

Softfoot will not survive this winter. Windwhisper did not need to be a healer to know the truth of her own thoughts. *And then what?* It was clear that Swift-Spear had through necessity blocked the reality of his sister's death. Now it would settle upon him. They had been close, Dove and Swift-Spear—or as close as the young elf could be to any other person. Something in Swift-Spear was always remote. How would he handle losing his mother?

Will it kill my chief, to lose her on top of his adored Dove? What was between the chief and his lifemate was beyond words. Prey-Pacer was not demonstrative by nature—and even more reticent about his children—but Windwhisper had seen him looking at his eldest when he thought no one was watching him. His pride in Dove had been visible, while the competition between the younger siblings grated on his nerves and will. *Someday Swift-Spear will decide he should rule, my chief, and he may not let you pass on naturally.*

And then Windwhisper gave herself up to the howl, to the pain of losing the friend she loved above all others. To the honor of her passing, defending the cubs who were the future of the Wolfriders. To the uncertainty of a future where Swift-Spear was the heir apparent.

The strength of Starfall's grip roused her from thoughts of life without Dove. Without turning her head, Windwhisper knew Skyfire was studying her. Was she drawing the same attention from Swift-Spear? No—he was bunched with Graywolf and Stonethrower, his special friends, wrapped within the wolfsong. But then Swift-Spear saw only what he wanted to see . . .

When he wanted to remember the rockshaper who had offered him a way to humiliate the humans without bloodshed, then he would remember. Until then, she might as well be invisible. A preferable state of affairs.

And Skyfire? She, too, saw what she wanted to see, although Windwhisper suspected that when backs were pressed to a blind canyon, Skyfire was the stronger of the two. In the ways that mattered most, she was the more intuitive, more thoughtful, more aware of the pair. She would not forget Windwhisper's help. Was she strong enough in herself yet to value the contributions of the tribe?

Dove, I wish I knew what you said to her. Lend her your wisdom, friend of my heart, because Swift-Spear wants followers, not companions—and someday he may try to lead us to our doom.

Windwhisper shivered, and even the press of Starfall, Stars Dancing, and her wolf Moonwalker was not enough to warm her thoughts.

Riders of the Storm

by Mercedes Lackey

Willowgreen dozed, curled in layers of fur, daydreaming that she was inside a giant egg. "Here—" A bowl filled with steaming broth materialized under Willowgreen's nose, startling her. "Eat," Two-Spear urged, gesturing with the bowl, so that the broth sloshed. "You need to keep up your strength."

Willowgreen closed her eyes for a moment and manufactured a sweet and vapid smile for Two-Spear, taking the bowl of broth he had brought her and obediently sipping at it. With not even a breeze to disturb it, steam from the hot broth hung thickly above the surface of the liquid. Light coming from the entrance and filtering through the thick white walls of their snow-shelter made it look as if she was sipping from a bowl of mist.

You'd think no elf ever had a cub before this one, she thought testily, curbing her wish to snap and snarl at him like an irritable bitch. All the cosseting and attention her lovemate was showering on her would have been welcome—if she were as round and burdened as Mother Moon at the full. But at the moment she hardly showed at all; she was *certainly* capable of all of her normal duties, and she did *not* need to be treated as if she were fragile and likely to break.

Especially not when there were others of the elves who could use that sort of attention. Rellah, for instance, who could well use some devotion and cosseting. Assuming she'd accept it from a half-blood like Two-Spear. Willowgreen swallowed as an unwelcome surge of despair from Rellah's direction washed over her, a cold despair no amount of hot broth could warm.

The deepest moon-dances of winter were always the hardest on the Wolfriders, even when, as now, they had good shelters, plenty of game, and hadn't yet needed to dig deeply into their stores of smoked meat. The first snow of the season had been a deep one, trapping deer in yards across the length and breadth of the forest. Hunters were able to go from yard to yard, picking the weakest and thinning the herds so that the deer would be able to survive until they could break out—yet gleaning plenty of game for the Pack. And the deep snow had an additional aspect: the Pack always made snow-caves to shelter in, but this year Graywolf, watching the cubs make hard-packed balls of the stuff to play with, had hit upon the idea of using those balls to build snow-domes over earth scraped bare. Padded with evergreen branches and skins on the floor, these snow-shelters were surprisingly warm. Some of the Pack had been uneasy about making something so obviously artificial, fearing discovery, but a few heavy snowfalls disguised the shelters, making them look like perfectly natural drifts. Camouflaging the entrances with brush—another idea of Graywolf's—ensured that the clearing looked very little different from any other.

But the cold was still hard on the true elves, and some of them suffered during the long nights with evil dreams, memories of that first, horrible winter when they had struggled every day for barest survival, with hands unaccustomed to labor and minds ill-equipped for the savagery of humans and weather alike. Willowgreen sometimes woke stifling cries of her own as she inadvertently shared those dreams. Worst of all were Rellah's—

Not only did Rellah dream of that first winter, she dreamed of another harsh winter, eights and eights of seasons ago, when she had seen her own daughter die in the jaws of a great long-tooth cat. Rellah's daughter had been the last of the pure-blooded elves to be born to the

Pack, and the Way of this world had found no place for her in its web. That first Willowgreen should have lived—forever, or nearly. Instead, her mother outlived her. And mourned for Willowgreen, the daughter for whom the present Willowgreen had been named. And sometimes, although Rellah never told anyone, the likeness of this Willowgreen and that one was too much to bear, and Rellah curled inside her shelter and mourned—shunning food, sleep, company.

Like now. *And I feel it, too*. Once, Willowgreen would not have had to bear Rellah's sorrow like a lump of ice beneath the breastbone with an aching void no food could fill in the belly. No longer. Now she was as sensitive to the thoughts and feelings of those around her as she had been insensitive before—and that sensitivity had increased with the coming child, rather than decreasing.

Perhaps it would not have been so hard for Rellah to bear if only Willowgreen were less like that dead daughter. *I never planned to be a healer*, she told herself, once again. *I never knew Rellah's daughter was a healer when I came to her and asked to be taught.* But like her pale hair and deceptive fragility, it could not be changed. Rellah saw the daughter she had lost in Willowgreen, and in the darkness of moonless winter nights she despaired her loss.

Willowgreen wanted to comfort her—if Rellah would have allowed it—but any words of comfort she might have given would be lies. There was no comfort on this world for the true elves. They were alien, outside the web of life here; the blood of Timmain and her wolf-mate that ran in the veins of the half-bloods of the Pack gave them a place in the web of life, a place that no true elf could ever earn. And the world would never cease, in its mindless, pitiless way, to be rid of them.

A two-edged knife, indeed. That wolf blood that doomed the half-bloods to mortality and lessened stature, that made magic a chancy and difficult skill to master, was what made it possible for them to survive here.

Hunting skills, lupine instincts, the ability to *kill,* to eat and enjoy raw meat—those were important. But Willowgreen had seen what Timmain had seen, that without native blood mixed with theirs the elves would be rejected by everything that lived in this place.

Willowgreen sometimes wondered, in the dark hours before dawn, if it were not so much savagery and fear that had driven the humans to try so desperately to kill the elves as it was the world itself, moving through them. Trying, like a wolf infested with fleas, to be rid of the alien pests.

She sighed, and Two-Spear touched her cheek, with a tenderness she would have traded a hand or a foot to have a few seasons ago. Now—when she only wanted to be left alone—

But if he's here with me, he's not *out hunting down humans,* she reminded herself, forcing herself to be patient. *And if he's not hunting humans, he's not likely to bring them down on us.* Even Skyfire thought of Willowgreen with grudging approval these days—she saw that the young healer was not shirking her work, but she *also* saw that she was keeping Two-Spear from his self-proclaimed war against the humans. And although Skyfire burned to have the chiefship, she also knew that winter, the hardest of seasons, was no time to bring a challenge. Not when the Pack needed every hand and hunter that could be mustered.

As long as Two-Spear stayed anxious over the welfare of his cub-to-be, he stayed as close to the model of a proper chief as he was ever likely to get.

She sighed again, but smiled and touched his hand. "I'm fine," she said. "Truly. Are there hides to scrape? It seems a pity to waste all this sunshine."

He frowned, his brows coming together into a solid bar across his forehead. "Are you sure you want to go out? Are you sure the cub will be all right? It's bitter out there—dry as an old twig, and the air cuts your throat when you breathe it."

"If I stay cooped up in here I'm going to go—" She stopped herself before she said the word. *Mad.* It was what they said of Two-Spear, that he was mad, and it was best not to provoke him into a display of that madness. Not now, when he was calm, rational, and not even his bitterest rival Skyfire could find fault with his actions. "I'm going to start biting my claws, like a bored wolf," she finished instead. "If there aren't any hides, I'd love to take a short run with Windwalker."

His frown deepened. "I don't know . . ."

She widened her eyes at him. "*Please,* lovemate," she begged. "I need the exercise, I really do. And how could I be safer than with Windwalker? He's the biggest wolf the Pack has!"

"I don't like it." Two-Spear chewed his lip. "I have to lead the hunt—I can't go with you." He pondered a moment more, as Willowgreen did her best to look crestfallen and disappointed.

"I have to get some fresh air and exercise," she protested. "How will the cub be anything but weak if I don't?" As he continued to frown, she fished desperately for something that would make him agree with her. "Send someone with me. One of the hunters who's resting—"

His face lightened. "Of course! Graywolf. *He* can go with you!" And before she could stop him, he wriggled out of the entrance to the lair and was gone.

Graywolf. She had managed not to flinch at the name, managed to keep her face straight. Managed not to show her mingled fear and joy. Of all the ironies—

The one person I dared not name. A thrill of elation made her shiver, and she hugged her arms tight to her chest. After days of silence, to have a chance not only to talk to him, but to be *alone* with him! And it was Two-Spear's idea!

She pulled her furs on, wrapping herself up well, determined to give Two-Spear no excuse to cancel the outing. When she struggled out through the brush screening the lair's opening and stood squinting in the sunlight, there was no one in sight, but a simple sending brought Windwalker bounding toward her through snow deep enough to hide all of him but the tip of his single ear. Once she had known him only as One-Ear, half-grown foundling of the animal-healer Shayana. That was before Shayana's murder—before she'd heard his true-name in her mind, and he had spoken her soulname in return.

Hunt? he asked eagerly, plowing to a halt in front of her, his tail wagging furiously, his one ear erect and his jaws stretched in a lupine grin.

Just run, she replied, burying her hands in his thick ruff and rubbing noses with him. Windwalker didn't lair too near the den she shared with Two-Spear; the chief's wolf, half-mad No-Name, was of too jealous and uncertain a temperament. With no urging on Willowgreen's part, Windwalker kept his distance. *He* didn't intend to provoke a fight, and he wouldn't permit No-Name to force one on him—but still, it was better that he stay away, though within sending range. The rest of the Pack accepted Windwalker and gave him a great deal of the deference they would have given a Pack-second if No-Name's madness hadn't prevented the existence of one. In fact, Willowgreen had the feeling that the new pups this spring might well be fathered by Windwalker.

They could have worse sires; Windwalker was tall, strong, and very, very bright—able to send as well as some elves, though only in simple thoughts. Willowgreen had never thought to have a wolf-friend; now she couldn't imagine being without him.

Running is good, Windwalker confirmed happily. **Good for Tyrr, good for cub. Tyrr play in snow, make blood sing. Maybe chase ravvit.**

That *maybe* was a clue to just how bright Windwalker was. He was the first wolf that Graywolf had ever heard of who could think in terms of *might be*. If Graywolf was "more wolf than elf," perhaps Windwalker was his lupine equivalent—more elf than wolf.

He was also the only other creature in the world with whom Willowgreen could share the memories of her secret friendship with one of the hated humans—the most *un*human animal-healer, Shayana. Like Willowgreen, Windwalker had been rescued and nursed back to health by the odd creature—and like Willowgreen, he had been too far away to come to her aid when her fellow humans had killed her.

She brushed away the shadow of sorrow at the memory; this was no day for mourning, sulking in the dark like Rellah. A hint of movement caught her eye, and she looked up from Windwalker's bright blue eyes to see a Wolfrider on the ridge above, waving to her. Too shaggy to be Two-Spear—the chief must already have gone off to lead the hunt.

She narrowed her eyes and sent out the merest touch of a sending. **Vrenn?**

The reply was short—but not curt. **Yes. Come up.**

She needed no urging. With an ease born of much practice, she slid onto Windwalker's back, fastened her hands in his ruff, and set her feet just in front of his hindquarters. The wolf plowed sedately between the drifts this time, refraining from bounding through them as he had earlier, out of consideration for his rider. Once again, Willowgreen was struck by how intelligent he was; not every wolf-friend would have thought of that. She'd seen plenty of riders sent tumbling by their wolf's exuberance.

The snow was thinner up on the ridge, barely ankle-deep. Through the bare bones of the trees, the sky shone as bright and blue as Windwalker's eyes, with not even a trace of cloud. No wind stirred among those leafless branches, and Windwalker's breath frosted on his whiskers. Willowgreen was glad of her furs; where bare skin poked through, the air was as bitter cold as Two-Spear had promised.

Windwalker trotted up to Moonfinder and sniffed noses amiably as his rider answered Willowgreen's greeting with a short nod. Graywolf would not meet her eyes, and she kept hers fastened to Windwalker's ruff, mingled joy and sadness tumbling in her heart and making her short of breath.

They had to be careful, so close to the camp—careful to let no one see that they were anything more than uneasy allies, casual acquaintances, held together only by love for Two-Spear. But they could send, if they could not speak, and as Graywolf turned Moonfinder down a game-trail, his thoughts touched hers, tentatively.

Are you well? he asked, keeping his eyes on the trail ahead, a deer-track that wound beneath the trees. **I— I did not dare come to you.**

I know, she replied, ignoring the bite of sorrow. **If you had, we would have slipped somehow, I know. And—**

And we dare not risk that. For the sake of the Pack. Graywolf's sending was grim and determined. **He acts like a chief now, and not like a mad thing.**

He needs us, she agreed sadly. **Else Skyfire—**

Else Skyfire will go off dream-chasing instead of man-chasing, he answered firmly. **One is as bad for the Pack as the other. Of the two of them, he is the saner, when he is not man-baiting.**

She nodded, and followed him in silence, watching the fur-covered back, slender and wiry, and wishing she dared to touch him. Although their presence on the trail held whatever winter birds there were in silence, off in the distance she heard crows calling to each other, and once, the scream of a hawk. After a time she glanced around covertly. They were far enough from the dens now that there was little chance of their being overheard or seen. She touched Windwalker lightly with her heels and he pushed up to walk beside Moonfinder instead of behind the other wolf.

Graywolf glanced at her, his face stone-silent and unreadable. But she no longer needed to read his face to know what he was thinking. "I miss you," she said simply.

He hung his head, and the pain in his voice cut her. "I can't stand being near you, not able to touch you—not able to act as if I even like you. So I stay away. It's easier."

Easier? she thought, her own pain echoing his. *Easier for Two-Spear, maybe. But not easier for anyone else.*

Graywolf hid the ache in his heart as best he could, but in the end there was no hiding it from Willowgreen. And he knew the attempt was futile. But he couldn't bear to cause *her* any pain—

This wasn't just Recognition, this tie that bound the two of them and had formed the cub she carried. This was something more. He'd Recognized before, of course— with as much wolf as there was in him, he'd fathered more than one cub, and all on elves with more of the pure blood in them than *he* had—elves who couldn't *wait* to be away from him as soon as the needs of Recognition had been satisfied. Merewood, others before her, others after. Always they mated, stayed together with him standing as protector and provider until the cub was birthed, and then they slid apart, quickly, like oil and water that would not mix. The true elves held him in quiet contempt—those who patterned themselves after the true elves mimicked that attitude. Even Willowgreen had—

Conscience stabbed him. It was doing that a lot, of late. He'd never thought so much in all of his life as he had since Willowgreen had walked through his thoughts and showed him what he was and was not. And he knew that last thought wasn't fair. She'd simply been afraid of him, as she had been afraid of everything. He had fostered that fear, as a wedge to use to drive between her and his dearest friend, Two-Spear. He had never lost an opportunity to snarl at her, to reinforce her fear, hoping Two-Spear would see her for the weak thing she was and reject her. Sometimes he wondered what it was that had caused the changes in her; she never spoke of what had happened to her when she had been washed away in the storm—except to say that she had been found by a solitary, crazed healer of animals who tended her and sent her home to the Pack.

"I stopped being afraid," she said, startling him. Her voice was soft, but very clear in the silence of the snow-covered forest. He looked up at her, eyes wide, his chest tightening at the sight of her.

"What?" he stammered, unable to say more.

She blushed and tossed her head, the little braids in front of her ears lying golden against the brown of the ravvit fur she had wrapped around her head. "I'm sorry; you were thinking so hard I couldn't help hearing you. You were wondering why I changed so much—and I've been thinking about that a lot." She looked up at a crow winging overhead, then back down at him. "I spend so much time alone—I— I have a lot of time for thinking. I think I changed because I stopped being afraid—when I stopped being *afraid* of everything, all the things that had been in the way of hearing wolfsong, for instance, were gone."

She tucked her hair back under the fur of her hood. "My healing-magic got stronger, and so did everything else, when I started relaxing."

"Like—learning how to throw a spear without tensing up?" he hazarded.

She nodded, her lips parting in a smile, her eyes sparkling. She was so beautiful; his hands ached to touch her, to comfort her for all those days spent alone when he dared not come near and Two-Spear was leading the hunt. Now it wasn't just his heart that was throbbing . . .

He swallowed, and told his body to behave itself. When he glanced back at her, he saw that she had flushed an even deeper red, and was staring at her wolf-friend's solitary ear.

"I can't stand this!" he blurted angrily, not certain if he was angry at himself, at her, or at Two-Spear. "I can't *stand* this! How can I watch you, moon-dance to moon-dance, loving you, knowing the cub you carry is *mine,* not his, and wanting you, and—and not go mad myself?"

Her flush vanished, her cheeks paling, and she looked up at him with eyes like a dying deer's. He flinched away from the hurt his unthinking words had caused her—but he could not unsay them. They were true, though they hurt. "How can I watch *you?*" she replied in a choked whisper. "How can I see you lurking at the edges of the Pack, never daring to speak to you—" She broke off, and shook her head violently. "It's no good. I love *you,* but I love Two-Spear, too. And so do you. You loved him as his dearest friend long before he and I became lovemates. Would you break his heart—or worse, his mind—by forcing him to see what's happened between us? Do you think that *he,* of all people, would be willing to share me with you? *Some* elves might, but Two-Spear? He's the Pack-leader! The *Pack-leader doesn't share his mate!*"

His anger died. Too-vivid memories of one of Two-Spear's rages killed even the thought of lust. There was no choice, for either of them. They would bear it, because they had to. For the good of the Pack. Two-Spear was not the best chief they could have had—but he was better than the alternative.

For the alternative was Skyfire. As given to rage as her brother, but without the ability to see when a dream was futile. Who sought magic, when magic was a dead end, a twisted, warped power that served no one but itself. As obsessed, and yes, *mad* as her brother, but in her the madness turned inward instead of outward.

No. Not Skyfire. Not until *she* learned different ways.

"He was never willing to share even a worn-out deer hide," he replied, trying to make a joke of it and failing, as his voice died away in the frosty silence.

Their breath hung in clouds about them, and Willowgreen brushed at her eyes. "Perhaps I should never have spoken," Willowgreen whispered pensively. "Perhaps—perhaps I should have said nothing, let Recognition have its way and let you go, thinking I still hated you . . . thinking I was like the others. I would have been miserable, but better that than to hurt you."

But silence would have brought its own form of misery. Even if she had not spoken, *he* would have loved her. In silence. Thinking that he would always love her, and she would never know it. Now it was his turn to shake his head. "No. That would have been even harder to hide."

"Two-Spear hasn't Recognized me," she murmured, and he saw tears sparkling on her lashes. "Not as long as we've been lovemates. I've never heard his soulname and he has never heard mine. Perhaps he'll—tire of me. He might be glad to have me turn to you—"

"No," Graywolf interrupted fiercely; certain, though he did not know why. "He loves you. He can't show you, but he loves you. And he *needs* you. So the Pack needs you to stay with him. Whatever happens. However much we hurt. We will bear it in silence, and he will never know."

She looked up, met his eyes, and nodded, slowly. Only then did he notice that their wolves were no longer moving—had not been since the conversation started. He was glad to have an excuse to turn away before the pain grew too great and he howled his despair and loneliness.

"Lazy one!" he said, mock cuffing Moonfinder's ears. "I thought we were supposed to be exercising!"

The wolf whined, halfheartedly, and trotted down the hill, following the game-trail beneath the black, skeletal branches, Windwalker right on his tail.

* * *

So.

Rellah moved slowly up out of her dream-trance, holding her secret, the prize she had sought for so long, like one of Zarhan Fastfire's delicate little glass disks.

So. The wolf-boy is the father of Willowgreen's child, and it is not her lovemate. That made a certain amount of sense; Willowgreen was the nearest to the true elves in her appearance and talents of any of the Pack—and Graywolf the most wolflike. It should have been inevitable that they Recognized. It explained her odd silences, and the strange way they had treated each other since they had returned together from a hunt for plants last summer. It explained why a mating that had been fruitless until now should suddenly become fertile.

But that Recognition should become love? Not possible.

Not for Willowgreen, the delicate, the bright, the sensible. It was a mismatch of dreadful proportions.

Worse than that: obscene. If Willowgreen had tired of Two-Spear and his indifference, his cruelty, Rellah would have been overjoyed to see Willowgreen turn to—say—Rellah's own lovemate, Talen. Now that she carried a cub, the chief had changed his ways somewhat, being more attentive and a great deal calmer, no longer hurting her with hurtful remarks. And she, in turn, had managed to blunt his temper until even Rellah was inclined to look on him with grudging favor. Two-Spear was not so bad a choice for a lovemate, if he could be taught to act in a civilized manner; at least he was chief.

But Graywolf? More beast than thinking being?

She shuddered, as much in anger as in distaste. Horrible. *Horrible.* Delicate, sensitive Willowgreen, in the paws of—*that?* Her Willowgreen? The idea made her ill with anger.

She had argued against this interbreeding with *animals* at the beginning, but her arguments had fallen on deaf ears. Too many of the others had seen that the half-bloods were hunters, survivors, *protectors.* And as the seasons passed, and Timmain's offspring flourished, fewer true elves were born with every passing year; her own Willowgreen, her little Darrel, had been the last.

And little Darrel had no sooner reached maturity, come into the fullness of her healing powers than—

Her mind closed against the memory, but in this shallow half trance she had less control over her visions than she did when waking. Again she looked up from drinking at the spring to see the long-tooth cat, crouched on the limb above her. Again she froze, and breathed a sigh of relief as its eyes passed over her without a flicker of recognition. Long-tooths hunted as much by sight and sound as smell; she had been downwind, and as long as she held perfectly still—

Then she heard the light footsteps down the path, saw the branches move, and heard Darrel call her name—

And the cat leapt.

For a moment she was lost in sorrow and agony again; hugging herself and rocking back and forth to ease the pain she carried inside, like a child that would not be born. But there was nothing to ease this pain; not the passing of the seasons, not the comfort of her lovemate— nothing. Nothing . . .

After a time she came back to herself, her resolve and anger sharpened by the memory of her daughter. *Her* Willowgreen had known better than to give her heart to a half-beast.

What of the Willowgreen who wanted to be a huntress? whispered another memory. *What of the Willowgreen who tried to howl with the rest, befriend the wolves, eat her meat raw? The Willowgreen who even tried to forget her soulname until Cat's quest showed that even the half-bloods had soulnames?*

She ignored the memory. That was the folly of childhood, wanting to be like the leaders of the Pack. Her daughter would have outgrown such nonsense in time, would have gloried in her power, would have scorned the mindlessness of wolfsong. *Her* Willowgreen would have submitted to the demands of Recognition with Graywolf, as Merewood had, and others before and since—and then she would have driven the half-blooded creature from her side.

Would she? Or would she have sought him out, as Zarhan sought Rahnee? Driven to him as this Willowgreen is driven?

No. This Willowgreen was a child, a child in wisdom and experience as well as stature. A baby bearing a baby, with an unnatural attachment to the father. A foolish infant, who could not know what was best for her.

No child could. Not without the experience of centuries, not without the true wisdom of her heritage—the heritage of the High Ones, who had sailed the stars. Willowgreen could never know what was in her best interest.

But Rellah knew what was best for her. . . .

And Rellah still had a command of magic that these half-beasts could only dream of.

True, it would drain her—but there was food aplenty, and she would recover. True also that she must go deeply into trance, as deeply as those who had driven the city between the stars had gone. This was not a task undertaken lightly, not here, where magic fought the wielder and was apt to go awry given the slightest opportunity. She would have to remain here in seclusion for a day and a night, at least.

Still, no one would guess at what she was doing and she would not be missed; the rest of the Pack thought her sulking in her shelter. Her belly was empty, as it should be before starting a great work of magic; full bellies held one back, stifled the flow of power. But she was not in any need, nor was she weak with hunger—that, too, made the magic go awry. This was as perfect an opportunity as could be, here and now.

She would set a trap; not something that would harm, oh no, indeed—beast though the wolf-boy was, he was still an excellent hunter, and the elves had need of him. But she would weave a trap that would lure him in when he was in the presence of Willowgreen, and reveal him for the animal that he was. Then Willowgreen would see and reject what she saw. And all would be well again.

Perhaps if you had done this before, memory whispered, *Darrel would not have been so drawn to the half-bloods. Perhaps she would have turned away from them. Perhaps she would never have died—*

Conscience and will now united as one, Rellah drifted down into trance for a second time, seeking not secrets, but power.

The deer broke from their yards as the season progressed, and the hunters needed to go farther and farther afield to find game. After a dance of Child and Mother Moon, the Pack fell into a pattern of sending out two hunting parties alternately, so that one could rest while the other hunted. Graywolf led the first, Two-Spear the second—and when Two-Spear's hunters were foraging afield, the chief entrusted the care of his lovemate to his best friend, quietly pleased that Graywolf's animosity to the slender Willowgreen had faded. Perhaps, he confided cheerfully to his lovemate, as he readied himself in the relative warmth of their shelter for the next hunt, they might even become friends.

"If you were friends, we could do things together," he told her, unconscious of the feelings that thought raised in the healer. "That would be even better when the cub comes."

Willowgreen somehow managed to keep from betraying herself, and nodded. "Maybe it's the cub," she said truthfully. "Maybe she has something to do with it—now that I'm pregnant he feels, oh, sorry for me, or that I'm worthy of you. I never *wanted* him to hate me, he just did, and I never knew why."

"Oh, he was just jealous," Two-Spear replied carelessly as he checked the leather thongs holding the flint heads of his spears to their shafts. "I'm just about the only real friend he has; we're almost like brothers. It figures he'd be jealous of anyone else. Besides, you were like the very opposite of the first Willowgreen—you kept trying to be like the old ones, where she kept trying to be like one of us. *You* know how the old ones treat him, and you can't blame him for not liking them or anyone like them. But now you've got a wolf-friend of your own, you hear wolfsong—you're Pack. And you're carrying this cub. I guess he's decided you aren't so bad after all." He frowned at the wrist thong on his second spear and bit through it, taking up a new piece to replace it. "In fact, I bet he'll help you with taking care of it when it comes."

"What?" she said, startled. "But—why?"

"He *likes* cubs," Two-Spear replied, testing the replacement thong. "You wouldn't know it to look at him, but he's good with them. Once they get wandering-high, forget it, but he really likes the little ones. He helped Merewood with hers. After a while, she appreciated it, too."

"Oh," she said faintly. She hadn't thought beyond *having* the cub—this revelation opened up a world of possibilities— and difficulties. How could Graywolf hide the fact that he was the father if he was with the cub all the time? But if he avoided her and the little one, that would cause comment as well. . . .

She changed the subject quickly. "Is it a good idea to have Skyfire with you?" she asked timidly. "Isn't she likely to cause trouble? She—she doesn't like me, and the cub hasn't made any difference at all to *her*."

"Better where I can see her," he said, looking up and frowning. "If I have her under my eye, she won't be off making trouble somewhere else. Besides, she's a good tracker, almost as good as Graywolf. If I can't have him, I'd as soon have her."

Then he actually laughed, a little sourly. "Don't worry. I'll keep her so busy she won't have time to cause me any problems. The game's getting thin; she'll have to really work to find anything of any size."

Then he was gone, with no warning, picking up his spears and slipping out the entrance of the snow-shelter before she could even wish him luck. But—that had always been his way. His affectionate gestures were swift as his spear; he seemed to be content with a quick caress, a violent bout of lovemaking—then he was off, on to other things. But she no longer doubted that he loved her. . . .

The difficulty was that she had to be careful, so careful—walking a slender branch above a torrent. She had sensed lately that he was uncomfortable with a lovemate who was too— assertive. There had been signs of that before her pregnancy, but the advent of the cub had so excited him that he had forgotten about her change in temperament.

But attempts to suggest things—or worse, to interfere in what he considered to be the area of his chiefship— made his brows draw together and threatened an angry outburst.

So Willowgreen had learned, over the past dance of the moons, to mimic her old, pliant, gentle self. To only suggest, meekly, and use the excuse for the suggestions that she was afraid for the welfare of her unborn child. Impending fatherhood was enough—so far—to keep Two-Spear from launching another war with the humans.

How much longer it would be, she had no idea. If the humans came closer—or worse, attacked an elf themselves—she didn't think she would be able to stop him.

The sounds of the hunting party gathering and leaving did not interrupt her brooding. *Perhaps the game will*

*move away from the humans, or will thin out, and we'll
have to move. Maybe Graywolf could even drive it away
somehow, and we'd have to follow. . . .*

She felt tired, suddenly. Worn out by the complicated
web of deception and control she had to weave and keep
intact. She wasn't even very hungry, so as the light
dimmed and vanished and an orange glow beyond the
entrance to her snow-shelter told that Talen had kindled
the evening fire, she stayed where she was, wrapped in her
furs, drowsing. The craving she'd had for ash-baked roots
was gone, and there was a store of tough, smoked jerky
here. There was no need to go out to face the rest of the
Pack and try to keep the mask she had shaped for herself
between her soul and them. Between that, and everything
else, lately she had felt as if she and Graywolf were like
birds, flying at the very edge of a great storm, liable to be
sucked in if they made one wrong move. Most especially
she did not feel up to dealing with Rellah—the elf-healer
had grown sharp-tongued since her last bout of depres-
sion and Willowgreen was not up to a bout of verbal
fencing.

Not tonight.

If only . . .

The dream of wolfsong was very seductive tonight. She
let it lure her into its timeless *now,* a place where she
drifted above the life-web of this world and could survey
it dispassionately, without feeling. She wondered, in the
elf part of herself that was left to wonder, if all the
half-bloods saw the web as she did. Or was that an
enduring legacy of Shayana's mushroom, which had given
Willowgreen back her healing powers after she lost them.
Not that it mattered—here there was no pain of keeping
half of her love silent, of hiding secrets, of dancing
deception. No storm to fight. There was no hurt of
wanting to touch and denying that need in the name of
secrecy. There was no ache of heart and agony of
loneliness.

From the dream of wolfsong she drifted into another dream, one in which Two-Spear had somehow learned of the bond between herself and Graywolf, and miraculously accepted it. She dreamed of the three of them, united against Skyfire, winning over every member of the Pack, Two-Spear's terrible vows of vengeance long forgotten in his joy at their threefold love. She dreamed of her little one, her cub, a miniature of herself, watched over with pride by both of her lovemates. And she dreamed of long, delicious nights, when she would lie between both of them, wound in a knot of passion that ended in a tangle of limbs and blissful sleep. . . .

Someone crept into the furs beside her and wound her in his arms, waking her. She started—and Graywolf stopped her cry of surprise with a hand over her mouth.

"The hunters haven't come back," he whispered, "and I don't think they will until late tomorrow, at the earliest. My hunt couldn't find anything bigger than a ravvit within a day's ride of here."

"But—" She hardly dared believe he was here, beside her. "Rellah—the others—"

"They think I went off to sleep. The old ones decided to start their stories and songs again." She smiled sadly at the open contempt in his voice. But when had Rellah ever been anything but contemptuous of him? Not surprising that he should return the "favor."

And the stories of the days before their exile—tales of magic and wondrously easy lives, songs of the stars and mourning for what had been lost—those things bored Graywolf and no few of the others. What was the *point,* after all? Oh, both Skyfire and Two-Spear shared the same wild dream, that of returning to the stars, but few enough of the others did. And that dream was the *only* thing, besides loyalty to the Pack and the Way, that the siblings had in common.

But sulking and weeping over the days and powers long lost would do nothing to aid their survival here and now, nor would it return them to their former home. Skyfire felt that regaining magic would somehow give them the power to *wish* their way into contacting those of their race who still roamed the stars, so that those High Ones could come to their rescue. Two-Spear simply wanted to destroy all the humans, so that they would have no real enemies left, and could learn to do more than merely survive. It was his hope that one day they could re-create what had been lost, and, rather than returning as the rescued, return as equals who had triumphed over terrible adversity.

Both dreams were futile. . . .

In that thought, she and Graywolf were united. And perhaps now it was time to tell her lovemate a little more of the truth, to test it on him, and see if she should impart it to Two-Spear.

He was still talking; she'd missed a little, lost in her own thoughts. "Anyway, they all think I got bored and went to bed. I made sure no one saw me slip back here." He shifted, tucking the fur in around them both. "I— couldn't stay away. It was so dark and lonely—"

The wistfulness in his voice convinced her. "When I was gone, that first time?" she said tentatively, and felt him stiffen a little as his arms tightened about her, as if he feared some kind of unpleasant revelation.

Or maybe he was just conscience-stricken, since he had no small part in the quarrel that had resulted in her running off into the storm that had caused her accident.

"I hit my head," she said, carefully keeping her thoughts to herself so that none of her real memories would leak through to him. He was a great deal more sensitive than he realized he was; though he did not like to send, except to his wolf-friend, he was quite adept at picking up thought-images. "When I woke up, I couldn't heal anymore. Magic healing, I mean."

He relaxed a little. "But you can heal now," he protested. "You could when you got back—"

"The healer that helped me—she had this mushroom. It was like dreamberries, only a lot stronger." Here she was on safer ground, and she relaxed, too. "She sent me off with some of it, to try and get my healing back—she said that I'd have to be by myself so that I wouldn't be distracted, because I'd have to find out what was wrong with *me,* and dreamsharing with her wouldn't help me do that." That wasn't exactly what Shayana had said, but Willowgreen felt she was within the spirit of what had been meant.

"It gave me my healing back—I mean, it helped me find out what I'd broken and fix it—but I saw something else." She groped for the right words.

And was surprised by his reply. "I—remember that, I think," he said slowly. "What you saw. You showed it to me, when I was hurt and I wouldn't let you heal me."

"You do?" She was relieved and grateful beyond telling. It made what she had to say so much easier. "Tell me—so I know that we're talking about the same thing."

"It's—it's the whole world, all the life on it. Like a river, with fish and stones and plants, all belonging." *That* was a surprise; she had seen the life of this world as a great web, but this made as much sense as her vision. "And the old ones—the High Ones—they don't belong. They kind of float on the top, like chips of bark, and sooner or later the river is going to toss them out. But us—the ones with Timmorn's blood in us—we're like—I don't know, plants that have learned to grow in the water, at the edge. Like reeds or something. Part in the water and part in the air. We *belong,* though, and they don't. The river won't get rid of us. . . ."

His voice trailed off, as if the implications of that only now occurred to him.

"Which means?" It was her turn to prompt.

"They're going to *die.* The world keeps trying to get rid of them, and it won't stop until it does," he said, faltering.

She turned in his arms and faced him, her head resting on his chest. "Yes," she said simply. "Exactly. Now—do I tell—and show—Two-Spear that?"

"Would it make any difference?" Graywolf replied, his voice full of doubt.

"It might," she said. "But I don't know what direction he'd go in. He *might* be kinder to them—but—"

"But he might not," Graywolf interrupted. "If the game grows thin—if living grows hard—who should the food and shelter go to? The young ones, who *will* live, or the old ones, who are doomed anyway?" His voice grew hard. "It's tempting, you know. If I told him—after the way they have treated me, as something less than an animal—it would be a very sweet revenge."

That was something she had not thought of—that Two-Spear would see what she had learned as a reason to rid himself of the true elves—and that Graywolf would use that information as a means to his own revenge. Her blood chilled, but his next words warmed her.

"No," he said, with a touch of regret, but still quite firmly. "No. Not even for revenge. If only because *they* would expect it of me."

She answered him, but not with words—and at least half of her earlier wish-dream found fulfillment in his arms. And in loving she could forget, for a little while, all her sorrows.

Rellah wound her furs tighter about her and frowned into the darkness. The trap had been laid—but the bait had not been taken. In fact, the wolf-boy had actively *avoided* the area, as if he somehow sensed that the trap was there. Perhaps he was more sensitive than she had given him credit for.

She would have to be more subtle, then.

In any case, there was a disadvantage to the site she had first chosen. Willowgreen hardly ever went on long rides anymore. With the snow so deep, she was staying close to the camp. And it would be better, far, if she actually saw the transformation with her own eyes.

Rellah's conscience hurt her for a moment, and she stirred restlessly. It wasn't as if she was going to *harm* the wolfling, she told herself. All she was going to do was trigger the change, the same change that Timmain herself had undergone. For a half-blood, it should be simple. It might be that he would merely drop completely into wolfsong, and be lost in it, but more likely he would become as Three-Toes, and run off to join a wild pack. In either case, Willowgreen would see what it was she had tried to join herself to, and her natural revulsion would drive her away from Graywolf—assuming the wolfling *didn't* run off himself.

Rellah frowned again. It was a pity that she didn't know more about shapeshifting. The magic she had created was not as specific as she would have liked. It drove what fell into it to *change,* into the shape that was the opposite of the one it now wore. That should be enough—but she wished that she could have keyed it to Graywolf alone, and forced it to call up the wolf-shape, and that only. But magic did not obey here, and she felt fortunate to have shaped it as closely to her intention as she had.

But she would have to conceal it better—and it was time to move it. If Graywolf would not come to her magic, the magic would come to a place where he would pass it and be drawn in. A place such as—the path to the camp, the game-trail that the hunters had taken. She would plant it beside the trail, so that nothing fell into it by accident, and she would weave a second spell that would attract the wolfling to that place.

Yes. That would do. That would do nicely.

She sank deeply into trance, putting all thoughts and emotions from her mind. There could be no distractions to taint the magic, for power responded oddly to emotions here. No matter how she felt about the wolfling, what was important was Willowgreen. Only Rellah could make her see the truth. Only Rellah could save her. And, by the power she held, Rellah would.

The magic grew. . . .

The Naming of Stonefist

by Allen L. Wold

The day that Greentwig was finally given his adult name started out just like any other day at Halfhill, though it didn't long stay that way. At first light the youngest elves, the cublings, came out of their dens, where they'd slept the night away with their parents and older siblings, and went down to the stream to wash and play. After a bit some of the older children came down to join them. And some of the wolves, who'd slept in the forest above the hill or across the stream, came around to find out if anything was up. It was a cool morning, but clear, and would get hotter as the day went on.

Many of the elves were away that day, as was frequently the case, on hunting trips, or in pursuit of materials for clothes and weapons, or just wandering around, the way Freefoot often did, though he was at Halfhill that day. He wasn't up yet, but was enjoying a quiet hour with Starflower, his lifemate, while Feather, his younger son, nearly an adult, was out with the cubs and cublings. His elder son, Fangslayer, had moved into his own den long ago.

In time the noise of the children became louder, and the elders began to stir themselves. It was a good season; there was no need to hunt every day, no need to be constantly out and about. Every day since late spring had been about the same, and everybody assumed the days would continue to be the same until the first frost. And that was good, and the way it should be, since that was the way it usually was, year after year.

If Greentwig's coming-of-age had been the only unusual event that day, it would be exceptional enough, and would have been remembered for many turns of the seasons following. After all, Greentwig was more than twice as old as any other elf had been when they became adults and assumed the responsibilities of being an elder. It seemed that he just never quite grew up. He was tall, and well built, and quite good-looking, but he had never developed any skills, he showed no special talents, and seemed content, much of the time, to play with the younger elves, the juveniles.

Like the wolves who shared their lives, the elves did not bear the burden of an incompetent, did not support those who could not carry their own weight, and in the course of the years there were many occasions when Greentwig's parents, Fernhare and Glade, had feared that this time he would die of his own ineptitude. His peers—Brightmist, who had been Sundrop as a child and was now lifemate of Shadowflash; and Deerstorm, known as Faun when a youth, now mother of Ebony, a cub halfway to maturity, and lifemated with Fangslayer—despaired of his ever growing up at all.

And yet he somehow managed to survive, somehow managed to avoid catastrophe, was able to hunt well enough to feed himself and share with others. No one expected that he would ever stop being an overgrown child, certainly not today. And though they could not coddle him, they accepted him, as best they could, and did not drive him away. But he was a sadness for them, and they all knew that someday he would find himself in a situation, which any other adult elf could easily survive, that would kill him. It was some comfort to them that he did not seem to be aware of that.

In fact, Greentwig was very much looking forward to the day. He was going on a special hunting expedition, with Fernhare, his mother, and Fangslayer, and Brightmist, and Two Wolves, and young Starbright, who was almost an adult, though she was less than half

Greentwig's age, and for whom this expedition had been planned.

Coming-of-age was a difficult time for a young elf, when one had to prove one's competence, and maturity, and ability, and responsibility. Starbright had been dancing around the edges of it for half a turn of the seasons, ever since Silverknife had somehow crossed that imperceptible threshold. Starbright wanted to be an adult too, but didn't know just exactly how to go about it. And so Fangslayer, the best hunter at the Holt, had planned this trip, to the forested mesa just north of the edge of the forest. It would not be a long trip, and the mesa was not a dangerous place, but the hunt he had planned would be a test of strength, cunning, courage, and endurance, and if Starbright did well, she would be that much closer to gaining her adult name.

As it was, things were not to turn out the way anybody had planned. Maybe if Freefoot hadn't been so busy that morning things might have happened differently. If he had not been so preoccupied with other problems he might have calmed Starbright when things began to go wrong, might have encouraged her to follow through so that the hunters, when they got to the mesa, would have been better able to deal with what happened. On the other hand, if he had, Greentwig might not have been given his one and only opportunity to prove himself.

Starbright was still young yet, and whether she took her name this hot season, or during the snows, or with the next coming of the green, it wouldn't have mattered much, except perhaps to her pride. For Greentwig, though nobody could know it, there would be no other chance.

The first thing that happened to upset everybody's plans began when Two Wolves was roused from a languid late slumber by his special kind of second sense. Rainbow, his lifemate, had been awake for some time but had not awakened him. She was thinking of the hunt on which her mate would be going today, thinking of a place where she'd found bright red clay for painting, thinking of a way to paste thin sheets of bark together to make a large, empty surface for painting, just quietly waiting while her mate slept so lightly, uncovered in the cool morning. Without warning, his eyes came open all at once, and, though he did not move, he became as tense as a hunter at the moment of a kill.

"What's the matter?" she asked him softly.

"Whitecollar is afraid," he answered, just as softly.

He had a special knack with wolves. It was his only exceptional quality. Every elf had a wolf-companion, but Two Wolves had two most of the time, this time a mated pair. He was the only elf who could communicate comfortably with another elf's wolf, and besides his two he was on friendly terms with three other wolves who were unattached and lived alone in the forest. And so he was able to feel Whitecollar's fear, though the wolf was not in the den with him.

"But what could possibly frighten Whitecollar?" Rainbow asked.

"I don't know," he said, but he got up quickly and dressed.

"Where's Brushtail?" she asked, naming Whitecollar's mate.

"There's something wrong," was all he would say, and he left even while he was pulling on his vest.

He stood for a moment in front of the high clay cliff that gave Halfhill its name, and into which all the elves had dug their dens. The stream, beyond a stretch of grassy lawn that served as the common yard, ran from the right, as he stood facing it, and it was toward the downstream end of the cliff, toward the left, that he felt the presence of his wolves. Whitecollar was definitely fearful, though Two Wolves could not tell of what, but Brushtail's wolfish mind was somehow murky, skittery, angry, and confused, and very hard to read. He strode in that direction, ignoring the other elves he passed, not running, but taking long steps to get there as quickly as possible.

At the eastern end of the clay cliff, where the upper bluff came down to the river lowland, was a cluster of small trees that formed a kind of ring, just four paces across. The two wolves were inside this ring. Whitecollar, a brownish gray wolf with a circle of white fur around his neck, was crouched down, tail low, hackles up, head down, half curved around himself, against the far wall of the ring, through which he could have escaped if he had wanted, staring with frightened eyes at Brushtail. She in turn was standing in the middle of the dark, branch-covered space, snapping at the air, turning around and around, her heavy tail with its black tip twitching, her jaws dripping white foam.

There was nothing he could do by himself; what he needed was a healer's help. Carefully, so as not to frighten the animals, Two Wolves backed out of the clearing and went quickly to Deerstorm's den. "May I come in?" he called from the entranceway.

"Yes, of course," he heard Fangslayer answer.

He went through the narrow passage, with its corner to keep out stray drafts, to the main chamber, where he found Deerstorm helping Fangslayer get ready for the hunt. Fangslayer was tightening the bindings on his spearhead while Deerstorm was wrapping some ravvit meat in berryvine leaves.

Two Wolves clapped Fangslayer on the shoulder, but turned his attention at once to Deerstorm. She was very large with the child that would be born very soon now. "Brushtail is sick," he said. "She's acting strangely, and she's foaming at the mouth."

"Oh, dear," Deerstorm said. She put down the bundles of meat and leaves and Fangslayer put down his spear. "I suppose she could have gotten into some soaproot."

"Whitecollar is acting afraid of her. She keeps circling around and around herself."

"Owl pellets," Deerstorm said. "I suppose I'd better go

and see." She had to work to get to her feet, her belly was so huge.

"I'm sorry," Two Wolves said. "Do you think it's the fever?"

"I'll know for sure when I see her." She turned to Fangslayer. He stood up to kiss her. "Have a good hunt," she told him. "Keep him out of trouble." Meaning, as they all knew, Greentwig.

"I will," Fangslayer said. "If Brushtail has the fever, you stay clear of her."

"I will," she said, and followed Two Wolves out of the den.

As they emerged onto the lawn between the cliff and the stream they saw Silvercub come out of Two Wolves' den. He ran up to them. "What's the matter, Father?"

"Brushtail is sick," Two Wolves told him. "I think she has the frothing fever."

Silvercub's eyes got quite large. He was in the middle of his childhood, and took things quite seriously. "I'm coming along, Father," he insisted. "Maybe I can help."

Two Wolves reached out and tousled his son's silver-white hair. "Maybe you can," he said. "But we'd better hurry. Whitecollar is with her." Without further discussion the three went downstream toward the circle of trees.

As they approached the place, they could hear strange growling, not like the sounds wolves usually made, and Two Wolves leapt ahead. When the other two pushed their way into the little clearing they saw Brushtail, foaming at the mouth, stalking Whitecollar, who backed away from her with his head down almost to the ground and his tail between his legs.

"She's bitten him," Silvercub exclaimed, and sure enough there was blood on Whitecollar's shoulder. "So now he's got it, too."

"I'm afraid you're right," Deerstorm said. "Now quiet a minute." She stood watching the two wolves, who paid no attention to her at all, and concentrated on her skill. To affect a healing she had to lay her hands on the afflicted, but even from this distance she could make a diagnosis, especially with an illness as terrible as this. "It's the frothing fever," she said after a moment. "I'm sorry, it couldn't be anything else. And it looks like Brushtail has been ill for several days."

"What can we do?" Silvercub asked, while his father stood grimly, silently beside him.

"We might be able to save Whitecollar," Deerstorm said, "but I'm afraid there's nothing we can do about Brushtail."

"Will she die?" He clutched his father's hand.

"Yes, she will," Two Wolves said, "but it's worse than that. We can't let her just die of the disease. You can see how wild she's getting; it will get worse. She'll become like Stringsong's wolf Rage was, so many years ago, biting at everything and everybody. She will have to be destroyed before then."

"Oh, Father, no."

"It has to be," Two Wolves said softly. His voice was choked, and Silvercub looked up at his face, which was strained and pale. "I was there when Rage got the frothing fever," he said with an effort. "Stringsong didn't want to put him down, though Graywing told him he had to. We thought we could keep Rage confined, maybe he would get over it. But he got worse and worse, and it seemed like he got stronger and stronger, and at last he broke free from his tether one evening when Hickory, Stringsong's father, was walking by, and bit him severely. Stringsong had to destroy Rage then. We had no healer at that time, and Hickory got the fever and began frothing and going wild and attacking people, so we bound him, rather than killing him, to let the fever run its course. We know now that that was wrong; a swift death would have been preferable to the madness and the pain that Hickory suffered until he died at last, screaming and biting himself."

Silvercub was very subdued. Deerstorm heaved a great sigh and held her belly with both hands. The two wolves, across the small clearing, jockeyed back and forth. The three elves had to move around inside the small ring of trees to keep the two wolves as far from them as possible.

"I'm going to need some help," Deerstorm said.

"Get back to the Holt," Two Wolves said to Silvercub. "Get whoever you can." Silvercub gave his father's hand another squeeze and left.

Whitecollar's fear of Brushtail was apparently overcoming his fidelity to his mate, since now he seemed to be trying to leave the circle of trees. At the same time, Brushtail appeared to be losing interest in the other wolf and looked like she might try to leave the small clearing at any moment. Two Wolves tried to keep the two animals together within the circle of trees while Deerstorm kept out of the way.

It wasn't long before Silvercub came back with Treewing, followed a moment later by Freefoot. It took only moments for them to comprehend the situation, and the two elder elves worked with Two Wolves to herd the animals into the one corner of the clearing where they couldn't escape between the trees. Whitecollar was confused and hurt, and did as he was directed with little resistance, but Brushtail was getting violent, lunging at the elves, backing, snapping at the air.

"Her disease is very far advanced," Deerstorm said.

Treewing paused to look at her. "Should you be here at all?"

"I think I can save Whitecollar," Deerstorm said, "if I can get to him."

Two Wolves called Whitecollar and the wolf came, frightened and uncertain. "See if you can calm him," he told Silvercub, "but be careful not to let him nip you or lick at you."

Silvercub subdued his anxiety and knelt before his father's wolf. This was not what Whitecollar was expecting, and this let Deerstorm come up on the animal's other side. She put her hands on the wolf's shoulders, a healer's hands, so that the animal did not flinch, but let himself be touched. Whitecollar was very nervous and in some pain, but the two elves attending to him meant that Two Wolves was free to do what he had to do.

Two Wolves, Freefoot, and Treewing consulted quietly for a moment, then they all sent to Brushtail, the same thoughts from all three, to calm her, to make her lie down and be quiet. The sick wolf had little resistance. She did, after a moment's confusion, what she was bid.

"Are we sure there's nothing we can do?" Treewing said when Brushtail had quieted as much as she could.

"Remember Hickory," Two Wolves said. "Nothing we did for him helped at all, and he was not as far gone as this."

"We didn't have a healer then," Treewing said.

"—that's true," Two Wolves said uncertainly.

Then Freefoot said, "I have seen the frothing fever several times before. Once the wolf, or elf, or other animal begins to spit white foam, it's too late. Even a healer can't repair the damage inside. Whitecollar has a chance, but Brushtail is beyond our hope. I don't know how to describe it in a healer's words, but Rellah, once very long ago, told me it was like trying to catch a school of shiners in the river with your bare hands. There are always more than you can hold at once, and the school as a whole always gets away, and when you grab at them they slip through your fingers. She was a strong healer, and I believe her."

Two Wolves stood uncertainly for a long moment.

"I'll do it for you," Treewing offered.

But Two Wolves knew that if it had to be done, he must do it himself. He drew his knife. He looked at Freefoot, who returned his glance, and once again the three elders shared a sending. And while Freefoot and Treewing kept Brushtail distracted, Two Wolves moved around beside and behind the animal, and with one stroke to her heart, killed her.

Whitecollar had been watching nervously, in spite of what Silvercub and Deerstorm could do to keep the wolf calm and distracted, and when Two Wolves struck, Brushtail yelped in surprise and pain. Whitecollar's reaction was instantaneous and violent. The wolf lunged across the tiny clearing toward Two Wolves, who was half crouched over Brushtail, holding her dead body. Treewing was between them, and Whitecollar leapt upon her in his desperation, snapping and snarling. She drew her own knife as the wolf bore her to the ground, and though she didn't want to strike, she had to kill Whitecollar in self-defense.

She pulled herself from under the dead wolf. Deerstorm rushed up, clumsy as she was, and knelt beside her.

"Have you been bitten?"

"No," Treewing said, and turned to Two Wolves, who was standing in shock. "I'm sorry," she said, "I . . ."

Two Wolves stared past her at Whitecollar, trying to catch his breath.

"Let Deerstorm make sure you are unscratched," Freefoot said to Treewing. Then he went to Two Wolves and put his hands on the stricken elf's shoulders.

Two Wolves came back to himself and looked into his chief's eyes, but could say nothing. He was a strong elf, but tears were streaming down his face.

"It is my fault more than Treewing's," Freefoot said, "that Whitecollar is dead. I should have taken him from here."

Two Wolves shook his head. "It's not her fault. He would have torn her apart, and me as well, and I couldn't have defended myself. But what do I do now?"

"You will need healing, too, of a different nature," Freefoot told him gently.

At that moment Ebony came crashing into the clearing, calling for his mother, and stopped short when he saw the dead wolves and the grief-stricken elves.

Deerstorm rose, with difficulty, from where she had

been examining Treewing. "What is it, my cubling?" she asked. There were tears in her eyes.

"Fangslayer is about ready to get the hunting party together," Ebony said. His voice was almost inaudible, as if he could not completely comprehend what had happened here, as indeed he could not.

"I'll be with you in a moment," Deerstorm said. She helped Treewing to her feet. "You have not been infected," she told the older elf. "But it is important that all of us wash carefully after this." Then she knelt to look at Whitecollar. "He died instantly," she said to Two Wolves. "Treewing's blow was right to the heart." She went to Brushtail and knelt close to the wolf without touching her. When she stood up she said, "Keep her from the forest until she begins to swell. That will make sure that the fever will be burned by decay, and will not contaminate those who eat her flesh."

Ebony was very upset and wanted to know what had happened, so Deerstorm told him briefly. Then she turned to Silvercub, who was in a state of shock where she had left him, and asked Ebony to come help her. Ebony went to Silvercub and they consoled each other for a moment.

Then Deerstorm said, "I think I need your help to get back to my den." So with the two children supporting her, perhaps more than she really needed, she let them take her back home.

Two Wolves sat in the center of the small clearing, his elbows on his knees, his face in his hands. When an elf and a wolf become partners, they form a bond almost as strong as that between lovemates. An elf's life is long, very long indeed, while a wolf's life is short, a few handfuls of years, so all elves know that they will lose their wolf-friends, and while this does not make the pain any less, it makes it bearable. Another wolf will come along. But to lose a wolf suddenly, through disease or accident, is a terrible thing. Two Wolves was special in this regard, more in touch with wolves in general, and his in particular. And he had lost both, in a single day.

Treewing and Freefoot came and sat beside him, put their arms around him, and helped him feel his grief.

"You should go back to your den," Freefoot said after a while.

Two Wolves did not say anything, but Freefoot could feel his acceptance of that simple bit of wisdom.

Treewing and Freefoot helped Two Wolves to his feet, and stood beside him to steady him. He looked at the two bodies.

"I'll take care of them later," Treewing said. "They'll be all right here for now."

Then, one on either side, Treewing and Freefoot helped Two Wolves out of the little ring of trees and walked with him back along the clay cliff toward his den. Other elves, having seen Deerstorm pass with the two children, were watching now, and their sympathy was evident in their expressions and postures.

As the three passed the den where Greentwig was still living with his parents, he came out and asked them what was wrong.

"Both Brushtail and Whitecollar died this morning," Two Wolves said simply. Treewing and Freefoot quickly told the rest of the story.

"I'm sorry," Greentwig said. "Is there anything I can do?"

"Thank you," Two Wolves said. "What I need right now is to be with Rainbow."

"Does that mean," Greentwig said, "that you won't be able to go hunting today?"

Two Wolves could only stare at him incredulously.

"Yes," Freefoot said, "it means that."

The disappointment on Greentwig's face was obvious. Treewing, Freefoot, and Two Wolves went on.

"He just doesn't understand," Treewing said softly.

Greentwig watched them leave, then went back into his den. His parents looked up and saw his disappointed face.

"What's the matter?" Glade asked him.

"Two Wolves can't go hunting today," he said and told them what had happened. Glade and Fernhare were shocked and saddened at the news. Greentwig was more than sympathetic to Two Wolves' plight, but he was also disappointed that Two Wolves wouldn't be going on the hunt, so he left the den again, looked around to see who was about, and saw Brightmist working just in front of her den.

She was knapping some flints for arrowheads in preparation for the hunt and she looked up when she noticed Greentwig coming out of his den, and watched as he came toward her. She had been sort of aware that something bad had happened regarding Two Wolves, and was concerned, but this hunt was important, not only for Starbright, but for Greentwig as well. He was her age, though she had become an adult when she had been something more than half as old as they were now. She could see that Greentwig was upset and guessed it might have something to do with Two Wolves.

But as he drew near she began to feel strange, as if she were somehow larger than herself. Her arms felt long and seemed to float beside her. Her mind was shrunken inside her expanding self. Greentwig sat down beside her and spoke to her, but she was so preoccupied with these strange sensations that she didn't really hear what he was saying. He spoke again, but the strange feelings got stronger and she lost track of him altogether.

Greentwig looked at her face, saw the faraway expression in her eyes, the subtle jerkiness to her movements. Even to his slow mind it was obvious that there was something wrong here. "Brightmist," he said again, quietly, but more insistently, "what's the matter, can you tell me?" He reached out and touched her shoulder gently.

She tried to tell him what was going on, but found it hard to verbalize. She didn't really have the vocabulary to describe what she was feeling, both in her body and now, more and more, in her mind. And what she did say,

Greentwig wasn't able, or didn't want, to understand—
she didn't know which, and at the moment didn't care.
She was feeling very strange now, as if she were floating in
a place in between the lawn and a dream, and the whole
world around her was somehow separated from her by
more than physical distance. But Greentwig seemed
insistent about something, so she forced herself to pay
attention, looking at his mouth as well as listening.

"Will you be able to go hunting today?" he was saying.

"No," she said. "I'm sorry, I don't think so."

Greentwig looked at her silently for a long moment.
Her eyes were unfocused, her face worked, and her hands
were twitching as if there were something in them. He
had never seen her behaving like this before and it
frightened him. He touched her shoulder again and
waited until she looked at him.

"Brightmist," he said, "are you all right?"

"I'll be okay," she said, but her voice was very odd.
"We'll hunt together another time."

He rocked back on his heels. He knew that she was
trying to be kind to him in spite of her distress, knew that
whatever was troubling her was not her fault. But he was
disappointed again. Now his hunting party was down to
four, and he knew that would make it more difficult, more
dangerous, less likely to succeed. He tried not to feel sorry
for himself—Brightmist looked so uncomfortable, so
unhappy.

"Are you sick?" he asked her. "Should I call
Deerstorm?"

"No," was all she said.

He watched her a moment longer, then bid her good-
bye, though he doubted she heard him, and went away.

He couldn't stop worrying about her though, so when
he came to the den where Fangslayer and Deerstorm
lived, he called out to the healer. After a moment
Deerstorm, huge and ungainly and now looking a little
wan, came to the entrance. Greentwig immediately re-

gretted calling her, but she assured him that she was okay. Greentwig told her that Brightmist seemed to be ill, that she didn't want help, but that he was still worried.

"If she doesn't want help," Deerstorm said, "then let's leave it at that."

Fangslayer, dressed in unusually plain, greenish clothes, came out to see what was happening, and Greentwig told him about Brightmist. "And her hands were moving like this," he finished, moving his own hands as if he were breaking invisible reeds into small pieces. "So she won't be coming with us."

"That doesn't sound good," Deerstorm said. "I'll try to look in on her a little later, but right now I'm not feeling so well myself."

"Maybe I shouldn't go," Fangslayer said.

"No, I'll be all right. Besides, Starbright is counting on you."

Fangslayer met her eyes, and for a moment they shared a private sending.

"Okay," Fangslayer said at last to Greentwig, "we'll go hunting anyway." He ducked back inside the den for a moment and came back out with his weapons, the bundle of meat wrapped in leaves, and something that looked like a lot of knotted rope. "Stringsong's best net," he said, showing it to Greentwig. He turned to Deerstorm and put his arm gently around her shoulder. "Let somebody else do the work for a while," he said. "We'll be back tomorrow."

"Good luck," Deerstorm said, then went back in to lie down while Fangslayer went with Greentwig to his den.

There Fernhare, with Glade's help, was finishing the preparations for Greentwig. They had some meat in a bag of clean intestine, had his ax and bow and arrows ready, and coils of light rope, Stringsong's best, which would be needed for this special hunt.

Fangslayer's news about Two Wolves was distressing, and Greentwig's news about Brightmist was disturbing, but Fernhare was determined to go on with the hunt as planned. "Even with only four of us," she said, "we have a chance, and besides, it's not whether we get anything, it's how well we hunt that counts."

"I think you're right," Fangslayer said, "though I wouldn't give up our chances just yet. Two Wolves is in good hands, and as for Brightmist, she's strong and I think she can take care of herself."

But at that moment, Brightmist wasn't so sure about that. She felt power in her, not her own minor talent as a stoneshaper, but something from outside that touched her talent and was working through it. She was the Holt's flint-knapper, not so much because of her skill but because of that bit of talent, just enough so that when she worked a flint, or whitecrystal, or other stone, it came out right. Now she picked up a piece of granite that she had been using as an anvil, against which she laid the flints to hold them steady as she worked them with a piece of antler, and started to work with it. She did not strike it with other stones, nor make it flow like she sometimes could in an uncontrolled, fluid sort of way, but molded it in her hands, as if it were pottery clay, shaping it with her fingers.

As she worked, aimlessly at first, Shadowflash, her mate, came out of their den behind her. He spoke her name, but she didn't hear him. She was sometimes like that when she was engrossed in her work, and he came up quietly behind her to see what she was doing and stopped dead still, his breath caught in his throat, when he did. The speckled gray-black stone in her hands was slowly taking on the shape of an elfin face.

Shadowflash knew that something was wrong. Brightmist had done nothing like this before. He touched her shoulder. She didn't respond, but he felt an odd tremor running through his own body at the contact. It frightened him, and he went off for help.

And who should be coming out of his den at that

moment but Puckernut, with Rillwalker, his lifemate, and their cub Dayshine, a youth of Starbright's age. Puckernut was as bitter and grouchy as his name, but he knew things, knew where things came from, where they had been, what was inside them, and Brightmist's behavior was something that Puckernut might just be able to make sense of. So Shadowflash stopped him and told him what he had seen Brightmist doing with the granite.

"That doesn't sound right," Puckernut agreed. He could see Brightmist, not that far off from where they were standing, and what he saw didn't look natural to him.

"Can we be of any help?" Rillwalker asked.

"I don't think so," Puckernut said, so Rillwalker and Dayshine went on to the stream to wash up. Puckernut wanted a bath, too, but he didn't like the way Brightmist seemed so entranced with her work, so he went over to her with Shadowflash and watched for a while.

"Is she just coming into her talent?" Shadowflash asked. Brightmist was now holding a chunk of flint, slowly pushing it into a bowl shape.

"It doesn't feel like it," Puckernut said. "If it were, she shouldn't be so oblivious to us. This is magic, and it's from outside her somehow. I can feel it."

"But where has it come from?"

"I don't know. Brightmist?" he said. She didn't respond. "Brightmist," he said again, louder this time. Her attention did not waver. She was making the bowl larger, thinner, working the white rind of the flint up to the lip, leaving the main part of the bowl transparent black. Puckernut reached out and touched her shoulder. She seemed to be completely unaware of him. Then he took her hand and felt a sudden thrill run through him, as if lightning had struck somewhere nearby. He jerked his hand away and sat back on his heels.

"What is it?" Shadowflash asked, his voice a hoarse whisper.

Puckernut wiped his hands on his thighs, as if to remove the contamination. "It's very strong," he said. "We'd better stay with her, at least for a little while."

Even as they settled down to watch Brightmist working the stone in front of her den, Rainbow, Freefoot, and Treewing were getting Two Wolves settled. He had held his grief for his dead animals in check, but now was the time to feel the pain, the loss. His mate and two good friends were with him, and he needn't be ashamed. It would be many days before he could begin to think about finding another wolf-friend, and before then the grief of his loss had to be worked out.

Rainbow stroked her mate's forehead, cooed at him wordlessly, just letting him know she was there and that she cared. But as she did so she began to feel weird, as if she were somehow both expanding and shrinking inside herself at the same time. She kept up her comforting reassurances, but as the moments went by her arms began to feel long and buoyant, and she held them up to look at them. They didn't look any different. The other people in the den seemed somehow faraway and unimportant. She turned away from Two Wolves and took out her art materials—pigments and white bark. It was as if she were watching herself from the outside—or from the inside, rather. She started to work, oblivious to Freefoot and Treewing, who were looking at her oddly, mixing red and yellow clays with a pine resin, which would make them waterproof when they dried. She didn't hear when Treewing spoke to her. She just mixed up some blue berry-juice with the resin and turned the bark over so the white side was up. Then she took a small twig of blue oak and chewed the end so that the fibers split small and fine, making a brush.

As she worked, Freefoot and Treewing watched, uncertain what to do. Two Wolves was curled up in a ball now, not really aware of them, so they left him and went over to see what Rainbow was doing. Her behavior was so bizarre that they hesitated to disturb her, but just looked over her shoulder, and stopped, astonished at what they saw. She had made a picture of the two dead wolves, as they had been in life, but drawn so realistically that it was frightening.

Meanwhile Greentwig, in his own den, was putting on some greenish clothes, like Fangslayer's. Elves usually hunted wearing their everyday apparel, bright as it was, but this hunt was different. Fernhare had already changed into something gray, and Glade, with Fangslayer, was just waiting for Greentwig to finish. As he was lacing up the front, Starbright called to him from the entrance.

"Come on in," Greentwig called back, and she did.

"Are you about ready?"

"Sure," he said with a broad smile. "How do I look?"

"Just fine. How about me?" Her own clothes were a muted brown.

"You'll do just fine," Fernhare said. She had been on this kind of hunt before.

"Has Brightmist come by?" Starbright asked.

"She can't come," Greentwig told her with a sudden drop in his spirits. "She's sick or something."

"Oh, no," Starbright said. "And we were counting on her, too."

"You're going to have to get along without Two Wolves as well," Fangslayer told her, and then explained why.

Starbright, who had come in full of excitement, slumped against the wall in bitter disappointment. "Why did that have to happen now, of all days?"

"Why, Starbright," Fernhare said, "I'm surprised. There's no good time for the sudden loss of your wolf-friend."

"I know, I'm sorry. It's just that I've been looking forward to this hunt."

"And so has Two Wolves," Fernhare said. "And so has Brightmist. And not only are they going to miss out on the hunt, but they have their other problems to deal with, too."

"Well, owl pellets," Starbright said. "I'm sorry for Two

Wolves, and for Brightmist, but if they can't go then there will be only two adults on this hunt, and there's no chance we'll succeed."

"I'm still going along," Greentwig said.

"Oh, you don't count." She seemed to be totally unaware of his feelings, or those of his parents. "I guess we might just as well call it off." She stood away from the wall and slouched out of the den.

The day, which had dawned so bright and fair, now seemed to her unpleasant, too hot, uncomfortable. She had been looking forward to this hunt for a long time, and she was intensely disappointed. Without really thinking about it, she headed down toward the stream.

Dayshine, as he came up from the stream with Rillwalker on the way back to their den, saw Starbright, and it was obvious that she was upset. He spoke briefly to his mother, then went to join his friend.

Starbright turned away from him, angling downstream, toward the east, but Dayshine fell into step beside her. He didn't say anything as they walked. But when they got to the big flat stone downstream, the one that hung over the edge of the creek, she told him about her disappointment.

"I'm sorry, Starbright," he said. "That's really too bad."

"It's more than too bad. I was hoping that maybe they would give me my adult name today."

"You want that pretty badly, don't you?"

"Sure, don't you?"

"Not as much as you do. It will come. But it's sure not fair that you're missing out on a chance like this."

"That's what I think. And you know, if it weren't for Greentwig, I could probably go ahead and go."

"How do you figure?"

"Don't you see? If Greentwig goes on a hunt, the others have to watch out for him. Fangslayer and Fernhare will be so busy keeping him out of trouble, there'll be no chance for me to do any good hunting at all."

"I guess you're right," Dayshine said.

As the two youngsters talked, Greentwig sat quietly in his den. He was hurt by Starbright's anger, by her dismissal of him as unimportant to the hunt. Maybe he wasn't as clever as the other elves, but he could feed himself. And he had been looking forward to this hunt, too. He knew it took the cooperation of several elves if it was going to work, and now that Starbright had dropped out there were only three of them left. "Maybe we should call it off," he said softly.

"Do you want to?" Fernhare said. She was half hoping he would—a hunt like this could kill him—but she and Glade had long since given up trying to protect him from his own ineptitude.

"No," Greentwig said after a pause. It always took him a moment to finish a thought.

"Then we'll go."

"Just the three of us?"

"I don't see why not," Glade said. "It will make it harder, but then what you do accomplish will be all that much greater."

"Will you come along with us?" Greentwig asked him.

"I've thought about it," his father said, "but there's someone else who really needs my help right now."

Greentwig thought for a moment. "Two Wolves," he said.

"That's right. As many of us as can should spend some time with him. He would appreciate your help, too, but he knows how much this hunt means to you and you can see him when you get back."

"I think you're right," Fangslayer said. "And I think we should start out as soon as possible."

"Okay," Greentwig said. He looked wistfully at his father, then picked up his weapons and supplies. Fernhare and Fangslayer did the same, then the three left the den and went around the west end of Halfhill and turned north into the forest.

Stringsong saw them go. He was sitting at the top of the bluff overlooking the Holt below. He liked to be by himself on occasion, but still liked to keep an eye on what was going on. He'd seen Two Wolves go out and come back, had seen Brightmist become entranced with her work, had seen the various elves go into and come out of Greentwig's den. He wished the hunters luck, knowing it would be hard with only three of them.

He turned his attention back to the work at hand. What he'd seen on the lawn below made him guess that there was some trouble, but there were enough people running around so that he didn't feel compelled to come down and add to the confusion. Right now he was busy making bowstring from sloth hair. Occasionally he plucked the string to make sure it was uniformly spun and sufficiently strong, and when he did so it made a kind of music. It was the kind of thing his predecessor Songshaper, in Prey-Pacer's time, had done, though Songshaper had used a bow with several strings. Mostly Stringsong used just one string, on a bow he could flex, which gave him all the notes he needed. He felt a kinship with the long-dead Songshaper. Their names were similar for a good reason: they both made music.

Stringsong was extremely good at cord-making—that was his special talent. He could twist hair, bark, grass, leather, tendon, intestine, almost anything, into the best kind of cord that could be made from that kind of material, and he could make whatever kind of cord or string was best for the job. Other elves marveled at his patience, but he enjoyed it. Sometimes he preferred to sit with the others and talk, but sometimes, like today, he preferred to be by himself.

Today, besides a goodly supply of sloth hair, he had some fish guts for fishing line, some deer entrails that he had cured, some fine deerskin as well, and a large hank of razor grass, which he would turn into a surprisingly soft cord that could be dyed bright colors and woven into cloth.

But even as he worked he started to feel odd, rather

distant from himself. The feeling persisted as he finished the bowstring. He began to feel larger than himself, and shrunken at the same time. His arms felt swollen, clumsy, and detached, and he watched his fingers move, fastening the bowstring to the bow as if of their own accord. He plucked the cord, making the music for which he was named. It sounded strange to his ears, as if there were more to it somehow.

The weirdness increased, and he took a different bow and bound several strings to it, the way Songshaper had done, and began to play, hesitantly at first, but with more confidence as his fingers found the notes. On the lawn below him other elves stopped to listen. He changed the notes by tightening or bending the bow, as he did when it had just one string, but it didn't work the way he wanted it to. It changed all the strings at once, and most of them too much or not enough.

Puckernut, who was still sitting with Brightmist and Shadowflash, heard the music too, and it sent shivers up his spine. He knew it was Stringsong, but he moved back from the steep clay cliff to see for sure. The music stopped for a moment, but he could see that Stringsong was just doing something with more wood and cord. After a bit Stringsong held out a different kind of harp and he started to play again, and all those who could hear, Puckernut observed, were both thrilled and disturbed. To Puckernut, the magic of the music was obvious, so he left Brightmist in Shadowflash's care and went to the upstream end of the cliff, the way the hunting party had gone, which was steeper and nearer to him, to investigate.

He came up the steeper slope, which blocked Stringsong from his sight for a moment, but still he heard the music. It stopped. He hurried on, and when he came through the bushes at the edge to where he could see Stringsong again, the other had rebuilt his harp yet another time. Stringsong started playing again.

Puckernut came up to him. He had his own special

talent, which was that he could feel magic, and he could feel that the magic was in Stringsong, the same as it was in Brightmist.

He knelt down beside Stringsong and tried to speak with him but, as it had been with Brightmist, there was no response from the entranced elf. Puckernut touched him gently on the shoulder and upper arm. Still there was no response. He even tried to take away the harp, but Stringsong held on firmly, though almost as if he were not aware of what was happening, and continued to play.

Puckernut rocked back on his heels. How did these two have the same magic? It seemed to be getting stronger. Where would it end? He had no answers, so he went down to look for Freefoot.

Meanwhile Starbright and Dayshine were still grumping on the flat rock down by the stream when Feather, Freefoot's younger child, came to join them. He was the same age as they, and their frequent companion. "What's the matter?" he asked when he saw their faces.

With much complaining, interrupting, and laying of blame, they told him.

"Now hold on just a minute," he said. "What are you getting so excited about? The way you're talking, you'd think it was all Greentwig's fault. He hasn't lost his wolf. He's not feeling weird. He's still going on the hunt, so what are you angry at him for?"

"But don't you see?" Starbright said. "Fernhare and Fangslayer will have to spend so much time taking care of Greentwig they won't have time for me."

"But that's not the way it really works, is it?" Feather said. "Greentwig has survived so far without being taken care of."

Starbright turned away from him. She didn't know what to say. She was just angry, and disappointed, and feeling so sorry for herself that she wasn't really thinking straight. Dayshine was silent, too. He recognized the truth of what Feather had said and he was ashamed of

having such bad feelings about the older Greentwig, even
if he wasn't very bright or competent.

"I'll tell you what we should do," Feather said. "Let's
go find Silverknife and see what she has to say."
Silverknife had been born at about the same time as
Feather and Starbright and Dayshine, and up until last
summer had been known as Warble. Then one day
something had happened—she'd changed, and had gone
off on a hunt and come back with her adult name. The
four youths were of an age, but Silverknife was an
adult.

"I think that's a great idea," Dayshine said. "Come on,
Starbright, she might be able to help with your problem."

"I don't have a problem," Starbright said sullenly.

"Is that why you're so cheerful?" Feather asked gently.

"Oh, all right," Starbright said. "Let's go find her."

As the three youths started back toward the Holt,
Puckernut came down from where Stringsong was still
sitting, around the upstream end of the cliff, and saw
Freefoot and Treewing as they came out of Rainbow's
den. He went over to them and told them briefly about
Stringsong, but even as he spoke he felt the same sense of
external magic, coming from inside the den.

"What's the matter?" Freefoot asked.

"Is everything all right in there?" Puckernut asked in
turn.

"Rainbow is behaving oddly," Treewing said. "Sort of
like the way you say Stringsong and Brightmist are."
From where they stood, they could see Brightmist sitting,
working her stones, and could hear Stringsong's music.

"Let's go inside," Puckernut said, and entered Rainbow's den with Freefoot and Treewing behind him. He
found Glade and Two Wolves in the main chamber,
watching while Rainbow worked. They looked up when
he came in, but didn't speak. Puckernut knelt beside
Rainbow, watched her for a moment, spoke in her ear,
touched her forehead, her arm, her hand.

"It's the same," he said and looked up at Freefoot. "This is serious."

Freefoot nodded, then went over to sit beside Two Wolves and told him about the other two entranced elves outside.

Two Wolves was still distraught—indeed, would continue to grieve for many days—but he knew that his pain must now take second place until they could find out whether this infection of magic was a threat to the Holt and what they could do about it. "Where were these three all together," he asked, "so that they could all become contaminated in the same way?"

"I don't know," Puckernut said, "but it's fairly obvious, isn't it, that they all became touched at the same time. Otherwise the effect of the High Ones' magic would have been different in each case."

"Are they the same?" Freefoot asked. "I mean, each one is doing something different."

"Each one is under the influence of their talent, made stronger somehow, so yes, it is all the same." He bent down to Rainbow. He could feel the magic around her, growing stronger. He thought for a moment, then he whispered the question, loud enough for the others to hear, in her ear. "When were you and Stringsong and Brightmist together? Where were you that was different?"

Perhaps it was that he was not trying to distract her from her painting, but he seemed to get through her focused attention. She kept on painting, but her expression became faraway, as if she were thinking, and her brush strokes hesitated once or twice. Then she spoke, in a voice that seemed to come from a long way off. "Stringsong and Brightmist and I," she said, "and Greentwig, too, we all went on a hunt together."

"Where did you go?" Puckernut asked softly.

"Down by the dry lake, about five days ago . . ."

They had been hunting, with their wolves, for red deer, but had startled a magnificent black-neck buck instead, at the verge of the dry lake. Twice as big as a red deer, the buck was far from its usual range. They decided not to pass up an opportunity like this, and Greentwig especially, since he had hunted black-neck before. So they chased it along the dry rill toward the Great River until they came to a place where the ground was low and damp. The buck sought escape in the boggy ground and floundered through the dense bushes and bog plants to the center of the soggy area, where a sinkhole opened up.

They all went into the bog after it, though the wolves were strangely reluctant, and the ground gave way some more, pulling the bushes and even some trees down with it. Eventually the sinkhole enlarged to three times its original width before the ground stopped moving and became stable again.

They couldn't see the buck anymore—the churned-up brush and plants were a dense tangle—but when they listened they could hear it, still moving somewhere ahead of them. They followed the sticky sounds the rest of the way down into the sinkhole, now more than twice as deep as it had been, and at the bottom saw the buck struggling through the soft mud toward what looked like the entrance of a dry cave, which had been revealed by the sinking of the land around it.

The buck, hearing them coming, made a great effort to pull itself through the mud, and entered the cave. They could hear its hooves striking hard stone and they followed it into the darkness. But they went only a short way because it soon got too dark even for elvish eyes. The echoes of their footfalls and the buck's hooves were strange around them, the floor of the cave was uneven, and though they could not see for sure, they thought there were side passages in which they might get lost. And besides, they were afraid, so they came back, disappointed.

The wolves were waiting for them just outside the cave and would not go in, so they climbed out of the sinkhole and went on with their hunt. They later got the red deer they had originally sought.

"Then that's where it was," Puckernut said when Rainbow had finished. "There was a bit of magic in that cave, left over from the time of the High Ones, and these three became contaminated. And the black-neck buck, if it got out, would be affected, too."

"But what about Greentwig?" Freefoot asked.

"He, too," Puckernut said. "But how the magic would affect him, I couldn't guess. He doesn't have any natural talent as far as I know, and that is what the magic has been working on, and enhancing. Where is he now?"

"He's on the hunt Brightmist and I were supposed to go on," Two Wolves said. "What will happen to him?"

"Who knows?" Puckernut said.

"But how long will this last?" Two Wolves went on.

"I don't know," Puckernut said, "but I suspect that it's temporary, just by the way it feels and the way it took so long to come on."

"It seems like it happened rather quickly," Treewing said.

"You mean today. But it's been five days since they were exposed. That's a very long time indeed for even ancient magic to have an effect."

They sat in Rainbow's den while she painted, and listened to Stringsong's music coming in from the top of the cliff outside. "I don't think there's anything we can do," Puckernut said. "It doesn't feel evil. It's their talents that are being enhanced. Let's just hope that something good comes of all this."

Each of the three afflicted did, of course, produce something great that day. For Rainbow it was not a painting, but a beading, the bright pieces of shell and stone and wood stitched one by one onto the fur side of a yellow cat skin, three handspans wide and four high. The beads formed a picture not so much of an object as of an event, though it wasn't until much later that anybody, especially Rainbow, was able to interpret the radiating lines as antlers, the arched and doubly forked green shape as an elf, the background patterns as indicative of a particular kind of motion. It was the kind of picture that, once you knew what it was about, you saw more and more in it, though the shapes were quite abstract.

Stringsong perfected not only his harp, but also certain ways of playing it so that the elves could develop their own singing scale of five tones, which sounded like wolves but like music at the same time. He created a tradition that was incorporated in their howls down through the generations.

And Brightmist, working not with granite or with slate but with a translucent white stone that was sometimes found in great crystals, made a simple sphere through which the light shone, diffracted and rainbowed, changing according to how it faced the sun.

Each of them finished these marvels shortly after midday, and then their gifts began to fade. Eventually each of them became what he had been before, though Rainbow had a new appreciation of beads, Stringsong remembered how to play his harp, and Brightmist got considerably better with her flint-knapping.

Starbright, Dayshine, and Feather got back to Halfhill long before any of this came to pass, of course. They went to the den nearest the downstream end of the cliff, where they found Silverknife just getting ready for the day. She still lived with her father, Stringsong. After all, though she was an adult, she was still young. Her mother had died long ago and they were not immediately related to any of the other elves.

Though she was the same age as the other three youths, she was obviously more mature. She carried herself with a confidence and sureness they didn't have. Her clothes, though bright and fancy, were better suited for hunting in the brush. Her den, and especially her sleeping chamber, was neat and orderly. And there was something in her expression, in her face, that just, somehow, to them, *looked* like a grown-up. She greeted them as they came in.

They told her the problem, all three more or less talking at once, but at last Silverknife understood that it was Starbright's perception of the situation that was the real problem. Silverknife thought for a moment. Then she said, "I think you should rejoin the hunt."

"But what's the use?" Starbright said.

"Suppose it was just you and Fernhare and Fang-slayer," Silverknife said. "Do you think you could do it?"

"Not just the three of us."

"Don't you have confidence in their ability?"

"Yes, but that kind of hunt needs more than just three people."

"Apparently they think that three is enough. And besides, you have Greentwig."

"But he's just a big baby."

"Which never bothered you until now. It's not him that's the problem, it's you."

"But Two Wolves and Rainbow dropped out," Starbright insisted. "It's their fault."

"You dropped out, too, and for no good reason. You didn't lose your wolf, you're not beset by ancient magic, you just got upset. You're not proving the maturity you seek by your behavior, and you're letting the other three hunters down—voluntarily, unlike Brightmist and Two Wolves, who had no choice."

Starbright was upset by this accusation and wanted to argue about it, but she was somewhat in awe of Silverknife because Silverknife had "done it," and because she recognized the truth of the accusation. She said, "So you think I should just go running off after them like nothing happened."

"Like nothing had happened, yes, but not just you."

"All three of us?" Dayshine asked.

"All four of us," Silverknife said. "I will go with you. It will help make up for those who couldn't go."

"But we need permission," Starbright said.

"We can't go that far alone," Dayshine added.

"I give you permission," Silverknife said, "and you won't be alone because I will take you. After all, remember, I am an adult and I can take the responsibility. Now let people know where you're going." And the three youngsters ran off to do so.

Meanwhile, Deerstorm was resting in her den with her boy-child Ebony when she suddenly realized her time had come. The cub in her belly was beginning to drop and would be born not in three or four days' time, but that afternoon. Fangslayer was off on the hunt, so she sent Ebony for her mother.

Ebony went to Dreamsnake's den, but she was not there. He came back by Rainbow's den, where he saw Freefoot with Puckernut, Treewing, Glade, and Two Wolves, just coming out. "Please, come," he said to them. "The cubling is about to be born."

"You go on back to your mother," Freefoot said to him. "I'll get Starflower and send her right over." Ebony ran off. Freefoot turned to his companions. "Will you be all right?" he asked Two Wolves.

"I will. Glade and I will stay here with Rainbow."

"I'll go sit with Brightmist," Treewing said, which left Puckernut to look after Stringsong.

"All right, then," Freefoot said, and went back to his own den to fetch his lifemate. She quickly gathered up a few things and went with him toward Deerstorm's den.

They met Fire-Eyes on the way, asked her to help, which she agreed to at once, and the three of them got to Deerstorm just as she was starting to labor. Starflower and Fire-Eyes went to her at once while Freefoot waited in the main chamber just inside the entrance. After a bit Ebony snuck in to see how his mother was doing and Freefoot decided it was time to leave. He went outside, where he found Treewing talking with Suretrail about what had happened to his son's two wolves. Suretrail was upset, not only by the death of the wolves but by the fact that Treewing had killed one of them, though there was nothing else she could have done. Freefoot joined his two friends and was about to go with Suretrail back to Two Wolves when Ebony came running out of the den behind them.

"Freefoot!" Ebony called. "Come quickly."

Freefoot and Treewing, with Suretrail following behind, hurried back in to Deerstorm. It was not the rule for males to be present at a birthing, but Freefoot had attended several—his presence seemed to have a calming effect when things got tight—and again he assumed a confidence and sureness that was not questioned. Treewing knelt beside Deerstorm, but Suretrail just waited out in the main chamber.

A few moments ago the birthing had seemed to be easy, but now Deerstorm was having trouble and it was all Starflower and Fire-Eyes could do to help, and Fire-Eyes wasn't much help at that. Something about Deerstorm, or the child being born, was making her hysterical. After a moment Freefoot drew her aside so that Treewing could take her place.

Freefoot held Fire-Eyes by the shoulders, then folded her in his arms. "What's the matter?" he whispered.

"I don't know," she said. Her voice shook. She took several deep breaths and pushed herself away from him a bit. "I don't know that there's anything wrong," she said, "but there's something about that child . . ."

"Take it easy," Freefoot said. He looked into her face. "What about the child?" Over on the bed, Deerstorm was thrashing and grunting while Treewing and Starflower did their best to help. "Don't look around," Freefoot told Fire-Eyes. "Just tell me."

She took another deep breath and looked into Freefoot's eyes; he could see, in hers, the strange light that gave her her name. She could look at an elf and know things about him or her that she shouldn't have been able to know. Sometimes she could look back along the line of ancestors, and sometimes bring back stories. "I guess a path just opened up," she said. She took another breath, her eyes fell. "That's all it is. I usually can't feel back unless I've had a lot of dreamberries, but this time I can feel Fangslayer in the child, and Deerstorm, too, of course, and you and Starflower and Grazer and Dreamsnake . . . I think that's it. Starflower is helping, but I can feel her through the child's life, too. Or something."

"Is Mother going to be all right?" Ebony asked. He was trying to keep his face calm but the difficulties were making him anxious.

"I think so," Fire-Eyes said. "I'd better go back to her."

"You stay with me," Freefoot told Ebony while Fire-Eyes did as she said. Then he took Ebony back out to the main chamber.

"I think I'd better be going," Suretrail said. "Two Wolves has had a hard time. He'll need some help getting over it."

"I agree," Freefoot said.

"Is everything all right here?"

"She's having some trouble, but I think it will be okay." Suretrail nodded, and left.

After a while Starflower came out, looking tired but happy. "It's a boy," she said.

"Is he well?" Freefoot asked his lifemate.

"He is, and so's Deerstorm. The cubling just got a bit turned around."

"How's Fire-Eyes?"

Starflower laughed. "She's really excited. You'd think the baby was hers. He has eyes like hers, they have a special fire, and they were open when he was born. Deerstorm is going to call him Glitter. It seems like he can see everything."

"Will you need me for anything?" Freefoot asked.

"No," Starflower said and turned to Ebony. "But you

can go find Dreamsnake, wherever she is, and bring her back."

"Can I see Glitter first?"

"Of course you can," Starflower said. And while she took young Ebony inside, Freefoot went off to attend to other business.

Meanwhile, Greentwig, Fangslayer, and Fernhare were involved in their special hunt. They had gone north through the forest to the glade, a broad area where no trees had grown in anybody's memory. There were flowers in abundance, and grasses, and some low shrubs, but no briars or brambles, and nothing taller than an elf's shoulder. No one knew why. From there they had gone on north to the clearing at the edge of the prairie, where grasses rippled in the summer breeze. It was an ocean of green. Then they went west along the verge between forest and prairie until they came to where they could see the mesa, then across the prairie, single file through the tall grass, to where the ground began to rise at the foot of the mesa, and around the far side to the easy slope up between the two halves of this high, steep-sided, flat-topped double hill, and by noon they were on the larger, southern, forested flat. Certain creatures lived here and nowhere else, and it was to hunt one of these that they had come.

Just as the prey which they sought was not an ordinary sort of prey, so the methods of hunting it were not ordinary. When they found what Fangslayer thought was a good spot, among tall trees with high branches and near the southern edge of the mesa, the three elves went up, climbing as high as they could. Their clothing blended with the foliage so that they could hardly see each other, and they moved with utmost caution, even Greentwig making hardly any noise. And then Fernhare spotted one of the creatures they sought.

But as careful as they were, it was aware of them and

was keeping its distance. The sound of its movements was not that much different from the breeze in the leaves and it carefully kept to shadow, on the far side of branch and trunk. They pursued it and it continued to elude them for something like an eighty part of the afternoon, climbing ever higher to where the branches were so slender that even an elf had difficulty keeping from falling.

It was a ghost ape, a kind of large, white, flying monkey that could not walk on the ground and could only be hunted up in the treetops. They had maneuvered so that it was moving toward a tree that was cut off from the others on three sides, and since the ghost ape could not really fly but only glide, it would be trapped, and then they would move in. Had there been six of them, as planned, it might not have taken so long, and the certainty of capture would have been greater. A hunt like this was supposed to be a challenge, and it was, more challenging than Fernhare or Fangslayer really liked. Greentwig had more than once almost slipped and fallen. But they went on.

This high off the ground they needed to use ropes, since the branches tended to be too small to hold their weight, and they swung along the ropes from trunk to trunk. Once they cornered the beast, it would try to defend itself, and though it was smaller than an elf, it had terrible talons and fangs, and absolutely no temper at all.

Their concern at the moment was to keep the beast moving in the direction they wanted and not to let it cut around the side, or climb above or drop below, or run between them—or glide away. Three more hunters would have made a stronger line. But they took their time, and though Greentwig was having trouble, as usual, he was in the middle position, the other two keeping close, and it was going well, all things considered.

When they finally got the beast where they wanted it, and had identified its most likely escape route, they set Greentwig in place. Then Fangslayer and Fernhare moved out to the sides, closed in, and deliberately frightened the beast. It charged, and when it passed Greentwig he dropped the net which he had been carefully instructed to prepare and, to his immense surprise, caught it. The three of them came together, dragged the net to the ground, and under Fangslayer's instructions Greentwig drew his knife and dispatched it.

They extricated the ghost ape from the net. Fernhare and Fangslayer praised Greentwig for his part and he felt good. The beast had a good fur, long and soft and very white. It was extremely valuable, though the ghost ape was seldom hunted. It was too dangerous a hunt, and the animal was too rare.

They were about to begin the process of skinning, which had to be done very carefully since the skin could easily tear, when they were interrupted by the sounds of something coming through the forest. They looked up and saw a black-neck buck, which seemed to be moving purposefully toward them. When it saw them it paused, and looked from one to the other. It was huge, even for a black-neck, and its antlers were gigantic, and its eyes shone with an intelligence and a fury far beyond that which a normal deer could express. Its muscles were bunched, its hooves scored the forest floor. This was not a normal animal; it had been transformed somehow and it was terrible.

"I've seen that deer before," Greentwig said in surprise. "But it's not the same."

"What do you mean?" Fangslayer said as he and Fernhare slowly got to their feet.

"See how that antler has a twist in it?" Greentwig said. "Brightmist and Rainbow and Stringsong and I hunted a black-neck just like that five days ago." He told them briefly about the encounter and losing the deer in the cave at the bottom of the sinkhole.

He, too, was on his feet by now, and he stepped toward the black-neck buck, and as he did so realized, belatedly, just how big it was, far bigger than he had remembered it being. It lowered its head and lunged almost casually forward and knocked Greentwig to the ground. Greentwig lay there in surprise, not really hurt, and watched with growing terror as the buck backed up a step, the better to stomp him with his two huge, sharp front hooves.

Fernhare felt almost as dull as Greentwig, but at last she broke out of her trance and leapt to the rescue, brandishing one of the climbing ropes as if it were a whip. The buck lurched at her, swung its head to one side, and caught her in the side with the tip of one of its antlers and threw her to the ground. She struck her head as she fell.

Fangslayer seemed to be faring no better. It was not like him to be the last to react to danger, and yet today it was all he could do to make himself move. He leapt at the creature, waving the net, which startled the beast and kept it from attacking Fernhare with its antlers. By waving his arms and the net and yelling at the buck, he managed to hold the beast at bay, at least for a moment.

Greentwig got to his feet. He felt guilty and clumsy. He looked around for the wolves, but they were nowhere to be seen. He remembered how they had been afraid of the sinkhole, and the cave.

Movement brought his attention back to the present and without thinking about it he tried to attack the buck with his ax while Fangslayer had its attention. But it turned too quickly. Greentwig ran; it turned on Fernhare. Fangslayer leapt between and was himself wounded by the buck's antlers, but he managed to wound the buck in turn with his spear, hitting it high in the shoulder.

Greentwig came to Fangslayer's assistance as the buck staggered off a ways, and they went to Fernhare. Her ribs were scored and her head was bleeding. As they tried to get her comfortable the buck attacked them from behind and Fangslayer was impaled through the side on the forward points of the animal's antlers. Greentwig beat at the buck's flank with his ax, which was twisted around so that he hit it with the flat instead of the edge, but it made the buck turn on him, which gave Fangslayer the chance to strike at the buck with the shaft of his spear. Two flank attacks in succession were too much, and the buck turned and ran off into the brush.

Greentwig was about to pursue when Fangslayer fell over. Greentwig went to him. "Are you all right?"

"No, but I'll live." Fangslayer held his arms around his sides. Greentwig then went to his mother. Fernhare was just barely conscious. "You've done well," she said.

"I haven't, Mother," Greentwig said.

He did the best he could for them, cleaning their wounds and finding a place, between two large trees at the base of a rock, where they should be safe. When the two wounded adults were as comfortable as they could be, Fangslayer told Greentwig to go back to the Holt for help.

Greentwig started back as he had been instructed, though he was not really sure of the way. When he was out of sight of the others, he stopped and tried to remember which way they had come, and then he thought, *Downhill.* He let the slope of the ground guide him, and found the draw between the two halves of the mesa.

But as he started down the draw he heard a crashing behind him. It could have been anything, but he knew it was the buck, back by his mother and his friend, and he stopped. He had hoped that the buck would not come back. And though he had been told to go to the Holt, and was deathly afraid, he couldn't stand the thought of leaving his wounded friend and mother alone with the buck, and so went back to them instead.

Meanwhile, Silverknife had found that getting her three age-mates up to the mesa was perhaps a bit more than she had bargained for, and that though she was, in fact, an elder, she was not as experienced, as patient, as resourceful, or as strong a leader as one who had been an elder for even five years or so. Just getting Starbright,

Dayshine, and Feather organized had taken quite some time, getting them properly dressed, their weapons ready, the ropes and nets properly coiled and tied.

Then, once on the way, the three juveniles had a strong tendency to think about other things, such as lunch, bright birds, what had happened that morning at the Holt, and so on, and they did not make very good progress. By the time they got to Round Hill, which was just to the west of their route, they were all getting a bit impatient with each other—Silverknife with the juveniles for still being so much of what they were, and the juveniles with her for what they perceived as overbearing control, though had any elder of their parents' generation exhibited such control they would not have noticed, let alone minded.

And then, on the hill, when they were all tired and frustrated and angry, they happened on a family of gobblers, the huge birds with the long bronze tail feathers who yelled and bobbled through the trees as if they were demented, yet which were incredibly difficult to shoot, capture, or trap. Remarkably good eating—even the wolves were interested—and in spite of Silverknife's warnings that the hunt on the mesa was needing them, the three youths just had to catch one of the big male gobblers, and by the time they did it was way past midday. They ate the bird, saved the best of the tail and wing feathers, and at last went on their way again.

Silverknife did not talk much, but stalked ahead of them, and after a while the three youths began to quiet and remember the purpose of their outing.

"Do you suppose they've caught a ghost yet?" Starbright wondered.

"If they haven't," Silverknife said, "it's because they needed our help."

And though by now everybody was rather more tired than they should have been, and rather sluggish with the meal, they hurried on until at last they came to the edge of the forest. Ahead of them, to the north, across the prairie, was the mesa, the flat hill that rose above the grass, crowned with a miniature forest of its own.

None of them had ever been there before, and the only time they had been on the prairie had been with elders, hunting for antelope. Even Silverknife had to admit that she was just a bit apprehensive, being out of the woods and all. The wolves seemed eager, though, so they started across.

The grass at this time of year was just about chest-high and very green. It took a while to wade through it, and they had gone no more than an eight-of-eights of paces when they all began to receive what felt, at first, like a sending, except that it was not directed at any one of them; it was nonverbal, had no other symbolic content, and was just an expression of fear. They paused, feeling the sending.

"That's Greentwig," Feather said at last.

"How do you know?" Starbright started to say, but she recognized the clumsy simplicity of it, too. Greentwig had never been a very good sender.

"But where is he?" Dayshine asked.

"Pay attention," Feather said. "What is he sending?"

"Fear," Silverknife said. "What else?"

"Trees," Feather said, "he's among trees, and he's hurrying, and he's afraid."

"So what else is new?" Starbright said.

"Come off it," Silverknife told her. "I've never seen him afraid like this."

"What are we waiting for?" Feather asked.

At the same time, back at Halfhill, while he was attending to Brightmist as she was finishing the crystal, Shadowflash got the same odd kind of sending, remote and conceptless, just fear. He looked at Brightmist, but she seemed to be only minutely disturbed by it. He saw the children, on the lawn and down at the stream. They were paying no attention at all.

But Glade called down from the top of the cliff, where he was with Puckernut and Stringsong. "Do you feel that?"

"Yes," Shadowflash said. "What is it?"

Puckernut said, "It's Greentwig."

"So it is," Shadowflash said. "I thought he had gone to the mesa."

Freefoot came from upstream, where he had been with Two Wolves. "He did," he said. "I think the sending is coming from there."

"I didn't know he had such power," Glade said.

"It's not him that has the power," Puckernut said, "it's the magic."

Beside him, Stringsong stood up somewhat unsteadily, plucked a few more notes. "It was that cave," he said. He sounded as if he were recovering from a night of dreamberries.

"It was that," Puckernut said, "but how do you know?"

"I can feel it," Stringsong said, "in the back of my teeth."

"But what about Greentwig?" Glade asked.

They all looked at each other and they all seemed to be getting the same thing—fear, determination, woods, movement.

"What do we do?" Shadowflash asked.

Even as he spoke, Greentwig returned to the "secure" place just as the buck was about to attack Fangslayer, who couldn't even stand. The buck was dancing forward on its hind legs, its front hooves pointed at Fangslayer's chest. The blow would crush the elf, the hooves penetrating all the way through his body and into the soil. Without thinking, Greentwig yelled as loud as he could, so that the buck lost its balance and its front feet came down several handspans from Fangslayer's body. Fangslayer groaned and rolled away, and the black-neck buck, startled and frightened, ran off.

Greentwig ran up to Fangslayer. "I'm not going to leave

you," he said. Fangslayer just moaned. Greentwig went to his mother. Her eyes were open, and she watched him. "You can't take care of yourself," he told her.

"You should leave," she said, her voice a whisper. "The buck will come back."

"That's why I can't leave," he said. He was terrified, but he was determined. He made sure that their backs were secure, then he took Fangslayer's spear and Fernhare's arrows and sat down in front of them with his own ax and bow, to wait.

He was not aware of his sending, or that the four age-mates were receiving his heightened emotions as they hurried across the prairie toward the mesa. Though there was no visual imagery in the sending, they knew through Greentwig's feelings, rather than his thoughts, that Fernhare was wounded, that the other, who must be Fangslayer, was wounded, and that the menace, whatever it was, was out there somewhere, and still a threat. They felt Greentwig's determination, his fear, and what they realized was his courage. All of them were upset and hurried as fast as they could through the thick grass, and Starbright was especially ashamed, as a consequence of what she was perceiving, of her earlier thoughts and comments.

At the Holt, as Greentwig's projected feeling intensified, Shadowflash, Glade, Stringsong, Puckernut, Freefoot, Brightmist, and Two Wolves, who had gathered together in front of the cliff, came to realize that it was not a sending as they knew it, but a kind of projected empathy, Greentwig's feelings only, which were now of stronger determination: anxiety for his mother and Fangslayer, and apprehension and fear of whatever moved in the forest.

Stringsong had always had the ability to feel an elf-child's potential talents, and all through Greentwig's life he had recognized nothing in him, just a kind of sluggish dimness. But now that he could feel Greentwig's projected empathy, enhanced as it was by the magic from the cave, he recognized that he had in fact felt this thing in Greentwig all along; he had just never recognized it for what it was—the ability to have others empathize with him—which up until now was all that it took, the tiny bit necessary for everyone to do just enough to help Greentwig survive, when another elf might have died of ineptitude while still a child. He had a special talent after all, and though it could not be used to anyone else's benefit, it had served Greentwig well and was what now enabled all the adults to know what was going on in his heart, if not his mind.

And so they knew that when the buck came again, Greentwig was terrified. But he held his ground and stood between it and the two wounded elves in their poor shelter between the trees. He expended all his arrows, and those he'd taken from Fernhare. His shots were enough to keep the buck from closing too quickly, but few of them hit, and those that did caused only superficial wounds. Greentwig, as usual, was just not very good.

When the arrows were gone he dropped the bow and took Fangslayer's spear. The buck reared; its hooves crashed down on branches and rocks, its antlers glittered.

"Set the butt," Fangslayer shouted.

Greentwig almost turned to ask for clarification, but then he remembered and set the butt end of the spear against the ground and crouched down to aim the head at the buck, which now attacked. But his aim was poor and the buck, striking the spear off center, impaled itself through the shoulder. The butt skidded along the ground, knocking Greentwig down. The buck reared back, dragged the spear out of Greentwig's hands, and crashed off into the brush.

By this time, all the other adults at Halfhill—Deerstorm, Treewing, Fire-Eyes, Suretrail, Starflower, and Rainbow—had joined Freefoot and the others at the base of the cliff on the lawn. The children, the cublings, watched them curiously, anxiously, but kept their distance.

Everybody who was able to receive the bizarre sending was in full accord with Greentwig's perceptions and could almost see and hear through him as well as feel, as he climbed to his feet panting, his hands raw, his body sore. He went to Fernhare and Fangslayer, ashamed of his failure. Fernhare could not talk anymore.

"You did as good as you could," Fangslayer said. He seemed to be more comfortable now.

"But it was not good enough," Greentwig said.

"It's not over yet," Fangslayer told him, and handed him his ax.

"I know," Greentwig said, and back at the Holt they all witnessed his utter terror and absolute courage as he turned away from Fangslayer and Fernhare, listened to the crashing in the bushes, and stepped forward to meet what was coming.

The buck came back, and, with an ax in each hand, Greentwig met its charge and delivered the killing blows on either side of its skull, right through the eyes, even as its forward horns, the ones that had speared Fangslayer, opened his belly, spilling his guts on the ground. The deer fell. Greentwig staggered back, and went to his knees.

He knelt there, knowing that it was his death he saw before him, gray and red on the ground. He felt nothing yet, an odd kind of pressure, perhaps, an ironic emptiness. Fangslayer crawled up to him, saw that the buck was dead, then saw that, though he still breathed, Greentwig was, too.

"You are a hero," Fangslayer said. "You struck with your axes as if they were your own hands. Stonefist, that's who you are."

"How is my mother?" the elf who was now Stonefist asked.

"She's all right," Fangslayer said, "she'll be just fine."

Then Stonefist, who had been Greentwig, closed his eyes and slowly leaned forward into the mess of himself and died, and everywhere, people felt him fade.

Finder

by Nancy Springer

Bathed in the light of two moons, caressed by summer breezes and pillowed by his own plumpness, Finder lay at ease amid an Everwood meadow of blue pawflowers. Most of the other young elves were hard in pursuit of some hapless animal, on the hunt. But Finder was not nearly as good at hunting as he was at eating. Nor was he adept in leathercraft, or arrow fletching, or fishing or healing or treeshaping or any skill of much real use to his tribe. His only contribution to the Wolfriders was of a peculiar, not very important sort.

"Finder." The chieftain of the Wolfriders stood over him.

With wide eyes the same soft blue as the pawflowers, Finder looked up at his leader owlishly and smiled. Tanner was nothing to be afraid of. As an orphaned cub, raised by the tribe, Finder had depended more on Tanner's kindness than anyone's.

Tanner asked, "Finder, would you happen to know where I hid that pit of ravvit skins a few seasons ago, when we last passed through these glades? I'd forgotten all about it until now."

"Um." Rolling up to a sitting position, Finder blinked and thought. It was not necessary to ask Tanner any more questions—where were the ravvit skins last seen, etc.—but merely to consider his request. It was not necessary for Finder to point out that the few seasons had been more like seven years, or to draw a map, or to exert himself in any way, because the finding process was not difficult. Before Tanner came, Finder had been dreamily, effortlessly locating the few rare four-fingered pawflowers amid the masses of their five-fingered kin. Even as a tiny cub he had been able to walk up to a field of pawflowers and pick a lucky "elf-hand" within a moment, when other cubs might take all night hunting for one. This minor magic was so simple for him that he no longer bothered to gather the lucky flowers, but merely lay and mentally located them.

He got to his feet, having done the same for Tanner's missing and forgotten tanning pit. "I'll show you," he offered. This was easier than trying to describe to Tanner the place where he needed to dig.

"Good. Thank you." The two of them ambled into the Everwood, a young, dreamy elf and an older, absent-minded one, both on foot; Finder rode his wolf-friend even less often than Tanner did his.

Finder had been finding missing items for Wolfriders long enough that most of the elves had forgotten he had another name, the one his sire and mother had given him. He had nearly forgotten about it himself. And he did not remember his parents at all, though he had been several winters old when they had disappeared. But of course he knew who they were, for the tribe remembered them and had told him. Brightlance, his father, had been a fierce and energetic Wolfrider, tireless on the hunt, fearless in defense of the tribe against humans—not at all like his languid son, as had been pointed out to Finder on occasion. And Moonway, his mother, had been a fine shot with the bow and arrow and a healer as well. The tribe had been without a healer since the day the two of them had left their cub in old Fallfern's care and ridden off to hunt together, never to return.

"There." Finder pointed out to Tanner a place under a jigglebranch tree that looked much like all the other jigglebranch trees around it. "Your arm's length under-

ground." He contemplated a moment, seeing not what
was before his eyes but what lay out of sight. "And I might
add, they will be quite fine, even after all this time."

"Yes, this is the place." When Finder blinked and came
back, Tanner was looking around with rising excitement.
"Yes, I remember now! What I don't understand is how I
could forget." Tanner shook his head, not understanding
what every other Wolfrider did, that as Tanner got older
he drifted more and more in wolf time. It was unavoida-
ble and not a problem, really. These were peaceful times.
The Everwood was vast; humans kept to its fringes and
seldom threatened. In recent years there had been a few
strange incidents of kills inexplicably stolen, and there
had been a missing wolf or two, but nothing really
disturbing. So Tanner could putter with his leathers and
be Tanner, especially as Finder was able to locate his
forgotten pits for him.

Tribemates? the hunt leader, Joygleam, sent from
not far away.

Here, Finder replied.

With a patter of huge, padded wolf paws the hunt rode
into the grove of jigglebranch trees. Over Joygleam's
wolf-friend's shoulders lay the body of a fine treehorn,
and all the young hunters looked bright and fierce of eye,
with the flush of success riding high in their elated faces.
By Joygleam's side rode her lifemate, Scarp, and nestled
against Scarp's chest and protected by his arms was the
pug-nosed cub Redstar. Though far too young to hunt,
already the little one was an eager rider on the chase. And
to hear Scarp and Joygleam tell it, little Redstar yelped as
eagerly as anyone at the kill.

"Good dark, my chief. Good hunting to you, Finder,"
Joygleam hailed the two of them. Finder felt the cheerful
sarcasm in her greeting, too good-humored to really sting,
but still . . . Joygleam wore the leather-and-feather hair
ornament he had found for her a few days before, after
she had lost it deep in the Everwood. But apparently that

did not count as hunting to her. No danger. Therefore, no glory.

"You have had good hunting," Finder replied courteously. "There will be a feast."

It was an unwise thing to say. All the hunters laughed, and even Tanner smiled. Everyone knew how much Finder loved to eat meat that others had brought in.

"Yes, Finder," Scarp said with just the right wicked emphasis, "there will be a feast." The cub in his arms, little Redstar, was too young to understand the joke but laughed because the others did, his golden eyes wide and shining.

Tanner put in, "Does anyone have a broadknife? Something I can dig with?" He was trying to turn the talk for Finder's sake, probably. Tanner was kind.

Several were offered. When Tanner had selected his, Finder took one also. "I will help you dig," he told his chieftain.

"Don't cut yourself, Finder," Joygleam quipped. "Knives are dangerous. And don't miss the feast." The hunt party rode off in high spirits.

For a while Finder dug with grim, unaccustomed energy and was silent. Being around Joygleam and Scarp always bothered him, but for what good reason? Because they were fortunate? Because they were lovemates *and* lifemates *and* soulmates, everything an elf couple could possibly be, their cub the product of Recognition, whereas he, Finder, was an orphan with no family and no lover? Perhaps. Perhaps this was the cause of his prickly feelings, but it was not a reason good enough. Finder felt ashamed of his own bitterness because he knew to his bones that any Wolfrider's good fortune was his, Finder's, good fortune also. He was a Wolfrider, and any elf's happiness was the happiness of the tribe; that was the Way. Wolfriders shared, which was why he, Finder, had never suffered. Others brought in meat for him to eat.

Why did he not feel right about eating it?

Finder grew tired of thinking and, simultaneously, of digging. He sat back on his heels to watch a while. Tanner dug on. Concerning leathers, Tanner could be quite single-minded.

A foul odor went up as Tanner opened the pit. "Ah," Tanner breathed, whiffing deeply, as if the stench were essence of honey to him. He reached in and drew out one of the leathers, holding it up and spreading it in the moonlight. It was perfect: soft, supple, and as blue as Finder's favorite patch of pawflowers.

"Very fine, just as you said," Tanner remarked to Finder.

Finder nodded, smiling.

"But small," said Tanner regretfully. "Why must ravvits be so small?"

"So? Fallfern will make them into small, beautiful things. And then Joygleam will lose them." Finder tried to speak lightly, but his discomfort seeped through. "And then I will find them. But apparently there is no worthiness in finding such small things."

Tanner gazed at Finder almost as if he understood. But before he could speak they both heard the sound of a Wolfrider speeding toward them at a hard, reckless run.

Scarp? Tanner hailed.

"My chief." Scarp brought his wolf-friend to a panting halt by Tanner and he was panting himself, though with emotion, not exertion. "My chief, please. The cub. He is not here?"

There was no need to answer. Plainly no cub was with Tanner.

"He is lost, then." Scarp looked straight at Finder, begging. "Redstar is lost."

There would have been worthiness in finding such a small thing as a cub. And it should have been the easiest thing in the world, no different from finding a bodkin dropped on the ground. Finder knew exactly what the cub looked like—his pale chestnut hair, those golden eyes—even down to the fawn-colored tunic and yellow fringed belt Redstar was wearing. It should have been a matter of blinking a few times and thinking a moment.

It wasn't.

Sureness should have simply come to Finder, a sense of where the cub was, as if he had known all along. But he knew nothing. And meanwhile Scarp was explaining frantically to Tanner, "I thought he was with Joygleam, and she thought he was with me, and then—none of the others knew where he was either—so we sent and sent, but he didn't answer—and we thought maybe he came back here to see what you were doing—"

Tanner was summoning his wolf-friend. **Ayooah! Stagrunner!**

Off in the distance toward camp Joygleam was sending for her lost cub. **Redstar! Beloved, please answer me!**

Scarp exclaimed at Finder, "You don't see him? You can't find him?"

And Tanner was staring, too, and others had arrived to gawk and mutter at the elf who could find lucky flowers and hair ornaments and lost skinning knives but apparently not lost cubs. Finder whispered lamely, "Maybe if I go off by myself, away from all this noise . . ."

"Please," Scarp begged. "Whatever you need to do. Please, Finder, find him."

Back in his pawflower patch, Finder sat with his head down, his face hidden in his pudgy arms atop his equally pudgy upcocked knees. Child Moon and Mother Moon hung far apart in the sky. Sometimes in the distance Finder heard the sounds of the others searching on wolfback. Their calling was hard to listen to, but even worse were the voiceless cries of their sending for the lost one. Finder could not think. For some reason, trying to think of the little cub lost was just too hard.

The sounds of the search reminded him of—*something*.

Finder sat in his meadow through dawn, when the heartbreaking sounds faded away, and through the glaring light of day, not caring that he should have been hidden where humans could not see him. The next night, when Tanner came to him, Finder still had not moved.

"I've brought you some meat," Tanner said, sitting beside him.

Finder shook his head. He was not hungry. "Redstar?" he asked, though he knew the answer. If Redstar had been found, he would have heard the glad shoutings, he would have known even if no one came to tell him.

Tanner said in a low voice, "No, nothing. He's just— gone. It's uncanny."

"Did they—did they say that when my mother and father disappeared?"

Tanner stared at him. "Yes," he answered slowly, "yes, they did. Though it was not exactly the same. A lost cub—"

"Yes, I know. I've tried and tried—" Finder swallowed and made himself stop because he heard the self-pity in his own voice. It was the cub who was to be pitied, not him, the finder who had failed. More levelly he said, "It is not that Redstar is not there. I should be able to see him, but there is something in the way."

"What sort of a thing?

Finder sat staring at the field of blue blossoms and slowly answered. "Something about—my parents. I keep thinking about them instead of Redstar. It's—whenever I close my eyes—I'm sitting in the dark, and there's a search going on—"

"Do it," Tanner urged gently.

He tried. He blinked, and for that eyeblink he was a cub again, helpless, abandoned, hurting—where were his mother, his father? And he cried out, "I have to find them!" Elves didn't just vanish, but no sign had been found of Brightlance and Moonway. "They're gone, I need them, why can't I find them? Curse me, I can find four-fingered pawflowers and stray arrows and dreamberries hidden in a thicket, but—I—can't—" Finder choked to a stop and shook his head hard, sending it all away. It was just too painful. He would remember his parents next, and that would be worse yet.

Tanner was watching him thoughtfully. "You stiffened," he remarked. "For just a moment before you broke away, you were in a healer's trance."

"I'm not a healer! I'm not—anything."

"I think you will find that you are more than you know, Finder." Tanner got up and left him there.

Finder sat where he was two more days. Each night Tanner brought him meat, and each night he refused to eat it. He was fasting in hopes of a vision that would tell him where to find Redstar, but he did not say that. "I have let Joygleam do the hunting for me too long," he said.

"Joygleam does not begrudge you."

"I begrudge myself."

"The Wolfriders have lost one tribemate," Tanner scolded. "You think it will help if we lose another?"

It seemed a very long time to Finder since he had lolled smugly at his ease on this same patch of flowers. So thoroughly in despair was he now that the chieftain's tone, quite harsh for Tanner, did not affect him. He heard only the words, and swiveled to look at Tanner. "Lost for good?" he asked. "You have given the little one up for dead?"

Tanner sighed, and his voice when he spoke again was much softer. "We will camp in this place for as long as we can." Probably they were the same words he had told the others earlier. "But game is getting scarce. For the sake of the tribe I can spare few Wolfriders from hunting any longer. Joygleam and Scarp must go on searching, of course, but the others . . . we need food. And with the long-tooth cats prowling . . . how can a cub on his own survive in the Everwood?"

A cub on his own.

A cub . . .

No, Finder thought, *no, I was never a little cub lost.*

He looked around. Tanner was gone.

My parents were lost. There is a difference. I always had the others.

But he was beginning to feel a sense that he could not go back to the others, to the tribe, until he found something that was badly missing in him.

A day and a night later, under the pale light of Child Moon but before Mother Moon had risen—and before Tanner could come again with meat in his hand—Finder stood up and walked away.

Wobbly with hunger, he walked slowly and with no particular sense of where he was going except that he had to—find something he had lost a long time ago.

In a few days he would be too weak to walk. Better call his wolf-friend.

Ayoooah—

No. Puckernuts, no. Little Redstar lost in the woods had no wolf-friend to call on, so neither would he.

Finder?

He was already staggering, and the sudden, gentle sending staggered him more. It was Joygleam.

Yes, it's me. Joygleam, I am sorry. Sorry about Redstar, he meant, and sorry he had ever resented her happiness, and in his half-starved condition fuzzily sorry because he assumed his abortive sending had disturbed her. **I woke you up?**

No. No, we mothers seldom sleep. Her tone of mind was wry and tender, though there were tears in it. **Where are you going, Finder?**

I don't really know.

Come back as soon as you can. I will have meat waiting for you.

It was much the same, half-joking way she had always spoken to him, but suddenly Finder understood: she did not scorn him—in fact she might have been rather fond of him. She was mothering him, that was all.

Slice me and dice me and stew me on a fire, am I a cub still?

Finder had stood his vigil, experienced his vision and found his soulname, all long since. But perhaps these things were not enough to make him truly an adult.

Very well, then, he vowed suddenly and fiercely, *I will be a cub, and cry for my mother, and see where that gets me.*

He wobbled on into the Everwood, past the glades he knew, past the place where the treehorn had been killed —his sensitive nostrils caught the whiff of its heart's blood still on the air. Past the jigglebranch-tree grove and on, beyond the woods the Wolfriders had been roaming he walked, far beyond. Finder tottered his way through dawn and the next day and on into the night after, until he had lost any sense of where he was and knew himself to be utterly alone in the vastness of the forest. Then, finally, instead of holding the pain at arm's length any longer, he sank down where he was and simply let it happen.

His mother, Moonway—he remembered her now. Remembered her dreaming eyes, pawflower blue, like his. Remembered the soft burr in her low-pitched voice. Remembered her moods—her sudden angers quick to pass and her sharp-toothed, teasing smiles. The day she—died, he might as well say it, she had died for him that night, though when and how it had actually happened he might never know—the day she died, before she left to go hunting, she had woven a dream catcher with him, a sort of spiderweb of sinew in a willow loop, for him to hang above his head as he slept so that it would catch all his dreams and he could keep and tell them to her when she got back. She had kissed him, then lifted her bow to him from the back of her great, gray, deep-chested Stormranger as she rode away. "Catch me a whole nogginful of dreams, Bluestar," she had called to him. That was the name she had given him, Bluestar. Finder did not know where the dream catcher was now. Someday, if he lived, he would try to find it, or what was left of it. But at least he had the memory. And it was a good memory, almost worth starving for.

And his father, Brightlance—he remembered him as well. Remembered his fierce eyes almost as black and shining as a clear winter nighttime sky. Yet he remembered how those eyes gentled when Brightlance looked at Moonway. Those two—Finder remembered how all forms of Wolfrider love had met in them. They were lovemates, lifemates, soulmates—and thinking of it, he felt the ache of knowing the truth: it could all end in an eyeblink. No wonder he sometimes felt uneasy when Joygleam and Scarp smiled at one another. It was a reminder, if he would let himself know it.

What a disappointment of a Wolfrider he had become, hiding behind his own fear. He, Finder, the product of Brightlance and Moonway's Recognition.

It was hard to believe he was their cub—he, Finder, the useless one, weeping with his face pressed into the forest loam. Hard to believe he was his father's son. Brightlance —that one was all elf, all Wolfrider. He had faced humans in desperate combat. He had held off long-tooth cats with the lance. He had once snatched a poisonous snake away from harming Bluestar with his bare hand. Brightlance had been brave.

Brave . . .

It was time to try. Groaning, Finder sat up, wiped his face with his hands, and struggled up from the ground, because far away in his mind's ear he heard the crying of a cub.

Himself, yes. It was the lost cub Bluestar that he heard. But also perhaps . . .

Redstar?

There was no reply. Yet there had been something . . . Finder stood where he was and blinked, deeply in thought.

A lost hat, a hair clip, a flint knife, they were simple things to find. Sturdy, inert, with no passions and little mutability, they lay where they had been dropped and waited to either be picked up or rot. But a cub—a cub squirmed and laughed, or screamed and ran away. A cub was another matter altogether.

It had not been sufficient to know how Redstar looked. But now that Finder remembered what it meant to be a motherlorn cub . . . there was a chance.

He stood and shut his eyes and searched, letting his mind reach out for tears, for wide terrified eyes, for heartache, for grief. This was what had frightened him away before: the grief, the pain. This reaching out for it was what he had not been able to do. Now, he could manage. It was not easy, but he could do it.

Redstar, where are you?

There was still no answer. But slowly, slowly, in hurtful flashes, knowledge began to come to Finder, flickering visions of the young elf's naked body—still alive, still breathing, but very weak—and of the dark den underground where he was kept, and of the human who imprisoned him there.

The human was so sick of mind that he had been driven out even by his own kind. Solitary, a lone predator, he had learned to hide the secret of his existence. The dank hole where he lived—and sometimes toyed with captives—could barely be seen at all from outside once he had pulled a branch or two across the concealed entrance. He wore hardly any clothing, and had learned to rub his skin with wolf musk to disguise his human scent. It amused him to crouch in a thicket and watch the human hunters, his former comrades, tramp by with not a notion of his presence—sometimes he killed one just for fun. But it amused him even more highly to fool the pointy-ears. Elves, demons of the forest, bah. What were elves to him when he could sneak up on their camp and snatch one of their brats along with a helping of their venison? They were pretty to look at and pleasant to break into little pieces. That was all he could say for elves.

Seeing his long, matted, filthy hair and beard in that first dim vision, Finder thought the human was some sort of vile yellow-toothed beast hidden in the bowels of the Everwood. A few moments later he understood that he had dishonored the most brutish animal of the world of two moons by thinking so, and he stood shaking with the horror of what he had seen.

Tanner! Finder sent for all he was worth.

Nothing.

Wolfriders! Redstar needs you, come, quickly!

Nothing. He was much too far from the tribe for them to hear his sending.

Therefore it was time to be an adult again. Finder made himself stop his shaking and got himself moving at the best pace he could manage toward where he knew the missing cub to be. Even at a jog trot it would take him most of the night to get there, and meanwhile he had to give all his attention and his skill to locating himself something to eat. He had been a fool to let himself get so weak. Now time pressed, yet he would need strength in order to help Redstar. The solitary human's muscles were ropy but strong.

Finder coaxed his shocked mind to scan the forest all around him, being aware of everything in it. He found a patch of sweetberries only a little bit aside from his way, and he stopped and snatched a double handful of them to eat on the run. It was not enough. But there, farther aside—on a moonlit hilltop a pack of wild wolves were eating at their kill.

"Ayooooah, brothers!" Finder tossed back his head and howled out his rage and grief to the Mother Moon.

Never before had his howling been so heartfelt. The stranger wolves ceased snarling into their meat and lifted their heads from their feeding to stare yellow-eyed at him.

"My brothers. My sisters." Finder strode up to them. "I am in great need. Howl for me, brothers! Tell the others to tell my tribe. Call the Wolfriders to me!"

First one of them pointed her muzzle skyward, then another. The howl went up, and in a distant valley another pack answered it and picked it up and carried it onward. *Sorrow,* the howl cried. *Sorrow and great need.* Now if only Tanner could understand.

Tanner, with his quiet smile and his fine leathers neatly laced and tied, seemed very far away. There was a madman on the prowl in the Everwood, and Finder might just as well have been a mad elf. He plunged in, taking his place at the wolf kill with teeth and claws. He hunkered down and tore himself a piece of bristleboar flesh to eat; when the pack elders snarled at him to dispute his right he snarled back until they let him alone.

A short time later, feeling stronger, headed toward Redstar again at a run, Finder wiped the grease from his face and gave his attention back to the cub.

It was dawn now. Dim daylight filtered into the human's den through airholes between the roots that made up its ceiling. In his mind's eye, Finder saw the little one lying unconscious or nearly so on his prison's bedrock floor, and his small, pale body was mottled with bruises. At one point his hands and feet had been tied—Finder could see the bloody marks left by the thongs. But now he was too weak from hunger and abuse to flee.

The human was sleeping at the moment, lying between the cub and the entry with his back turned. Sleeping. When was the last time Finder had slept? He couldn't remember.

Redstar? Finder tried again.

The cub lifted his head, and his bruised eyes widened.

Redstar, hang on. I'm coming.

Who—who is it? The cub's sending faltered, as weak as he. **I want—I want my mother!**

Shhhh. She's coming, too. Finder hoped this was true. **Just lie there and be quiet and be ready.**

But—who are you?

Bluestar. Why had Finder said that? It meant nothing to the little one. **Finder.** That meant not much more.

Redstar sent, **I—I just want to die.**

No! I am coming. Hold on to life. Blyw is coming. Finder gifted the cub with his soulname to sustain him. Perhaps it meant more than the other names.

Seemingly it did. Though Redstar laid down his head and was silent, Finder sensed the pulse of life beating more strongly than before in the cub.

Now there was the matter of dealing with the human. At his belt Finder wore his short knife, a little thing never meant to be a weapon. Until lately Finder had not expected to ever combat anything larger than a bumble-bee, and he used the knife most commonly to cut meat or the stems of flowers he was gathering.

Puckernuts. I will just have to make do.

Make it do *what?*

That indeed was the problem. Just going down into that den after the man would be no use; Finder knew his abilities. Any such attempt on his part would simply get both him and Redstar killed. There had to be some other way.

Near enough now that the human might hear his thudding feet, Finder slowed his pace to a soft-footed walk and began to blink and think.

His leather tunic flapped around his middle as he walked. Apparently he had lost some pudge.

Finder took the thing off and contemplated it. Also he contemplated the entry of the human's den—near enough now for him to see in fact, not only in his mind's eye. The den was placed under the lip of a high stream bank. Atop the bank grew many trees, and one of them looked as if it might serve a purpose.

Finder smiled and started to cut his tunic into a long leather rope.

Setting a large snare was really a two-elf job, but Finder

managed. Climbing the tree and fastening his rope to a springy branch was no problem. The hard part was pulling the branch down while securing the snare's business end, and being very quiet in his movements the whole time. And keeping a mental eye on the human below.

The human who, curse it, was up and moving around now, and starting to pay unwelcome attention to Redstar again.

At first it was not too bad. The man said, "Meat, little demon?" and dangled a strip of raw ravvit in front of the cub's nose. When Redstar reached for it, the human pulled it back and laughed nastily.

"Let me cook it first, my pointy-eared guest. Poor thing, can't you move?" That laugh again. "Look, I will bring the fire to you so you can watch."

The man picked up live embers from his hearth with his bare hands. Up above, trying to set his snare and watch at the same time, Finder started to shake because of what he saw: sometime this human's hands had been seared in fire. Whoever had done it to him might as well have seared his soul instead, because now this one no longer hurt and no longer cared what he did to any living thing. He was more dangerous than a marauding bear.

With those scarred hands the man put the coals into an earthen pot and carried it to Redstar's side. He tossed in the strip of meat, and it started to sizzle. Redstar's eyes went wide.

"What, you do not like cooked meat?" the human mocked. "You do not like fire?"

Now it was getting bad. There was clear, ugly threat in the man's tone. Finder jerked his attention back to what he was doing and tried to hurry. The noose was almost set. **Redstar, courage,** he sent.

Redstar might have had that on his own. "Cook me and eat me and be done with it!" the cub flared with fine defiance at the captor, who outweighed him probably ten times. "Toss my bones on your midden heap. I don't care."

"You don't? Very well, little one, we shall start." The human fished a scorching orange coal out of his pot and pressed it to Redstar's back, holding it there. The cub screamed and screamed again, but had no strength left to fight off that heavy hand.

"You lied, pointy-ears," the human crooned. "You *do* care."

Finder had choked back his own scream. He would do Redstar no good if the human became aware of him before he was ready. But what he was seeing in his mind's eye was so horrible, it staggered him like a blow. He blundered heavily to one knee atop the human's lair and the man heard him.

"What was that?" he hissed, and he left Redstar, snatched up a long, black-bladed knife, and started up his climbing pole.

"Fry me for a fool," Finder moaned. Because he had not seen the human wearing one—no belt, no weapon— he had not included the likelihood of a knife in his plans.

Blyw, kill him! Slice his head off!

The cub's anguished sending jolted Finder into action. He scurried into position to spring his mostly completed snare. Flattening himself atop the stream bank—and he really could flatten himself now—he waited.

The human came out knife first, lifting himself head and hairy shoulders out of his hidey-hole to have a look around. His glaring eyes turned to the intruder. There was a horrible instant while their stares met within a handspan of one another, while the human raised his long weapon. But in that instant Finder also moved, slashing the short length of leather that held down the tree branch overhead.

It swished up. The human yelped out a hoarse, startled shout as the noose jerked him into the air. Finder tried to maim or disarm the man's knife hand on its way past his face, but he missed. There was no time to berate himself. He scrambled to his feet, figuring he had about a heart-beat or two of safety now.

And then maybe an eyeblink of a chance when the human hit the ground.

He was right on both counts. The human, roaring with rage, swung from the rope for no more than two heart-beats' span before he managed to cut himself loose. And he fell heavily into the shallow stream. And, as good fortune would have it, his head came down against a rock.

Finder was there. He knew he had to be quick—that first missed blow had taught him as much. He was already running forward before the human hit the ground. In that half a moment while the human lay stunned, Finder reached him and stamped on his knife hand, hard. The man gasped and dropped the weapon, and Finder snatched it up.

Then the enemy was on his feet again, roaring mad and twice Finder's height.

Mother! The cub's sending cried out from the human's foul cave. **I—can't—climb out. Mother, Father, come, help me!"**

Anyone come, Finder amended, adding his plea to the cub's, and he lifted his captured weapon and sprang.

Afterward he had no clear conception of how the fight progressed, who struck first, who drew first blood—it was all just a mess of blood, human and his. He sliced away at whatever part of the monster he could reach, but meanwhile the man was pommeling him and picking him up and throwing him down again and trying to wrestle the knife away from him and trying to take his arms off at the shoulders.

And then there came a time when he could not get up one more time.

Finder? Finder, hold on, we're coming!

Tanner?

Finder found new strength somewhere. For the sake of

one final effort he struggled to his feet. Odd that the man had not simply smashed him dead. The human was just standing there, panting and hugging himself. Apparently at least some of his wounds were causing him some difficulty.

"Cub stealer," Finder said thickly, and as a huge, hard, scarred hand cuffed him away, he stabbed straight for the man's navel. For once the blow hit just the way he'd wanted. The human shrieked and fell to his knees.

"Ayooooah! Finish him, Finder!" Scarp yelled, charging across the stream on his wolf-friend.

There they were, Tanner, Scarp, Joygleam, Brook, half a dozen others. Wolfriders, charging to fight by Finder's side, his own wolf-friend, Bloodjaw, running along with them.

Finder could not do what Scarp had said. Something was making him dizzy and weak. He sat down on the ground.

"Finder!" Dismounting, Tanner took Finder by the shoulders and looked him over anxiously. Others were dispatching what remained of the human for him, then raising a howl of triumph over the carcass.

"The cub," Finder urged Tanner. Curse his voice, why would it not raise above a whisper? "Get Redstar."

But already Joygleam was emerging from the human's den with the cub in her arms, and when the others saw the look on her face all howls of victory ceased.

"Lifemate?" Scarp asked, his voice wavering into a whimper.

She could not answer him. Her eyes were huge with shock and fear and tears.

Finder searched himself hard and found strength to stand up. With a hand on Tanner's shoulder for support he tottered over to Joygleam and looked at the cub lying in her arms. The little one, unconscious. Beaten. Maimed. Barely breathing. Worse injured than Finder had seen him in his finder's eye.

Hesitantly Finder put out one bloodied hand and touched the cub's cut and swollen face. Something in that hurt and silent body seemed to answer him.

There was an odd instinct or urging moving in Finder, a sense that he needed to find another way to reach out to pain, this time to take it away. And what could happen to him if he tried, really? Already he had failed, again and again he had failed to be the elf he thought he was, and he had exiled himself from the tribe until something changed, and he had cried like an infant. He was past pride, he no longer cared what the others saw in him. His face was dirty, he had already made a fool of himself in every conceivable way, he had looked into the eyes of horror, he had nearly been killed—there was simply nothing to be afraid of any longer.

He whispered to Joygleam, "Give him here."

Her arms tightened on Redstar; she did not want to let go of her dying son. But Tanner touched her on the shoulder and looked at her, and she looked back and nodded. She relinquished the cub. Finder took Redstar and cradled him in his arms, and felt the small heart beating close to his own, and knew he had to make it pump harder. He sank down and laid the cub on the ground.

The Wolfriders had gathered around to form a circle. No one spoke.

Finder laid his hands on Redstar's small chest, closed his eyes and waited.

"Patience," Tanner said in a low voice. To him, or to the others? He didn't know. It did not matter.

It came slowly at first. And it turned out that Finder was afraid after all, terrified of the strange power taking him over and moving through him. It was all he could do to hold back the fear and let it happen, let himself stiffen into the healer's trance. Then the force felt no longer strange, but fated. And he knew what he had to do, and he started to do it.

He had to find the tiny invisible moth that was Redstar's soul and whisper to it to be comforted and forget the evil it had seen and stay a while. He did so.

He had to find the hidden bleeding inside the cub's belly and coax it to stop. He did so.

He had to find the cub's heart and urge it to beat valiantly, and find Redstar's lungs and will them to breathe strongly on. He had to find the cub's broken bones and smooth them into straightness with his hands and start them knitting. He had to find the bruises, the burns, the cuts, the swelling, and take the pain away from them, and start them mending. He did so.

Then there was nothing more to find or do, and he blinked and looked at Redstar, and the cub opened his golden eyes and looked back at him. **Blyw,** the cub sent, **I knew it was you. Thank you.**

And Scarp was shouting to the sky, and Joygleam was gathering her son into her arms and weeping with happiness. More than one Wolfrider was weeping those tears of joy. But Finder had no tears left in him. There was nothing left; he had spent it all. Like an empty waterskin he folded onto the ground, and the others were saying things to him, but he could not hear them. He could not hear or find or do anything at all.

When he awoke, he was lying on a thick bed of furs in a comfortable tree hollow and old Fallfern was watching over him.

"There, you are awake at last," she scolded as soon as his eyes opened. "You simply must eat something. I never thought I'd live to see the day I'd have to coax you to eat."

"Is Redstar all right?" Finder asked. For a moment it had felt all too familiar, too much like that other day when an orphaned cub had woken up to find old Fallfern grumbling over him. But only for a moment. So much had changed, most of it inside him—he could feel the difference. He was not a motherlorn cub any longer, and never would be again. Redstar was the cub who had been lost.

"For the umpty-ump time, the little one is just fine!" Judging by Fallfern's tone, Finder must have asked the same question before, though he did not remember doing so. "Will you eat now?"

"Do I need to?" Finder held up his hand and studied it. It was thin.

"Yes!" Fallfern snapped. She whisked out. A moment later Tanner came in—Tanner, the chieftain who was seven hundred years old and still had not lost the shy smile of a stripling. Through his beard he smiled that way at Finder now.

"Well," he said awkwardly, "my eyes see with joy, lad. We were worried."

"Is Redstar really all right?" Finder asked him.

"He is really and truly and indeed very much all right. Those bad days are like nothing more than a bad dream to him. It is you we have all been scratching our heads over. Who is going to heal the healer, that is always the problem."

"Healer?"

As soon as he said it, he knew: of course he was a healer, as his mother had been. That was what it meant to be Blyw. Redstar had understood. Though Finder had never fully understood it before.

"Don't you remember?" Tanner sat down beside him.

"Yes, I— I do, I was just—surprised for a minute."

"You remember how you found Redstar?"

"Yes."

"And how you slew that ghastly huge human? You fought as fiercely as your father ever did in his life, Finder. You are going to have a few interesting scars to decorate that new slim body of yours. I think you ought to begin considering yourself a very attractive elf, youngster."

Finder shrugged this off. "I didn't kill the human. Scarp did."

"Scarp merely sped things along. It was your kill."

Finder lay silent. Tanner sat watching him.

"What is it?" the chieftain asked after a while.

"Redstar wasn't all I found," Finder said in a low voice.

"No?"

"No. I saw—in the bottom of that pit—the bones of my parents are lying there."

Silence. Tanner laid his hand on the thin, pale one curled on the furs, and Finder turned his palm to face his chieftain's. Fingers clasped.

Finder said, "When I am better, I must go back there. Give my parents back to the wolves, and destroy that pit. End it."

"I will come with you, if I may."

"Of course."

Across the glade they could see Fallfern hurrying back with the meat. Tanner stood up to go.

"You found a lost cub out there in the Everwood," he said to Finder.

"I know."

"I don't mean Redstar." Tanner smiled once more in that shy way of his and turned to go. "You found a lost elf. Yourself."

"I know," Finder whispered after him.

Turnings

by Diana L. Paxson

Egaruk held on to the whitebark tree, listening to the voice of the waters. All around the low ridge where he stood great sheets of water mirrored the gray sky. He shifted his weight and spongy soil squelched beneath his feet. They had run out of fat for greasing boots some time ago, and he could feel new damp soaking through the rotting hide. He took a deep breath of moist air, coughed, and wondered if his lungs were dissolving like his shoes.

At first he had welcomed the warm south winds—old bones ached when the great prairies were locked in ice. But the spirits of the land were angry and spring had come too quickly. Snowmelt outran the capacity of the land to absorb it, turning the peaty soil to bog. Instead of late snowfall there had been rain, and with nowhere to run, water collected in every indentation in the rolling plains. For generations Egaruk's people had roamed the prairies, following the great herds of branch-horns. But this year the herds had not come. The only creatures that moved on the plains now were the stinging flies.

Egaruk looked up at the blank face of the sky. *What sin have we committed, Gotara? Why have you turned your face away?*

Behind him the sagging skin tents of the People clung to the ridge. The sounds of the camp came faintly, as if muted by the air's moisture—a woman scolding, the thin wail of a child. The shaman who taught him had said that in the beginning there had been nothing but water, until Ifana, the First of the Graywings, brought up mud from the depths to make a place to lay her eggs. But nothing lasted forever. Perhaps the gods had decided to turn the world back into water again.

Once men had called Egaruk "the Bear," and he had sung luck for the hunters and healing for the sick, but he was an old bear now. The last of the warriors who had been young when he was a boy were dead. His wife had been taken by a fever the year before. Everything living must die when its season was done, and he would not be sorry when his time came to journey to the spirit world. He could face his own death, but not watching his people drown.

He turned from the watery wasteland of the prairie to look back at the tents. A thin haze of smoke hung sullenly above them, but when the whitebarks were gone even that must disappear. Egaruk closed his eyes, dazzled by a sudden memory of sunlight through green leaves.

Where had that been? As he grew old he found himself remembering the details of his youth with painful clarity, while the seasons just passed grew dim. He could remember hunting camps beneath the narrow-leaved fever trees, and the hillock where an ancient oak spread gnarled limbs. But what he was remembering now was a forest . . . where many trees fought for sunlight or clung to the rocky hills.

Had he dreamed it? There were trees enough to feed the fires of generations in that forest. And surely its slopes were steep enough to keep it above the waters even in a year like this one. This was not like the visions of his trances. But perhaps the spirits were answering his prayers at last. He had lived in such a forest, in the long-ago days when he had been stolen by the Woods Demons, when he was a little child.

If the People could reach the forest, they might survive. The headman, Gayag, would fight him over this, but it was the only chance that he could see. Wincing as stiffened joints took his weight once more, Egaruk hobbled back down the slope.

*   *   *

"The last time we saw humans in the Everwood was long ago," said Acorn, stretching out his leg to ease its aching.

"In the time of the High Ones?" asked little Spark, his red hair glowing even beneath the cloudy sky.

Spring had come wet and early to the Everwood, filling the world with the sound of rushing waters hurrying down to the plain. Trees were breaking into leaf, but the ground was treacherous; a misstep in the mud had lamed Acorn two days before. He would heal soon, but in the meantime he had found an unexpected pleasure in watching the cubs in the Hurst while the others went hunting.

"Not so long ago as that—" He laughed. "But many turnings ago, just before your mother was born!"

Spark stared up at him in amazement, his eyes the same deep blue as Speedwell's. Acorn understood his disbelief. When he had been a cub he had known that some of the Wolfriders, like Longreach the storyteller and Fangslayer and Brook, chief hunter before Joygleam, were really old. But once an elf reached maturity, the turnings all blended into the wolfsong, and Stormlight had seemed as old as Tanner to him.

"Were the Tall Ones ugly?" asked Waterfall.

"The old ones were, but their cubs are cute, just like you—" He reached out to ruffle the little one's brown curls.

Waterfall looked dubious, though she did not quite dare to doubt what the lifemate of the Wolfriders' chieftess said.

"I think you are making up a story. If the Tall Ones are real, where are they?" Spark's eyes darkened and Acorn blinked, reminded suddenly of Speedwell's stubborn childhood. Goodtree had eyes like light coming through spring leaves, but Stormlight's midnight gaze had skipped a generation and turned up in her granddaughter, and now Acorn saw it in Speedwell's boy-cub as well. And not one of the three of them seemed to know how to enjoy what the world had to give.

"Humans are real," Acorn said gently. "But elves and men can't share the same territory—no more than wolves and wild dogs. And as for their cubs, well, Goodtree fostered one of their children for a time," Acorn explained. "She called him Bearling. That's how I know."

Four pairs of slanted Wolfrider eyes grew round. Even Spark's disbelief wavered, for if Acorn said it had happened to the chieftess, it had to be true.

"Would you like to hear the story?" he asked, and was rewarded by their gap-toothed grins; the unease that had stirred at Spark's challenge faded away. He had loved Speedwell through a tumultuous cubhood. There was little she would accept from him now, but at least he could care for her cub, though she seemed to be having as much trouble being a mother as she had being a child.

Acorn was just telling them how Goodtree had given Bearling back to his own people to stop them from attacking the tribe when he heard Fang's howl. The hunters were returning with meat—a fat springer buck— and after that, of course, the only thing anyone thought about was food.

In the flickering light of the headman's hearth, the faces of the People appeared and disappeared as if they were already spirits floating in the final dark. Sick spirits, thought Egaruk, seeing faces gaunted by winter starvation and the illnesses of the spring. Even Ogan, mightiest of their warriors, looked like an old man.

"Life is hard here," said Danik, always a cautious one, "but at least these dangers are those we know, and when summer comes the water will go away." He sat with the other hunters in the inner circle around the lamp, the women and children huddling behind them.

"What use will the summer be," asked sharp-featured Agli, "if all that's left for the sun to warm is our bones?" In the silence, they could all hear the patter of rain upon the stretched hide roof.

"I have never seen a forest . . ." said Danik, "or a Woods Demon. How shall we find our way into a shaman's tale?"

"The spirits have reminded me," said Egaruk, "how we traveled down from the forest to hunt the branch-horns. The Demons went faster than men can travel, riding on the backs of their wolves, but it seems to me it took only a day to reach the plains. When we came out from beneath the trees and made camp there I saw the sun setting to the right. It was the first time I ever saw that. In the forest the sun is swallowed by the trees. I have never forgotten how it seemed to melt, little by little, into the sea of grass."

"Can other men walk in a shaman's dream?" muttered Danik, but the others were looking at Egaruk wistfully. He had spent much of the time since the idea came to him sorting through old memories. He had told them of feasts where the Demons gorged on fresh meat until they could not move. He had told of nuts that fell out of the trees into one's hands.

"We are the People of the plains," said Fen, who was Danik's brother. "We belong *here*, not fighting Demons among the trees!"

Bone ornaments clicked softly as Egaruk moved, and all attention returned to him. "The gods of the waters are too powerful, even for me. But the Woods Demons favored me when I was a child. My spells will protect you now."

"And if not," Gayag spoke finally, scratching his thatch of ginger hair, "we can kill them. We cannot kill the rain. I agree with Spirit Man," he said reluctantly. "We will go." There was a mutter of approval from the men.

Egaruk sighed. Why did he feel sorrow, now that the People had accepted his plan? As he emerged from the tent into the rainy darkness he realized it was because of Gayag's words. Why had the headman given in so easily?

To the People, the Woods Demons were evil. Egaruk had grown up with the story of how one had turned into a bear, killed his grandmother, and stolen him away. It was only when the Demons had ventured onto the People's hunting grounds that his own kind had been able to rescue him. From that moment, the old shaman had claimed him, sure that one who had survived such an ordeal must be marked by the spirits for special power. But among Egaruk's reclaimed memories was furry warmth surrounding him, and the painful beauty of wolfsong beneath the moons. Was that memory a message from the spirits, or the delusion of a man who had outlived his time?

Goodtree lay back against Lionleaper, rubbing her belly, which was stretched tight as a waterskin over the meat on which she had gorged. The rest of the Wolfriders were in a similar condition, though some still chewed reflectively, gazing into the fire. They were too full even to sing, but the silence was filled by the low growlings of the wolves as they gnawed the bones. Now that she was finally full-fed, Goodtree could reflect on what a hard winter it had been. Though the cold had broken early, wet weather had retarded growth, and only now were the beasts beginning to fill out enough to be good eating again.

"Longreach, think back—can you remember such a soggy spring?"

The old elf closed his eyes, reaching into his memories, and Acorn, who was sitting on Goodtree's other side, pushed himself up on one elbow to listen to him.

"Owl, who was my father, had a tale from the time of Prey-Pacer of a turning when it rained so long the wolves took some illness and nearly died. We lived to the west of here then, in caves," Longreach answered. "And there was a bad flood when we were living at the Holt at Halfhill. Freefoot was chieftain then."

There was a little murmur of wonder from the younger Wolfriders, who could not imagine living anywhere but here.

"That's why we moved to this spot, though it's farther to water," said Longreach. Others nodded. Moisture had collected in a few of the dens during the worst of the rains, but the roots of the beech trees had held the soil securely, and the water had quickly drained away. He looked around him, smiling. "It has been a good home."

Goodtree sat up, disturbed for no reason she could name. "And will be for many a turning to come," she said sharply.

"Of course—" The old elf turned to her. "But there have been times when we shifted camp every few turnings, not just on our summer journey to hunt the plains. We have a good life here, but this is not the only way that Wolfriders can live."

Unbidden, Goodtree saw the Golden Valley where she had found her name. She had always meant to go back to it, but the tribe had grown through these good years in the Everwood and there would not have been enough game to support them all. The Wolfriders needed her, and so from turning to turning, revisiting the Valley remained a dream. Maybe when Speedwell had grown mature enough to lead the tribe, Goodtree could go away.

If she ever *did* mature. Spark and some of the other cubs were gathering around Longreach, asking for more stories, but Goodtree did not hear them. The thought of her daughter had destroyed the last of her contentment.

"What is it?" Lionleaper laid a strong arm across her shoulders.

"Speedwell—look at her—is that how a future chieftess should behave?"

With a forked green stick, Speedwell had nudged a coal from the fire, which she was slowly moving toward the toes of Brightlance, who lay in a satiated stupor with his arms flung wide. Silvertwig and several of the other young ones watched with bated breath; her lifemate, Fireweed, who was enough older to have known better, looked simultaneously amused and guilty.

"A cub's trick," said Lionleaper, stifling laughter.

"Exactly, and if Spark were trying such a trick you

would know what to say to him. But Speedwell is Spark's mother! She should be keeping him out of trouble, not playing cruel games!"

"I'm sure she won't let it—" Acorn stopped as the coal rolled against the old hunter's big toe. Howling, Brightlance leaped upright, arms flailing, tripped over a bone, and went down again in a tangle of startled wolves.

For a moment there was silence, then Speedwell and her friends burst into laughter.

"She's scarcely more than a cub herself," Lionleaper said, a little weakly. "It happens sometimes. Stormlight was no older when she gave birth to you. . . ."

"That's what I'm afraid of," Goodtree said darkly. These days she was remembering her mother only too well. The Wolfriders could survive a few such wild spirits, but not when one was their chieftain. Skyfire had been one such, and according to the stories her passions had nearly destroyed the tribe.

Ignoring Acorn's pleading look and shaking off Lionleaper's restraining hand, she got to her feet and stalked around the fire.

"Did you see?" Speedwell looked up at her mother and gradually her giggles stilled.

Goodtree had never been overfond of Brightlance, who had been Stormlight's lovemate for a time, but as she watched him blearily pulling himself together, too confused even for anger, she found herself quivering with anger of her own.

I saw— She put all the force that had made her chief into the locked sending. No need to force the rest of the tribe to listen to this little scene. **If you have no respect for your elders, at least you should show some gratitude! How many times have you eaten meat Brightlance killed?**

I didn't hurt him. Speedwell's reply was sullen. **He's always such a stiff old stick, and he looked so funny, like a ravvit with a burr in its tail!**

You could have! And you did hurt his dignity . . . A chief should *care* for her pack—for their spirits as well as their bodies—

She stopped, for Speedwell had drawn herself into a tight ball of denial.

"Speedwell, are you listening to me?" Goodtree said aloud.

"I am not a chief . . ." Speedwell said in a hoarse whisper. All around them pointed ears were pricking, though the Wolfriders politely pretended not to see. "I don't want to be chief . . . and I *won't* be!"

"I don't understand you—" Goodtree began, but her daughter leapt suddenly to her feet, glaring.

"You don't have to!" she said furiously. "Just leave me alone!" She turned on her heel and stalked into the darkness, whistling to her wolf-friend, Briarpaw, who heaved herself to her feet with some effort, for she had gorged as heavily as any, and followed.

Goodtree shut her mouth with a snap, but before she could move she realized that Lionleaper and Acorn were beside her.

"Let her go," said Acorn softly. "Let her be—"

"She's just like my mother! She makes me afraid—" Goodtree felt Lionleaper's finger on her lips and stopped, shaking her head.

"Is she? I remember a cub who ran away rather than let us tie the chieftain's topknot in her hair . . ." he said softly. "Be patient. There is plenty of time. . . ."

Goodtree sighed and let them hold her, drawing strength from Lionleaper's force and Acorn's gentleness equally, as she had ever since the three of them had become lifemates so many turnings ago. But anxiety, harder to digest than the meat she had eaten, made a hard knot in her middle that would not go away.

The journey of the People across the flooded plains was harder than even Danik's and Fen's worst fears. Two of the children died from the coughing sickness, and Agli's wife was drowned when she stepped in an underwater hole and, weighted by her burdens, went down. There were times when Egaruk thought that if they had not all been so miserable they would have drowned *him,* and he wondered if his spirits had lied, as the journey northward went on and all they could see was the waterlogged expanse of the plain.

But there came a day when younger eyes made out a smudge of gray on the horizon. By sunset of the next day, they could see the fringe of branches sharp against the dimming sky. On the third day the ground began to rise, and they camped that night on new grass at the edge of the trees.

"This is a good place," said Ogan when he brought in a springhorn that had been driven, like the People, up from the plains. "We can learn to live here."

"Make magic to protect us, Spirit Man," said Gayag, looking around him as if he were expecting Woods Demons to materialize from the trees. Egaruk nodded, but as he breathed deeply of the scent of moist earth and leaves, he felt younger than he had in years.

That night he dreamed of a hut in the forest. He saw each tree clearly, and felt a sudden certainty that he would know them again. In the dream, he was hungry; then the world fell apart in a terrible roaring. A gigantic taloned paw swept past, then small hands grabbed him. A sense of swift movement became a nightmare of pain. He almost woke then, but the dream still held him, and he stilled as it passed into a vision of golden light shining through leaves, in which his belly was full and he laughed as he snuggled against a slender, agile body with soft breasts and gentle, four-fingered hands.

At last the weather had broken. Kissed by the sun's radiance, the trees seemed almost visibly bursting into bud; the scents of a hundred different flowers mingled in the soft air. In such weather simply being alive was an ecstasy that was almost pain. Speedwell ran through the Everwood, slim legs flashing as she raced her wolf, Briarpaw, through the trees. She had started running to get away from her mother's scolding, but now the joy of running was its own justification, a release from the tensions of a winter cooped up in her den. She was leaving her confused concern for Spark behind her, her reluctant passion for Fireweed, and, above all, the mingled love and fury that shook her when she remembered her quarrel with Goodtree.

At some level below the conscious, she was aware of moving southward; the ground sloped gradually and the trees were growing sparser, their branches gnarled by the winds from the plains. Here she could go even faster. She sucked in the clean wind and leapt forward as if she could outrun memory.

If Speedwell had been going more slowly, the new scent on the wind would have warned her. As it was, the message of her senses reached her awareness just as Briarpaw growled, and it was at the same moment that both of them ran full tilt into the strange creatures that were crossing the clearing between the trees.

She felt leather and skin and sharp bones beneath them as she went down. But wrestling with wolves builds quick reactions. As she hit the ground she was already rolling. She glimpsed the spreading tangle of a puffbush and dove beneath it, wriggling furiously forward, heedless of scratches, and not until she had put several clumps of trees between herself and the clearing did she halt, gulping air.

Briarpaw, what was that?

In a few moments the tawny female had joined her, hackles still bristling. **New thing. Smells bad!** came the reply.

That was certain. Speedwell sniffed at the arm with which she had shoved the stranger away, grimacing at the scents of sweat and rancid fat and woodsmoke. She had never smelled it before, but she would know it again. It was not an elf, but neither was it an animal. A horrible suspicion growing in her belly, she backtracked her trail. But this time she moved like a leaf on the breeze.

Deep gouges in the leaf mold and a trail of torn branches would have shown her the way, even without the smell. There had been three of them, hunters, for the body of a ravvit had been dropped in their panic, and not very good ones, for it had not been a clean kill. She followed the trail with all the skill that Lionleaper had taught her until she came to the imprint of a foot very like her own, though much larger, with five clearly defined toes.

But by then she could hear shouting, and the smells of woodsmoke and burnt meat and stale urine were tainting the clean wind. Heart pounding with excitement, Speedwell left the trail and circled, moving gradually closer until she could see.

The prairie steamed in the growing heat of summer, and hordes of insects drove the People deeper into the forest, despite their fears. Egaruk fasted and drummed, praying to the spirits, and after that first horrifying encounter with the Demons, no more were seen. The forest resounded to the *thunk* of stone axes, and soon the shelters were surrounded by a stout palisade. Each day the men ranged out, hunting. Women and children wandered closer to home, looking for edible roots and leaves.

But only Egaruk dared to walk alone, naming the things he saw in a language no other human knew. The others watched him with narrowed eyes, but he was a Spirit Man, protected by his spells. While he did the magic that kept them safe they did not dare to question him.

But though the humans saw nothing, not one of them

left the shelter of the palisade unseen. Speedwell and her friends had at last found an outlet for their energy, and they took turns watching the village, saving their laughter for the tales they told the rest of the Wolfriders when they returned home.

"The Tall Ones look at the forest as if the trees might eat them!" exclaimed Speedwell. "Especially when it gets dark. Every night they build a big fire and dance around it, and the one who wears all the bits of fur and bone sings."

Goodtree listened carefully, pleased with the way Speedwell told her story even as its content made her frown.

"Sounds like fun," said Freshet, who thought the Wolfriders ought to dance more often, especially if they could pass the dreamberries around.

"I don't think they're doing it to enjoy themselves," said Fireweed slowly. "There's a kind of desperation, like the way they built the log wall. I think they are dancing from fear . . ."

The others stared at him. The Wolfriders danced to celebrate the birth of a cub or their own identity as a tribe, or simply because the world was so beautiful. What other reason could there be?

"I don't understand." Lionleaper spoke for all of them. "You say they are growing fat and healthy. Why should they be afraid?"

Fireweed shrugged. "They shouldn't be. They are eating well, and two of the females are pregnant."

"But the forest is strange to them," said Longreach. "Humans always fear what they do not understand."

Goodtree sighed, remembering the odd arrangement of bones and red-painted arrows with which the humans had decorated the stones they had heaped over the body of the old woman who had taken care of Bearling.

"It's funny to watch them looking over their shoulders," said Speedwell. "Only the man who wears the bones is different. He walks in the forest as if he liked it, and every day he goes to visit a clearing where there's a funny mound."

Goodtree stiffened. She had been thinking about Bearling a lot since the humans came, but she knew better than to assume these were the same ones to whom she had returned him.

"Is he a strongly built man, with brown hair?" she asked.

"No." Speedwell seemed puzzled by her mother's intensity. "His hair is white, what's left of it, and he is old. . . ."

Egaruk glimpsed sunlight through the trees ahead of him and quickened his pace. On the plains he had been ancient, but here in the forest he felt himself growing young again. It had taken half a day the first time he had come this way. Now he could make the distance from the village to his grandmother's grave before the sun was well above the trees. He thought that the place where he had lived with the Woods Demons was farther to the east. If he had known the way, he would have gone there. Only a chance remark from one of the hunters had shown him the way to the old mound. The people thought he came here to pray to his grandmother's spirit and work magic, but he did not even remember her. Egaruk came here to dream of those whom his people feared, and there was a special urgency to his dreaming today.

He ducked beneath a low-growing oak branch and straightened carefully, then stilled. The clearing was not as he had left it. A wreath of summer asters and clingsilver lay upon the mound.

Egaruk took a few careful steps forward, looking around him. There were no footmarks, but he had not expected them. No hunter of his people had time to play with flowers and the women did not come so far from home. It had been a spirit, or one of the Demons. He wondered by how long he had missed him—or her—and found his vision blurred by the quick tears of old age.

"Mother . . . where are you?" he murmured in that tongue that no other human knew. And then, though no sound alerted him, he became aware that he was not alone.

Wiping his eyes, he looked upward. Startled slanted eyes, luminous as the leaves themselves, stared down at him from the tree. Egaruk blinked, and as if their owner had materialized out of the branches, he saw slender limbs half covered by a fawn tunic with insets of a darker leather in leaf patterns around the edges, the gleam of an elk-tooth necklace, the glimmer of sunlight on golden hair. And in that moment Egaruk understood that the folk whom his people called Demons really were magic, for though he had not remembered she was so small, she still looked exactly as she had in his dreams.

"Mother!" he whispered again, trembling.

"Bearling, is it really you?" Goodtree slid to a lower branch of the tree.

Egaruk looked at his veined hands, painfully aware of how he must appear to her. Her speech sounded strange, but already more of it was coming back to him.

"I was, once," he said bitterly, "then was called Egaruk the Bear, Speaker to Spirits. Now I am only an old man. . . ." Abruptly he sat down on a fallen log.

Goodtree stared. "So, it is true. The Wolfriders die, but they do not grow old. They told me, if I kept you, that this pain would come. Was I wrong, Bearling, to give you back to your mother? Were you happy with the tribe of men? The Hurst is nearer than you think—you have only to follow the stream to the falls and then cross the beechwood. Do you want to come home with me?"

Egaruk sighed, and then he smiled. "I was happy. I was a great spirit talker. My woman gave me many children. She is dead, and only one son lives, but he gives me grandchildren. It is enough. They carry my life when I am gone."

"I also have a grandchild," said Goodtree, smiling. "He thought that humans were only a cub's tale until your folk returned. Did your people believe what you told them about the Wolfriders, and me?"

He looked up at her, and his face changed. "I learned young to tell nothing. Old shaman, he beat me when I said different from what the People believe. They call you Woods Demons, Mother—say that you can change into wolves—"

As if her laughter had been a summons, the bushes stirred and a large, brindled she-wolf emerged. Egaruk froze as she sniffed him thoroughly, then she gave a disgusted snort and flopped down at the base of the tree.

"No—or at least, not now. The wolves are our friends."

"Then guard them!" he said with sudden intensity. "All my songs of power don't free my people from fear of the forest, not when they see wolf tracks in the morning dew. Gayag, our headman, knows poisons. He and the warriors will kill the beasts, put wolfsbane in bodies for wolves to find!"

"But we have not harmed you!" Her green eyes went wide.

Egaruk shrugged. "Gayag hates any power he cannot control. If he hurts wolves, what will your chieftain do?"

"*I* am the Wolfriders' leader . . ." she said slowly. "But what can I say to an elf whose wolf-friend dies?" Her attention returned to him. "Oh, Bearling, I wept when I lost you. Have I found you again only as an enemy?"

"Not your enemy," Egaruk said tiredly. "I do what I can, but I am old. Men fear the forest more than my magic. I do not think they will listen to me."

Speedwell jerked upright, pointed ears twitching, as the howl of anguish split the warm air. The sound had come from an elf's throat, not a wolf's, but all her watchers had sworn to be silent. It must be something terrible. The wail was repeated, and women who had been hunting for starflower bulbs in the meadow just beyond the palisade snatched up their children and ran for the safety of the walls. But the headman's door flap was thrust aside and the man himself emerged, shading his eyes as he looked around him, and it seemed to Speedwell that he smiled.

She eased backward through the stand of redgrass from which she had been watching the village with scarcely a quiver to mark her passing, and in another moment she and Briarpaw were speeding toward the source of the sound.

Wanderfoot came here, and Silvertwig, came Briarpaw's sending as they reached the stand of whitebarks above the stream. **Smell meat . . . smell man-scent,** and then, **Smell death.**

But by that time Speedwell could hear Silvertwig's sobbing. In another moment, they were in the clearing. The half-eaten carcass of a springbuck lay beneath the trees. Nearby, Silvertwig was weeping, the body of her wolf-friend in her arms.

"She ran ahead . . . " Silvertwig looked up and Speedwell held her. "The humans must have seen her, for they dropped their kill and ran. When I got here she had gobbled most of the beast down. I scolded her, but what wolf could have resisted? We settled here to see if the hunters would return for their kill, and I dozed off for a little while. When I woke, Wanderfoot was coughing, but she couldn't seem to bring anything up. Then she got stiff. She fought it, but she couldn't move, she couldn't breathe—"

The elf eased her grip and Speedwell touched the body. Though it was still warm, every muscle was rigid, and the wolf's muzzle was wrinkled in a silent snarl of agony.

She straightened and saw Briarpaw nosing at the remains of the springer.

No! Don't touch! Speedwell put all her force into

the sending. Ears flattening, the she-wolf backed off.
Bad meat, killed Wanderfoot. Stay away!

Silvertwig stared at her, eyes widening as she began to understand.

"We must bury that thing where none of the other wolves can dig it up again," said Speedwell, her belly beginning to burn with anger. "The Tall Ones have poisoned it!"

They were still digging when Freshet and Fireweed and the others who had been within earshot of Silvertwig's cry arrived.

"You think this was a deliberate killing?" asked Fireweed, reaching out to her.

"The humans weren't taking a poisoned beast home to feed their cubs!" Speedwell snarled at him, and he looked hurt and took his hand away.

Silvertwig began to cry again and Speedwell hugged her, her own heart aching with pain for her friend. Was this what Goodtree had meant when she said a chieftess must care for her tribe?

"They are bad! They don't belong in the Everwood—we should drive them away!" cried Oakarrow.

"Let's go after them, give them reason to fear!" Silvertwig cried.

"I don't know," Fireweed objected. "The whole tribe should discuss this. Goodtree—" He stopped as he met Speedwell's furious glare.

"Are you a cub, to go running to your mother the first time it meets a ravvit? If this were a bear or a long-tooth, we would know what to do! But even a long-tooth kills only to eat or to defend itself or its young. The humans killed Wanderfoot for no reason at all! Freshet is right—they don't belong here, and it is up us to make them go away!"

A low growling came from elf and wolf throats alike. In moments they had mounted, Silvertwig riding double behind Speedwell, and were trotting along the path the humans had already worn into the forest soil.

The sun was setting by the time they came in sight of the palisade. But the gate was still open, and skin-clad figures moved in and out, dragging logs for the nightly fire. Silent as the lengthening shadows the Wolfriders slipped through the trees. Two humans came out of the gate laughing, followed by a smaller one.

Now! Speedwell's sending flashed from mind to mind.

"Aaoowh . . ." The howling of the wolves resounded, and three gray-feathered arrows flickered through the air.

The humans' heads turned as the first arrow thunked into the ground; at the second, one cried out and staggered, and the smaller figure, leaning forward to help him, took the third in the throat and fell. From the village, folk came running with torches in their hands. Yells of fear and anger changed to cries of grief as they took up that still form, mingling painfully with the Wolfriders' triumphant howls.

Oakarrow and Silvertwig nocked more arrows, but the humans were already scurrying for the shelter of their palisade.

"Enough—" said Speedwell. "They're safe for now, but perhaps they'll think twice about putting out poison again!"

"I hope so," said Fireweed, but as the forest grew silent Speedwell could feel the others beginning to wonder.

"Let's get back to the Hurst," said Freshet. "We'll have to tell the others what's happened."

We'll have to tell Goodtree . . . No one had said or sent it, but Speedwell's heart sank with an uneasiness she could not explain.

"Where is your magic now, old man? What use your spells?" Gayag's blow crunched into Egaruk's cheek, but the others kept him from pulling away. "You swore that your charms would protect us, but see—see there!" His voice rose to a shriek as he pointed to the boy's body laid out beside the fire. "You failed us, and it is my son they have slain!"

For a moment Egaruk closed his eyes. This, then, was the dread that had haunted him as he returned through the forest. Better if he had wandered into the wood and died there before the two peoples he loved warred this way. It did not need a shaman's vision to see this scene repeating itself again and again until death was victor over both Wolfriders and men. But was this a fated future? Could it be stopped, even now?

"Well?" Another blow shook him and he tasted blood. "What have you to say?" He opened his eyes, and men flinched from his stare.

"I said that you must not attack the Demons!" he said sternly. "You were safe while you did not harm them, but you moved outside my protections when you set poison for the wolves. It is your own disobedience that has brought this on you, Gayag!"

"Is it? Now I begin to wonder just who you were protecting!" The headman's face thrust close to his, contorted with rage. "Is this why the Demons spared you so many years ago? Did they give you power to lure us to this place where they could kill us all?"

For a moment sheer amazement kept Egaruk from a reply.

"We were dying anyway," said Fen. "Have you forgotten? The hunting is good here. Let the Spirit Talker give us new magic so that we can stay."

"You have killed at least one of them—" Egaruk seized the opportunity, "or didn't you hear that howl? A life for a life—let that satisfy your honor. If you will seek no more vengeance I will strive with the spirits and make magic so that this does not happen again!"

"And whose son will die next time if you fail?" Gayag said dangerously, and there was a little mutter of agreement from the other men. "These hunting grounds are ours. We would fight other men who tried to dwell here.

Surely our gods will turn against us if we allow these abominations to live. . . . Our sin was to spare them for so long!"

"You are mad," Egaruk said furiously. "My brothers, will you die for Gayag's pride? For death is indeed what will come if you follow him!"

"Are you cursing me, old man?" Gayag's foul breath blasted him. "We can deal with Demons, and we can deal with sorcerers!"

For the first time Egaruk understood his own danger. He would have welcomed death, but if he let them kill him, too much else would be lost.

"Can you?" he hissed, and men's eyes flickered with unease.

"A noose will strangle your curses," answered Gayag, "until we can drown you in the marshes with a stake through your heart and withies to tie down feet and hands. Neither body nor spirit will walk again after that treatment, Spirit Talker. Oh yes, we can deal with you!"

"Perhaps," Egaruk replied with a terrible smile. "But can you control the spirits who will be released when I die? Can you make hunting magic? Can you sing the souls of the dead to the spirit world?" Gayag had always hated him, but the People needed his services. Egaruk suspected that was the only reason he had lived so long.

"My son is dead!" the headman growled. "But yours is living. You will serve us, Egaruk the Bear, if you want him and his children to survive." He paused, grinning evilly at the horror Egaruk could not hide. "Spirit Man, we need a new magic. You will make a spell to destroy the Woods Demons, whether they take wolf or spirit form. And then you will lead us to their lair. Put him in his tent, and guard it," he said to the other men. "He will do what we want now."

As the hours of darkness passed, the fires in the human camp burned high. The space between the trees of the

Hurst was lit as well, by the Mother and Daughter moons as they glared at each other across the sky. And in the clearing, the same baleful light gleamed from elf eyes as Goodtree faced her child. How could their pleasant life have been destroyed so quickly? wondered Goodtree, searching for strength to face the defiance she sensed from her child. In an eyeblink, it seemed, everything was different, as sometimes in one night the world can turn from summer to fall.

"You *talked* to him? You should have killed him!" cried Speedwell. "Mother, don't you understand—one of our wolves is dead!"

"If Bearling had not warned me, we might have lost more." Goodtree strove to keep her voice under control. "Do you think that springer was the only poisoned meat the humans left for them to find? While you and your foolish friends were off making trouble, I was warning the tribe. Pounce got sick, but the other wolves were stopped before they ate any at all."

"The humans are dangerous—" Freshet was saying. "Their village was humming like a hive of angry bees!" There was a chorus of agreement from the elves who had been with Speedwell.

"Indeed," said Goodtree coldly. "And who stirred up that hive? You have *killed* one of them, a child. Do you think they will forgive that? Would we? I doubt that even Bearling can calm his people now—"

"Bearling . . . " Speedwell's voice dripped scorn. "Your wonderful Bearling didn't stop his folk from setting out the poison. Were we supposed to slink away with our tails between our legs and let them do it again? Has it occurred to you that your pet human might have been sent to lull us while they made plans to kill us all?"

"He didn't have to tell her about the poison—" Acorn began.

"By the time Goodtree got back to the Hurst, we would have known about it anyway. The Tall Ones are treacherous, and we should get rid of them as we would a nest of brown snakes, before they can breed!"

That was a little strong even for angry Wolfriders. As they began to mutter, Goodtree caught her breath and stalked toward her daughter, summoning the force that had made her chieftain. She had worried that Speedwell would take after her own mother, but it was far worse— the cub was a throwback to Skyfire, who had split the tribe!

"Listen to me," she said softly, but green eyes blazed as they met blue. "I have no love for humans. They killed my mother. But those are thinking beings. To exterminate any creature is not our Way—if we destroy the humans, we become worse than they!"

Will strove against will as they stared. Goodtree felt an unwilling flicker of satisfaction as she faced a strength in her daughter she had not known was there. If Speedwell did not get them all killed, the cub might make a chieftess after all.

"No love . . . for humans . . ." Speedwell gasped. "But what about . . . Bearling? You didn't want to give him up before. You always wanted . . . your stupid human cub . . . instead of me!"

For a moment Goodtree gaped. Then a sound she did not know she could make burst from her throat and she leapt. Taken by surprise, Speedwell went down; Goodtree pinned her, glaring, and this time the younger elf's gaze flickered and slid away.

"Who is the chieftain of the Wolfriders?" Goodtree demanded in a tone that set hackles to bristling in every wolf that heard.

"You are . . ."

"Then hear me! We will defend ourselves," growled Goodtree, "but we will not destroy! And especially we will not destroy the one human who has tried to help us. Do you understand?"

There was a tense silence. Goodtree could feel Speedwell trembling beneath her hands. Then all the fight seemed to go out of her. Goodtree let go, shuddering with reaction, and after a moment Speedwell drew herself together and rolled away.

"I understand," she whispered, getting herself upright again. "But you are wrong. That human brings disaster, and I will rub your nose in it before all this is done," she added with a flash of her earlier defiance. For a moment it seemed as if she would say something more, then she turned, and before Goodtree could speak again she faded into the shadows beneath the trees.

I meant to tell her that I love her . . . thought Goodtree, but in her daughter's present mood she would not have heard. *When she comes back I will. Meanwhile, if we're not going to follow Speedwell's advice, we had better decide what to do!*

Egaruk had been imprisoned for a day before he recovered enough to pick up his drum. His family would be safe while Gayag thought the shaman was doing magic. And if he could give his spirit wings, no man could say where it might fly.

Egaruk drummed, seeking first to still the frightened voices within him. He drummed until awareness of his body faded; only his hand continued to move while his spirit swung free. In vision he saw the village and the folk within it. Gayag was the evil spirit that drove them. To save his family, death or disappearance must free the shaman from Gayag's power. If he went to the Wolfriders, perhaps he could guide them all to a peace that they could survive. But he would have to escape before they tortured him for the location of the Woods Demons' home.

When Egaruk came back to normal consciousness, it was night once more. His arm ached from drumming. Coughing once or twice to get his throat working again, he called. The warrior who pulled open the door flap was Sarn, whom he had treated for a hunting injury not long ago, and Egaruk began to hope once more.

"I have labored mightily with the spirits," the shaman said portentously. "And now I require food."

When Sarn withdrew, Egaruk scrabbled furiously among his herbs for a skin packet tucked in the bottom of a leather sack. Taking care not to breathe it, he poured the fine powder into his hand. Presently the door opened and he smelled some kind of stew.

"You must bring it to me," Egaruk whispered. "I am too weak to move."

The young man nodded and knelt by the fire to set the bowl down. As he did so, Egaruk took a deep breath and flung the handful of powder on the flames. Instantly a dense smoke billowed upward. Sarn started to draw back, but Egaruk was behind him, holding him there for the moment it took for the smoke to take him. Sarn swayed, coughing weakly, and Egaruk picked up the stone he used to grind herbs with and tapped him expertly behind the ear.

Neither smoke nor blow would hold the man long, but before he could recover, Egaruk had bound hands and feet and gagged him securely.

"Be still . . ." the shaman whispered as the warrior began to stir. "You will live if you do not struggle, but my spirits will devour you if you try to get away—"

The young man's eyes dilated and he relaxed. With the sweet-smoke in him, he would probably be willing to swear that the shaman had turned into a spirit himself and flown away. Fighting dizziness, Egaruk gathered a few herbs, his warmest cloak, and a mask he used in the rituals to frighten demons away. He crept to the door and peered out, breathing deeply of the clean air. The man who was watching by the bonfire seemed half asleep— there would never be a better time.

Egaruk could not move like a Wolfrider, but even in his

old age he stepped more softly than most men, especially now, when fear suppressed awareness of his body's pain. No one challenged him as he made his way through the shadows to the gateway, but the barrier with which they blocked the opening was heavy, and he could not prevent it from squeaking painfully as he pulled it aside.

The man by the fire jumped to his feet and grabbed a branch to stir up the flames. In that moment Egaruk slipped on the grinning demon mask. Leaping firelight showed the guard a creature from nightmare. He yelped and knocked over his spear. By the time he got ahold of it and looked back at the gateway, the apparition was gone.

Speedwell tensed as a branch rustled behind her, then she caught Acorn's scent and relaxed against her tree. For a night and a day and most of another night she had waited here, watching the path to the village. Fireweed had brought her food and Silvertwig a skin of water, but neither had been able to persuade her to come away.

"Did *she* ask you to come argue with me?" Speedwell said as Acorn swung himself up into the tree and found a perch just below.

"No . . . " He sounded amused, as if she were a cub who had gotten into a jam.

"It was your own idea then, to save her pain?" She knew she sounded petulant, but she could not help it.

"I thought you might be hungry—" He handed up a piece of dried click-toe. "And tired. If you want to go find a place to curl up, I will watch the path for a while."

Speedwell tried to chew the dried meat, but there was a lump in her throat and she could not get it down. Acorn seemed content to sit in silence, leaning against the tree.

She looked at him and felt a burning behind her eyes. "I'm glad that I had two fathers, and that you were one of them. . . ." she said at last.

"I think it is love, not lineage, that makes a parent. I have always thought of you as my own."

The tension that had kept her to her task snapped suddenly, and the easy tears spilled down her cheeks. Sobbing, she slid down from her perch to join Acorn, clinging to him while the shudders ran through her body and he stroked her tangled hair.

"Spark sends his love," said Acorn. "He caught a ravvit and wanted to save it for you, but we persuaded him it would be better to let the wolves eat it now and stretch the skin. Do you think he might have inherited Tanner's gift for working with hides?"

Speedwell laughed through her tears. It occurred to her that the females of her line were not very good at motherhood. Stormlight had run from the responsibility; Goodtree had reacted so far in the other direction that Speedwell felt stifled. She herself had borne Spark when she was still half a cub, and he was growing up wild because she did not know what to do for him. She gulped, suddenly aware of how much she loved him, and Acorn made a small sound of affection and continued to stroke her hair. For a singer of songs, he was astonishingly good at communicating without words.

They were still sitting in silence as the night began to fade. They could just make out the silver veils that the night-breath of the moist earth had left between the trees when they heard footsteps on the trail.

**A man . . . ** sent Acorn, ears pricking.

But not as heavy-footed as the hunters, Speedwell replied. **He is old, though, or sick, or very tired . . .**

They swung down from the tree and woke their wolf-friends. In the mist, even elf eyes were half blinded, but as the man drew closer, Speedwell heard the click of bone ornaments, and in another moment caught a familiar scent on the heavy air.

It's Bearling! Her sending had a vicious snap.

Don't hurt— Acorn stopped himself.

No—I'll get proof before I strike again!

The two elves faded back among the trees as the old

man passed. He was leaning heavily on a stick, pushing himself, though he wheezed with the strain. At this rate, thought Speedwell, he would kill himself before she touched him. But what in the name of the two moons had brought him out at this hour? She parted the branches, saw old blood on his face, and frowned.

Men come— came Briarpaw's sending. A few moments passed and the elves heard a distant clamor like wolves on a hunting trail. But it was several minutes before the human paused, panting, and started back the way he had come. Then he moaned and began to hurry once more.

**They are hunting him . . . ** sent Acorn, and Speedwell had to agree.

They were almost to the place with the mound. As they reached it, the human looked back down his trail, and shook his head despairingly at the clear set of footprints he had left in the damp soil.

He is running to us for safety, thought Speedwell. *And it's Goodtree's fault for telling him where to go. . . .* She thought of Spark, curled in unsuspecting sleep in the den, and her grip tightened on her spear. Even unwilling, the old man must not be allowed to lead the other humans there.

But Bearling was fumbling in his pouch. Speedwell scented the same acrid taint as she had smelled on the poisoned meat as he unfolded a bit of leather.

"Mother . . ." He spoke aloud, and in the Wolfriders' tongue. "I would help you, but I can run no more. At least they won't find you by following me!" He grimaced and lifted the poison to his lips.

"No!" Without volition, Speedwell found herself leaping forward, snatching the packet from his hand. The human blinked, his expression changing from anguish to delight to amazement as he realized he had never seen her before.

"Acorn—take him to Goodtree!" she called. "The

wolves and I will give these hunters some music while we hide your trail!"

Before Bearling could speak, Acorn was dragging him into the trees, and a quick call from Speedwell sent Briarpaw and Twitchear dancing down the trail. With a little luck, the humans would think the old man had turned into a wolf and run away.

But the Tall Ones kept coming. Speedwell added her own howl to the wolf chorus and, as she flitted through the trees ahead of them, heard other elf voices joining her. *A whole pack of wolves, that's right!* she thought gleefully as round human eyes gazed nervously at the trees, *and they're going to gobble you up if you don't run back to your walls!*

But either these humans were mad, or numbers had made them brave. When the trail disappeared at the mound they spread into an uneven line and continued to blunder forward, hoping to pick it up again. And they might well do it, thought Speedwell, if Acorn, counting on her ability to mislead them, ceased to cover his trail.

They're getting awfully close to the Hurst, came Fireweed's sending from somewhere to her right.

Throw stones, she answered. **Make a ring around them and howl!** In amazement she realized that she was following Goodtree's orders. Though the humans clumped together as if they wanted to make themselves targets, they kept on.

An arrow hissed past her, struck a human's leg, and hung, quivering.

"Goodtree says to hold them until she can get the cubs away," shouted Briar. Lionleaper appeared behind him, shaking his spear.

Speedwell stared at them. She had convinced Goodtree that Bearling was a danger, but there was no joy in being proven right. When it came to the test, she had been as softhearted as her mother, and now they were all in danger. She fought back an image of Spark, writhing on the end of a human's spear.

A Tall One screamed as Joygleam's spear hit his belly. Another leapt forward, and Speedwell collected her wits and jabbed at him just in time to spoil the cast that would have brought the huntress down. More arrows came from the forest, but the elves never made many heavy hunting barbs at one time, and the ones they had were soon gone. They were quickly reduced to spearwork, and that gave an advantage to the humans' stronger arms and longer spears. All the anger and frustration of the past few moons exploded through Speedwell's arm as the world fell apart in a tangle of jabbing points and snarling wolves.

As the light strengthened, Speedwell saw two of the humans down and groaning, but Fangslayer lay still beside them. And beyond—a thatch of red hair had been dyed a deeper crimson. Her sending met silence, and she knew that she would never find Fireweed's soulname now. But there was no time for her to feel the pain. Her stomach clenched. The refrain echoed through her awareness—*No elf must die . . . no elf must die!*

Silvertwig was jabbing furiously at a big hunter, eyes blazing with grief for Wanderfoot, and as Speedwell started forward to aid her, the man's spear slammed into her breast and bore her down. Snarling, the man leaned on the spear. Pinned to the earth, Silvertwig convulsed; for a moment her eyes met Speedwell's—she was trying to send—but all that came was a chaotic mixture of pain and fury. And then the light went out of her eyes and there was nothing at all. Speedwell shrieked and drove her own weapon upward into the human's belly while he was still trying to free his spear.

She leapt back as he fell. For a moment, nothing moved around her. Her nostrils flared at the stench of blood, but she herself was unwounded. She seemed to be rather good at this business of killing, though it sickened her. Briarpaw leaned against her, panting and rubbing her muzzle against her own foreleg as if she did not much like the taste of whatever had reddened her jaws.

Not like hunting, is it, old girl? Speedwell sent, but got only a "whfft" of disgust in reply.

Then a knot of struggling figures lurched toward them. With a shock of horror Speedwell realized that though most of the Tall Ones were bleeding, there were still more of them than there were Wolfriders. They had gathered around a big man with gingery hair who slavered like a rabid wolf as he waded into the fray. And now she saw Briar's body lying across that of his wolf, and Snowfall, huddled against a tree, trying to stop the blood that flowed from a gash in her thigh.

Acorn appeared on the other side of the clearing. **Are the cubs safe?** He nodded, then someone moved behind him, and Speedwell saw Goodtree, hefting a yet unbloodied spear.

"Mother! Run! If we stay to fight, everyone will be killed!"

For a moment, the older elf's green eyes widened, mirroring the horror in Speedwell's own, then the younger elf blinked at the power of the sending, a chieftain's sending, that blasted through the consciousness of every elf and wolf that could still hear.

Fade into the forest! Scatter! The cubs are safe at the caves on White Rock peak! Cover your trail and meet there—get away!

The humans shook their heads, blinking, as their foes seemed to disappear before their eyes. But not everyone could run. Through a haze of branches Speedwell saw Lionleaper holding Oakarrow on the back of his wolf-friend. Snowfall had made it to her feet, but could get no further. The big warrior with the fox-colored hair grinned nastily and started toward her, raising his spear.

Then gold hair flickered in the pale sunlight and

another figure was between them, snarling like a she-wolf defending her young.

"Mother, *no!*" Speedwell sprang out of hiding to join her. **Acorn, Lionleaper! Help Snowfall, and get Goodtree *away!***

"Do you think I can't fight?" growled the chieftess as her daughter sank into a defensive crouch beside her.

"I think the tribe needs you alive!" Speedwell replied. She was aware of sounds behind her, branches crackling and Snowfall's whimper of pain, but the Tall Ones were coming at them. She jabbed, and the foe on her side flinched backward. But the big man's spear was plunging toward Goodtree, batting the chieftess's weapon aside like a twig. Speedwell tried to get her own weapon around, but there was no time— She threw her body in front of her mother's and gasped as the heavy stone spear point glanced across her ribs, caught in the soft flesh below them, and drove in.

Mother! Goodtree did not know if the cry was Speedwell's or her own. She saw the weapon blur—it was a club, no, a spear—and past and present became one as it crashed down and blood splashed pale hair. She rolled, heard a wolf howl beside her, then more shouts and a cry from one of the men. Now she was upright, standing over Speedwell's bleeding body, with Lionleaper and Acorn at her side.

The Tall Ones shook their spears, yelling, and they all had a single face, imprinted beyond forgetting in Goodtree's memory—the face of the human who had killed her own mother, Stormlight, when she took the blow that would have struck Goodtree down.

Like Speedwell . . .

Goodtree shrieked, grief stirring depths untouched since the day she found her name. Elves and humans alike trembled, and in that instant, Goodtree's magic wakened. The tall grass began to quiver. Treetops rustled where there was no wind. Grass stems twined about the feet of the Tall Ones as they tried to charge and sprouting branches tangled in their hair. Goodtree's fury swept through the forest and the Tall Ones screamed as the earth beneath their feet grew a thousand grasping fingers to drag them down.

The power that was surging through Goodtree peaked and then began to pass. Their enemies had forgotten them. Screaming, they were slashing hysterically at bushes and trees. Acorn lifted Speedwell. Emptied, Goodtree swayed, unable to protest as Lionleaper caught her in his arms and dragged her away.

"Humans die, go live in world of spirits . . . " said Bearling. "We bury our dead with tools and food—things they need along the way. We live so few turnings, we need hope for another life. I have believed I saw those spirits, in visions. But I am old. Soon I will know."

Goodtree heard him without emotion. While Speedwell lay between life and death she had no interest even in Bearling's words. The others coaxed her to eat and watched her with anxious eyes, but she scarcely noticed. Only Speedwell's labored breaths had meaning now.

Acorn nodded and put another stick on the fire. Wind whistled through the crevices of the White Peak caverns, making the fires burn too swiftly and whirling their warmth away. The younger Wolfriders were kept busy gathering fuel.

"I have lived . . . two hundred turnings . . ." said Acorn. "Speedwell was born just after we returned you to your people. But the Wolfriders do not grow old, and any death is too soon."

And soon she will be part of the wolfsong, thought Goodtree, hearing the words he did not say.

"I brought this on you," said Bearling somberly. "Trying to save my people. Now both lose too many hunters. You say you found Gayag with his neck broken—that is good, but without him my folk won't dare go back to the plains. I should return to them. Help them, if they don't kill me because of you."

There was a change in the sound of Speedwell's breathing and Goodtree hurried to the sheltered darkness at the back of the cave.

Mother . . . hurts. The sending was blurred.

"She wakes," said Goodtree sharply. "She needs more of your herbs for the pain!"

Bent double beneath the low ceiling, Bearling made his painful way back to them, felt the fluttering pulse at Speedwell's wrist and touched her brow. "Not yet—too much, and she dies now."

Goodtree bit her lip. The other Wolfriders who had survived the battle were recovering. Speedwell lived, but she did not heal. Only Bearling's potions had kept her alive so long.

"She is my age . . . " He sighed, looking down at her. "But I am old, and she is young. I would give the blood of my heart to save her. Now I cannot even ease her pain." He sighed. "All things change . . . and die. Only good is to know the time. . . ." He shook his head and crawled back to the fire.

Goodtree spooned a little water between Speedwell's cracked lips and sat back again, shivering at a stray touch of wind.

Mother—you must let me go.

"You will live," Goodtree said aloud, afraid of what she might reveal in a sending.

How? There was a painful humor in Speedwell's reply. **You would have given the final mercy days ago to any wolf who had suffered so long!**

"My mother died to save me—I should have died for you!" Goodtree continued as if she had not heard. "You must lead the Wolfriders after me."

To war? That is what I was good at, but that is not the Wolfriders' Way. Why do you think I jumped in front of you? We cannot live with the Tall Ones. Lead the Wolfriders away from here, maybe to that valley of yours. They would have fought me, but they will follow you.

"But I love you. . . ."

Speedwell tensed against another surge of pain, then turned her head away with an implacability that made Goodtree cold. **You are the chieftain, and you know what you must do.**

Goodtree listened to the harsh drag of her daughter's breathing, feeling the weight of every turning she had walked this world. She roused only when Bearling returned, bearing a bowl of beechwood whose contents he had heated with stones from the fire.

The Tall Ones go to their spirit land, but Timmain's children become part of the wolves and the world's magic . . . or perhaps nothing. . . . Neither man nor elf could be sure where that thing which caused a creature to live and move—and love—went when the body failed. But she had seen the same knowledge of the time for ending that she sensed from Speedwell in the eyes of a king stag when it faced the wolves. This was only another turning. . . . Goodtree rocked, hugging herself with cold.

You are the blood of chiefs, she sent. **I accept your will.** She leaned forward, and with trembling fingers twisted Speedwell's hair into a chieftain's knot. From her daughter she sensed a wonder beyond words.

"Let her have all of it—" The words scraped her throat. Acorn straightened, and she knew he was calling Lionleaper. For a moment Bearling looked at her, then he emptied the packet into the cup, took another and stirred it in.

It was Acorn who lifted Speedwell's head so that Bearling could hold the bowl to her lips. Lionleaper was weeping beside her, with Spark, eyes wide and uncomprehending, cradled in his arms. But Goodtree felt as if she had been turned to stone. She had given in, but she could not help her daughter die. . . . Then she heard Speedwell's breathing grow softer and, panicking, reached for her hand.

**Love Spark for me—teach him to make trees grow. . . . ** Those midnight eyes—Stormlight's eyes—were smiling. For a moment Goodtree felt her love, and wonder at the release from pain. Then, as if she had seen something that surprised her, Speedwell sighed.

It was only when the wolves began their howling that Goodtree realized that her daughter was not looking at anything anymore.

"That was not the herb," said Bearling. "Too quick. She chose her time."

"She chose . . . " Goodtree's voice cracked as she echoed him. "Lionleaper, gather the tribe. When we have howled for her we will move southward, to the Golden Valley beyond the plains."

Egaruk the Bear clung to the whitebark tree, gazing out over the plain. The wind blew chill from the northlands, flattening the dry grass like a wolf's coat stroked by a strong hand. Soon there would be snow. Somewhere out there, the Wolfriders were moving. He hoped they would reach their valley before it fell. He thought they would make it. Goodtree had looked like a winter-blasted oak when they parted, but surely she would put forth new leaves when the world finally turned toward spring.

The People had praised him for making the Woods Demons go away, and gave him the best they had, but Egaruk did not think that he would live to see another turning. Individuals died, but the tribe lived on. If only this one season remained to him, then he must use it to leave a memory of wonder to temper the fear.

He lifted his face to the silver sky, listening for spirit songs, but what he heard was the distant howling of wolves.

The Long Hunt

by Len Wein and William Rotsler

A chill gust of autumn wind sent the stiff red leaves tumbling around Mantricker's boots. He squinted at the solemn gray sky, virtually featureless yet somehow threatening, and knew it would not be long until the snow came, thick with all its isolation and danger.

Mantricker wrapped his heavy cloak tighter about his throat and hunched against another swirling attack of dead leaves as he slanted toward Bowmaker's shelter, snuggled close against the base of the Father Tree. There was a scent of dying dreamberries in the air, of smoke and sweet decay.

The elfin warrior liked the changing of the seasons, with their attendant dramatic skies and ever-changing colors. Summer was a pleasant time, but the skies were most often a dull blue bowl. Still, the worst was what the skies were now, lumpen gray, a looming threat against tomorrow.

"Ho, Bowmaker!" called Mantricker.

"Ah! Come in, my boy," came the warm reply. "Come and share my fire."

Mantricker ducked through the hide-covered portal and straightened up, his sensitive nostrils assailed by the heavy smell of wood and oils, of resins and a hardwood fire. Bowmaker was holding up an unstrung bow still gleaming with polishing oil.

"Look," said the older elf proudly, "I'm almost finished with the new bow for Woodtrack. And just in time, eh?"

Mantricker was full of praise, for the bow was indeed a work of art, far more useful, he thought, than any pot or necklace. "Is that the wood Brownseed brought from the far valley?" asked Mantricker.

"Yes, yes, she definitely has an eye for it." The older elf nodded. "As Watersheen did in the long ago."

"Fine wood, the finest wood could Watersheen find," the older elf continued, muttering, rubbing at the polished wood with a distant look. Finally he shook himself and smiled at Mantricker a bit sheepishly. "Good mates are not as hard to find as good woodhunters, you know, and Watersheen was a fine mate indeed."

Mantricker nodded too, for it had been Watersheen who had taught him how to hold the bow, to hold the shaft, to bring it back until the feather tickled his nose, to sight on the bight of straw, then let the arrow fly straight and true.

"Yes, well, what brings you here, Mantricker?" asked Bowmaker gently, still somewhat embarrassed. "Don't tell me you've lost that latest bow I made you."

"No, I learned my lesson after I lost the last two," answered Mantricker sheepishly, "but I do need a new bowstring, and an extra as well, if you can spare one."

"Ah, yes, of course. The winter hunts." The old elf heaved himself to his feet and shuffled to a bench heaped with bags and boxes. He rummaged around, squinted nearsightedly at Mantricker again, measuring him, then pulled two narrow rolls from a leather bag. The rolls trickled out into seasoned bowstrings and Mantricker smiled.

"Ah, from the hide of the longmane, right?" asked Mantricker.

"Yes, the one you and Longreach brought in last spring. A useful animal, the longmane." Bowmaker nodded thoughtfully. "So much of him one can use . . . and so pretty, too. The meat is tough, but then that is what stew pots are for, eh?"

Bowmaker tossed the young elf his bowstrings. "I am still in your debt, Mantricker, so use them for the good."

As Mantricker left Bowmaker's burrow, Woodtrack waved to him from the burl of a nearby fallen oak where he was selecting arrows, aided by his daughter, Fairfeather. Near them, Moondance called out to Mantricker, but the wind swept away her words. Mantricker trotted over to the eager young huntress. "I said we should leave before the sun rises much higher," she repeated. Mantricker agreed.

From the corner of his eye, Mantricker spied a sudden movement and looked between two tall oaks, to where Thornflower was cutting thongs from a deer hide. Though she seemed preoccupied now, Mantricker could not escape the feeling she had been watching him. This made the young elf uncomfortable, as he had yet to decide his true feelings toward her. For weeks now, Mantricker had been trying to ignore Thornflower, but he was finding it more and more difficult.

And yet, how she irritated him. At council, she constantly argued and contradicted Mantricker. He was convinced she did it intentionally, if only to annoy him. Yet outside of the council fires she ignored him, barely nodding if they passed. He could not understand why the other males his age considered her so desirable and actively pursued her. Oh, Thornflower was attractive enough, Mantricker admitted, certainly not ugly by any standard, but he had more important matters to concern him now.

Still muttering, Mantricker returned to his burrow and shrugged into his heavy winter coat, leaving it open, for it was not yet that cold. His pack and his weapons were ready. He strung a new line to his bow and stuffed the spare into his pack. Then, slinging the bow and his quiver across his back, the heavily laden young elf stepped outside. For a moment he felt vaguely lost. He had no female to bid farewell, to joke with or cry with. Shrugging off these unfamiliar feelings philosophically, Mantricker trudged up toward Old Crone Rock, and the hunters' rendezvous.

"Good hunting," said Suncatcher as Mantricker passed. She was smiling, twirling the ends of her long hair, the color of polished maple wood.

The young chief smiled briefly in reply, for Suncatcher had the air of a wood spirit about her: here now, yet gone in a heartbeat. He continued up to the rock where the other hunters waited.

Mantricker found young Windsong there, bright and eager as always, her long hair in a braid under a red-fox cap, anxious to begin her second hunt. Behind her, Mantricker observed Woodtrack coming, his new bow strung and tight across his back, his ever-present daughter following behind him, taking long strides in an effort to keep up. Moondance was still adjusting her belts of equipment as she strode up to the others. "Where's Dreamwalker?" she asked.

Mantricker tilted his head back toward the Holt. A slender elf was hunched down talking to a wolf, trying to explain that this was that rarest kind of hunt, where the scent of a wolf would vacate the countryside. The great gray creature was sullen but accepting, and Dreamwalker was soon striding up the hill, shrugging his narrow shoulders to adjust his pack.

Assembled now, the hunters turned without another word and started climbing the hill, Mantricker first, then Dreamwalker and Windsong, followed by Woodtrack and Moondance. Fairfeather stood by the rock, watching them go, her small body hunched into the wind. At the tree line they glanced back for an instant, then they turned onto the trail and were quickly gone.

The hunters went on without a word. It would be a hard climb to the saddle of the ridge, then down into the nameless valley beyond, where game abounded, where there was a hot spring and a sheltered copse where snow would not smother the grass.

None of the hunters noticed the lumbering figures who

were watching them depart from the shadows. If one of them had, he would have instantly sounded an alarm.

For the unexpected appearance of humans in the wood had never been cause for anything but trouble.

Their leader was a big man, far larger than the others, even dirtier and more hairy. His cold eyes, under deep brows, watched from a sheltered rock ridge as the hunting party climbed out of sight. His name was Ugarth.

Beside him, another of the human interlopers suddenly started and reeled back, his eyes wide and terrified as they stared at a fat spider casually scuttling along the rock. He recovered quickly and, with a hoarse cry, smashed a stone ax down on the hapless spider, splattering it.

The leader snarled, thrust himself back from the rock ridge, and slammed the spider-killer in the chest. "Quiet, fool!" he snarled in a harsh whisper, even as he whirled back to study his target, glancing down at the vast, sprawling tree below them to see if they had been heard.

"But, Ugarth," protested the spider-smasher, "it was one of *them,* the eight-limbed demonspawn!"

"Someday your cowardice will be the death of you, Ahrah," snapped the leader. "Now be silent! We must be still until the hunting party is out of sight. They must not hear us."

Now another big man crept up to where Ugarth was kneeling. "Will there be food, Ugarth?" he whispered eagerly. Then, without waiting for an answer, "Of course there will be food. Look at how many of those vermin there are! They will have much food. I'm sure of it. Do you think they'll have *much* food, Ugarth?"

"Shut up, Kordo. You're as bad as Ahrah!" hissed Ugarth. "When the moment is right, we will know all. Until then, we will wait."

Now a woman slithered close, her furs matted and dirty. "Where do we go when we are done here, Ugarth?" she whispered fearfully, pulling her filthy furs closer about her throat. "Surely not back to the valley of Yurthor? Surely not there? They would kill us there, Ugarth. They would kill *me* there! It was not my fault, Ugarth. You know that. The child just cried *all* the time, *all the time!*"

"Will you all just be silent?" Ugarth thrust the woman back angrily and they settled into a grumbling group of almost a dozen humans, homeless nomads, unaware of their stench, suspicious and afraid.

Ugarth watched the doings around the Father Tree gloomily, waiting for the sun to complete its long crawl across the sky. There would be food here, of that much he was certain, but the clothing of these forest demons would be too small, their weapons too complex and puny.

But there might also be slaves to be found here, and there were those over in the Washeen Valley who needed slaves. They didn't care for the forest demons much— nobody did, as they were more trouble than they were worth. But at the very least, these strange, small, forest dwellers might serve well as a sacrifice to the humans' arbitrary gods.

By the time the elfin hunters reached the top of the ridge, there were snow flurries blowing about them. They went quickly down into the northern valley beyond. Already the fur on the few animals they glimpsed was thicker. There were thin transparent sheets of ice crusting the surface on small pools that were sheltered from the light. Reluctantly, Mantricker finally fastened his coat.

They had not visited this valley since the previous winter, but they knew where the cave was, halfway toward the far side, in an island of rock thrusting up through the pines.

The elves reached their destination before sunset and, as the first of the two moons began to rise, Mantricker hurried out to set a few traps. Dreamwalker and Windsong set up camp as Moondance gathered firewood, and Woodtrack, with his new bow, went in search of dinner.

It was a rich valley, almost untouched. As far as Mantricker knew, the only ones to ever hunt here had been elves the previous winter. There was no sign of humans, and human sign was easy to find, as they left bones and trash all around their campsites—even an occasional body.

Mantricker moved softly along the stream, circling around so as not to backtrack, and at last returned to the cave. He helped Windsong put a sewn skin curtain across the cave mouth to hold in the heat. At length, when Woodtrack returned with a deer haunch, Mantricker and Moondance went back out with him to retrieve the rest of the carcass.

"It is going to be a good hunt," said Woodtrack, and everyone agreed.

Back on the rise above the Holt, the nomads found they were too cold and too impatient to wait for dawn. Below they could see warm campfires and the small people eating. Rumblings in Ugarth's own stomach convinced him it was time to take action. Slowly, clumsily, the nomads crept down from their hiding place, and it was only the snapping and crackling of the elves' own fires that kept them from being heard.

The humans came from downwind, for they were aware of the wolves, and they had their long spears ready. Ugarth knew that once a wolf leapt at him, if he was swift enough and did not let fear guide his feet, he could use the animal's own speed to impale it.

Suddenly a young female elf emerged directly in front of them from a tangle of brush they hardly recognized as a shelter, thinking it a windfall. She whirled, but before she could raise an alarm, Ugarth struck her in the head to silence her. She fell limply to the ground, but still the silence was not long-lived. Even as Ugarth turned, a low growling filled the air, and he found three wolves charging straight at him, snarling, ferocious.

The lead wolf, sleek, gray, leapt and Ugarth caught her on the point of his spear, its butt wedged solidly in the dirt. The wolf was carried upward, snarling, whining, then slid partway down the spear and died. Another wolf was on Ugarth before he could free his spear, but the animal's fangs only caught a trailing edge of the nomad's dirty robe and Ugarth's stone ax crashed down heavily on its head.

All around Ugarth were cries of fear and pain, the screams of females, the shrieks of children. An arrow sank deep into the chest of a nomad standing right beside Ugarth, and the startled wanderer coughed, fell limply to his knees, then forward onto his slack face, driving the arrow deeper. Ugarth saw a slender elf, an old one, standing outside a crude shelter beside the vast tree, calmly loosing arrows.

Heavyset Orach gasped as an arrow sliced through his upper arm. As a sleek shaft penetrated his thigh, timid Sumra cried out, tumbling into a fire, then scrambling in panic to get out. A young elf ran from the shelter of the Father Tree and crashed a thick pot across the back of Sumra's head. He moaned once, collapsed, and lay still.

Ugarth ducked behind a tree, then heard an arrow rip away the bark beside his head. Startled, he ran gasping to yet another tree. Before him, a pale figure rose up as if from nowhere. Reflexively, he struck it down. Across the clearing, a well-kept burrow suddenly burst into flame and the arachnophobic Ahrah ran out, patting at his robe and carrying a bag. He grinned briefly at Ugarth and ran off.

Ducking again, the brawny human leader raced between two trees. He could see the aging bowman clearly now, and also noticed that fat Urga was down, sprawled on his side, his hands clutching at an arrow buried deep in his middle. Ugarth charged at the bowman, uttering a fierce cry. But, rather than terrifying the old elf, the sound merely warned him. He swung toward Ugarth, gracefully pulling back another arrow.

Unable to check his headlong lunge, Ugarth instead tripped over a jutting root, the hard-swung blow from his battle-ax coming down a full foot before the slender bowman. Still, Ugarth's rolling momentum carried him forward, to crash into the elfin archer, bowling him over. Together they struck the side of the archer's shelter, collapsing it, their momentum carrying them inside. Still struggling, Ugarth clawed at the neck of the slender bowman, then savagely wrenched the old elf's head to one side. There was a sickening snapping sound, and the old elf went slack.

Ugarth released the elf, and the body dropped to the dirt like a sack of loose meat. Still, to be certain, Ugarth recovered his ax and struck the limp body a few more blows before he stepped back outside. Two females and a male elf lay motionless nearby, as did a wolf and an elfin cub.

Now Ugarth heard the snarling of other wolves and turned to peer at the forest. The remaining elves were scattering into the underbrush, their retreat rear-guarded by a line of snarling, mad-eyed wolves. The elves were mostly limping, or carrying wounded. Realizing pursuit would prove more dangerous than productive, Ugarth shouted at his men to let them go.

"Take whatever you can find of value from these hovels before they all burn!" he cried. Then he went back to examine the remains of the elf-archer's shelter.

There wasn't much left intact. Oh, there were several of those strange small bows such as the old elf had wielded, but Ugarth had learned long ago that one had to have a talent for this weapon. His arrows were more likely to hit an innocent bystander than any target.

No, either you have a talent for these things, or you do not, he thought. *My talent is my ax, and my leadership. I*

*was born to be leader because I can destroy anyone who
dares defy me. I know it and they know it. And that is good.*

Ugarth flung aside an artfully crafted bow and instead
gathered up what little food he found, stuffing it in a
leather bag. Then he went to check among the wounded
for those who might still be suitable for slaves. Or
sacrifice.

Thornflower's head throbbed as if a boulder had
bounced from it. She didn't want to open her eyes against
the fierce brightness. She felt cold, stiff, and sore everywhere. The sounds penetrated first: moaning and harsh
laughter, harshly shouted orders, and pitiful cries.

From the corner of one tightly slitted eye, Thornflower
saw that the humans had been the victors. They were all
over the Holt, great hairy, smelly creatures covered in
moldy old furs and sweat.

Thornflower attempted to move and found her hands
were bound behind her with a stout leather thong. So
instead she feigned unconsciousness and inventoried her
surroundings.

Near her, Longfang lay dead, her dark fur matted with
blood. It would be twenty long steps to the Father Tree,
another thirty to the shelter of the woods. Brownseed lay
on her back nearby, unmoving.

Now slowly, very slowly, Thornflower turned her head
the other way. She saw Bowmaker's feet. His shelter was
smoking, but not yet ablaze. Two of the humans also lay
nearby, unmoving. Another moved, but ineffectually,
needing help, knowing a bad death was not far off. Good.
At least the other Wolfriders had not sold their lives
cheaply. Her eyes alone moving now, Thornflower saw
old Rivertrail alive, her own arms bound behind her. For
an instant Rivertrail's glance caught Thornflower's own.
Then the older she-elf turned her gaze away, her eyes
gesturing urgently for Thornflower's gaze to follow.

Slowly Thornflower peered in the direction Rivertrail

had indicated. The humans, what remained of them, were eating. Gorging themselves on the winter's food the Wolfriders had worked so hard to put away. Two, four, six, seven in all. A woman, too, and she was laughing.

Slowly, almost imperceptibly, Thornflower began to move, to edge back from the spot where she lay. Over what seemed an eternity, she had moved several feet toward the clearing's edge. Then, unexpectedly, she backed up against something she could not recognize, started to work her way around it.

And was stunned when it suddenly kicked her painfully in the ribs.

A human stood over her, the unwashed Ahrah, leering down at her with smug confidence. "Going somewhere, are you?" He laughed cruelly. Thornflower could not understand his words, but even a fool could understand their meaning.

Beyond Ahrah lay Suncatcher, also bound, with a smear of dried blood in the hair above her ear. Her eyes were wide, staring questioningly at Thornflower, who found somewhere inside her an old worn smile and used it.

"Keep watch," she said. "The others will be back soon."

And Ahrah kicked her again, though not hard.

One of the humans, the biggest of them all, got up and walked over, wiping his brutish face on his furs. He studied the two female captives quietly. Suncatcher, who was young and still somewhat unsure, tried to look defiant. Thornflower was impenetrable.

"Good. They will fetch a fine price," Ugarth said. "We leave soon."

He glanced over to where Kordo and Oggula were lashing together a travois from two poles they had ripped from one of the shelters. Sumra was tying layers of bear robes to it. Ugarth told Ahrah to take the two young female captives over and rig a way for them to pull the travois.

Thornflower realized she and Suncatcher were not to be killed, but perhaps a worse fate awaited them.

At dawn Mantricker made a circuit of his traps, emptying and resetting them. One had been tripped, the bait stolen, and triumphant pawprints led off into the underbrush.

"Good for you, wily fox," Mantricker said with a wry smile.

Returning to the cave camp, he helped prepare the hides and meat, then went out with Woodtrack to lie in wait along a deer trail.

At dusk the elves' bows thrummed and two proud bucks lunged into the air, arrows buried in their hearts. The two hunters made a quick drag from the trunks of young trees and carried their prey back to the cave through a light snow. They were harvesting the hides when Fairfeather thrust aside the hide curtain, white and gasping.

"Humans!" she said, and slumped to her knees, exhausted.

Mantricker's mouth was set in a grim, hard line as he viewed the ruins of the Holt. The bodies of the humans had been laboriously pulled to a freshly dug pit, to be burned. The bodies of the slain elves and their wolf-friends had been laid across the backs of the surviving wolves, then carried off into the forest's darkness to become part of their spirit and their blood forever. Woodtrack was comforting his frightened daughter. Dreamwalker trotted up, snugging a pack into place.

"Ready," he said, joining Longreach and Treetop.

Mantricker turned to Rivertrail. "Two only? Thornflower and Suncatcher?" he asked. "No cubs? They sometimes take cubs."

The old she-elf shook her head, her face wet with angry tears. "No, the two is all. It seems I was too old for them to even bother with me."

"All right, then," Mantricker snapped. Woodtrack patted the old she-elf on the shoulder and then picked up his two spears. "The trail leads that way," Mantricker said, cocking his head in the indicated direction. The wolves leapt to their feet, tongues lolling. Longfang's mournful mate, Bentclaw, growled.

Rivertrail watched them go until she could see them no longer. They were heading toward the pass the elves called the Shield of Arrows, where the stories said the elf-chief Skyfire had once held the high, narrow pass against a relentless enemy.

"It is growing colder," she said.

But no one responded.

The travois was heavy and awkward to maneuver on the trail as it climbed. The humans poked at the two elfin females to prod them along, but occasionally, reluctantly, they helped the elves pull the travois through the roughest areas. Thornflower's head still throbbed. Suncatcher was young and not terribly strong. Neither was wearing her warmest clothes, and the snowfall had increased.

"I cannot feel my fingers," said Suncatcher, and Thornflower nodded.

"Watch your hands as you work," the older elf warned her.

"My feet are numb, too," added Suncatcher. "Are we ever going to stop?"

So far Thornflower had seen two reasonable opportunities to escape. Ahrah was careless about letting his blade come within her reach, and the new guard, Kordo, was almost as bad. They seemed to have an air of arrogance about them, feeling these elves posed little danger, being both small and female. The third human guarding them was more suspicious, more alert. But Thornflower did not believe Suncatcher was in any condition to succeed in escaping, and she would not leave without her.

The natural path of escape would be downhill. Not

only was it the swiftest, but it would ultimately lead the two elves back to the Holt. How to bring the fragile Suncatcher with her was Thornflower's problem.

But right now there was the more immediate problem of the cold and snow to be dealt with.

The wind was growing stronger, more harsh. And though the humans had not said where they were going, both the elfin females were fairly confident they knew.

They also knew it would be almost impossible to reach their destination as the snow increased.

"The pass will be closed," Treetop said, holding her hood open a crack. Mantricker nodded. They crested the top of a snow-crusted ridge and saw Bentclaw waiting there for them. As soon as the wolf saw the first of the party approaching, he whirled and went on, the other four-legged members racing along behind.

"What do we do if it's closed and they've passed through?" Dreamwalker asked.

"We go through," Mantricker shouted against the wind.

"But that pass has always been closed from the first snow," Dreamwalker said. "Maybe we should go south, go through the Cleft."

A flurry of new snow brought them all to a temporary halt. At this height, no one wanted to take a blind step. Then they trudged on, following the path determined by the sensitive noses of the wolves; all previous tracks had long since disappeared.

And if the pass *was* closed and the humans *had* gotten through with their prisoners? Mantricker's icy face was grim. Suncatcher was such a sweet child. A woman, yes, but still a child in so many ways. Thornflower, on the other hand, was different, a fierce warrior. Both would be a sad loss to all.

But no more of Mantricker's tribe would die at the hands of the human scavengers! he swore silently.

Many humans were all right, for their kind. They didn't go out of their way to harm elves. In fact, they feared them. But there were these others, these who were cast out even by their own kind. Those who would murder elders and cubs deserved no mercy.

And Mantricker would show them none.

Suncatcher fell near the crest of the rise. Fell and slid and was motionless. Ahrah's hand grasped the arm of Thornflower's jerkin, but she bit his wrist and squirmed out of the travois straps, flinging herself down at Suncatcher. The travois slid back, turned, and flipped, spilling some of the bags.

Suncatcher's skin was cold, but then everyone's skin was cold. Thornflower's hand snaked into her wrappings and felt for her heart. She could sense nothing.

"Suncatcher! *Suncatcher!*" Thornflower shook the young elf as she shouted, but only the snow around them moved.

Ahrah yanked Thornflower to her feet. "Get away!" he shouted. "Get back, you worthless whelp!"

The humans righted the travois and gathered the spilled bags as Thornflower was forced to don new skins against the bitter cold. Already Suncatcher was being lightly covered by snowflakes.

Forcing back her tears, letting her anger build, Thornflower moved as if to once again slip into the harness straps as the last of the spilled bags was being tied into place.

And, at that moment, Ahrah finally came too close.

Thornflower slid the crude blade from the human's belt and slashed at his face to make him back off. The big knife was like a short sword in her hand as she yanked the travois around. Holding the straps, she jumped off the trail to a ledge below, carrying the travois with her. The heavily laden sled shot past Thornflower, hit a rock, slammed sideways and knocked her off her feet, then disappeared down the steep hill with a crunch and a rattle.

Ahrah scrambled down, seized his knife from Thornflower's hand, and knocked off her fur hat. He grabbed her hair and bent back her head, his knife swinging back to begin a deathstroke.

"No, Ahrah! *No!*" shouted Ugarth.

"*Yes!*" Ahrah snarled. "She has cost us *all* our food, all our treasure, everything. All our dead—for *nothing!* I say kill her! And kill her *now!* She's a jinx!"

"And I say no." Ugarth spread his gloved hands. "You kill her, she suffers little and for only a matter of moments. But take her to the valley and she suffers greatly, and for a long time."

Breathing heavily, Ahrah turned his angry gaze from Ugarth to the she-elf and found her glaring defiantly at him. "Pfah!" he growled, and threw her back.

Quickly, Ahrah pulled a thong from his coat and whipped it around her wrists. Then he yanked Thornflower to her feet and shoved her up the cliff to the narrow trail. "Get going," he growled.

Bentclaw was sniffing at Suncatcher's body or they might not have seen it, lying down off the trail as it was, half buried in the snow. The other wolves just stood there, some looking up the trail, others down at the body. It took the hunters only seconds to uncover her. Mantricker stood and stared at Suncatcher's cold blue face for what seemed an eternity. Finally, Woodtrack came back from up the trail and trudged over to the assembled mourners.

"The pass was closed," he said. "I couldn't get through."

"That's it then," murmured Treetop, turning back downtrail.

"In the spring," said Dreamwalker, "in the spring we will track down and slay every one of them."

"Yes," Woodtrack agreed without enthusiasm. "I suppose so, though how we will know by then which . . ."

"I'm going on," said Mantricker quietly. There was a heavy drift of snow on his shoulders and fur cap. "Dreamwalker, may I have your spear for a stick? The rest of you, give me what food you can spare."

"You'll die," Woodtrack said over the wind. "Another loss . . ."

"And perhaps I won't. No one has gone through the pass before because there was never enough need. Now there is.

"Since the passing of my mother Goodtree, I am chief of the Wolfriders," continued Mantricker. "Thornflower is my responsibility. But you are also right. There is no reason to put us all at risk. They will have need of the rest of you back at the Holt. I will carry on alone."

"At least wait until this storm passes," suggested Treetop. "They will be held back by it, too."

Mantricker shrugged. He gave his companions a curt wave, then went up the slippery trail, using the spear to test the snow-capped ground before him, and was soon out of sight. Bentclaw glanced at the other warriors, then leapt off after Mantricker. The other wolves howled, then followed their elf-friends back down the trail.

For an interminable moment, the Wolfriders turned to watch their young chief vanish into the swirling snows, then they turned again and continued their trek back to the Holt. Woodtrack hesitated the longest, then his shoulders slumped and, reluctantly, he followed the others.

As the storm grew worse, the humans huddled together in the niches and cracks of the rock walls in the pass. Thornflower was huddled on the outer side of one crevice and certain she was going to freeze to death. The crevice was really only large enough to hold Ahrah and one other, so the body heat generated by them was small. The wind had died down, but the snow was piling up slowly and there was no sound.

There was nothing, nothing but cold.

Farther back on the trail, Mantricker found a leaning rock that created a small natural cave and then some brush to burn. The fire was very small, but any fire was welcome. Bentclaw lay against Mantricker, panting, his presence a great, warm strength. The wind died as Mantricker chewed some dried meat and thought about Thornflower and what he would do if she was still alive. Or if she wasn't. She could still be back where they had found Suncatcher, he realized, just another mound of drifting snow.

Curse these humans. One way or another, they would have to be taught to leave the Wolfriders—to leave *all* elves—alone.

Ahrah stirred and grunted and Thornflower awoke. She groaned to find she was still among the living. It had been peaceful being dead. The humans rose stiffly in the morning sun, and embraced themselves. They kicked the snow out of the way and waddled into the light.

The sunlight was dazzling. The sky was clear. One moon was up, pale and mottled against the bright blue sky. As Thornflower watched, the humans counted their new dead. There were three more to leave behind without benefit of burial. The bodies were quickly stripped of anything worth carrying and the humans broke trail.

Coming upon the humans' abandoned camp, Mantricker peered into every niche and crevice. Sniffing with distain, Bentclaw ran quickly from corpse to corpse. No Thornflower among the dead.

Mantricker trudged on, probing the thick snow with his spear.

* * *

The neck rope chafed, but Thornflower would not let her captors know it. The wanderers were down from the drifts now and there was only snow in the dark places where the sun had not yet pierced.

"I still say we should have a feast and eat her," said Kordo.

Ugarth grunted dissent. "No, we will *sell* her," he replied, "and then watch them eat her!"

"But . . ."

The argument had been going on since they had stumbled out of the final drift. Thornflower knew that if she could get her hands on a blade and a few unguarded moments, she could sever her wrist bonds and escape. But for the cursed rope about her neck, that is. It was made of thicker hide, woven and stiff. It would not be cut that easily.

"Come on, you she-demon!" Ahrah snapped.

Mantricker saw the valley, lightly covered with snow, and off to the right, a thin line of smoke. Bentclaw sniffed cautiously and started in that direction.

Ugarth and his people attacked the small village at midmorning. They just walked down off the mountain and into the spaces between the huts as if visiting, and began striking down whomever was in their way. Women screamed, children wailed, and men bellowed, but the band of outlaws were merciless.

They lost Raghor to a well-wielded spear and hungry Kordo got a painful burn from a boiling pot. They siezed half-cooked food and gorged themselves. Thornflower stole bits of food, for she, too, was weak from hunger. She felt some pity for the humans lying about wounded. But they were, after all, humans, and should have rid themselves of this band long ago.

"Tonight," Ugarth bellowed, waving a pig's leg over his head, "tonight, our captive will provide entertainment!"

There was a rush of laughter and some sporadic yelling. Someone said something to Ugarth, who answered in a hoarse whisper, then they all whispered to one another and glanced over at Thornflower, who stood in the firelight, looking at them impassively. They laughed again, and the elfin warrior felt her heart sink.

I know I can get someone's knife, she thought, *and then some of these filthy five-fingers shall perish with me.*

Mantricker put his hand on Bentclaw's bristling fur and kept him down. **Wait,** he sent to his wolf-friend. **I know you want vengeance, but we must wait.**

They slipped closer through the brush, leaving a noticeable trail in the thin snow, which could not be helped. The village was before them. One hut was burnt, another was still smoking but mostly intact. There was no Thornflower in sight.

Maybe she *was* up in the pass, lost and gone.

He froze and he felt the muscles of his wolf-friend tense. *Thornflower!* She had been hidden by the smoking hut. Two of the hairy, hulking creatures took her inside, and after a few moments came out alone.

Grinning now, Mantricker patted Bentclaw, and the two began to creep closer.

Thornflower was tied to the hut's center post by the neck rope, her wrists and ankles bound around the post. She was angry, tired, cold, and bored. The hut stank from the fire, and she had no idea of what the night would hold for her, but she was certain she wouldn't like it.

Suddenly her sensitive ears picked up an unfamiliar noise and she noticed a familiar, comforting smell. *Wolf!*

Mantricker sent, **Greetings, Thornflower. Are you through playing with these wretched humans?**

Mantricker! And is that Bentclaw with you?

Careful now. I'm coming in. Can anyone see into this hut?

Thornflower glanced surreptitiously around each side of the post, out through the broken doorway and the section of still-smoking wall. **Only one of them, and he appears to be having a love affair with a roast pig.**

Seconds later, a sleek shadow leapt effortlessly over the open section of burnt wall, and bristling hair tickled Thornflower's leg.

Bentclaw, dear Bentclaw! she sent. **I am so sorry about Longfang. She was a fine, brave wolf. She will be missed.** The wolf panted, staring out the door, ears forward, body on alert.

A sharp blade began cutting through the leather thongs that bound Thornflower, and Mantricker grinned. The two young elves gazed into each other's eyes.

And, suddenly, everything stopped.

Bentclaw whimpered softly.

Recognition.

The two elves groaned.

No, she sent. **Not you. Not now.**

It can't be, sent Mantricker in reply.

But it was there. They couldn't deny it.

Recognition was something every elf desired and all elves feared. It was the Recognition of the other half of you, of your lifemate, Recognition of the father of your children and the mother of your heirs. Recognition was natural for some, awesome for others. Right now, it was just damned inconvenient.

Some faced Recognition gracefully, accepted it, grew with it. For others, it solved all problems. But for some it was a strange kind of slavery, a bonding to an undesired love. All knew Recognition was inevitable, all bowed to their relentless destiny, for all attempts to deny Recognition, to fight it, had come to an unpleasant end.

But *her—!*

Him!

No, please, not that, not *now!*

Why now?

Suddenly Bentclaw growled low, and Mantricker

roused himself from his momentary stupor as he realized there were voices drawing near.

"I still say we should sell her to those River People!" Ugarth said.

They lumbered through the door after Ugarth, three large, hairy humans. Thornflower glanced back to where Mantricker had stood but an instant before; both he and his wolf-friend were long since gone. Thornflower struggled to regain her poise, but a great chill wind had just ruffled her mind. She wrinkled her nose. It was bad enough outside, but in the close confines of the hut the sheer stench of the humans was hard to take.

"When you said she'd entertain us, I thought you meant the fire," said Sumra, who was still limping.

"Well, I'm saving her for the River People, or maybe that tribe that killed Urga last summer. They had good food."

The argument continued as the humans untied Thornflower, never noticing that the thongs that bound her were already partly cut through. The she-elf had a glimpse of Bentclaw's dark fur rising from the brush outside the hut and a curving glint off what must have been Mantricker's bow.

Now the humans dragged Thornflower outside. The sun had almost completely set now and one of the humans torched a nearby hut to provide light.

And suddenly there he stood before her, great, hairy, and grinning maliciously. The one they called Huk had won the draw for the right to fight the diminutive elfin warrior. He thought this was all great fun. So did all the others.

All that is, of course, except Thornflower.

Roughly, Ugarth handled the startled she-elf a hard-wood pole, which was roughly as tall as she was. Thornflower noticed that Huk had one as well, only his staff was much longer, as long as he was tall. *Human humor,* thought Thornflower. Now they cut away her remaining wrist and leg bonds, and lifted off the neck rope. Thornflower wanted desperately to rub at the irritating chafe marks, but restrained herself.

"Remember, do not kill her," Ugarth reminded Huk. "We won't get nearly as much for her if you do." He made a great show of starting the face-off between the two combatants, then stepped back into the semicircle of shouting humans.

You would think that they'd get tired of this sort of thing, thought Thornflower. She felt the heft of her staff as she watched her opponent's feet. *But Mantricker, why Mantricker? that egotistical dolt!* The human was the sort who liked quick, easy victories, she quickly realized. *He'll attempt to rush me, hoping to use his size and reach to his advantage. No, Recognition* must *be wrong this time*!

Uttering a fearsome cry, Huk charged, the staff held at one end like a club. Thornflower did not flee. Instead she ran straight at her foe, dropped to one knee, and thrust her staff between his legs. Unable to halt his charge, Huk stumbled, tumbling end over end, his staff flying out of his reach, until he crashed headlong into a stump.

There was silence. It had all happened so fast. Then Oggula roared and stepped forward. "Demon! Demon!" he cried.

Oggula drew back his arm, preparing to hurl his spear at her. He roared again, and an arrow suddenly sprouted from his breast. For an instant, Oggula stared at the small shaft uncomprehendingly, then the spear fell from his limp fingers and he toppled to one side.

Now the other humans drew back in horror. Ugarth stared at Oggula's body. An *arrow!* An elfin arrow? He had not seen it strike. Suddenly it was just there.

This cursed elf-woman has to be a demon, he thought, *and you can kill them. But not in the usual ways.*

Why had she not struck them down with her magic arrows before? he wondered. At the village? In the pass? Why had she not slain them all before? What did she want here in the valley of the humans?

"Seize her!" Ugarth suddenly bellowed.

But no one moved, not until he beat at their backs with the haft of his spear.

At Ugarth's command, they bound the struggling Thornflower in the center of the clearing. When she winced at the tight bonds and made a small moaning sound, another arrow streaked across the fire and into the lower back of Forog, who screamed and sank to his knees.

They stayed awake all night, all of them, with Forog pleading for help at Thornflower's feet. At last, just before dawn, he grew quiet, then groaned no more.

It was a very jumpy band of humans who took to the trail the next morning. They proceeded slowly, approaching every dark patch of forest carefully, fearfully. Thornflower was in their midst, still bound, her chin up, covering her fear with an icy facade.

They believe me a demon now, she thought, *and they might decide to rid themselves of me the easy way.*

But, to Thornflower's relief, nothing happened all day. She could still smell the faint aroma of wolf, but she doubted the humans could. Their senses seemed dulled somehow. *He's out there. My fated mate! My lifemate! I simply cannot believe this!*

By late afternoon, the nomads were more relaxed and didn't stay grouped around her. Kordo lingered a bit to gather some nuts he'd noticed scattered on the ground, then hurried to catch up. He'd gone only a few steps before he paused, his eyes wide, jaw slack. There, lying by the trail, was a rawhide bag from which jutted a haunch of fresh meat. Realization dawning, Kordo uttered a squeal of sheer delight and stepped off the trail to claim it.

The others didn't even miss Kordo at first. Like lice, Kordo had simply always been there. When Kordo finally was missed, Ahrah was chosen to backtrack a few yards down the trail to find him. Bored after walking several yards, he squatted on his haunches for a while, watchfully waiting. Toward dusk he finally gave up and trotted back to the others to report Kordo's disappearance.

Those remaining made camp on a cliff near the river. They lit an unusually large fire and tied Thornflower near it. Nobody spoke much, but all eyes kept darting surreptitiously back to the she-elf, who remained as impassive as she could. In those moments when she caught them watching, the humans quickly averted their gaze, to stare instead into the darkness. At length, the camp quieted, until there were only the sounds of snoring and night owls and the crackle of the fire.

Then, suddenly, Ahrah jerked to his feet with a loud, incoherent scream. Standing on his toes now, the brutish figure wiped desperately at his body with jerky, frightened movements. As if dancing insanely, Ahrah staggered closer to the fire and everyone could see that his body was spotted with great, dark spiders.

Now Ahrah ran, blindly, screaming. One human woman tried to stop him, but he knocked her aside and blundered off into the brush. They heard a gurgling scream, a scraping of small rocks, then a sickening splash.

Slowly, everyone turned to peer at Thornflower.

"Somehow she knew Ahrah hated the crawly things," the woman said accusingly, rising once more to her feet. For an instant, Ugarth put his hand on his knife, then he glanced into the darkness and thought of what might be waiting there, and quietly changed his mind.

That night, none of the humans slept, and before dawn Ugarth had them up and on the trail. "The River People must not know about this," he muttered to himself, again and again. "Let them find out the worst for themselves."

Ruhr was younger than the rest, and Ugarth's son. He was constantly hungry and kept stepping off the trail to gather nuts. Ugarth feared for him and put Ruhr in charge of holding on to the elf-woman's neck rope.

When Grah, in the rear, screamed and fell, an arrow through his neck, Ruhr whirled and dropped the rope. Instantly, Thornflower leapt for the brush, but Ugarth stepped on the trailing rope and brought the she-elf up short with a strangled cry.

Ugarth slapped Ruhr across the face and angrily handed him the rope, even before he went back to strip the late Grah of his few valuables.

Now the nomads stretched out along the trail, each more nervous than usual about being in close contact with someone who might die at any moment.

Softly, barely perceptibly, Thornflower began to whisper to Ruhr about the Great Revenger. Her command of the human tongue was weak, but there were a few words in common, and signing helped.

The Great Revenger, Ruhr quickly discovered, was not a protector of the elves, for he lived on a mountaintop and thought about where the stars should be and moved them along at night. He thought about which of the forest animals should be sacrificed to the creatures that roamed the darkness. The Great Revenger, Thornflower haltingly explained, was the one who shaped the moons and made the night flowers open.

But during the day, the Great Protector was free to help the elves, who were his special friends. It might take him a while to find out his elf-friends were in trouble, then to get there to help, but in the end he always came.

"Always?" whispered Ruhr.

"Always." Thornflower smiled.

At length, the wanderers came to a place where the cliff had fallen and the water of the river was not too far away. "Agar, help Huk get some water," Ugarth ordered.

Huk, who was still limping and still seemed a bit confused, nodded and started down. Agar hesitated.

"Ugarth, you know I hate the water," protested Agar. "I . . . I am afraid of it. The water spirits hate me."

"I am in no mood to argue," growled Ugarth. "Just do as you are told." Ugarth hated always having to argue with his people to get them to obey.

Agar's shoulders slumped and he followed Huk down through a path that led between tumbled rock and trees that bent at odd angles. Near the bottom of the path, Huk coughed and staggered, his hand outstretched as if seeking purchase.

"Huk—!"

The big man turned and Agar saw the small arrow jutting from Huk's side. Suddenly another blossomed in Huk's throat and he staggered back, collapsing in a lifeless heap. Agar screamed and turned, racing hysterically up the rocky slope.

Suddenly a tree before him rustled and whooshed as it snapped erect, and Agar's feet were swept from under him. He narrowly missed cracking his head on the rocks as he swung upside down from the crude snare, his feet tightly bound.

There came an angry whispering in his ear, then a violent push, and Agar found himself swinging out over the depths of the treacherous water. Then somebody cut the other end of the rope from which he dangled and he was falling, screaming, into the cold, wet arms of the river spirits. Agar tried to kick back to the surface but his feet were still tied, and the river mud quickly clogged his ears and mouth.

Mantricker watched from the brush as the humans stared at the spot where the rope still disappeared into the water. The bubbles had stopped rising from the depths long before the humans reached the water's edge. Mantricker felt no remorse, no guilt. He hardly even felt much anger. He had a job to do, that was all.

Of all the humans he had ever met, these were by far the worst. He felt that even the humans he had known would be afraid of these and hate them. They were making much of these new deaths because they were directly touched by them, but they had made little of the deaths of others, either human or elf.

Finally, with a roar and a great waving of arms, the humans charged back up the bank. Mantricker noted with contempt that they hadn't even bothered to bury their wet comrade, no more than they had bothered with the others. He patted Bentclaw, who crouched beside him, watching it all with ears up and tongue lolling.

Now the humans moved on quickly, casting fearful looks behind them, having no way of knowing that Mantricker was already well ahead. They crowded around Thornflower, as if guarding or perhaps even protecting her, but Mantricker knew that they merely huddled with fear.

The part of him that had been shocked by Recognition was calm now. There was no use fighting it, both he and Thornflower knew it was there. Of all the elves on this world of two moons, they two had been selected for one another. But why now, when it could easily cloud their thinking? Why not earlier? They had known each other for some time, but there had been no spark between them before, barely even civility.

Mantricker thought of those who had known Recognition even as cubs and had grown with it. He remembered Silverknife and Sunsong, old and white-haired now, who had shared what Recognition had brought seemingly forever. It came when it came and you bowed to it. Better than those who had not yet found Recognition, or worse, those who talked themselves into believing they had when all could see that they had not.

Don't fight it, survive it. Survive this day, in this place, and then figure it all out later. *But Thornflower! She hates men, she's rude and contemptuous! How am I supposed to deal with this?*

The humans came to a low range of hills, where a long-trod path cut into a pass next to a burbling stream. They made camp, but their actions were different this night. More purposeful, more grim, and far more frightened. They argued among themselves easily, over trifles.

The big leader set a pair of his fellows to finding stout limbs or logs and then dragging them into camp before it got too dark.

Mantricker made the sound of the owl-who-likes-berries and a small smile came to Thornflower's lips.

He is out there. But he is only one against so many!

Elfin bows are good, she thought, *but their range is a little on the short side. To use his well, Mantricker will have to get into close range, and then they may see him.*

In point of fact, Mantricker did not have many arrows left. He had not had the opportunity to recover his shafts from his targets. He wanted to save those he had remaining, and tried to think of other ways to deal with his foes. Silently, Mantricker and Bentclaw circled the camp, laying traps.

But, as darkness fell, none of the humans had ventured out beyond the safety of the firelight.

The elfin warrior watched as the humans widened a crack in the ground and set a stout limb into the opening, hammered the stake down and braced it with rocks. They tied Thornflower to it, her bound wrists high into the branching, helpless. Mantricker nocked an arrow and waited, alert.

But the odoriferous humans did nothing more, merely bedded down around the fire. They set sentries, but the nearest of them went to sleep almost at once. Mantricker crept closer. Better to release Thornflower as quickly as possible and escape. These were irrational creatures who might decide to kill her in a fit of madness. He sent to Bearclaw, ordering the wolf to stay.

Now Mantricker crept up silently beside the sleeping sentry and tied his feet together with a thong. The human snorted and *humph*ed and settled back into sleep. Mantricker slowly slipped the sentry's stone ax from beneath his arm and cut almost through the leather bindings of the stone.

The sentry who remained awake stood up with a yawn and walked aimlessly around a bit as Mantricker hid behind the sleeping sentry. Suddenly the sleeper threw a burly arm around Mantricker and hugged him close, murmuring something obviously intended to sound romantic. The startled elf found the human's stench almost overpowering.

The conscious sentry frowned and muttered something into the dark. Mantricker snaked up a hand and pinched the sleeper's nostrils shut. The sleeper snorted and stirred and Mantricker slipped from his grasp, melting into a still, dark shape a few feet away.

As Mantricker watched, the dutiful sentry kicked the sleeping one savagely awake. They had a short hissing fight before the wary sentry lumbered back beside Thornflower and sat down. Within moments, the sleeper had gone back to his dreams, undisturbed about either his duty or his fears.

Mantricker watched for some time, and although the wakeful guard's head would often sag in slumber, it always snapped back up again and he stared about him wildly, clutching a hefty cudgel.

From the darkness, the elfin warrior gave Thornflower a reassuring wolf-call, then slipped away to get some sleep himself. He could not free Thornflower without rousing the camp. An arrow from the darkness would eliminate the guard, but not the noise.

It was a long, stiff, cold night for Thornflower. Though it was reassuring to know that Mantricker was out there, so far his actions had only alerted the humans, making any escape less likely.

About midnight, the wind changed, heralding the rise of the second moon, and the scent of the humans came to Thornflower more strongly than before. She simply could not understand them and their curious ways.

Silently, Thornflower studied the human who sat near her. He was tall, like all humans, maybe taller than many.

She believed he was called Morgo, but she was not certain; for the most part, their guttural language was beyond her.

Morgo was hairy, strong, and with sharper eyes than most. He had crude tattoos on his bare arms, a pattern of circles and lines, and a crude depiction of some sort of beast on what she could see of his chest. A thong around his neck held a small bag made of animal hide.

Thornflower had seen the contents of these bags before. A bone, a claw, a feather, a bright stone or two. Sometimes a piece of shaped and sun-dried clay. A tooth or boar tusk, often carved. The combination of these things made no sense, but they seemed to mean something to each of the humans who carried them. She had noticed many of the humans touched their leather bags for reassurance when they woke, or in times of greatest danger.

Thornflower thought about Mantricker for a while. Perhaps the stories of his prowess as a wily warrior were not exaggerated, after all. He had done more thus far against these humans than any other elf she knew could have. He was the one who was free, and therefore the one capable of action. But, even though a prisoner, she would have to find a way to help.

The captive she-elf pondered the possibilities as the two moons sank into the sea of night and the predawn hunting of the forest's smallest creatures began.

Mantricker came awake suddenly. But what had awakened him? Thornflower! Thornflower's voice. Bentclaw was already alert, sniffing, a low growl rumbling in his throat.

In the eastern sky overhead, the low clouds were tinged with a brittle crimson. Mantricker wiped the sleep from his mind and twisted to peer through the sheltering brush.

Thornflower was singing. She faced east, toward where

the sun would soon rise, and she was singing. The song was obviously improvised, though the words were put to a tune usually associated with preparing for the hunt.

"*Oh, rise, great and golden god, rise from the bed of night,*" she sang. "*Cast your smile over the land, over all the creatures before you! Let your vast light cover us all, even to the creatures who crouch in the brush alone, who might hear my voice and wonder.*"

Ugarth yelled as he sat up, but Thornflower continued. "*O great shining orb, create the Great Revenger, for I have prepared the way! Create the Great Revenger who will smight the enemies of the elfin folk!*"

The humans were all sitting now, staring. The sleeping guard awoke with a start, leapt to his bound feet, tripped, fell on his stone ax and broke it. The guard who had been sitting by Thornflower gaped at her until a bellow from Ugarth brought him shakily to his feet.

"*Create the Great Revenger, O mighty golden orb, bring terror and haunting until the—*"

The guard hit her in the face. Thornflower spat out blood and glared at him. The guard took a hesitant step backward, shaking his club at the defiant she-elf.

Mantricker's bowstring went taut, but the guard moved away from Thornflower, scanning both sky and brush. The sun rose in a blinding arc over the distant hills and suddenly Thornflower let out the gathering cry of the wolf.

Instantly, Bentclaw answered and Mantricker joined in. Then he ran, down the hill, out of sight, with Bentclaw bounding along beside him. Mantricker paused for an instant to let out another long, quavering cry. Bentclaw ran ahead, stopped, and let out a howl of his own, an anthem to the rising sun. Between them, they almost appeared to circle the camp, creating a ring of phantom wolves answering one another's howls. Then Thornflower emitted the short, yapping bark that was the mating cry, and all fell silent.

Mantricker peered through the brush. The humans stood in a circle, clubs and knives and axes in hand, even the woman. They faced out from the circle, hunched and fearful. One held a knife to Thornflower's throat.

Slowly, as nothing else happened, the humans relaxed, made food, and gathered up their camp. Thornflower was not fed, but Mantricker did not notice, for he was busy at the edge of the small stream.

Sometime the following morning, Ugarth pointed into the hills. "We are almost home," he said. "It is here we must make the sign."

There were nods, and Ugarth again noted to himself how few comrades he had left. So many now dead, or vanished. Those who remained would return in defeat, but at least they would return. Well, he would return, anyway. And, to Ugarth, that was all that really mattered.

Still, they really should have left these strange small creatures alone.

Now Ugarth pointed at the elf-woman still bound to the post. "She has called upon her gods, called her evil friends, the wolves," he snarled, "but she is still in our hands, helpless."

"Make her the sign," Ugarth's woman cried.

"Yes, let her cries warn them away!" said Oggula.

"Very well, we have spoken!" Ugarth said. "Make ready to move the camp! We return to the valley of Yurthor!"

As the humans gathered up their furs and pots, Ugarth plotted. That the wolves and spirits were out there in the growing morning he was certain. Wolves and wolf-spirits hunted either by day or by night, it didn't matter which. The she-elf had sung to her wolf-gods, or perhaps to the sun-god. But, at night, the sun-god at least was weak. Should they wait until moonrise to make their move?

No. They could be lost in the night, if they had to run.

Ruhr, Ugarth's son, came to him timidly. "Great Father, let us leave this creature here. Unharmed," he muttered hesitantly. "I . . ."

"What?"

"I . . . I know only a few words of their language, Great Father," said Ruhr. "Remember when you gave me that elf-slave when I was not much more than a crawler?"

"Yes? She magicked you and escaped. So?"

"Um, yes, Great Father, but I learned some of her words. This one," said Ruhr, gesturing toward their captive, "this one spoke of a god, or perhaps not a god, but a spirit. The Great Revenger. Something not like us. A protector of the small ones. One who kills and cannot be killed."

Ugarth growled and shook his ax. "Pfah! Anything can be killed!"

"Not spirits, Great Father."

"No, perhaps not spirits," the man agreed, "but anything that can harm us can be killed in turn."

"Yes, Great Father," the boy agreed, though his voice had no conviction. "But I still say we should just leave her."

"Oh, do not worry, my son," Ugarth said grimly, as his dark gaze turned to the small, defiant figure strung up by her wrists. "That is precisely what I intend to do."

Thornflower watched as Bentclaw stepped out on a ridge, then was gone. So they were there, she thought, they were ready.

But so were the humans, ready to leave. Ugarth stepped up before her and faced the small, nervous band.

"We leave now, but we will leave behind a sign, a sign that will tell all that we are not to be trifled with." Without looking, he pointed back at Thornflower. "Aye, we will leave her as a sign, once we have freed her spirit."

There was a murmuring and shifting among the humans, and more than one nervously eyed the brush and rocks around them.

"Orach!" commanded Ugarth impatiently. Orach put down a hide bag and stood before his leader.

"Orach, you were wounded by the elfin spirits, yet survived. So you will have the honor of freeing the creature's spirit." Orach smiled uncomfortably and his slight smirk quickly vanished.

"But, Ugarth," Orach stammered, "she is a demon."

Ugarth snarled, pulled Orach's knife from his belt, and forced the frightened man to take it. "You will do it!" Ugarth ordered. "Blood for blood! Use the arm that is unhurt."

Thornflower suddenly yelped. Yelped, then howled, her head back, the quavering wolf-cry scattering birds in a flurry of wings. A wolf-cry answered her, then came another from elsewhere.

"Quickly, Orach!" Ugarth snarled. "Just do it!"

Orach trembled, his shoulders hunching, afraid of the slender elfin form. What would he free? Night spirits, pale in the sunlight? Swooping, dark, demon creatures that would carry him off? Spiders, like those who came to Ahrah?

Fear drove Orach. Fear of Ugarth, fear of the unknown. He raised his one good arm, hesitated, took a tight grip on the knife.

And screamed as another arrow penetrated his good arm. The knife clattered to the ground as Orach stumbled to his knees, staring with wide, deeply frightened eyes at the shaft that jutted from his biceps. The pain was intense, worse than before, horrible.

Ugarth snarled again and whirled. There was another wolf-cry, then another. The humans began to run. Once one ran, they all ran, all but Ugarth, who bellowed for them to stop. Even Orach staggered to his feet and fled after them, cradling his newly injured arm and moaning.

Thornflower let out a warbling cry of victory, of the kill. Ugarth turned on her, his knife bright in his fist. Their eyes met and Ugarth saw the demon within the elfin figure, the untrammeled spirit, the magical fire.

But still he had to kill her, to dam the flow of fear. He drew back his knife, focused on where her heart should be, but before he could plunge his blade into her chest, there came a horrible sound from behind him.

Once again, Ugarth whirled, staggering, panting, sweat dripping from his brow. "Who—?"

And the creature was there. The Great Revenger his son had spoken of, the guardian spirit of these accursed little people. It rose up from the grass, a demon of sticks and mud, of leaves and muck, part of the earth, and yet nothing the likes of which the earth had ever known.

It made a sound that was both wolf and man, and yet neither. Like both spirit and wind, the creature cried out and moved toward them.

Ugarth turned again, almost falling. His knife slashed at the straps that held her, and Thornflower fell forward. "There! Take her!" he cried. "She's free!"

The demon creature moved, rustling, snapping, tearing its roots loose from the soil and planting them instead in Ugarth's mind.

Stiffly, Thornflower rose and stood like a chieftess, unafraid. Just beyond the nearest hill she could see the terrified humans, frozen in their tracks, staring.

Glaring at Ugarth, but speaking to the shambling demon creature, Thornflower said, "They must learn to leave us alone."

The creature murmured in assent, and Thornflower picked up the knife Orach had dropped. Ugarth stared, his lower lip quivering. His hunched body twisted as if in physical pain. He desperately wanted to flee, but his feet were leaden, rooted to the spot.

Thornflower saw the small bag on the thong around his

neck. With a snakelike movement, she seized the bag, severed the thong, and dumped the contents into the dust, stepping on them, crushing the fragile bits.

Ugarth stared, then his eyes rolled back up into his sloping brow and he collapsed. The humans saw what had occurred.

And they ran.

Bentclaw trotted up and whuffed at Mantricker and Thornflower as they topped the rise. They looked back. On the post where she had been held captive, facing the valley of the humans, hung what remained of Ugarth, who had been transformed into a sign that all could understand.

"Well," sighed Mantricker, "they wanted a sign, and we have given them one. Perhaps now they will learn to leave our kind alone."

"Perhaps," replied Thornflower, "though in my heart I sincerely doubt it."

"It is several days' journey back to the Holt," said Mantricker, "But I think we will make our way unmolested."

"That's good," said Thornflower impatiently. "That's very good. Because, my reluctant lifemate, we have a great deal to discuss along the way."

Five-Finger Exercise

by Esther M. Friesner

Bearclaw would always remember that spring as "the itchy season."

Though the "now" of wolf-thought allowed precious few moments of recollection, it was a time out of the wolf-chief's youth that would live forever in his mind. Even without Longreach's carefully hoarded store of dreamberries to provoke slumbering memory, all that came to pass in those strange weeks on the prowl would occasionally leap into Bearclaw's mind uninvited, with all the glory and beauty—and, yes, all the peril, too—of a skyfire storm.

And yet it had all begun so simply . . .

"Timmorn's Blood, what's wrong with you?" Mantricker demanded, at his patience's end.

Bearclaw stood before his father with downcast eyes, his mouth a thin, sullen line. He didn't dare meet the chief's gaze—not because he feared that the action would be taken as challenge or met with swift punishment, but only because in his inmost heart Bearclaw knew he could not look Mantricker in the face without bursting into wild, foolish laughter.

It had been that way ever since the whitecold season had departed from the Holt. On a day of sweet smells and newgreen beginnings, Bearclaw had roused himself from sleep, shaken himself all over like his wolf-friend Crest, stuck his nose out of his den in the Father Tree, taken a deep breath of springtime and . . . laughed. When

Longreach poked his own sleep-muddled head out of a nearby bole and grumpily inquired what was so funny, Bearclaw only laughed louder, which rousted more elves from slumber.

"Foamsick," said pretty Joyleaf, yawning. "Definitely foamsick, or why is he up and about when sane elves sleep? He'll be running around and biting us, next."

"Only if you ask me nicely." Bearclaw gave her his most wolfish grin. "You might like it."

"Or I might just hand your pelt over to Blackbark for a proper tanning," Joyleaf responded, but she was smiling.

Bearclaw had no idea what possessed him, bantering like that with Joyleaf. So slender and sweetly made, she was the fairest of his tribe's elf-maidens.

Too fair, or so it seemed to him lately. Just looking at her dried his throat to leather. When chance paired them in a hunting party, he was all business, keeping communication between them limited to signs, gestures, and the odd growl. Sending to her was out of the question, to be avoided at all costs even should the circumstances of the hunt require it, though if anyone asked him for a reason he would come up empty-skulled and snappish. Even after the hunt, when silence was no longer necessary and all the other elves were trading good-natured gibes over arrow-shots missed or spear-thrusts bungled, Bearclaw rode as far apart from Joyleaf as he could and still share the same forest path.

All that was changed now, and he still couldn't say why. All that he felt this newgreen dawn was an itch, a powerful itch, a nasty, insinuating, unreasonable itch that ran down his spine and up to the tips of his ears and lodged in his chest until it could only be dislodged by laughter. Powerless, he let the laughter reply to Joyleaf's smile.

"Foamsick," she repeated, ducking back into her den. "Let me know when it kills him," came the last muffled echo of her voice. After that, he was wholly lost to the laughter.

"Well? I am waiting for an answer." Mantricker paced back and forth before his apparently penitent son. "It's not as if what you did was so bad . . . but it might have been! You endangered yourself, and you could have endangered the whole tribe! Briars and deadfall, what possessed you to walk into the humans' camp like that?"

Bearclaw shrugged. Mantricker's rage was hot and very, very real. The bitter lash of his sire's disappointment was enough to shave the edge off of Bearclaw's ungovernable attack of quirky humor.

For a while.

"I thought I'd help you, Father," he said, still talking resolutely to his toes. "Give those five-fingered ones one more reason to pack up and move on, out of our territory. You yourself have done it eights of eights of times: upsetting their gather-baskets, undoing the thongs that hold up their skin houses, sending the wolves to howl around their camp, setting out stones and branches in mean-nothing patterns right near their fires as 'spirit signs' to scare them—"

"But never," Mantricker said with clenched jaw, "*never* in all my life did I ever think to go dancing in among the round-eared filth in full daylight, blowing on a clutch of hollow reeds, *bare as a treewee's behind!*"

Bearclaw felt the laugh scramble nimbly up his throat and tried to stifle it, but too late. It escaped, bursting from his lips as boldly as he himself had burst from the undergrowth surrounding the humans' camp when he appeared to them just as skyclad as his father's accusation painted him. A moment more and the laugh was his master, riding him harder than ever he rode Crest, shaking him like a sapling in a gale, turning all his bones into twiglets too fragile to support his weight. He felt his knees buckle with the force of the laughter and he let them go until he was rolling around on the ground before Mantricker's outraged stare.

"Oh, Father, if only you'd seen their faces!" he gasped, holding his aching ribs. "If only you could have heard the jabber that went up when they saw me! The women screamed, the men stood like rocks, the cubs all ran away to hide behind their mothers. That's not the way they're used to seeing us, bold and by daylight. I was in and out of their midst faster than a darting silverfin." With an effort, he hauled himself back onto his feet, wiping moisture from his eyes as the last few chuckles left him. "It was done between one breath and the next, but it's something the five-fingers will be talking about over their cook-fires for more turns of the seasons than you and I together could count."

"Between one breath and the next," Mantricker said slowly, "is when the spear point reaches the heart." His eyes glowered at Bearclaw with too much anger for the offense. Only by building up the blaze of wrath could the wolf-chief hope to sear away what was truly troubling his soul: the fear he felt for his wayward son.

"Father, I tell you there wasn't time enough for me to be in any danger! You've lingered near the humans' camp longer, many times. It was just the sort of thing you would've done yourself—"

Silence!

Mantricker's sending struck Bearclaw like a blow, toppling the younger elf from his feet. For an instant, Mantricker was startled by the force of his own action. He had meant the sending to be no stronger than the mental equivalent of a she-wolf's reproving cuff to a froward cubling. But Bearclaw's recent prank on the five-fingered ones was only the last of a series begun soon after that first bizarre outburst of springthaw laughter. Mantricker feared too deeply for his son's life if these escapades among the humans continued, and in the terror born of love he had lashed out too hard, without thinking.

Bearclaw sprawled on his back in a thicket of bracken, narrow eyes glaring up at his sire, lip curled in a snarl. Every limb trembled, the way a wolf's will when it tenses all its muscles just before it springs. Then, more frightening to Mantricker than any attack, any ill-thought challenge, Bearclaw once more burst into laughter.

"I just don't understand him," Mantricker said to his lovemate Brightwater as they lay still entwined in their comfortable nest of bedfurs.

"I thought you were more than a little distracted," the female elf replied, drowsily replaiting her long, amber-gold hair.

"Something's got hold of the cub and I don't know what it is." Mantricker sat up and stared out of his den at the leafy canopy of the Holt, only now beginning to show the first light of false dawn. Soon all the tribe should be safely denned up inside the Father Tree, sleeping away the daylight hours. Should be . . . but these days *should be* meant less than nothing to Mantricker's suddenly ungovernable son.

"He seems so much more lighthearted," Brightwater observed, finishing the braid and securing it around her head like a burnished crown. "I wouldn't call that a bad thing. The cub always had a tendency to be grim; this new way of his seems better to me."

"If his heart gets any lighter, he'll float away like a fur flower," Mantricker muttered.

Brightwater laughed. "It's the springtime, that's all."

"I wish I could believe that." Mantricker's eyes were as keen as any Wolfrider's, but the eyes of his heart could see further still. Now they tried to pierce the solid wood of the Father Tree standing between himself and his son, tried to burrow still deeper, all the way into Bearclaw's skull to read the reason for his careless pranks, his apparent willingness to hazard his life for a joke on the humans.

Not just his life, Mantricker thought. *Ours.*

Aloud he said, "Maybe Joyleaf was right."

"What, that Bearclaw's foamsick?" Brightwater scowled. Bearclaw wasn't her cub, but she had always had a gentle fondness for Mantricker's child. Perhaps it was the way the youngling always went about looking so scruffy, his shaggy brown hair forever in need of grooming, his glance more like that of an old, suspicious, ever-snarling lone wolf than an elf, even when he was still a tiny cub.

"I think that Joyleaf should mind her tongue before she says something truly foolish," Brightwater said so hotly she surprised herself. "Foamsick! As if that were anything to mention lightly. She's too young, that one, to know what she's talking about. And you, Mantricker—you and I are both old enough to remember the last time the foamsickness ravaged our tribe. Wolves and elves died mad, in agony, our healer helpless to save them!"

"I remember," Mantricker said. *And I remember, too, that you lost three fine cubs to the foamsickness, lovemate,* he thought. *One, our own.* But he did not send those thoughts, for fear of renewing the pain.

"As our chief you should have gone to Joyleaf the instant you heard what she said about your son—your own cub!—and taught her a thing or two about discretion."

Mantricker drew his legs up close to his body, rested his chin on his knees, and curled himself into a ball. "Joyleaf has more common sense than elves many turns older than she. She spoke in jest."

"Her jests are acceptable, Bearclaw's are not?" There was a sharp edge to Brightwater's words.

"Bearclaw's jests are more than words!" Mantricker sprang to his knees from his pensive pose, seizing Brightwater's shoulders to shake the seriousness of it all into her mind. "Bearclaw's jests could kill the whole tribe!"

With a huntress's grace, the female elf slipped from his grasp and leapt naked to the rim of the den's entrance, her eyes blazing. "And Bearclaw's father's temper could do the same!" she snapped. "Shout and shake, that's your way, Mantricker. You can't live quietly and you can't solve any problem quietly. If you keep silence on the hunt or when you're prowling around the humans' lairs, it's only because you're waiting to make another one of your great, pouncing, thunderbolt strikes. You steal out of the Holt in secret, solitary hunts just so that when you return, your wolf so laden with blackneck meat the poor thing can hardly walk, we'll all gasp and praise your skill and courage. But Strongbow brings down more game with his silent ways than you, for all your boldness. 'Look at me! Look at me!' That's what your whole life's become. Now your son's dared to say, 'No, look at *me* for a change!' and that's put a burr under your tail." She tossed her head and dropped from sight, her last bitter words still hanging on the air of Mantricker's den long after she was gone.

Mantricker dug himself deep into the now lonely bedfurs. His anger had grown like one of the human's cook-fires, the first small sparks of Bearclaw's misdemeanor stoked to flame by Brightwater's accusations, further fed by the unwilling but inexorable knowledge that she was right. Realizing this made Mantricker mad at himself, and that was the hardest fire of all to extinguish.

So it was that when next he called for his son to attend him as part of a hunting party and Bearclaw did not instantly respond, Mantricker's reaction was perhaps a little out of proportion.

"With the trolls? *Again* with the trolls?"

The Wolfriders stood in an uneasy circle around their chief and his son. Mantricker had called all of them to witness this confrontation, for reasons of his own. None wished to disobey the chief, but more than a few among them wished for some excuse to be elsewhere. Brightwater found herself standing beside Joyleaf, and sensed the younger elf-woman tense with each word of reproof Mantricker shouted into Bearclaw's averted face.

At Bearclaw's side, Crest whimpered and went down on his belly, getting ready to roll over and show the furious elf-chief his underside in submission, even if Bearclaw would not. A loyal wolf-friend, he, too, had been troubled by his bond-companion's recent excess of risk-taking. Yet listening to Mantricker rant and shout, Crest had a feeling that no visit to the humans' campsite had ever put his elf-friend in as much peril as this.

"Amber asked me to," Bearclaw replied. "She'd made a pact with Old Maggoty to deliver four good hides of her own hunting in exchange for a new brightmetal blade of trollwork. Blackbark only just returned the tanned hides to her, and she had no time to go to the caverns herself because she was supposed to be part of the hunting party, so—"

"The same hunting party *you* were supposed to be part of, too!" Mantricker bellowed like a wounded treehorn. "You've gone to the troll caverns on errands before this and come back before anyone missed you. What took you so long this time?"

Bearclaw looked at the ground. "Stns," he mumbled.

"What?"

"Stones," he repeated more clearly, lifting his chin. "A game the trolls have got: six-sided stones, it's called. It's easy, once you know the way of it, and you should have heard how Gaptooth yowled when I won—"

Gaptooth's yowl was a pitiful peep next to Mantricker's inarticulate cry of rage. Yet still more frightening to the Wolfriders gathered around father and son was the intense silence that followed.

Brightwater could almost feel the weight of Mantricker's hostile sending to the youngling. It hung on the air like the distant rumble of an oncoming flash flood: a peril real enough, but impossible to gauge. Father and son faced each other, jaws set, faces equally grim. For once, Bearclaw's laughter had deserted him. Only the fact that both elves carefully kept their eyes from meeting let their tribesfolk breathe a bit: this was no challenge, though for all the tension present it might as well have been.

Then Bearclaw relaxed without sagging. Brightwater thought she could read the signs of what had passed: he had met his father's sending with strength and accepted it—maybe not as the chief's equal, but as one worthy of his sire's respect. She laid a long, four-fingered hand to her breast and was surprised to feel her heart still beating at its regular pace. She expected the poor thing to be racing, as it sometimes did after great stress.

"Very well, my chief-father," Bearclaw's gruff voice rang out, so loud after the enforced silence of sending that more than one Wolfrider jumped in his skin. "So be it, then." He turned his sharp-featured face from his sire's and made a short, sharp hand sign to Crest. The big wolf rose up from its uncharacteristically timorous crouch, tail wagging, eyes bright. Without another word, Bearclaw mounted, and wolf and Wolfrider turned from the assembled tribe, heading for the deep woodland. Though they moved without haste, there was a dreadful air of finality to their going.

"Bearclaw?" Brightwater called after them. Crest paused, checked by a thought from his elf-friend. The older elf-woman darted up to place a staying hand on Bearclaw's arm. Behind her she heard Mantricker directing the rest of the tribe to see to various small make-work tasks around the Holt. Her name, too, was among the roll he called, but she ignored it. "What are you doing? Where are you going?"

The other assembled Wolfriders re-formed their circle around her and their chief's son, as desirous as Brightwater to hear Bearclaw's answers. Only Mantricker remained aloof, arms folded, with ever-steadfast Strongbow at his side. The fair-haired huntress knew that her lovemate would call for repayment from all who followed her disobedient example, but she did not care.

"Is it exile?" came a shaky whisper from the ring of glowing eyes encircling them.

And, "Two-Spear's madness," came another voice, harking back to Bearclaw's ancestor whose insanity had grown to such legendary proportions that it no longer required the aid of dreamberries to evoke the memory.

Bearclaw regarded the whisperers in the dark with cool contempt. Then he fixed Brightwater with a lupine gaze that effectively dismissed all of the other Wolfriders to oblivion. Speaking as if he and she were the only ones present, he said, "Isn't it obvious what I'm doing? I'm going on the prowl for a while. It's . . . a good idea. Too often in the past we've had to move on the spur of the moment, when the Tall Ones got too close for comfort or the game thinned or wind and water turned against us. Badgers always have two doors to their dens. Shouldn't elves be at least as wise as badgers? So I'm off to scout us our 'door,' in case we should ever need it." He glanced back over his shoulder to where his father still stood like a rough-hewn slab of stone. "It seems I can be spared." Not another word did he say to Brightwater, or to any of them, as he and Crest vanished into the trees.

By ones and twos the remaining Wolfriders broke away from the circle, tardily going to do the chores their chief had assigned or else see to some personal task that would occupy them. Bearclaw's stated reason for leaving rubbed every one of them against the fur. Brightwater's ears were too keen not to pick up the muttered questions and irritated cavils. From the day of Bearclaw's birth, there had been Wolfriders ready to see the cub as one of those throwbacks to the hunt—offspring sired by Timmorn Yellow-Eyes who had seemed more wolf than elf. Yet here was Bearclaw, shaking off the "now" of wolf-thought like raindrops, speaking of making plans for the future. The future! It was a concept few among them could comprehend.

Brightwater.

Mantricker's sending was a warmth in her mind sweeter than dreamberries. There was a plaintive note to it now, a pleading quality that roused her pity for an instant. An instant only. Frozen walls taller and thicker than the rivers of ice that had forced the High Ones out of the northern lands clasped her soul, barring him. She refused to respond.

Brightwater . . . lovemate . . . I did not send him away.

Didn't you? Fire leapt under the ice but could not melt it.

I—

Mantricker's thoughts cut off abruptly. Silence glided through Brightwater's mind like the flight of bats at twilight. There could be no dissembling in sending, only the most naked of truths. Mantricker could not lie to her now, no matter how uncomfortable that made matters for him.

I— If I did, it wasn't on purpose. I told him that if he found trolls and humans so much more fascinating than the welfare of his own tribesfolk, maybe he should give them all his time. It was done in anger, a foolish thing, impetuous—

Impetuous sire, impetuous son, Brightwater thought in her inmost mind, where even her lovemate's thoughts could not penetrate without her leave.

He took my words at face value, Mantricker went on. **'Maybe I should do just that,' was what he replied. It was his idea, his choice. Whatever's taken over his spirit these days is too powerful for either one of us to control.**

You couldn't explain? Apologize? Brightwater asked. And to herself she wondered, *Or would you, even if you could?*

There is more to this matter than there are layers on a wild onion bulb. I think this last clash of ours gave him an excuse to do something he's been after for a long time. He told me, 'I have already made the journey to find my soulname, Father. But maybe it would be better for us all if this time I went out to seek myself.'

For the first time since Bearclaw's leave-taking, Brightwater turned to her lovemate. The distance of but a few strides separated them, a distance she crossed swiftly to say, "What self is there for our kind to seek but a soulname, beloved?" Her hands brushed his cheeks tenderly, as if her touch held some healer's magic strong enough to take away some measure of his pain.

Mantricker let his head fall back until he was staring up into the thickly leafed branches of the Father Tree, searching for his own answers in the light of the lone, vagrant star that twinkled through the greenery.

"I wish I knew," he said, sighing.

He let her draw him back into her own snug quarters within the Father Tree. Brightwater's den was one of the untidiest, only partially through her own fault. Her lastborn cub, Moonshade, still shared Brightwater's nest, even though the maiden was now full grown. These living arrangements seemed like a peculiar whim—Moonshade had developed a passionate interest in learning Blackbark's skill as a tanner and the den was fearsomely cluttered with her experimental leather stitchery and dyework. Only Brightwater knew the truth: that she herself had never fully recovered from the time of the foamsickness; that no matter how many of her cubs survived, she would be forever haunted by the three who had perished in those accursed days; that forever after, the one thing Brightwater could never do willingly or completely was let a cubling she loved go.

Not even when the cub was not her own.

She cleared a place for herself and her lovemate and did what she could to let the sweetness of joining soothe

the sorrowing thoughts from his mind. Later, while he slept, she spread one of Moonshade's better, larger hides on the den floor. As she laid provisions and supplies on the leather, she summoned her wolf-friend, Fireracer. The small, stocky-barreled she-wolf was waiting for her at the northern roots of the Father Tree when she stole from the shadows with her pack—her two favorite hunting spears strapped to her back—mounted, and rode.

Hunt? Fireracer queried. It was the perpetual question of Wolfrider wolves, and their perpetual hope.

Yes, Brightwater returned. **Hunt Crest.** A flurry of confusion and a brief shock reached her from her wolf-friend's mind. **Not kill-hunt,** she reassured Fireracer. **Find-hunt only.**

Knew that, Fireracer replied, tossing her muzzle haughtily, trying to recoup lost dignity. Pride salved, she set her nose to the trail Crest and Bearclaw had taken.

In spite of her name, Fireracer was not a swift wolf. Brightwater had so dubbed her wolf-friend for the twin reddish blazes running down the she-wolf's sides from shoulder to flank. Too, Crest had a head start and was one of the pack's better runners.

That doesn't matter, Brightwater told herself. _I don't want to catch up to them. If he knew I was following, Bearclaw would be furious. He has all his father's pride, and more. But even at the price of his pride, I will not allow him to go out from the Holt alone. Especially not when this strange new recklessness has him by the throat. It is the least I can do for my chief._ So her thoughts ran, though she was powerless to say whether she meant her good intentions to benefit the present chief of the Wolfriders, or the chief that Bearclaw might someday become.

Setting her knees more firmly to Fireracer's sides, Brightwater sent a restraining message to the she-wolf, stressing caution and to keep a discreet distance from their quarry.

Not find-hunt? Fireracer queried.

Find but not catch, Brightwater clarified.

Hunt, not-hunt; find, not-find; catch, not-catch— The she-wolf snorted. **Elf-friend gone all ravvity in head!** If ever a wolf had been fed up with her Wolfrider kin, it was Fireracer. **Other elves stay, hunt, find, catch, *eat*—!** Brightwater caught the hint of a mental sigh from Fireracer's mind and the lupine equivalent of a weary **Why me?**

On a forest trail leading north out of the Holt, Crest was feeling much the same disgust and bewilderment over his elf-friend's odd behavior as Fireracer was. He and Bearclaw had departed the Father Tree with no more provision for a journey than the dark-haired elf's hunting gear. Crest, therefore, according to the simple assumptions his nature allowed him to make, believed they were only venturing on a brief foray after small game.

But as they traveled on, their passage startled a family of four fat young ravvits from cover. The wolf tensed, ready to give chase, only to have his instinctive reaction brought up short by a terse wolf-send from his rider. Crest whined, questioning Bearclaw's decision, and got no further response. Knowing what he did of Bearclaw's moods, Crest merely adjusted his assumptions. If ravvit was not their game, then probably they were after clickdeer. He sniffed the breeze, seeking. No, there was no sign of clickdeer nearby. Did his elf-friend know something the wolf did not? Stoically, Crest walked on, waiting for Bearclaw to make all things clear.

Explanation never came. Elf and wolf left the shelter of the great forest and came to a land of scrubby growth and small hills. Here was no good hunting, except for the few whistlers Crest scented, just emerging from their winter burrows. Whistlers were famine fare, and whistlers in springtime were skin and bones, not worth the energy of the hunt. Still, Crest reasoned, a little something in the belly was better than nothing. But Bearclaw remained as indifferent to the skinny marmots as he had to the newgreen-plumped ravvits. Apart from pausing so that elf and mount might satisfy thirst from a rocky streamlet, he refused to interrupt the journey.

The sun was high overhead as they crossed the scrubland. Day had come upon them before they were completely out of the forest. Crest felt more and more bewildered. Although his kind preferred to do their hunting by daylight, as a Wolfrider's wolf he had long since adapted to his elf-friend's preference for night hunts. Now this! It was too great a change for his mind to comprehend, and so he slipped by degrees into the "always now." Only his empty belly refused to be distracted, objecting so loudly and persistently that without actually intending to, the big wolf found himself whimpering and sniveling like a cranky cub.

The constant sounds of complaint must have reached Bearclaw in whatever state of mental abstraction held him, for the elf abruptly dismounted and grabbed his wolf by the thick ruff-fur of the neck. "I'm sorry, Crest," he said, his voice hoarse. "I haven't been thinking of your needs, have I? Are you hungry, friend?"

Very hungry! Crest gave Bearclaw a reproachful image of a once-handsome wolf reduced to the ignominy of raw ribs sticking out through a dull, moth-eaten hide.

Of course Bearclaw laughed.

Crest didn't know much about humor, but he knew when his dignity was being insulted. He butted Bearclaw from his feet with one shoulder-thrust and walked away stiff-legged, bushy tail radiating resentment. Bearclaw laughed louder, not the brightest thing to do to an already irritated wolf. Though the bond between Wolfrider and wolf-friend could not be broken beyond repair by anything less than death, there was no past experience among Bearclaw's tribe to say that a wolf could not absent himself from his elf-friend for however long he chose, if something pushed him to it.

By the time Bearclaw stopped laughing, Crest was far gone. He leaned on his hunting spear and tossed a casual wolf-send after him, bidding Crest return. His shadow lengthened as he waited for any sort of reply.

Bearclaw's next wolf-send was a shade more emphatic. Crest's reaction was the same. A third summons went the way of the first two, no matter how much temper Bearclaw put behind it. Finally he gave up. "He'll come back when he's ready," Bearclaw growled. "Hunh! What did I do to him? Since when is laughter such a bad thing? He's worse than Father. Neither one of them can take a joke."

With a last send to Crest—**I'm going; follow me or don't**—he turned his face to the north and marched on.

In the shelter of the last few trees that formed the forest's straggly northern border, Crest stretched out to enjoy the feast of ravvit that the fair-haired elf-woman set before him. A small she-wolf with red blazes striping her sides lay a respectful distance away, crunching her own portion. Brightwater watched the wolves eat and smiled. She was never happier than when she was giving.

"He got your dander up, too, did he?" she said to Crest, scratching the wolf's ears in a friendly way. Crest snarled at her for form's sake and crunched ravvit bones. "He called it a joke, too, I'll wager," she went on. "As if that made everything all right. Laughter has become Bearclaw's excuse for defiance, for endangering himself, for hurting the feelings of others. His father was that way, too, once, only it wasn't laughter he used as his excuse. I am older than Mantricker by many turns of the seasons, so I still remember Goodtree's time. She was a good chieftess, but she refused to see that her cub was not herself. She sought peace for us by avoiding the humans' settlements. She never understood that Mantricker was not born to run from his enemies. She used her position as chieftess to keep her wild cubling in check. But if Mantricker could not attack the Tall Ones directly while his mother lived, he could play his little 'tricks' on them. And when Goodtree took him to task over a prank that came too close to starting all-out war with the humans, he shrugged and said it was nothing more than a jest."

Crest finished the last of his ravvit and rose, shaking his coat vigorously. The wolf didn't follow much of what this elf-woman had said, but he liked the sound of her voice and even more, he liked the taste of her kill. He swung his heavy head back toward the trail he had taken away from Bearclaw, intending to rejoin his elf-friend, but a send from his new benefactress touched his mind with gentle, irresistible insinuation.

Crest, stay with us.

Stay—? But elf-friend . . .

We are going after your elf-friend, too. Does it matter if you travel with him or with us?

Her reasoning did make sense to the big wolf, in a way. He *would* rejoin Bearclaw, and it was not as if his elf-friend were in any sort of immediate danger. Crest no longer recalled the cause for his leaving Bearclaw behind, but the impression of something rankling remained in the wolf's mind, like the time he'd tangled with a whitestripe as a cub.

If you stay with us as we follow Bearclaw, Brightwater coaxed, **there will be meat. Much meat.**

That did it. *Meat* was one thing Crest could understand. He wagged his tail and let his huge red tongue loll from his mouth in pleased anticipation. He returned to Brightwater's side and permitted her to groom some bits of leaf and twig from his pelt. He would eat well, and he would rejoin his elf-friend soon. That was all that mattered, wasn't it?

What did not—could not—matter to the wolf was the fact that his kind had no real grasp of *soon*.

Feeling a trifle guilty, Brightwater ministered to Crest

while Fireracer looked on, grumbling a bit with envy. *Now he will come back that much quicker,* she thought. *Without his wolf-friend, in alien land, he won't be able to hunt as easily. He left on the spur of the moment, with no preparation for a journey. Hunger will turn his head back to the Holt, and then . . .*

Then I will do what I can to make father and son see that sometimes there are conflicts where neither wolf needs to show throat and both can win.

It was a very good plan. It almost worked.

Without his wolf-friend to ride, Bearclaw no longer had the leisure to turn his thoughts inward as he traveled. Although outwardly Bearclaw seemed to have been transformed by his newly come sense of humor, at heart he remained unchanged, and his self's core was often darkened by a tendency to brood. On the first leg of the journey from the Holt, introspection overwhelmed him: the enormity of his break with Mantricker, the true cause for all his recent wildness, his own doubts that he really knew himself, soulname or no. But at last, beyond question, on his own, more immediate needs presented themselves.

The first thing he did was climb the highest of the small hills and get his bearings. In the distance he thought he saw a river meandering through rolling land that gradually became even more undulating on the far shore. Beyond that the peaks of a low-lying mountain range beckoned. It was a tempting prospect, made more tempting by certain chance remarks he had picked up during one of his many visits to the troll caverns.

They spoke in mutters and whispers, the Holt trolls did, of mountains to the north. Foolishly discounting the sharpness of elfin ears, they whispered scare-tales of other trolls, trolls expelled and exiled from the lairs beneath the Holt, trolls who had gone off adventuring and who had likely found rich lodes of precious metals and glittering gems. Or else the exile trolls had perished horribly, a warning to any young mump fool enough to desert the security of the home caverns.

If you're so fond of trolls and humans, why don't you spend all your time with them! Mantricker's sending still buzzed in Bearclaw's head like an angry wasp. Very well, if there was something skewed in the younger elf's nature that lured him into the company of the Tall Ones and the trolls, this was his chance to run down the length of that crooked path. As to where it would take him and what he would find when he got there . . .

My self, Bearclaw thought, and his right hand strayed to the bulbed hilt of the strange, moonbladed sword he had won from the Holt trolls in that last game of six-sided stones.

So it was to be the mountains, then, the mountains beyond the river. That was good: there would be silverfins to spear from the water. He was starting to feel the first aches of hunger that had troubled Crest, and there were places between here and the river where fingerlings of forest tentatively explored the scrubland. He could hunt small game there, snare birds or rig a sling from his belt and bring them down that way, reap mushrooms, dig roots, maybe have luck enough to find a patch of ferns topped by tender, tight-curled fiddleheads, catch mice if it came to that—but he would not starve before he reached the river.

"Well, well, what's this?"

Bearclaw rolled his head from side to side groggily. The voice he heard was harsh, the words foreign, obscure, half-known . . .

Human.

Bearclaw had dwelled within hunting range of humans all his life. As soon as he was old enough to dare, he had sneaked near the five-fingers' camps to watch and mock their crude way of life. Given enough time—and an elf had more than enough time—he had picked up a certain familiarity with their language. He had not been the only cubling fascinated by the Tall Ones' loud, smelly, filthy, intrusive doings in the forest, and on days unfit for hunting he and his age-mates would sometimes gather to trade gibes and insults against the humans in their own tongue. Such practice honed his knowledge until Bearclaw was nearly fluent in the humans' speech.

Fluent enough to pluck most of the meaning from the voice now addressing him. The pronunciation of certain words was queer, and there was an underlying lilt that made it all sound less grating to Bearclaw's ears than the way he was used to hearing the Tall Ones talk. It was as if this human were struggling to emulate the elves' own musical tongue.

Very nice, but still . . . human.

"Come on. Sit up, roll over, let's get the water out of you."

Bearclaw felt himself being tugged and pushed this way and that. He was hauled onto his belly, and big hands pressed hard against his back just below the ribs. He wanted to protest that there was a bulky lump sticking into his stomach, but a wave of nausea overcame him, growing stronger with each rhythmic thrust of the hands, until his unhappy insides spewed up what felt like at least twenty waterskins' worth of river, silverfins included.

Bearclaw flopped onto his back, gasping. Through strands of drenched brown hair he saw his tormentor. The human sat back on his hams, hands splayed on his skinny thighs. His skin was a deep tan, unlike the pale complexions of the forest-dwelling Tall Ones who camped near the Holt. The rich brown shade made his blue eyes and straw-colored hair stand out all the more by comparison. Even though the round-ear wore a short, loose deerskin tunic, awkwardly stitched and beaded, Bearclaw could tell that the body beneath was almost as slender and fragilely boned as an elf's, with the exception of the big hands and clumsy feet. He looked like a wolf cub trying to grow into its paws.

"That's better," said the human. It was nearly the last thing he ever said.

Bearclaw's hand darted to his side and found the moonblade still there. In less than an owl's blink the crescent-shaped sword leapt from its scabbard as its owner sprang up, knocked the human over backward, and pinned him to the wooden floor. "Don't move," he growled in his own version of the Tall Ones' tongue.

"Not even in my thoughts," the creature replied with a sick-looking attempt at a smile.

Safely master of the situation, Bearclaw took in his surroundings at a glance and didn't like them at all. Lashed logs were under him and all around, except for a flap of hide partially masking a cutout space on one wall. Weak daylight slipped into the human's den through the cracks, and the air was ripe with the damp smell of rotting vegetation. Above, a roof made of saplings overlaid with woven mats of reed kept the place in darkness, and from somewhere far below the bumpy floor came the gentle sound of lapping water. What little space there was within the lair was taken up by tumbled piles of clay vessels, mountains of poorly cured pelts, and strings of leathery dried fish festooned one corner of the place to the other. Bearclaw felt his skin crawl at how totally unfamiliar it all was. As always, he had one way of dealing with his own discomfort.

The elf snarled as he set the blade to the human's throat and demanded, "Where am I?"

Which, in turn, was almost the last thing *he* ever said. A gigantic paw lifted out of one of the pelt piles in the darkest corner of the human's lair and gave Bearclaw a mighty sideways buffet that sent him tumbling heels over head. The moonblade clattered on the logs, to be quickly retrieved by the human.

"Torgal! Stop! Get off him now!"

Bearclaw only partly heard the human's sharp commands. Most of his attention was centered on the close-up view he was getting of the inside of a bear's gullet. The bear was a youngling, not more than two turns old, judging from the keenness and whiteness of his teeth. Bearclaw was excellently placed to render such judgment, not that he appreciated it. The bear's maw gaped over his face, tongue tickling the tip of the elf's nose. If not for the astounding reek of old fish on the beast's breath, the situation reminded Bearclaw of friendly wrestling matches he'd enjoyed with Crest.

"Torgal! Torgal, obey!" The meagerly built human flung himself onto the bear's back and began tugging its ruglike pelt, keeping the moonblade clear. "Off, I said! Get off! He can't hurt me, and it's your fault he's here anyhow." Reluctantly the bear swung its muzzle back over one shoulder, stared at the round-ear with small, mournful eyes, and shoved its bulk off of Bearclaw's supine body.

"Better?" the human asked, squatting beside Bearclaw. The Wolfrider grunted and touched his ribs gingerly. "Oh, you're all right," his host pronounced. "Sitting on my enemies is Torgal's best trick. It's the only reason Headman Bogro hasn't had me killed yet." The human shook his shaggy yellow head. "Just because I compared him to a blind river rat in my last word-weave. Some people can't take a joke."

"A . . . joke?" Bearclaw ventured. The word was new to him in the human tongue, though he would have known it well enough in his own.

"Here, get up." The human offered him a hand. Five fingers clasped closed over four as he pulled Bearclaw to sit upright. The moonblade gleamed in the round-ear's other hand, and while he did not hold it expertly, he managed it with sufficient competence to keep Bearclaw on good behavior . . . for the moment.

"I'm called Aloki. Aloki." The human repeated his name several times, thumping his weedy chest so heartily he knocked the breath out of himself and had to gasp for more. Bearclaw found his thin lips involuntarily quirking up at the corners.

"Me, me big fish in this lake," Aloki went on. All of a sudden he was speaking to Bearclaw in the most primitive manner imaginable, even for a Tall One. Every word out of his mouth and into the elf's ears was like the provocative tickling of a tuft-reed. "Great hunter. Kill many animals with bare hands. Not use spear, spear for river rat like Headman Bogro." He squinched up his eyes and stuck out his front teeth until he was the comic picture of the rodent. (Bearclaw's lips quivered; he snorted a bit, fighting to keep control.) "Me get plenty food, plenty women. Me get this many women—" He flashed the fingers of his free hand four or five times (Bearclaw felt a warning tremor in his chest), then once more for good measure. "Many, many women. All women say Aloki great hunter, got big spear—" He pointed again, but most decidedly *not* at the bone-tipped fishing spear propped up near the hide-hung doorway. "Aloki got *much* big spear, got biggest spear women ever see, got spear so big—"

Bearclaw's mouth writhed, trying to maintain the stoic scowl his dignity as chief-son demanded. He might as well have tried to hold on to a mud-slick eel. The laughter erupted inside the human's hut and was a long time dying.

"There," said Aloki with much satisfaction, watching his guest wipe moisture from his eyes. "Now *that* was a joke!"

"Dreamberries, eh?" Aloki stirred the heap of dried fruit in the clay bowl with one finger. "We call 'em bearberries here. They grow well around the margins of most of the lakes."

"Umm hmmm." Bearclaw's head hummed pleasantly. "So that's why you build your dens out over the water, on waderbird legs. I didn't *think* it was to wash away your stink."

If he'd said something like that to one of the Tall Ones near the Holt, he'd have had to be ready to fight or fly on the next breath. But Aloki knew a joke when he heard one, even from an elf, and he only laughed.

"No, we—what d'you call us?—Tall Ones?" This, too, was a joke between them. Skinny Aloki was only about two finger widths taller than Bearclaw. "We stay near the water so we can push Headman Bogro into the mud anytime we want."

"This Headman Bogro sounds like he could use some more dream— bearberries himself."

"Him? Ha! He'd sooner eat a raw waterstinger, fangs first. The gods forbid *he* should ever remember what it was like to be young." He shook his head. "I don't know what Mother ever saw in him. Oh, well, at least she still held fast to being our spirit-woman, even after mating up with that bladderwort. Only way I get left alone to make my word-weaves is because the fat old muskrat's still a little afraid of Mother's power, even now she's dead."

"What's a spirit-woman?" Bearclaw asked, but all the dreamberries he'd consumed in Aloki's company soon reduced the human's explanation to a vague rumble of words while the elf sought his own thoughts.

He had stayed in the human's hut three dances of the moons for reasons that would have infuriated Mantricker and scandalized the other Wolfriders: he was curious and he did not find Aloki to be a monster. Already he had learned some things about the lake-dwelling Tall Ones that were frivolous, impractical, of no use to his survival skills, and poisonously fascinating. Worse: *entertaining!*

These past three days he came to realize that too much of his own tribe's diversions carried a weight of grim purpose. Forest games were to sharpen hunting skills, moonslit dances were to encourage joinings, on the off chance a longed-for cub might be sired outside of Recognition, howls were never for the unalloyed joy of reveling in their own animal spirits. Serious business must be transacted, the burden of ancient chieftaincies passed down.

No one ever tells a funny story about Freefoot or Prey-Pacer or Rahnee or— Puckernuts, I know the times were hard, but I'd bet my new sword to a single toss of the troll stones that even Two-Spear sometimes laughed. The ghost of a frown flitted over Bearclaw's brow. *When they howl for me, will they ever recall Bearclaw with laughter?*

"—and that's why no one's discovered you here yet. If Headman Bogro can't force me to move on, he can turn me into almost an outcast among my own tribe. Still, I don't mind having a hu— a hu— a hut to myself, and there's been one girl at least—her name's Panpa, I wish you could see her!—who's bold enough to sneak in here whenever the moons make owl eyes. She *says* she comes because Torgal helps me gather the most bearberries of anyone on the lakes, but I think she does it because my word-weaves make her smile, and the only way she can get to hear 'em is by coming here. Women are forbidden to share the mystery of word-weaves."

"I've heard you how-howl a few of those word-weaves of yours," Bearclaw drawled thickly. "I sh' say your women are lucky."

Aloki threw a fistful of dreamberries at Bearclaw, who let some of them patter into his cupped hands before devouring them.

"Ugh." Aloki made a face. "*There's* proof enough you're not human. Torgal's the only other creature I've known who can shhhh-*shtomach* them raw, but they make good eating when we soak 'em in plenty of lake water and let 'em stand around." He reached behind him for another, larger bowl, this one filled with water-covered dreamberries, and pushed it toward Bearclaw.

The elf lounged back against Torgal's flank, feeding the brown bear handfuls of raw dreamberries, which were eagerly snuffled up. For himself, he alternated munching the dried fruit with draining the frothy liquid from

Aloki's store of soaked dreamberries and drinking it "because we are brothers." He had become brothers with the human after four bowls of fermented berry-juice, and four more might see them become lifemates, for all Bearclaw cared at present.

He was also feeling rather fond of Torgal, even though it was largely the tame bear's fault that Bearclaw had wound up in Aloki's keeping in the first place. He and the big bear had met in the clump of woodland nearest the river. It wasn't bear country and, in any case, Bearclaw wasn't armed for big game. Therefore when Torgal reared up in front of Bearclaw without warning, out of a stand of sunfruit bushes, the elf had been spooked enough to flee first and wonder after.

"You—you train him to run like that?" Bearclaw asked Aloki. The dreamberries had summoned up the past while at the same time fuddling Bearclaw's head so that he thought Aloki as capable of sharing memory as a fellow Wolfrider.

"I trained him to run with me," Aloki replied. He took dried dreamberries from the bowl and arranged them in weird patterns. "Two steps ahead of Headman Bogro. Sometimes two steps *after* the old catfish, if we can surprise him without a hunting spear. I wish I had a bowl of berries for every time Torgal chased him into the lake!" Aloki chuckled.

"Like he chased me into the river." Now that it was over, Bearclaw could laugh about it.

"It's a tricky river to ford, if you don't know the bed," Aloki said. "Your feet must've found one of the bigger rocks. Your head sure found another. Good thing I was downstream to pull you out, Fishface."

Bearclaw siezed Torgal's ear and shook it in a friendly manner. "Hear that, round-ear?" he bellowed at the beast. "Insults! It's all your fault I'm stuck in this stinkhole, forced to—*urp!*—to waste my nights with— with one who doesn't even ha-have sense enough to o-o—*hic!*—own the *right* number of fingers and—and—" He lost the trail of his words, shrugged, and drank some more dreamberry juice. Torgal snorted wetly at such ravings and laid his snout across his paws in slumber.

"Hunh!" Aloki's snort of disdain was almost as soggy as his bear's, and his head almost as muzzy as Bearclaw's. "Blame poor old Tor-Tor—*hwup!*—Torgal! Just because *you* didn't have the brains of a stone-struck squirrel in the woods. Wh-wherever you gods come from I b-b—*ork!*—bet you can't tell forest from fish."

"Owl pellets," Bearclaw snarled. "Ow—*hrrrap!*—owl pellets to you. I was bor-*born* in foresht. To a—to a wolf, I was." He subsided into trollish mutterings against Aloki, reviewing the five-finger's insults until he recalled that they were brothers, which made him begin to howl.

"Whew!" Aloki winced at the sound and stuffed his fingers in his ears. "I believe the wolf part. 'Splains those ears, any-anyhow. 'Course, why you never heard Torgal crashing through the brush with ears like that—"

"I thought . . . he was someone else." Bearclaw tilted his head back against the bear's fur. Not all dreamberry thoughts were merry ones.

Crest, my wolf-friend, where are you? How far beyond send-range are you roaming? Did the river steal my scent, my trail? Or do you think I have forgotten you?

"I want to go," Bearclaw said aloud, and the sound of his own words surprised him.

"Thought you might." Aloki scooped up the scattered dreamberries and poured them back into their bowl. "My mother always said the gods never stay with us for long."

"The . . . what never stay?"

"Gods."

The elf scowled. "Ano-*anovver* word I don't know!" He regarded Aloki narrowly. "You sure you're not ju-jusht making 'em up as you go?"

Aloki struck an offended pose. "*I* am a word-weaver! *I*

don't go 'roun' ma-makin' big mesh—mush—*mess* of words. Jus' 'cause you're a shtupid god, don't even know what god means, you blame me. Jush' f'that, I won't sing you the word-weave 'bout the long-tooth anymore." He folded his arms and sulked.

"Ha!" Bearclaw's scorn reeked of well-aged dreamberry juice. "I don't need you t' sing that wor-word—thing again. I got 'nough dreamberries in my belly, I can remember when Child Moon was a cub. Show you." He tossed back his head and began to sing:

> *"There once was a long-tooth*
> *For whom I'll sing a song,*
> *But you hunters who knew him know*
> *It wasn't his* tooth *that was long!*
> *One day in the spring he came out of his den*
> *And every female he met, he pum-pa-pum-pum*
>   *again!"*

Somehow, before Bearclaw got to the verse about how the remarkably energetic long-tooth cheered up a whole herd of branch-horns (males included), he recalled that he still did not know what this "god" thing was that Aloki had called him.

"I'll tell you," the human agreed, "if you promise never to sing another of my word-weaves. You sound like an otter with his tail caught in a cleft stick."

"Pum-pa-pum-pum to you," muttered Bearclaw. But he promised, then he listened to Aloki's explanation, and when the five-fingers was done there was a very thoughtful look in Bearclaw's eye.

Alas for Headman Bogro, there was the same wicked gleam in the eye of Bearclaw's round-eared brother.

Brightwater and the wolves shared the same gnawing tension as they kept to the scanty shelter of the lakeshore willows, the closest thing to forest cover they could find so near the strange settlement of "floating Tall Ones" that had swallowed Mantricker's son. It was all the female elf could do to keep control over her own wolf's impulse to whine, let alone leash Crest's mounting urge to panic.

She could not blame the wolves. What they now saw was strange, even measured by the standards of a journey that went from one unfathomable incident to another.

It was a hard road that had brought them this far. Game was scarce and small, the uneasiness in Brightwater's half-empty belly accentuated by her concern for Bearclaw, hunting the same ungenerous land without his wolf-friend to help him.

The trio had traveled so far back on Bearclaw's trail that when they reached the fateful woodland where Torgal had surprised Mantricker's son, the signs of their meeting were already icy cold. Too, what remained was confused. Telltale clues of bear-scent made Brightwater's heart lurch painfully, for fear's sake. Several times on this trek she had found herself short of breath, her ribs tight, an unfamiliar tingling in her arms. This, too, had held her back, keeping the wolves with her, refusing to let them run.

Not once Fireracer read the smells of the grove and sent her the irrefutable message **Bear!** Then Brightwater threw herself onto her wolf and demanded speed, even knowing that it had all happened days past. As the she-wolf bolted forward, Brightwater was still able to make a quick survey of the thicket: no blood, simply evidence of flight. Where the younger elf had run, scarcely a sign, but where the bear had charged after there were snapped twigs and broken saplings aplenty.

Run, run, setting the wolves to follow the scent all the way down to the river. And there to lose it in the water. There to see the nearly weathered-away impression of bear paws in the mud, entering the water, none leading out. There to lose hope in an abrupt assault of despair, only to regain it with the sharp, scolding voice in

Brightwater's mind demanding she stop her silly, pointless mewling to recall that prolonged chases were not in the nature of the big brown bears.

"That's right," she said aloud to the wolves. "A short charge, enough to scare away the hunter, unless it's a she-bear with cubs." She checked the size of the paw prints. "Too small and young to be bearing cubs, even if this is the mark of a she. Too young to attack a hunter! And if it did attack, why plunge into the river? Unless they fish or seek to cool themselves in high summer, bears turn from the water. High Ones, help me read this riddle, something's peculiar in these lands." She studied the rushing river's flow a moment, then added, "Timmain, grant Bearclaw didn't die trying to find the answer."

Now, keeping to the willows, a gape-mouthed, disbelieving Brightwater saw that Mantricker's cub had not only survived the solving of his riddle, he had created an eight-of-eights more, of his own howling.

Brightwater and the wolves had crossed the river, had found no elf-sized prints leading away from the far bank. They returned and cast up and down the near bank until Crest stiffened, bringing Brightwater and Fireracer to the spot far downstream where the marsh reeds were still bent with the impress of a small body being dragged from the water. They had shared the anguish of finding Bearclaw's scent mixed with a five-finger's stench and the repeated evidence of bear, but Brightwater alone experienced the creeping sensation of to-the-bone, inexplicable weirdness the combination of smells implied.

Brightwater and the wolves followed the trail. Here were no trees, only green reeds and bonny, fluff-topped rushes towering above the elf-woman's head. The ground grew more and more marshy, the scents sinking into the sodden earth. But a nose-blind elf could follow the bear's unsubtle passage, and the five-finger seemed to have feet of a size with the animal.

Passing through the reeds like a whisper, Brightwater

was haunted by her own thoughts. There were howls that told of High Ones' powers gone awry on the world of two moons, unwholesome places where the soured magic lingered. Had Bearclaw fallen afoul of such a spot? And if he had, how had it changed him? *Bear and human walk together in peace—unheard of! But the trail cannot lie to me. Can this be magic's doing? And Bearclaw . . . I think he must be riding the beast. No sign or scent of death, but do I dare risk a send? No. Not with so much unknown. We will follow, and learn the truth of it all.*

Brightwater was to learn that sometimes the hardest thing of all to believe is the truth.

The elf-woman pressed her back against the willow, wishing she had the power to draw the strength of the tree trunk into her own spine. Her hands lay one on each wolf's neck, the fingers knotted in the thick ruffs. What was she seeing? If she ever lived to return to the Holt, how would she ever be able to describe it to her tribesfolk without hearing one hushed word pass from lip to lip: *Foamsick.*

She was not so certain it would be a lie. Oh, the Wolfriders might believe her when she described the uncanny encampment these crazy round-ears had built for themselves over the waters of the lake. She had first seen it when she emerged from the reeds two days ago, at sundown. She waited until dark to pursue the bear's tracks, which broke away to skirt the lake and ended where the bank bore the imprint of a large, round shape. Keen elfin night vision and kind moonslight let her see several bowllike objects, tethered to the legs of the alien over-water dens. Which of those teeter-legged lairs held Bearclaw? If he was still Bearclaw, unaffected by the sick magic that ruled this land. Brightwater was a huntress; she could wait.

So she had waited until this night of madness, this night that began with shouts and excited cries wafting shoreward from the humans' dens. Next Brightwater saw a swarm of the five-fingers drop from their lairs into the round, buoyant shells, using long poles to propel them toward land. She and the wolves marked their direction and darted around the lake margin to meet them, melting into the place where the shadows were thickest.

Men, women, and children tumbled from the beached shells and leapt to their feet with glad cries. Some carried torches, some carried what looked like blocks of brown earth, but when fire was set to a great pile of these, they burned with an intense, smoky flame. When the fire was lit, other Tall Ones spread hides all around it, while their females took special care to arrange heaping bowls of fish, fruit, and dried meat on one hide in particular. Children splashed in the shallows to cull fragrant white water-flowers with which to adorn the place of honor.

All that, the Wolfriders might believe. They had seen the five-fingers' queer festivals before. But never, never unless the High Ones came again would they believe who came to sit in the place of honor, nor what he sat upon, nor how the Tall Ones all gathered around him and—and—

Brightwater closed her eyes and opened them again. It didn't change a thing. From his place, mounted on the furry back of the brown bear, Bearclaw accepted the Tall Ones' worship. All the sweetest portions of the feast were offered to him first, and bulging waterskins, whose pungent, fruity scent blew Brightwater's way and told her that they did *not* hold water. Bearclaw guzzled dreamberry wine while the largest and ugliest of the Tall Ones prostrated himself before Mantricker's son.

"Lord, we are your people, and we seek only your goodwill and the favor of your powers!" the human cried. Brightwater had to concentrate to understand his version of Holt-humans' speech, but she was certain she understood him. "What more may we do to please you?"

Bearclaw thought about it, the first sliver of a smile tweaking his whiskered lip. From behind the bear's flank, a pale-haired human with outsized hands and feet came sidling up to tug at Bearclaw's elbow and whisper in his ear. The elf's smile blossomed. "It is good for a man to make his gods laugh," said Bearclaw. "Sing the one about the long-tooth."

This simple pronouncement appeared to upset the big, ugly human more than necessary. He made several *grumph*ing noises, his blunt, strong fingers fiddling with the many strands of carved and polished bone bits around his neck. "Lord, I— the women are— it is forbidden that they—" he began.

"It is best," Bearclaw continued, "for the man whose gods have given him laughter to keep them laughing."

The big human's mouth opened, shut, opened again, then closed with a snap. "Very well, Lord." He looked as if he'd bitten into a whole handful of puckernuts, but he cleared his throat and all at once a most extraordinary combination of sound and words rode the bonfire smoke up into the moonlit sky:

> *"Now this long-tooth went on a journey,*
> *But a very sad thing he found,*
> *For the thing that made him happiest*
> *Was so long it dragged on the ground!"*

The other humans swayed in time, and clapped their hands, and rejoiced to behold their guest and god standing up on the bear's shoulders to join in lustily on all the pum-pa-pum-pums with their chief. If Mantricker's son had begun this journey to find himself, what on earth or of the stars was this self that he had found?

"Foamsick," said Brightwater sadly to the wolves. But whether she meant Bearclaw, the five-fingers, or herself, the wolves could not tell. The last thing she heard as she drew them farther from the firelight was the rich, joyful sound of Bearclaw's laughter.